# DARK HOPE OF THE DRAGONS

## ELYSIUM'S FALL – BOOK ONE

NIKKI McCORMACK

ISBN: 978-0-9983765-6-1
First Edition 2018

Published by
Elysium Books
Seattle, WA

Written by Nikki McCormack (https://nikkimccormack.com/) Cover Design by Robert Crescenzio (https://robertcrescenzio.artstation.com/) Typesetting and Design by Brian C. Short

•

*To my mom, Linda, for instilling a love of
reading in me at a young age and for giving
me free access to your vast collection of horror,
science fiction, and fantasy novels.*

•

{ For readers who are dealing with
trauma in their own lives, note
that this story contains a plot line
involving sexual assault that may be
difficult for those who have experienced it themselves.

*So did chaos find the lost*
*and give them purpose.*

The babe Dephithus drew his first breath...
...and the stone dragon in the graveyard of Imperious, a fixed reminder of another time, became flesh.

Cloaked in the shimmering beauty of a starlit night, it moved its hands much like the infant did, first discovering his body, stretching and clenching long clawed fingers scaled in crimson. Leaning forward, it braced itself on muscular forelegs, every movement careful and deliberate, like things forgotten. It stretched massive wings and the stars reflected brilliant light off the gold sheen overlaying its crimson scaling. It drew in a long, deep breath. Held it. Stretching out its slender neck, it opened its jaw, displaying rows of tapered teeth designed for the rending of flesh, and let loose a ground-shaking roar filled with pain and pride. The sound chilled and saddened the hearts of those who heard it, but was quickly forgotten, for it came from a creature lost to the memory of mortal men.

With precise movements, the dragon resumed its position and turned again to stone...

...and the babe Dephithus exhaled.

\*

1

Rakas startled awake, gasping and reaching for his throat, eyes wide as if he had dreamt of his own death and was shocked to find himself still alive. In the same moment, a tremor passed through Amahna. She fought the urge to wrap her arms around herself as she looked over her shoulder at him, disdaining him for reacting to the very jolt of panic she struggled to hide.

Haunting eyes, blackened over completely from long immersion in the daemon powers, focused first on her, narrowing as though suspicious of her presence there, then shifted to the painting behind her. Those pitch-dark eyes were mirrors, reflecting everything and revealing nothing, but she knew him well enough to recognize the distress in the cadence of his breathing, the slight tightening at the corners of his mouth, and the twitch of muscles in his jaw.

She turned to the painting inset over a natural opening in the limestone wall of the chamber. It depicted a magnificent blue dragon being driven back into the stone cauldron by warriors of the Imperious Legion, their long pikes tipped red with blood. The primal rage of betrayal in the beast's long-snouted face was so perfectly wrought that a pang of pity stung her for it even now.

"That power came from the dragon web."

Perhaps she should admire that he so readily put to words the alarming truth of what they had both felt. She did not.

The sound of water dripping and the gritty shuffle of someone moving through another part of the cave filled in the ensuing silence. Her gaze lingered on the painting. On the dragon. Wings spread. Intelligent blue eyes alight with exquisite fury, but also with hurt and confusion. Claws digging deep furrows into the earth, yearning to lash out but reluctant to harm those who had long been its allies. She could feel the black eyes of

Rakas upon her back like the heat of a fire, waiting for her to turn and acknowledge his words, to confirm the improbable truth. She let him wait, intentionally drawing out his torment.

Amahna felt a peculiar kinship with the great beast in the painting. Two awesome powers, dark and light, daemons and dragons. Forces opposed by their very nature both driven into imprisonment by the same betrayal. Now both yearned for freedom. She herself was not trapped in quite the same fashion as the dragon. Her imprisonment was self-inflicted by her choice to join with the daenox, the daemon power that once ran free through the soil and rock like blood. If she wanted, she could leave this place, but until the daenox was unleashed and her lord, Theruses, able to emerge from this cave system by her side, she would never truly be free.

"So it would seem." She turned to Rakas and he looked away, anger at her deliberate delay evident in the white-knuckled fist clutching at the blanket beneath him.

He rarely met her eyes anymore. The gradual darkening of her once deep blue eyes bothered him, more so because he had been the one to bring her here. One day her dark red hair and blue eyes would turn as black as his. It happened to anyone who immersed themselves in the daenox for too long. Until then the contrast of lingering color gave rise to guilt in him. Guilt she resented for the arrogance of it.

Did he truly believe she would never have come to this of her own volition? She belonged here, molding the daenox, serving Theruses. This was her fate. Her purpose. Rakas was merely the pawn that led her to it when the time was right. It could have been anyone.

He held his silence now with seemingly boundless patience. Or perhaps it was not patience anymore, but the distance that had grown between them over the last several years making him reluctant to engage her. She could almost feel the pent-up discontent that boiled up in him. Left to boil unchecked like a teapot with a broken whistle. Jealousy played a big role. Though he had been in these caves far longer, their lord favored her, a truth that took a heavy toll on his confidence and leached the passion from the once scalding heat of their relationship. Even the scent of him that mixed with the musty dampness of the cave had taken on an unpleasant tang, like some citrus fruit aged past its prime.

Before she could think of something to say that would not set off another argument, her skin prickled with the sense of something approaching and she spun to face the entrance.

Theruses entered the chamber cloaked in crushing silence, his very presence weighing down the air. His steps made no sound despite steel-hard talons at the end of long articulated toes that made his feet look more like those of a large reptile than a man. She could not tell his mood for the stillness of his expression and the eyes in that almost human face were as black as the deepest chambers of the cave, his pupils as lost within them as her soul. Perhaps if she gazed into that fathomless darkness long enough she would find herself again.

Brushing the thought aside, she sank to her knees on the cold stone and bowed her head as Rakas had already done. She could only see his feet now and the end of his tail lashing about them in apparent aggravation.

"You both felt the power?" His deep voice washed over her flesh like a phantom caress, making her shiver.

"Of course," she answered, showing devotion with the speed of her response. In the corner of her field of vision, she saw Rakas grind his nails on the hard rock and smirked to herself.

"It came from Vanuthan, the Mother Dragon. From your old home in Imperious, Amahna." The throaty rumble in his voice when he spoke her name could have been a purr or a growl. "You will send a message to your sister. Tell her how you have missed your old home. Ask her for any interesting news she can share to ease your sorrow. Perhaps her answer will provide some insight."

She licked her lips and smiled, the knot in her gut that always came with his unexpected arrival unraveling. How fortuitous that she could be of use to him in this. "Yes, my lord. It will be done."

Silence answered. He had already gone.

Without giving Rakas opportunity to comment, she rose and hurried off to another chamber to write a letter to her estranged sister. It had to be perfect. Contrite. Earnest. Her sister was soft and trusting. The right hint of remorse would win her over.

When that was done, she summoned a mountain hawk, binding the plentiful daenox within the caverns to call it and give it direction. Once the letter was securely fastened to the hawk's leg, she sent it on its way, her heart pounding in her chest like that of a child eager to please a tempestuous parent. If her sister's response provided insight into the mysterious surge of dragon power, she would climb even higher in their lord's favor. That was, if she got a response at all. She had abandoned her home and family long ago without a word of explanation. What if her sister had changed? What if she was not willing to forgive?

Her hand came up to her mouth, the urge to chew at her nails almost overcoming her careful control. One never knew who might be watching. She forced the urge back down and stood calm at the mouth of the cave, staring after the hawk. It was raining outside. A gray drizzle. It always rained in the cave. The moisture in the earth dripped through every crack in the stone. It was always dark as well, the only light the soft illumination created from the daenox. The gray light of the sky stung her eyes. She turned away from the outside world and walked back into the cave.

*

The response came several months later. Her sister had born a child on the night in question. Not only was the timing right, but in her sister's letter, after several long sentimental paragraphs about how she missed Amahna, she went on for some time about how special her new baby was.

Everyone believed their baby was special. Babies were not of interest to Amahna. Her sister's child, however, was very interesting. The child was born with faint silver scaling over his shoulders and down his spine and had slit vertical pupils in his silver-green eyes. All traits reminiscent of the lost line of Dragonkin. There was little doubt now that the dragons had come up with some way to influence the world beyond their prisons and this child was somehow a result of that meddling. Though she did not yet understand exactly what had been done or how they meant to use the dragon-child, she knew it had to be part of some plan to break free of their stone prisons.

Rakas sat upon the shelf that was his bed in the chamber they sometimes shared, absorbing the part of the letter she had read to him about the baby. The rest of the content did not concern him, so she kept it to herself.

It irritated her to look at him now, so she stared at the painting, tracing the jaws of the dragon with one long fingernail. "Perhaps we could use the dragon-child. If we can reach him on his sixteenth year, when he is old enough to wed and begin influencing his world, we could plant daenox within him. We could make him ours. At the very least, it might make the dragons writhe in their prisons."

Rakas shuddered, the sudden motion catching her attention from the edges of her vision and she narrowed her eyes at him to let him know that she had noticed, but she said nothing.

"Will you give this information to Theruses?" Respectfully, Rakas bowed his head and closed his eyes as he spoke their lord's name, but there was underlying mixture of sorrow and bitterness that dripped like a thick poison from his tongue as he said it.

She glanced around the cave, familiar unease sinking through her skin, but rather than retreat to a safe corner as she was inclined to, she walked to the center and sat beside the crystalline pool that filled half of the chamber. She traced the damp edge of the smooth, rust-orange shelfstone with her fingertips, knowing the daemon power would protect the vulnerable formations from the oils in her skin. Theruses liked his realm spotless and had bound daenox throughout to keep it that way. Within the caves where the daenox was imprisoned, pulsing within the rock all around them, its use was almost unlimited. Outside, the daenox could be used only in the most restricted of ways. The imprisonment of that power was not as complete as some might have hoped, and she now knew ways of gathering and storing it like one might collect sap from a tree. Theruses had taught her how.

"He hasn't paid many visits of late." Despite her rigorous self-control, she could not keep an edge of longing from her voice and she instantly dreaded his response.

Rakas had often offered himself as an alternative bedmate in response to such comments, as if he were at all a worthy replacement for Theruses. He must be growing weary of her rejections for he said nothing this time. It was hard not to pity him. She knew he had found many fine intimate companions to replace her with among the other residents of the cave, but whenever he dared favor any one slave too much, Theruses would take that one and use them until their flesh gave out. Perhaps it was their lord's way of punishing Rakas for his frailty. Regardless of the motive, it taught her former lover to be cautious and cold about seeking partners.

"I'm sure he's just been preoccupied." His voice faltered and another tremble shook him. He stood abruptly and started to pace with quick, jerking strides, then stopped just as suddenly and tensed like a startled deer before retreating to one corner of the chamber.

"Have I been neglecting you?"

The sensual voice was soft within her, though it filled the chamber with an almost overwhelming pressure of power. Even before he entered, Amahna could feel his phantom caress on her neck and the musky scent of him filled her nose, chasing away the smells of water and stone and Rakas. It numbed her thoughts and quickened her pulse.

She gasped in surprise when Theruses appeared before her and slid a finger under her chin. Her eyes closed as he lifted her from the floor, balancing her weight on daemon power. He kissed her hard, driving his tongue back to her throat as his tail snapped out, wrapping around her bare calf with a force that was both painful and arousing. She feared she might choke from the force of him, yet she longed desperately for more, yearning for him to do as he wished with all of her. Her muscles quaked with carnal need. Then he pulled back and kissed each eyelid, silently giving her permission to open them.

"Your idea is a good one."

She hung there helpless, dangling from his fingertip, but the sensation only heightened her desire. A hint of pale gold scaling showed on his bold forehead below a thick raven black mane of hair. His features were strong and commanding and her need for him caused her sex to weep with longing. The pale gold scaling showed again at his shirt collar and many other places she knew that could not been seen when he was clothed.

She shivered.

He responded with a feral grin. "When the dragon-child nears his sixteenth year, the two of you will go to attend his birthday celebration. You will bring him a very special gift from me. You will plant daenox within him and make him mine."

He kissed her again, choking her with his tongue and his power until she could think of nothing beyond the need to have him inside her. She whimpered when he bit her lip and licked once at the blood that welled there then drew back, his black eyes blazing feverishly.

"Leave us, Rakas," he commanded, the hunger in his voice promising unworldly pleasure and pain. A slight grin curved his lips then. "Or stay if you like. You might learn something."

Rakas hurried from the room as Amahna shivered again with dreadful anticipation.

*Since I am convinced*
*That Reality is in no way*
*Real,*
*How am I to admit*
*That dreams are dreams?*

**Saigyo Hoshi**

Dephithus meandered through the gardens outside the Elysium palace's west wing, basking in the warmth of a bright mid-summer day. A wide array of blooms bathed him in their perfumes and dazzled his eyes with their color. Blue and violet, red, orange and white. Cheerful yellows and soft pinks. Scents sweet and seductive, calming and invigorating. Greens to cover every part of the spectrum from the palest mint to the deepest forest shade. Amongst all that color, numerous palace residents and guests lounged or strolled, enjoying the fine day. They wore everything from casual finery to the bare skin they were born in, adding their own array of varied colors to the scenery.

"Dephithus, my dear."

He stopped before his mother, Avaline, where she reclined against one of the nude sculptures surrounding the central garden pool. Light brunette hair relaxed down over her shoulders, a few strands clinging to the stone of the sculpture. She patted the stone bench where he might sit beside her. Acquiescing, mostly, he sat on the stone curb just below his mother whose figure, softened by a life of leisure after many years retired from the Imperious Legion, was exposed to the sun through a thin silk dress of translucent sky blue. Most of those who rested around the gardens suffered from such a relaxed figure, except for the odd lounger who was on break from duty or practice time with the Imperious Legion. Even after generations of peace, the Legion maintained rigorous physical requirements for their active soldiers per his den-father's orders.

"What troubles you, Mother?"

Avaline leaned down and kissed his cheek, smiling with an open adoration that made him almost as uncomfortable as the stares he got from others when they thought he was not watching. They did it now, turning to watch him. He could see them in his periphery when he lowered his gaze to the stone walk.

Did his mother even noticed the things about him that made them stare? The vertical slit pupils of his eyes, the silver flecks in emerald irises, the pale silver scaling that ran up the back of his neck, peeking out at his temples and on the inside of his wrists. That same scaling ran over his shoulders and down the center of his back, appearing again on the upper part of his calves. Things that made him different. Things that made him unlikely to ever share in the comfortable nudity others of his class took for granted on days like this in the sunlit palace gardens. Things he pretended not to care about, but every time someone looked at him, he couldn't help wondering what they thought. What unusual trait did their eyes linger upon the longest?

They whispered about him. He couldn't help wondering which of them perpetuated the rumors that his markings were a throwback to darker times and an omen of darker days ahead even now, almost sixteen peaceful years after his birth.

He smiled at them all. What else was there to do?

"Your Dawning Day is almost here. You'll be sixteen," Avaline remarked as if it were a casual observation and not a major event she had been planning for since practically before his birth. "I've seen you admiring other young women, but still you spend all of your time with Myara."

*This again?*

Her remark had the inflection of a question, so he responded to it as such. "We both have other friends," he defended, playing obtuse and opting to ignore her insinuating tone as he eyed a brilliant green grasshopper that had landed on the walk.

"Have you given any consideration to marriage yet?"

He rolled his eyes, knowing she could not see it from her vantage, and turned his attention to gently prodding the grasshopper with the silver-plated toe of his boot.

She started to quote the words of a familiar song with a poetic cadence. "Marry money or marry none, my son, for we have more than enough to share. Marry one or marry many, but no more than seven for there are only seven nights in a week."

The grasshopper jumped and Dephithus followed it with his gaze.

Her tone turned serious. "But you must marry."

At the top of the jump, his eyes refocused on a mischievous smile and sparkling dark eyes peeking through an opening in the garden hedge.

"You are the most likely heir to an illustrious line... Dephithus, are you listening?"

He grinned at Myara and shrugged, a helpless gesture indicating imprisonment in yet another of his mother's lectures.

Mythan, High Lord of Imperious and Avaline's primary husband, walked up then, casting a shadow upon them both with his height and the strength of his presence. He quickly eased that regal pressure away by ruffling Dephithus's hair.

"I see your mother has your rapt attention." Dephithus glanced up, his brow furrowing with guilt, and Mythan cracked a conciliatory grin, his hazel eyes full of warm affection. Mythan's gaze moved to his mother then, the warmth in his eyes deepening. "Avaline, are you trying to fill his head with talk of lineage and marriage when he's almost old enough to enter the tournaments? There will be many a joust and melee championship under his belt before he has to prove the virtue of his seed."

Dephithus's face grew warm. He could only hope Myara had not heard that.

Avaline gave an exasperated exhale, but she gazed up at Mythan with open love and indulgence brimming over in her eyes. Brown eyes, not green, and with round pupils like everyone else. For all that she appeared not to notice, he could not seem to help seeing the differences.

Dephithus stood and inclined his head in a slight bow, noting as he did so that he could meet Mythan's eyes without looking up. He was tall enough now that he could muss up Mythan's head of neatly trimmed brown hair if he ever had the courage to do such a thing to the lord of the realm.

"Good morrow, Den-father," he greeted with enthusiasm, already contemplating the potential for escape in Mythan's fortuitous arrival as he straightened his hair with a casual shake of his head.

"Ever the gentleman my son." Avaline reached up from her perch to ruffle his hair again.

Her smirk told him she was picking on him, knowing how he disliked having his hair messed with like he was still a child. Dephithus tossed his head to settle his hair down again.

Another hand reached up from behind to muss his

hair yet again as Myara slipped into the gathering with a feisty smile and a soft giggle meant only for him. He requited with a playful bump of his elbow and a scowl of mock warning.

"Myara," Avaline greeted. "You have grown to be such a lovely young woman. Don't you think so Dephithus?" Avaline looked expectantly at him.

Even Mythan raised one regal brow as though curious what he might say to this unexpected query.

Myara shifted her feet, her gaze dropping as if the cobbled walk had very suddenly become a subject of great interest.

Obligingly, Dephithus turned a critical eye on her.

At fifteen, she had started to change dramatically from the boyish young girl he had grown accustomed to. She always had her father's natural strength and the structure of a fighter, something that was deceptively starting to hide itself beneath the emerging feminine curvature and beauty of a court lady. Her dark gold skin was kind to the eyes in the bright sunshine. Indeed, everything about her was a soft, dark gold. Her skin, her eyes, her hair, even her smile had a warm gold softness to it.

But she was still a fighter. Her family was one of the great military lines, highly respected for their martial history, though few could quite remember why that was so important anymore. There was no need to dwell on a violent past, Avaline once told him, when the present was such a wondrous time of peace. He remembered the words because it made him uncomfortable sometimes wondering what lessons were being lost in the forgetting of that past, but perhaps it didn't matter. Perhaps families like Myara's would eventually have to become something new or fade away.

After a proper period of awkward silence aimed at making his friend squirm in her boots, he shrugged and strangled back an inappropriate grin similar to the one he could see tugging at the corner of Myara's mouth.

"Pardon mother, but I really don't have the time these days to notice such things, what with all my training and my Dawning Day around the corner. There will be tournaments to compete in soon. I need to be ready." He offered Mythan a wink at that then faced Myara again. "Shall we be off to training?"

With a sly smile he offered his arm. Myara gave a hasty bow to Mythan and Avaline, then she slipped her arm into his and they tromped off, chuckling at his mother's impotent glower trying to burn holes in their backs. His laughter was a bit forced though, for now that his mother mentioned it, he did notice the woman his childhood friend was becoming. There was something alluring about the angle of her golden eyes and her high cheeks were tinted with a kiss of self-conscious pink after the encounter with Mythan and his mother. Her lips were full and probably quite supple. There was a healthy shine to her thick wavy hair and the glow of her skin made him curious if it was as silky smooth as it looked.

When she took her arm away, he let his fingers slide across the bare skin of her forearm. Yes, it was soft and pleasant to the touch. How had he not noticed these changes happening? Was he simply too accustomed to her presence to notice or had something changed in him as well? Perhaps one day while the weight of his sword or a flash of bright sunlight distracted him, life had simply stolen away her boyish awkwardness and replaced it with this.

He released a troubled exhale.

"What is it?" Her voice pulled him out of his reverie.

"What is what?"

"That woeful dramatic exhale. Is something wrong?"

He answered with a gentle smile, realizing after he had done it that it was not quite characteristic of him, at least not with her. He made his expression more serious. "We're doing mounted work today, right?"

She nodded, her eyes narrowed suspiciously, and stared at him a long moment as if still seeking the cause for his odd behavior. Just when her probing gaze began to make him uncomfortable, she gave up. With a small shake of her head, she turned her attention to the distant training grounds.

"Race you to the stables," she challenged.

In hopes of catching one another off guard, they both burst into a run. Giddy pleasure burned away the remains of his discomfiture. He reached over and pinched her side, making her stumble and giving him a few strides advantage. Glancing over one shoulder, he saw her lip twist into a playful snarl as she bounded after him. They hurdled two lovers who lay entwined in each other in the groomed grass of the lower garden where the hill sloped down towards the stables. Lighthearted threats followed them as they raced down the hill, but the lovers would soon resume their petting.

"Last one there has to ride tail," Myara announced as she lunged a stride ahead of him.

A broad grin split his lips and he plunged recklessly after her, but he held back his speed. Sometimes, he had to let her win.

He had always been stronger and faster than others his age. It was one more thing that made him stand out as different. Either a freak to avoid or a fascination to follow and study. It didn't bother him most of the time. The other students didn't seem to mind that he was born with advantages all that much anymore, unless they were on the wrong side of his practice sword.

Still, it was always better with Myara than with anyone else. She allowed him to go easy on her without calling him out for what he was doing and sometimes she gave him quite the run even with his natural edge. As ruthless as she could be in combat, he expected her to make an occasional jab at him for it, but she rarely did so. Most of the time she simply treated him like her best friend instead of someone different to fear or fawn over.

Her friendship was all he wanted, wasn't it?

As he let her pull ahead of him, he again noticed the ways in which she had changed. His gaze ran down the lines of her body. Where had the curves come from? The power of her strides only added to this new appeal. He found his eyes lingering on her slender waist and the soft curve of her hips until a stumble at the edge of the maintained road brought him back to attention.

Myara sprinted across to the side of the first stable and turned, panting as she broke out a broad grin and stuck her tongue out at him. There was the Myara he knew, her pretty face twisted up in a childish expression of taunting.

He slowed to a walk and rolled his eyes. "So uncivilized."

With a toss of her head, she turned up her nose and stomped toward the stable entrance, sporting a satisfied grin all the way.

I n one of the outdoor practice arenas, the oldest and highest ranked class of youth in the Imperious Legion Training Academy stood proud beside freshly groomed and saddled mounts. Their leather saddles gleamed in the sunlight of the outdoor arena. Area Commander Parthak insisted that her reflection show clearly in a properly polished saddle. The students of Imperious were required to clean their gear with their own hands twice a week regardless of social standing and how many capable servants one's parents had. A rule Dephithus appreciated, for it gave him one more way to build camaraderie with his fellow students.

Parthak strode down the line, short blond hair creating a frame around cool blue eyes and severe, angular features. As an area commander, she was only one rank below the lance commanders, who were, in turn, only one step down from the high commander. An individual to be respected. She scrutinized each aspiring soldier's equipment, checking everything for dust or signs of poor care. After several grumbles and an occasional satisfied grunt, she returned to her place in the center where her mount patiently waited and faced the lineup.

"Do I have a volunteer to ride tail today," she barked, eyeing them, as she always did, like unscrupulous rabble needing to be brought to hand.

"Commander," Dephithus piped up, not missing Myara's smug grin as he did so, "it would be my honor to ride tail for the troop."

"You are going to be a remarkable soldier, Dephithus. I must remember to put a word in to the high commander for you." Parthak beamed at him, though the gesture signaling him to prepare to mount was as abrupt as ever.

Now Dephithus was the one wearing the smug grin when he glanced over to see Myara rolling her eyes at him. He winked then positioned himself beside his mount. Upon command, he mounted the big chestnut courser. The horse stood solid as stone, unmoved by the sudden weight on his back and ready to respond to any direction his rider might give. Being one of the top students had its benefits, such as the prime choice of mounts for schooling.

The lineup waited, facing the area commander, as Dephithus gave a gentle squeeze of his legs to lift his mount onto the bit and into a delightful prance down the front of the line and into the tail position. He lacked Myara's natural seat and her rapport with the big animals, but he had enough drive and desire to succeed that he rode as well as the best of them.

"Myara, you and Chen will ride scout," Parthak ordered after running her icy gaze over the group several times.

Myara let out a gleeful little squeak as commander Parthak mounted her stallion and commanded the rest to follow suit. She then turned her mount toward the arena exit and moved the animal into a perfectly cadenced prance. The troop fell into line behind her in a well-choreographed pattern of movements. They had practiced so often that most of them could probably do it sleeping.

Dephithus watched from the rear as they left the arena. Myara and Chen trotted out ahead to scout the forest that bordered it on the south and west sides. Parthak held the rest of the troop back for longer than usual and a charge of excitement began to pass among them, bringing the horses heads up a little higher, when they realized the commander had something out of the ordinary planned. Once the scouts had time to disappear out of sight into the dense foliage of the spring forest, the commander turned to the troop and proceeded to split it down the middle, leaving Dephithus as tail of one half.

"Troop one," she pointed with her crop to indicate the half of the group Dephithus was tailing, "will circle wide to the north and come in ahead of the scouts. You are the enemy. Your object is to take the scouts captive and defend against the troop sent to retrieve them." As the first troop prepared to move their mounts off, she barked out, "Hold up. Let's see how good you really are, Dephithus. You will be their commanding officer. Now move!"

Dephithus didn't wait to be hollered at again. He spun his mount and galloped to the head of the troop. As they pulled a wide, galloping arch through the field and into the woods around where the scouts were likely to be, Dephithus started planning tactics. When they had gone far enough, he pulled the troop up and discussed his plan with the others then split the troop in half again, designating one person from each group to scout ahead and locate their respective targets.

His half of the troop moved out cautiously through the trees in the wake of one scout, leaving their horses behind so they could move with less noise. Predictably, one of the original scouts was following the deer path they were slinking along. Dephithus gestured for his troop to hide off the path and wait. He grinned as Myara rode into view humming a dance melody and peering through the trees. Before her sweeping gaze hit them, one of his troop threw something up into the trees, making a noise above her. She glanced up at the canopy of bright green that filtered the sunlight and Dephithus signaled the troop to swoop in. Her expression turned to instant alarm when he whistled his troops into action. She didn't have time to do more than wheel her mount in preparation for flight before they had her surrounded. To do her credit, she drew her sword to fight, but she recognized within a few seconds that she was grossly outnumbered and relinquished the weapon.

Dephithus stepped out of the trees while they bound her hands and one of the soldiers bowed his head, falling into character.

"We have captured an enemy scout, Captain."

Three short, sharp whistles let him know that the other scout was also in custody.

With a disapproving scowl and a shake of his head, Dephithus looked down on Myara. "Shameful how lazy a soldier can get in times of peace."

Myara stared up at him, the color fading from her cheeks. In that instant, her eyes widened, growing moist with the fear of one who truly faced an unknown and terrifying enemy. A chill moved through Dephithus and he shook it off, giving her a wink.

The look of terror faded, and she shook her head as he had to dash away the feeling before narrowing her eyes at him. "I thought you were riding tail."

Dephithus grinned, relieved that the odd moment was behind them. He made a show of puffing out his chest. "I was promoted."

Kathan, a lad from the local village, stepped up to Dephithus, clearing his throat to speak with an exaggerated solemnity. "Captain?"

Dephithus nodded to him. "What is it?"

"The other soldiers and I are concerned about your camaraderie with this enemy scout," his expression remained admirably serious, though his eyes betrayed him with the sparkle of laughter.

Dephithus chuckled. "Come, we have a rescue party to conquer. Gag the prisoner. We can't have her crying out a warning to them." He turned his back on Myara's sudden glower and led them back to the horses.

The other party arrived with Chen. They bound him and left the two with a guard. They would have better odds of winning if they hurried out to intercept the other troop rather than giving them time to put a rescue plan into action. Their opponents would be planning an offensive. He would force them into a defensive position. If he was correct, it would not be what they expected, and it would give his troop an advantage.

An eerie quiet filled the woods, broken by the soft shuffle of well-trained warhorses moving through the underbrush and the occasional snap of a twig that would hopefully be covered up by the sounds of the rescue party's horses. His troop moved in a slow and cautious line stretched across the section of woods with him at the center. The first of his soldiers spotted the opposing troop through the trees. She signaled him with a convincing bird call. He gave the hand sign to charge, nodding approval as the signal passed quickly along both sides and a predetermined set from each end moved out further to circle around the enemy. They charged then, letting the sound of hooves now crashing through the brush be their battle cry. The fragrance of broken foliage rose up under the salt and hay scent of the horses and the oily perfume of polished leather.

His troop drew their practice swords when he did, responding to his lead as if they had been doing so through years of hard battle. Their energy bolstered him, feeding into him like they were all connected in that instant on a new and deeper level. He felt stronger and faster than ever. When his mount surged ahead, he caught sight of Parthak. The commander was not just observing, she was calling out commands to the opposing troop. She was their captain. She had pitted herself against him, rather than putting command of the troop under another student.

Dephithus aimed for the instructor.

Parthak's eyes widened in an instant of surprise, then narrowed, homing in on Dephithus as she kicked her mount into action and met the charge.

Practice swords clashed. Dephithus heard the clash of real honed steel in his head and grinned when Parthak nearly lost her weapon before the force of his attack. Another student charged at Dephithus from the side and he nudged his horse's hindquarters around into that attacker's path while he thrust his blade at Parthak. The commander recovered with barely enough time to knock the strike away, but her balance was off enough to further her opponent's advantage.

Dephithus urged his mount into Parthak's horse and struck again, checking his attack just fast enough to stop the blade against his instructor's neck. Parthak lowered her own blade and nodded once. As she started pulling out the white kerchief on her shoulder to mark herself dead, Dephithus spun to face his next opponent.

\*

Horses and riders were slick with sweat and numerous students bemoaned their bruises as they rode back to the stables, the dead still wearing their white kerchiefs on their shoulders. Parthak grinned back at Dephithus and his troop every few moments, beaming with pleasure. Myara, free of sweat or bruises thanks to her captivity during the battle, brought her mount close and leaned toward Dephithus.

"Never in my life have I seen anyone so thrilled to

be defeated. You think she would have preferred to win rather than be outsmarted and outfought by a student."

Dephithus laughed and shook his head in disagreement. "Parthak has been boasting to my den-father over what a fine soldier she was going to make out of me since I was six. I don't think she sees my defeating her as a loss at all. As far as she's probably concerned, I proved her right today."

He scanned the opposing troop. Well over half of Parthak's soldiers and the commander herself were marked dead within a few minutes of the initial attack, having taken what would be fatal or debilitating blows from their enemies. His troop had followed his orders precisely and executed a flawless rout.

"Well," Myara scowled at him, "try not to be too modest."

He laughed again. "Can I help it if I'm perfect?"

She rolled her eyes and shifted her focus to the youth moving up on his other side.

Kathan tossed his head to get his overlong red hair out of his eyes and nodded a greeting. "Several of us were going to ride into town to my folks' tavern and celebrate our glorious victory under your command. Would you care to join us, Lord Dephithus? You can bring the captive." He added the last with a wink for Myara.

Dephithus glanced at her. "Myara?"

"I'm only the captive," she remarked, "I'll go where you please, oh magnificent warrior."

An unexpected urge to take her somewhere they could be alone struck him. Swallowing hard and hoping no one noticed the sudden warmth he felt in his face, he turned to Kathan. "That sounds grand."

"Fantastic! I'll see who else wants to join." Kathan moved off then to talk to one of the other students.

Myara pulled forward a lock of her hair and began

to braid it, keeping her mount in line with leg cues. For the first time in his life, Dephithus was uncomfortable having her by his side. He stared ahead, chewing at the inside of his lip.

"Is something wrong?"

He shrugged, refusing to look at her lest she see something of his thoughts in his expression.

"In less than a week you can start competing in the tournaments. You're one of the best jousters I've seen. Aren't you excited?"

"I am," he replied absently. He did feel the promised thrill that would come with finally entering tournaments, but it wasn't enough to take his mind off her, especially given his mother's focus on his future as a husband. He knew she was worried that he would have trouble finding a partner with his strange markings, but she had succeeded in disrupting a perfectly good friendship with her meddling.

"Myara, if you were me, would you marry right away?"

She stared at him for several strides, her hands pausing halfway through the braid. "Why worry over such things now? There's no rush. I mean, you are almost guaranteed to be named heir to the throne, but Mythan is still young. He's not going to be passing off the crown anytime soon."

He glanced over and caught the little frown on her face deepening as she fell into thoughtful silence, the braid forgotten. "It bothers you too, doesn't it? The possibility that some woman might come between us. Not at first, but eventually I might become accustomed to waking up beside her. I might forget why I spent so much of my time with you. If we had a child, then I would spend even more time with them. You and I would fade away like a pleasant memory that offers no images, only a warm feeling."

Myara laughed and the muscles in his shoulders drew tight with self-conscious irritation. Warmth spread up his neck and into his face. She glanced at him and started to laugh harder, curling forward and grabbing the horse's mane for balance.

He gritted his teeth and stared hard ahead.

Parthak glanced back at them with a raised brow and Myara sucked back the laughter, forcing composure, though the twitch at the side of her mouth told him she was fighting to keep it in.

"What's so funny," Dephithus asked under his breath.

"I went from being your best friend to a warm, fuzzy feeling in mere seconds and I didn't even get to have a parting spat. Where's the fun in that?"

Laughter bubbled up in his chest and he clenched his jaw making a small snorting sound as he tried not to let it free. She was right. It had been silly.

"I just want to know one thing," she pulled a serious expression, "did you and your wife have a girl or a boy?"

"Boy. I wouldn't have a girl for you to corrupt."

"You think that'll help? Being a boy doesn't seem to have protected you any."

Dephithus only grinned and she nodded as if the subject were satisfactorily resolved. He wondered, as he watched her go back to braiding her hair with a charming moue, how he was going to go on spending most of his waking hours with her given the new feelings she aroused in him. How she would laugh at him if she knew.

Amahna gazed into the mirror pool, her lips curving in a pleased little smirk. While her reflection smirked back at her, she practiced using illusion to mask the strangeness of her nearly black eyes, restoring their natural color. Her skill with the daenox and her willingness to serve had lifted her high in favor with Theruses, but simple luck secured her position now. The dragon-child, Dephithus he was called, was the son of her half-sister, Avaline. The letter she sent requesting to attend the boy's Dawning Day celebration was well received. Avaline's sap-soaked response expressed grotesque enthusiasm at the opportunity to see Amahna after all these years and reminisce upon their childhood. As Amahna recalled, it was a forgettable experience, but she would endure anything for Theruses.

Since the day of the dragon-child's birth, Theruses favored no lover over her and she savored watching him turn others away for her. She yearned for him even now, but he was with Rakas. A necessary pairing to pass on the potency that would sprout the seed of daenox they were going to plant within the dragon-child. Still, it was rare that a man could satisfy Theruses, so she would wait for the inevitable call to sate her lord's lust when they were finished. After that, she and Rakas would begin their journey to Imperious.

When the summons finally came, she was pacing the passages of the cave system, her hands balled into fists on the fabric of her skirt to keep from chewing at her nails. The sudden relentless compulsion to seek him out, an even deeper need than her own desire, drove her to change her direction. She followed that inner need through the passages with complete trust. Theruses ruled her. He was all she wanted or needed. She could not recall when the unconditional devotion developed, nor could she be bothered to question it.

Theruses awaited her in the immense chamber he called the Womb of Daenox. A space so vast and dark that even with a bright light one could not see any of the walls or the ceiling. Some daemon power had been bound to cast a faintly blue light over the center, where flowstone over an old pile of rock created a natural throne. Massive white columns that made up the back of the throne disappeared into the black above.

Rakas wore an even deeper scowl than normal and Theruses didn't appear any less irritable. The more Rakas succumbed to the weakness inside him, the more he and Theruses irritated one another, but Theruses allowed him to keep his place here in recognition of the many others, Amahna included, he had lured in to the daemon power to serve. Perhaps that weakness was all that aggravated the lord of the daenox now, that failing that demoted Rakas from his once glorious position as one of Theruses's most favored and trusted servants. She would hope that was all it was.

Glancing from one to the other, she could tell that she would not join with her lord before they left. Given the dark glower he wore and the violent twitching of his tail, she might not survive a pairing with him anyhow. Her nerves danced a little when she knelt before him in the low-cut, almost transparent red dress that clung in such a way as to leave nothing to the imagination, but his expression did not change. With a bit of a pout and a conflicting sense of relief, she stared at the floor and waited for his acknowledgment.

"You will be gone from here within the hour," he told them, not giving her permission to look up from the damp, dark stone at his feet. "The seed will be strongest if it is planted within the dragon-child on the night of his sixteenth birthday, as near as possible to the hour of his birth. That night, once your task is finished, you will return here without him. The seed will take root and bring him to us in time. As the seed grows stronger, it will draw out the daenox. We will watch and wait. I trust this task to you Amahna and I will know if you fail in any way."

The need to be away from him was suddenly overwhelming. He was compelling her to leave. Driving her away. It made her resent him, as much as she could resent he who was her life. It also left her confused. Did he seek to test her loyalty by making her angry with him before she left? Did he doubt her devotion?

If so, she would prove to him that no other was as dedicated and reverent as she was. Perhaps he knew Rakas wavered in his devotion as his body failed to adapt to the saturation of daenox and he wanted to see how much influence that had over her by sending her off in this way. She had believed she loved Rakas once, but he was nothing to her now. They would be better off without him once this was finished. Perhaps she would help Theruses to see that.

With a sly smile she ducked her head in a deeper bow, touching her forehead to the cold stone. Then she rose, swaying her hips suggestively as she walked from the chamber, using all her will to fight the compulsion to move faster and not bothering to check if Rakas followed.

The outside world was a place she visited quite rarely. It had been perhaps seven years since her last visit to the surface. The procurement of supplies for life within the caves was a task left to the lesser servants. There was no other need to leave the cave system, so she stayed within, immersed in the daenox and the nearness of Theruses. The outside world was harsh and bright. She liked it a little less every time she visited.

The cave entrance was a gapping maw at the base of the ragged limestone cliffs of the Dunues Mountains. Walking toward the entrance from within was like emerging from the throat of a sleeping giant, the brightness of the outside world searing her eyes and rampaging cruelly through her skull. The cave exhaled, air moved by the extensiveness of the passages within. Just inside that entrance, they made their careful way along a narrow strip of stone between two large pits several hundred feet deep that opened in the floor. For anyone without a connection to the daenox, the floor looked solid. An easy illusion used to deal with unwanted visitors.

They walked from the entrance to the bottom of the rocky dirt slope that rolled down toward a nearby ravine. Behind them, a mountain mist, also enhanced by daemon power, quickly obscured the cave mouth from view and a brief pang of loss twisted in her chest, an orphan without Theruses. Forcing calm, she squinted against the painful brightness and focused her awareness on the herd of horses that she knew would be near. They would use daenox to lure the stallion into range and fog his awareness enough that he wouldn't notice a couple of his mares wandering away.

The pounding of hooves preceded the herd as the stallion drove them through the valley, breaking through the mist with the dramatic roar of rolling thunder. Amahna breathed in the beauty of their natural strength, almost forgetting to select a mount until Rakas pulled his out and stopped it a few feet from her. Picking out a lovely bay mare who ran close to her magnificent sire, Amahna drew her from the herd and over beside the buckskin Rakas had picked. The stallion would notice that his herd had gotten smaller when the daemon power wore off, but they would be well out of his range by then.

Quickly, they equipped the horses with light tack pulled out of a storage chamber. The lord of the daenox was no fool. He kept what supplies he could within the cave and was well aware of the benefit of things he could not keep in his underground realm. Storage chambers were maintained for weaponry and other useful equipment, but he did not have the facilities to keep a full army within the cave's passages. What he did have was the ability to seduce people to his cause with the daemon power if the need should ever arise.

Amahna swung into the saddle, the motion a bit awkward after so many years without practice. She kept her wild mount calm and still with a soothing flow of daenox and smiled, feeling the warmth of that power flowing through her. True power. When the world returned to the old way, when daemons roamed free again, she would be on the winning side, and this time there would be no dragons to balance the daemon powers.

Without waiting for Rakas to study their map she kicked her mount ahead. He had always been challenged when it came to directions, but these mountains were her home and she needed no maps to navigate them. Cursing, Rakas hurried after her, folding the old map he carried as he bounced uncomfortably on the mare's back, at least as out of practice in the saddle as Amahna.

They would stop first in Kithin, a small mountain village that swore allegiance to Theruses, aiding him when needed in exchange for protection from rockslides as well as the rare roving daemon spawned by the concentration of daenox in the nearby caves. All the residents had black eyes and hair due to their proximity to the daemon power's prison, but they stayed here because they were shepherds and the mountain meadows were lush grazing for their herds. The shepherds of Kithin would provide food and other supplies for their journey.

Using daenox, it would take about three days to cover the several hundred miles to Imperious. Their second stop would be at the graveyard a couple of miles outside of Kithin. There, Siniva, the Fire Dragon, was entrapped in his stone prison. They could use daenox they had accumulated within themselves over the years in the caves to tap into the deep web of dragon power there and use it transport themselves to the graveyard in Derg where Cylan, the War Dragon, was imprisoned in his stone cell. Amahna and Rakas could travel all the way to Imperious this way using four of the stone dragons. They would go from Siniva to Cylan, then Cylan to Tikat, the Hope Dragon in Kuilen, and from Tikat to Vanuthan, the Mother Dragon in Imperious. It would be such a pleasure to use the dragon's own powers to foil their plan for freedom.

Amahna directed her mount only when necessary, letting the mare guide them around cliffs and other hazards hidden by the thick mountain mist. With her head held high, she let the moisture of the mist collect on her face and hair. It felt wonderful. Such things as this and many others—the color of the grass, the smell of the horses—they were things she loved, but somehow, she could not recall missing them when she was in the cave. Perhaps the wonder of the daemon power, the beauty of the cave, and the magnificence of Theruses himself were enough to compensate. It must be so, for even now, as she enjoyed the world around her, she was eager to return home to the cave and Theruses.

Not far out of Kithin, they encountered a shepherd tending his herd. The man knelt respectfully as they approached, his black hair falling into his face, and rose only once they had stopped before him and bid him do so.

"My Lord and Lady, how may I serve you?"

Amahna briefly considered demanding that he attend them in Kithin, knowing that he would even leave his flock untended to do so. Then again, it would bring little satisfaction to cause disruption in the life of someone who stood only one station below those who served Theruses from within the cave and whose people provided many needed services to their lord.

She dredged up a smile for him. "Keep at your duties, we will find someone in the village to assist us."

Just before he bowed his head to them again, Amahna saw a mix of relief and disappointment warring across his features. It was almost sad that she could relate to his conflict. The desire to serve Theruses was so great that she too was often disappointed to be left to her more menial duties.

The village of Kithin was bordered on two sides by high limestone cliffs. Upon topping the rise, it appeared in the valley like a mirage against the green of the fields and the cold gray of the cliffs. The log buildings had a warm and inviting look to them and the village itself would have seemed quite welcoming if not for the peculiar black hair and eyes of all its occupants. They milled about on various chores like worker ants, an assortment of black heads bobbing along their way. The children played in the streets while their parents shook their heads and smiled if one got in the way. Kithin was such a friendly place most of the time that it reminded Amahna, a bit uncomfortably, of her old home in Imperious. It was simply a massively downsized reflection of that grand city.

When they neared the village, a cry went up and most

of the younger generations dropped what they were doing and raced out to greet the guests. Rakas shied away
from the attentions, hanging back, but Amahna enjoyed
their special treatment as they gathered about, eager to
see who would be chosen to attend their visitors.

Amahna smiled down at a lovely young woman with
long, straight black hair, who stood quietly hopeful.
"What are you called?"

"Kara, my Lady and Lord." She offered a graceful,
if somewhat abrupt curtsy to each of them.

"You will attend us Kara."

The young woman smiled up at Amahna, gratitude
and pride giving a glow to her cheeks. Kara escorted them
into the town with a bounce in her steps and found them
a comfortable table outside the tavern to wait while she
visited the shops where she procured the best foods and
equipment and made certain that they were all packed
efficiently onto the horses under her very serious supervision. While this was being done, other villagers brought
them the finest foods and drinks to be found in Kithin so
that they might refresh themselves.

Amahna watched her chosen assistant with a
growing sense of pride. The girl was lovely and athletic.
She danced tirelessly around the village, enjoying her
tasks, but making certain everything was done right.

"I think I'm taking a fancy to her," she commented
sipping at the robust red wine they had been given.

"Unfortunately for her," Rakas muttered under his
breath.

Amahna ignored him, taking another sip of her
wine. He was not worth the hassle of getting her ire up.
She watched Kara and considered the young woman's
future.

Once all was prepared and the riders nourished,
Kara escorted them to the edge of the village.

"I bid you good journey, my Lady and Lord."

Amahna reached down from her mount and placed a hand on the young woman's soft pale cheek. "I will see that our Lord Theruses hears of your excellent service." Then she turned her mare and they started off.

"My Lady?"

Amahna stopped her mount and glanced back.

"What might I look like if I had not been born near the daenox?"

"You would be a beautiful brunette with green eyes like emeralds," Amahna replied without hesitation.

Kara chewed at her lip then beamed up at them. "I gladly sacrifice that for the pleasure of serving you."

*Enchanting.* Amahna dismounted and walked up to the girl, placing a hand on each side of her face this time and gazing into black eyes that held no secrets.

"I believe you." She kissed the young woman's forehead before returning to her mount and leading the way out of the village.

"A quiet and charming young lady, don't you think," she remarked as they traversed the steep path to the graveyard.

"Oh, certainly," Rakas did not try to hide his bitterness and Amahna had no doubt he was rolling his eyes behind her.

"You're just annoyed because she said, 'Lady and Lord' instead of greeting you first. Perhaps Theruses would allow me a lady's maid when we return." She grinned smugly, knowing he was probably rolling his eyes again.

In the meadow at the top of the path they navigated carefully around the graves. This near to the daenox prison it was not unlikely for the dead to come visiting, so they made a point of treating the mounds with respect. At the far side of the meadow the dragon, Siniva, waited helpless in his prison. His stature was very proud, his forelegs straight and settled between and just in front of his hind legs. His neck was arched and high so that his slender head looked out over the graveyard like a king surveying his realm. It was unnerving how noble he looked despite his dismal circumstances, as though he had nothing to fear. As though his power hadn't been ripped away from him by a cruel betrayal. As though the threat they posed to the dragon's future hope for freedom didn't matter.

Amahna suppressed a shudder and bit the inside of her lip. Such thoughts had no place here. They had a job to do and her nerves were not going to get in the way.

They stopped the horses at the Siniva's feet and Amahna watched while Rakas focused in on the power of the dragon web. Even in this form, the dragons retained a limited connection to their web of power, though not enough to do much of anything for themselves. Anyone who knew it was there and had the power to access it could tap into the dragon web. It linked the dragons like a spider web running though the ground in such a way that she and Rakas could travel along it, but such manipulation took time, usually a day or more, and a great deal of energy. They had broken up the trip in such a fashion that Rakas would take them to Derg, then Amahna would take them to Kuilen while Rakas recovered his strength. Rakas would do the final leg to Imperious so that Amahna would have her wits about her when it was time to present themselves to her sister and the other nobles.

The ground trembled beneath them so violently she could feel it through her mount, the raging of Siniva in his prison, unable to stop them from using the dragon web for their own ends. The travel experience itself was like falling asleep. You could even have dreams, but it was still exhausting for whoever controlled the process. The risk of losing awareness in the open always made Amahna's palms sweat and lit her nerves on fire, though she knew that the power moved them in a realm that could not be seen just as sound could not be seen by the naked eye. Before she even knew the traveling had begun they snapped awake in a different graveyard and she had to quickly calm the horses with a touch of daenox. It was noon or just before the next day and they were not alone.

A young lad stumbled back from the grave he had been kneeling at, his mouth hanging open, his blue eyes wide with fear. Rakas did not have the energy left to do anything about it, so she drove her heels into her mount and took after the boy when he began to run. She threw her dagger straight and true, a skill she had learned in the Imperious Legion, and sunk it through the back of his neck. The lad dropped instantly and Amahna jumped down to retrieve her weapon, wiping it clean on his shirt. They could not allow anyone to witness their passage.

Rakas exhaled heavily and shook his head as if to apologize for not helping, his eyes glassy with exhaustion.

"It is done. Let's hope our arrival in Imperious is not so disagreeable." She turned her attention to the stone dragon behind them. "Shall we?"

Dephithus leaned back in the comfortable crook of a big branch of the old Mother Tree and grinned down at his companion. They were both winded from racing to the meadow as they often did. Myara, who had lost the race, jumped up, grabbing hold of his boot toe with a war whoop and hauling him off the branch he had claimed. Dephithus landed on hands and knees in the damp grass by the brook. In seconds, he was on his feet again and charging after Myara as she struggled to get up higher into the tree before he could catch her. Like a hungry wildcat, Dephithus crouched and sprang, catching hold of the branch he had been pulled from. With a playful snarl he pulled himself up, his arms trembling with the exertion of their prolonged roughhousing.

Myara had claimed a seat and held her hands up in surrender, gasping for air. "Mercy," she cried, breathless, as he climbed up to her branch.

"It's about time," he replied, dropping back onto another branch with a sigh of relief. "I was afraid you were going to win."

"Sure, Dragonkin, as if that is even possible."

"You win races all of the time," Dephithus argued.

Myara turned her nose up and looked away, not pointing out that her victories were typically due to his letting her win.

38

He stuck his tongue out at her. "Fine then. Nobody asked me if I wanted to be a throwback to my mother's long dead ancestors."

"Oh, poor Dephithus," she replied teasingly with a shake of her head and a crooked grin. "So, tomorrow night is your night. Are you excited?"

"This again." He took a moment to adjust his position and pluck a leaf from the tree. Though Myara still gasped for her air, his breathing had already begun to regulate. As the intoxicating burn of his muscles began to fade, a twinge of the old guilt for his unusual physical abilities crept in, not that he had any control over them. Lacking interest in Myara's choice of subjects, he began to study the veins of the leaf as he answered. "I really don't see a need for all of the fuss. It is only a birthday."

Myara plucked a leaf and balled it up, using it to bomb the leaf he was inspecting out of his hand. His gaze followed the lost leaf as it twirled dancingly down to the grass below, then he plucked another leaf for inspection.

"Just a birthday." She rolled her eyes and he scowled mock anger at her as she bombed him with another leaf, hitting the back of his hand this time. "It's your Dawning Day. You can enter in tournaments now and marry all those girls and boys that swoon after you."

Dephithus chuckled as he let go of the new leaf, letting it float to the ground, forgotten. "Yes, and I can be called to stand gate guard or honor guard at any time. I can have kids and spouses to nag at me."

"What is wrong with being called to duties? You always enjoyed standing with the guards when you were younger."

True. He used to stand with the honor guards for fun as a child, staring up at them with reverence and dreaming of the day he would be one of them.

He plucked another leaf and another, crushing them into balls and piling them along the branch next to him. Myara observed this and began storing up her own ammunition while they talked.

"I don't know." Dephithus hesitated on one leaf, staring at the myriad veins weaving through it for a moment before crushing it down into another bomb. "I just enjoy our outings. I won't have as much time for this kind of thing once they start calling on me."

Myara tossed a leaf bomb, hitting him on top of the head this time. "In a few more months I will be joining you at those duties."

"It won't be the same."

Myara smiled over at him and he was caught up for a moment by the way the sunlight piercing through the leaves sparkled in her eyes. He sighed and bombed her shoulder to distract from his straying thoughts and her smile broadened.

"Shall we run away together?"

Dephithus shook his head with a serious frown, though their silliness made a giddy laughter bubble up, threatening his charade. "No. It's a fine idea, but I'm still tired from the last run."

Myara pummeled him with green leaf balls and he returned the onslaught, laughing as he tried to dodge her shots without falling from his perch. When they were each out of ammunition, they leaned back, grinning proudly at their own foolishness. Then she closed her eyes and turned her face to the sun. He watched in silence.

It would not be the same. He would be proud to do whatever duties he was called to and he would do them to the best of his ability, but he would long for their time together. They would have training together again once she had her Dawning Day, they just would lose much of the free time they spent enjoying each other's friendship. Marriage was an entirely different problem. He would be expected to wed soon, within a year or two at least, and the only woman he wanted to be with was Myara. There was the obvious solution of marrying her, but that might change their relationship as much as if he married another.

The sound of approaching horses drew their attention as a young serving lad rode into the meadow. He wore the blue and silver livery of the Elysium palace stables and drew behind his mount two geldings from Lord Mythan's private show stock decked out in royal finery.

"Lord Dephithus," he hailed as he pulled the horses up at the foot of the Mother Tree.

"Yes," Dephithus crushed a leaf in his fist. Their childhood together was nearing its end. The sixteenth anniversary of his birth was upon them.

"Your mother requests your presence at the palace. She asks that you come prepare to ride to the inner gates with her."

It was exactly what he had expected. His mother's half-sister, whose name he had never even heard before a few weeks ago, was supposed to be arriving with the noon sun. It was odd enough that she had not contacted Avaline in nearly sixteen years, not even to let her sister know she was alive and now she suddenly wanted to attend her sister's son's Dawning Day. His mother was excited, so much so that his birthday was the only thing she talked about more, so he would do his best to please her and hide his misgivings.

"Of course. Thank you. We will take the horses." Dephithus dropped from the tree, landing light on his feet and spooking the showy animals. He took the reins from the youth who bowed his head respectfully and cantered back the way he had come. The horses were a perfect match, dark blood bays with black stockings and thick black manes and tails. Their delicate, pointed ears perked forward with curiosity and, though their build was more refined, they were not much smaller than the Legion mounts. Overall, they were beautiful, but they each sported some flaw of conformation or temper that was not obvious to his untrained eye or they would not be gelded.

Myara dropped down beside him, landing harder and spooking the horses again. "Does this mean I'm invited?"

"It would seem so," Dephithus replied, nodding his head to the violet rose that had been fastened to a brass ring on one of the saddles.

She smiled at the thoughtful present, a bloom from her favorite rosebush, then swung up into the ornate saddle. Both mounts were garbed in black equipment worked over with blue and silver embroidery and adornments. When Dephithus swung up, the high-strung steeds made as if to bolt, but they held them back, forcing them to keep a reasonable pace.

Myara fingered a petal of the rose. "Do you ever wish Mythan was your blood-father?"

He shook his head. "I don't see where it would change anything. My father spends most of his time with his other wives in Derg and, since Mythan is sterile, I'm the closest thing he has to a true heir. Besides, Mythan also has the distant Dragonkin lineage, so most people think that somehow I really am his son."

She nodded, still gazing at the rose, pensive. "Do you think that's possible?"

"What, that Mythan could be my father?"

She nodded again.

He shrugged. "It is a strange world sometimes, I suppose anything could be possible."

Dephithus had considered the possibility many times. Avaline said there were rumored to be many history books stored in the library archive about the Dragonkin, though she herself had never seen them. Supposedly, the Dragonkin sometimes possessed unusual powers in addition to their enhanced strength and speed. Nothing truly exceptional, just subtle ways to manipulate things. Perhaps, if Mythan wanted a son badly enough, the distant Dragonkin blood in him could have made it happen. However, there was always so much to do being a student of the Legion, the undeclared heir to the throne, and a friend to Myara, that he never seemed to have time to ask about the library archives. Even if he did have the time, he was not sure he could convince Mythan to give him the key.

They picked up the pace, allowing the horses to move out into an easy trot. Anything faster might throw dirt up on the fancy trappings the animals wore and that might irritate Mythan, who clearly meant to make a good impression on their visitors. Outside the stables a line-up of twelve more horses, all decked out in formal gear, waited with the stable hands, shifting about impatiently. Their approach stirred up a chorus of snorts and whinnies among the waiting animals.

Six mounts would be for honor guards and two were for Mythan and Avaline. The other four were for Kent, Avaline's third husband, their two daughters, and Kent's husband, Vicard. His half-sisters, Kinny and Cinda, were both younger than Dephithus and lived primarily with their father and his husband. Lornin, Dephithus's blood father, would be arriving tomorrow to stay for a few days and attend the Dawning Day celebration.

They left their mounts with the others and went into the palace to change into more formal attire.

The palace was a towering structure with an open design. The entrance a wide sweeping staircase with low steps leading to the massive double doors. An elaborate half-wall ran along the sides of the staircase carved in the shape of waves rolling gently in toward the doors, done in stone that was a warm and welcoming beige color. The walls and floors beyond the doors were also done in soft elegant colors. Muted tans, greys and blues. The grace of the craftsmanship, the lines all done in gentle wave-like curves with no harsh angles, made it seem not so much as if the walls were flowing but as if the person walking there were flowing past them. The clumsiest of men could feel graceful within those walls. The structure was designed to exude welcome. Everything was crafted in such a way that the palace embraced the people who entered there, giving off the illusion it had been designed specifically for each individual who set foot upon its floors. People stood taller and walked with pride when they passed through that grand entrance.

Dephithus delighted in watching people make the transition. Most people were intimidated by the towering exterior, sometimes even cowering a bit as they approached, but they puffed up like nobles as they made the walk up those steps and came inside. Even Myara moved along with a little more confidence in her bearing as she strode along beside him.

Myara spent so much time with Dephithus and his family growing up that as much as half of her wardrobe resided in one of the guest rooms. When she had first started spending nights in the palace Mythan had placed her in the wing opposite the one Dephithus slept in. The two quickly made a game of trying to sneak through the halls to each other's rooms without being caught. It did not take Mythan long to break down and allow Myara a room just down the hall from Dephithus to keep their nocturnal adventures from waking others.

"What shall I wear?" she asked, stopping in front of her bedchamber.

He made a play of thinking it out for a moment, though he had already envisioned the dress she should wear. When her expression began to turn impatient he grinned.

"The royal blue split skirts," he said. She had already begun to frown. "The one with the v-neck and waist and the silver trimmings. Don't shake your head, you know you will look enchanting in it on back of that fancy mount, and the colors are appropriate."

"I'm not part of the royal family."

"You became an honorary member of the royal family for today when Mythan extended the invitation to you."

She scowled. "Fine, but you owe me one."

"No matter how you fight it, you are still a lady," Dephithus called as she stepped into the room.

Myara peeked her head back out and smirked. "Not a lady. A woman."

"Not yet."

He laughed as she slammed the door. With a smug grin he walked a few doors down and entered his own room. He had a similar outfit to the one Myara was putting on. The trousers were royal blue with fine silver embroidery running up the outside of the right leg. The jacket was the same color with silver embroidery on the lapel and around the cuffs. He stood before the mirror while pulling the lace of his dress shirt out at the collar and cuffs then ran a brush through his thick, dark hair.

Myara stepped out into the hall a few moments after him, responding to his approving smile with an exasperated sigh. Dephithus bowed down, holding one hand out to her. Myara's laugh was soft, almost uncertain as she took his hand and he wondered when the unease had spread through their relationship. Could it be that she had begun to notice in him whatever it was that made so many girls and boys swoon? Could it be that he wanted her to notice him in that way?

He rested his free hand at her waist and felt her hesitate again as she went to set her hand on his shoulder. He smiled, looking into her eyes and whirled her down the hall in time to the music in his head. They continued this way, laughing and spinning, until a deep voice startled them.

They stopped abruptly, stifling a few giggles and turned to face Mythan, whose outfit was the exact opposite of the one Dephithus wore, silver with blue embroidery.

"Pardon, Den-Father, we were just..." He trailed off. What had they been doing exactly?

"Acting childish."

Myara grinned. "Practicing for tomorrow," she countered, beaming at her own brilliance.

Mythan's stern expression broke and warmth infused his smile. "I do hope you have a little more restraint tomorrow, you'll run someone over dancing like that. Come, Avaline is waiting and she is dreadfully anxious."

*

Amahna and Rakas arrived at the inner gates of Imperious, the entrance to the Elysium palace grounds, a short time before noon. The gate guard inquired as to who they were and their business then waved them on with a friendly smile. Moments after they passed, the guard seemed to have forgotten them.

"How amusing," she remarked once they were out of earshot. "They didn't even consider the possibility of a threat from us. Has it been peaceful so long that danger does not even hold a place in people's minds?"

Rakas nodded. "And the history books praise the Imperious Legion as one of the most fierce and effective fighting forces of all time."

"Yes," Amahna chuckled. "Now they would be so

stunned to encounter hostility that they would forget their precious training and wet themselves."

They followed the main road through gradual rolling hills vibrant with spring grasses and flowers. In no time, they could see some of the buildings rising to greet them. She recognized the stables and training grounds off to their far right before the forest. The highest towers of the distant palace peeked up over gently sloping hilltops. Somewhere in the distance, to the east of the palace, were the lesser manors belonging to the few nobles esteemed enough to reside within the walls of Elysium. The surrounding forest and rolling fields were lush green, though they had to contend with a long rainy season to keep it that way. As she recalled there were plenty of things to do here in bad weather. Not the least of which were the frequent tournaments complete with jousting, archery, and melee competitions put on in the huge covered arena. All the silly, trivial things the nobility did to amuse themselves.

An assemblage of riders topped the nearest rise. A woman at the head of the riders waved at them and led the group down the hill at a swift trot. Amahna waved back and searched out a smile for them. Avaline was still lovely, if slightly plumper than she remembered her. The regal looking gentleman next to her was obviously the much-matured Lord Mythan, ruler of Imperious and Commander of her famed Legion. She remembered him as barely more than a boy. She had last seen him around the time of his own Dawning Day.

Amahna and Rakas held their mounts and waited for the group to pull up in front of them. The six mounted honor guard formed a perfectly spaced half circle around the rear of the royal party.

Avaline rode up close enough to reach out and hug Amahna from her saddle. Amahna suffered through her suffocating embrace with feigned enthusiasm and

quickly encouraged turning to introductions by pre-
senting Rakas to her. Avaline greeted him with genuine
warmth, his weary look prompting a comment on how
they must have travelled a long way, and began present-
ing her group, but Amahna had already spotted the
dragon-child.

When she met the young man's eyes he stiffened in
the saddle, and she had the uneasy feeling that, for a
brief second, he had seen through their illusions to their
blackened-over eyes. She quickly blurred his perception
with a touch of daenox and he frowned as if puzzled,
then he spurred his mount up to greet them, conjur-
ing up a truly charming smile. He was quite handsome,
with strength of presence that was tempered by the captivating beauty of his eyes. He had the dragon scaling
like Theruses, but over less of his visible body, and in
silver rather than gold. The only thing that delighted
her more than his beauty as he laid a kiss on the back of
her hand, was the fact that Rakas had suddenly come to
life, completely enthralled by the dragon-child.

"It is an honor to finally meet you. Mother has told
me so many good things about you." Dephithus spoke
the obvious lie graciously as he took his lips away from
her hand and released it. Something about her made
him uneasy, she could see it in the twitch of his lips and
the way he refused to hold her gaze. He did not want
them to stay. However, she was willing to bet that he
would not say as much to his mother. He was raised to
politeness.

"Likewise, Lord Dephithus. My sister could speak
of little other than you in her letters." She gave a faint
wistful smile as if something amused her. Let him
wonder at that.

Avaline also introduced one of the other gentlemen
as her third husband, which put Amahna's hackles up.
How many men did the woman need to claim as hers?

Then she introduced their two daughters and his husband and Amahna recognized that theirs was a marriage that allowed the two men to have children of their own. Still, after a youth spent watching her sister charm away every man she showed interest in, it only reinforced her loathing for the other woman.

When Dephithus turned to Rakas and reached to shake his hand, his smile slipped briefly at the way Rakas looked at him as though his favorite dish had been laid before him. Despite that, Dephithus did not allow his manners to falter. The dragon-child shook her companion's hand firmly, but abruptly, not lingering long enough to chance giving a wrong impression. The young man's brow furrowed once the attention was off him and Rakas greeted his pretty young friend Myara in an almost disinterested fashion. Amahna wanted to kick her companion for his lack of tact, but it wasn't so surprising given how tired he must be after taking them the last leg of the trip. To her surprise, it was the dragon-child who spared them any further awkwardness.

"Shall we go to the palace?" Dephithus suggested. "I imagine you both must be in need of some rest and refreshment after your journey."

Avaline beamed proudly at him.

"Of course," Mythan spoke up after a discreet nod of approval to his den-son. "We have refreshments waiting. Let us go to the palace."

As they turned their mounts, Amahna caught Rakas watching the young Dragonkin with that hunger in his eyes and smiled. His attraction would make the whole process much easier...for them.

The dark gaze of Rakas haunted Dephithus. That gaze had followed every move he made throughout much of the prior evening. Aside from the unnerving staring, the man had been polite, quiet, and soft-spoken. What bothered Dephithus most was that Rakas looked at him like he had found the object of his greatest desire...and he was heartbroken about it. Something about it made his skin crawl.

"What are you thinking?"

Dephithus was startled out of his ponderings by Myara's sudden question, making his mount to jump almost as hard as he did.

Myara offered a gentle smile, though he could see the temptation to laugh at his surprise shining in her eyes.

He knew she was putting out an effort to be supportive and resist the usual teasing banter they engaged in, but he did not want to talk about last night. "It's nothing really."

"Just wondering what to do about your newest admirer." She did laugh then, and he scowled at her. "Oh, come on. I'm not blind. I saw the way that Rakas fellow was pining after you yesterday. He is honestly attractive, if a bit thin. You should be flattered."

"I think this whole thing is suspicious. What made

my aunt suddenly decide to come back into Mother's life? And why now?" He offered her a sideways glare for her teasing. Try as he might, he could not shake off his discomfort remembering the way Rakas had watched him so intently through the afternoon the day before.

Myara tossed her thick dark gold hair in a saucy manner as Dephithus slowed his mount to move in behind so they could maneuver through a thick stand of trees and brush. "Why don't you concern yourself over more important things, like who to pick on at the dance tonight or making bets on how many braids you'll have on your belt by the end of the evening. You usually aren't this anxious."

Before Dephithus could put voice to his apprehension, a mountain cat lunged out of the brush to their right, swiping a warning at Myara's horse's legs with one deadly paw. Both mounts leapt sideways and Myara was knocked from her saddle by a low branch across her side. The tawny cat let out a bone-chilling cry as it leaned back into its haunches, preparing to pounce on the grounded rider.

Forcing his panicked mount around, Dephithus faced the cat, emitting a deep growl from his own throat. It was the same growl Myara had always delighted in when they sparred. Such sounds were another characteristic of the Dragonkin whose vocal cords differed slightly from those of a normal human.

The cat hesitated, though its muscles remained taut as it stared at Myara with deadly intent, long canines wet with saliva. Dephithus jumped down from his mount and growled again. This time the cat looked up at him, losing Myara as its focal point. It met his strange eyes for a few seconds then finally conceded, though its tail switched about in agitation when it turned and bolted into the trees.

Myara shakily exhaled the breath she had been holding. Her frame shook visibly with the panic that had flooded her system.

Dephithus hurried to her side, retaining his frightened mounts reins as he knelt next to her. "Are you hurt?"

"Just a little bruised, thanks to my hero." Perhaps it was meant to sound jesting, but the words came out in a bitter tone and she was too busy soothing her own nerves to acknowledge it.

He rested his free hand on her forearm and gave it a squeeze. "You know, Myara, I'm like everyone else. That cat could have just as easily ignored me."

She placed a hand over his on her arm and looked up at him, sporting a small scrape on her cheek that made her look irresistibly vulnerable. There was a moment of resistance in her eyes that said he was wrong. It said he was different and they both knew it, but the resistance faded and she glanced away.

"I know. Why do you think I'm coping so poorly?" She managed a smile then. "Help me up. I think we're riding double for a bit."

Another rider came weaving through the trees as Dephithus was helping Myara dust off. It was Amahna, leading their lost mount. She held out the reins to them.

"I hope you don't mind my interruption, but I was enjoying a pleasant ride when I was almost run over by this distinctly rider-less horse and I thought someone might be missing it."

"Thank you." Myara walked over to claim her mount, her gait hitching with a slight limp.

"Better work that out before the dance tonight," Amahna remarked conversationally before turning her all-too-expectant gaze on Dephithus. "I was hoping I might run into you. I would love to speak with my nephew a little before tonight's festivities."

Dephithus, though he tried to set aside his misgivings, immediately suspected that it might be more than a coincidence that she happened upon them at this moment. How likely was it that she would come upon them right when they needed assistance? But no, how could she have known they would be attacked by a mountain cat? It was extremely unusual for one of the relatively small predators to come after a mounted rider. But maybe it really was a chance encounter.

He said nothing and Amahna met his gaze with confidence. Her hair, colored like obsidian seen through a thin layer of blood, blew back from her face in a soft breeze as if daring him to find some secret in her features, though her dark eyes revealed no hidden agenda to him.

Myara swung stiffly up into her saddle and forced a little cough to get his attention. Dephithus slowly turned to her, reluctant to look away in case Amahna should disclose some secret in her expression when his attention was elsewhere. "Perhaps you two could talk now. I'm going to ride back to the training hall and work out this knot in my hip."

Dephithus frowned. "You shouldn't ride alone, that cat—"

"Would not linger around people," Amahna interrupted. "I think that is a sound idea. I look forward to seeing you again this evening Myara."

"Likewise, Lady Amahna. Take care of my boy." Myara gave him a teasing a grin before winding her mount away through the trees.

Dephithus watched Myara until he could barely see her through the trees then turned to Amahna and forced a friendly smile. "Where shall we ride?"

"I would like to visit the graveyard, if you don't mind."

Her choice of destination and her determined gaze

chilled him. "I'm not sure I know how get there."

"I do." She urged her mount ahead, not looking to see if he followed.

Perhaps she assumed his good manners would compel him. If so, she was right, he thought, resenting his etiquette training as he mounted up and urged his horse after her.

*

It had been all too easy to send the mountain cat after them with a touch of daenox. Though his appearance left little room for doubt, Amahna had known that if Dephithus were the dragon-child they suspected him to be, the cat would respond to him. The whole plan worked beautifully, proving him to be their target and giving Amahna a convenient way to get rid of his lady friend as well. It was a shame that he seemed to have no interest in men. If he were at all attracted to Rakas, it would make the planting of the seed of daemon power much easier, though likely less effective.

With a mental sigh she turned her thoughts to remembering the way through the trees to the graveyard from this side, letting him choose whether to converse or to quietly puzzle her over in his mind. It almost seemed as if he had chosen the latter option and she was beginning to settle into the silence when he finally spoke.

"Why did you come here?"

She smiled appreciation at his directness. He was not afraid and would that would make him a fine servant to Theruses when he turned. "You're the heir to the throne of Imperious, people from all over the kingdom have been invited to your Dawning Day. When word traveled my way of the occasion, it was as good an excuse as any to finally visit my old home."

"I was told you left because you'd fallen in love with Rakas and you're still with him, but you're obviously not a couple. Why is that?"

"Obviously? Do you say that simply because he can't seem to take his eyes off you?" She twisted in her saddle and looked him over like a cow that would soon be dinner then nodded approvingly, catching his resulting scowl before facing front again.

"I don't appreciate being appraised like a four-course meal."

She laughed. "You will be a man soon, and a handsome one at that. You had better get used to being appreciated by both women and men. Especially at court."

Dephithus blew out a frustrated breath behind her. She suspected he knew that he couldn't deny the truth in that statement. She let him think about it, hoping her frankness would earn her a little of his trust.

"Why did you leave?"

She hesitated a moment, but there did not seem much harm in telling him the truth. Avaline could have told him if she ever wanted to. "Your mother always possessed more natural charm and, as a result, was much more popular with the young suitors than I was. She caught the attention of every young gentleman who came around, even the ones I fancied. It happened so often I started to wonder if she were doing it on purpose to vex me. But I never let it worry me too much. I wasn't that serious about them. Then I started to fall hard for a particular young lord in the court. We had spent some time together and I was certain he returned my affections. The day I worked up the courage to tell him how I felt, I found Lornin kissing your mother."

"My blood father?"

Amahna smirked at the shock in his tone. "None other. She won his heart, as you know, and then she continued to drag him along, keeping him on a tight leash even after she gained the interest of the young Prince Mythan. Perhaps I could have turned my affection to women, but I hadn't explored that part of myself yet. I believed I needed a man of my own and I hated her for taking Lornin from me. I felt like I would never find someone as long as she was there.

"It was around then that Rakas rode through town. He was young and so darkly handsome. He took a fancy to me and, more importantly, he didn't even seem to see your mother. I suppose I was shallow, but that alone would have been enough to capture my devotion back then, but he also promised that he could bring me great power where he lived, and I wanted that. I wanted the kind of attention he gave me, and I wanted the kind of power my sister would have when she married Mythan, which I had no doubt she would. I was so hurt and angry over Lornin that I left one night with Rakas without a word to anyone."

"What happened between you and Rakas?"

She smiled wistfully. "Relationships change. We are no longer lovers. I have someone else in my life now. We still interact and travel together on occasion."

He was silent for a time, then, when the path widened, he moved his mount up beside her in a more open and confident position. "Why go to the graveyard?"

"That's better. You shouldn't ride behind me like a servant or a thief. Have you ever been to the graveyard?"

Dephithus frowned at her as if she had lost her mind. "We celebrate the dead in the palace while the Silent Watch buries them. You lived here long enough to know that."

"Indeed." She gave him a smug little smile designed to pique his curiosity.

The graveyard was in a large clearing amidst the thickest stand of trees in the forest. The graves were laid out in a circular pattern with the oldest at the foot of the statue in the center. Dephithus dismounted before the first grave and left his mount standing there, the animal's reins falling from his hand as though forgotten. His attention fixated on that center statue. Amahna stopped her mount inside the cover of the trees at the edge of the graveyard proper and watched him approach the magnificent Mother Dragon, Vanuthan, where she crouched protectively over the mass of graves as if her own children were buried there. Vines grew over that massive stone body in places, some dripping down over her great head like chains dragging her down.

Dephithus moved toward the Mother Dragon as if nothing else existed in the world. There was caution in his movement, despite his obvious fascination, almost as though he knew there was more to the dragon than stone. When he reached the foot of the statue, he sank to his knees there and caressed one of Vanuthan's clawed feet with a gentle touch. It was all Amahna could do not to laugh with delight when a single tear squeezed free of the stone eye and ran down the dragon's face to drop upon the boy's head.

Dephithus frowned up at the sky, searching for the offending cloud, and Amahna allowed herself a smile.

The dragon-child got hastily to his feet when Amahna moved her mount out into the open and he brushed his knees off, as though trying to hide what he had been doing. There was a tremble in the dragon's power then, stronger than she had ever felt from any one dragon. The Mother Dragon wanted very badly to protect her son. Rakas would probably curse her later for tempting the dragon's fury, but it amused Amahna to remind them of how helpless they really were.

Dephithus had cocked his head to the side, his gaze focused intently on the ground. Somehow, he too had felt something of the disturbance in the dragon web of power.

"She's a dragon, isn't she? I've never seen one before. I've only heard of them in children's stories."

Amahna said nothing, though she was surprised that he knew the dragon was female. There was a strong connection between him and the beast.

"Was I wrong to touch her? Is that what that trembling was?"

She made her expression solemn and imagined Theruses in place of the dragon so that she could gaze upon it with something like reverence. "No, there is nothing wrong with what you did. There is a dragon guardian in all the graveyards. It is shameful that we never come to appreciate them."

Dephithus turned his captivating eyes up to wonder over the long, slender head of the dragon. "She doesn't look so fearsome. She's quite beautiful. Why do people make them out to be so horrible in children's stories?" He faced Amahna and began to pick his way toward her after gently touching Vanuthan's foot once more.

"It's just another way of frightening children into behaving."

Amahna regarded the dragon-child with a prickling of dread creeping up the back of her neck. She could already feel herself becoming fond of him. No wonder the villagers and gate guards were so receptive when she had said she was his aunt. He was the kind of young man you could not help liking. He was handsome, kind hearted, honest. There was little about him that Theruses would like, though she found him quite enchanting. If only she could find some way of luring him from his home. Then maybe she could turn him to the daemon power in a nicer way. She could show him the wonders of the world as she knew it and lead him gently to Theruses.

"Have you ever considered anything other than your life here? Perhaps adventuring or offering yourself as a hired hero."

He swung up on his mount and settled himself in before turning to regard her thoughtfully. After a moment he shook his head. "Those aren't proper pursuits for a well-trained soldier and I am the expected heir to the throne. I can't go gallivanting off like I have no responsibilities. Besides, there's nothing to fight, not like in the fancy stories."

Amahna frowned. "I suppose those are all good points. Although, one might wonder what the point is of being a soldier in the Legion when there's nothing to fight."

He grinned, and she could see in that easy expression that she was winning his trust.

"Also, a good point. I will have to think on that." He looked up at the sky for a moment then his gaze drifted back to the dragon as if pulled there. "Mother will want to fuss over me for a few hours before the festivities, we had probably best get back, but..." He faced her again. "I thank you for this ride, it was unexpected and interesting."

Amahna bowed her head, as much to hide her pleasure at his words as to show her growing respect. "Certainly, my young lord. I do hope we get another chance to visit before I leave again."

She let Dephithus lead off, pausing a moment before following to breathe in the fragrant forest and remember her resolve. Picturing Theruses in her mind, she knew that she could and would do anything for him. Setting her shoulders and lifting her head high, she turned her mount and followed the dragon-child.

For Dephithus, preparing for the Dawning Day celebration consisted mostly of teasing his mother about the inappropriate things he might be inclined to do on this most auspicious of nights while she fretted and fussed over how he should act and what he should wear. Rothrik, the man fixing his hair at that moment, had already been redirected on how to do so no less than seven times.

"All of the eligible young ladies will be there." Avaline was saying. "The daughter of—"

"What about the young men?" Dephithus interrupted.

His mother stared at him for a moment as though surprised he had spoken. "What?"

"The eligible young men. Will they be there?"

She smiled reassurance. "Plenty of young men will be there, darling, but none hold a candle to you."

"I was hoping they'd hold themselves to me," Dephithus remarked, digging at a stubborn bit of dirt under one fingernail.

Rothrik, his back to Avaline, was biting his lower lip to fight back a smile.

"What?" She asked again.

"I feel like men are just better dancers," he continued, enjoying the forlorn look on her face. "I don't

60

know that I'll waste much time dancing with the ladies tonight."

"W… well," she stammered. She was silent then for a few seconds and he could see she was struggling for the right words. "It isn't that you shouldn't dance with the men, darling. As heir to the throne, however, it might be advisable to get to know some of the young ladies at least. There is the matter of future heirs after all." Her eyes widened as if she had just realized something. "Is that why you and Myara are only friends?"

Dephithus burst out with a laugh. "I'm only teasing you mother. I'll dance with every lady in the place if it pleases you."

Avaline let out a dramatic breath of relief. "You shouldn't torture your mother so. I'm going to go see how the food is coming along. Please see that he is presentable when he leaves here, Rothrik."

The man stopped working for a moment to offer her a gracious nod. "Of course, my Lady. I have such a handsome foundation to start with after all."

Dephithus cracked a grin. "Vying for the first dance I see."

Rothrik chuckled and Avaline shook her head at them before bustling from the room.

About an hour later, all decked out in his finery, Dephithus found himself a quiet corner to watch from. Servants bustled about preparing several long tables, set in the shape of a horseshoe, for the enormous assortment of foods they would soon bear. It was probably a good thing that they had gatherings of this magnitude very rarely, he could almost smell the weariness of the men and women as they rushed to make sure every detail was arranged perfectly and on time. There had been a miscount at some point that required the addition of two more table settings and a mass shuffling of every place setting at the tables. At least three people had adjusted the spacing of the plates and silverware on the long tables no less than five times since then.

This group of servants would move on to setup the dessert hall while the guests dined and would then be allowed to rest while a second group attended the guests and a third followed along to clean up. All things considered, he would rather be in the first group since the second had to keep the hours of the guests and the third would be up long after everyone else had retired.

The nobles who had arrived early were out enjoying the garden and Dephithus, as the guest of honor, chose to keep himself out of sight since returning to the palace. In perhaps an hour, he and his family, consisting of Mythan, Avaline, and his blood father Lornin—who despised large gatherings, but had agreed to attend only because it was a very special occasion—would meet their guests in the greeting hall. Kent, Vicard, and their daughters had tactfully declined seats at the greeting, choosing more appropriate spots standing below and to the left of the throne dais.

Here, among the servants, Dephithus was allowed his peace. They did not bother him, offering only a nod or smile in his direction when they noticed him watching. Though they were considered lesser by some, they knew the value of time alone as well as any lord or lady expected to host grand affairs. At ease among them, Dephithus laid his head back against the cold granite of a wall column in the dining hall and closed his eyes. With several deep, even breaths, he cleared his head. Tonight, he would be expected to behave with all the nobility of manner a king would possess, which seemed a lot to ask of a sixteen-year-old boy. Not to imply that he could not do it, or even that he would not enjoy it, but it would be exhausting.

He could feel some change in the air at Mythan's approach and wondered if he would ever have such presence as his den-father did. Before Mythan could speak Dephithus opened his eyes and regarded the lord of Imperious thoughtfully. Mythan returned the thoughtful scrutiny for a moment, his gaze hesitating on the silver scaling at his temples a second too long before moving to his silver-green catlike eyes.

"Pardon my boldness, Den-father, but you seem troubled by something."

Mythan nodded, his expression one of approval. "Yes. You trouble me, my son."

Dephithus sat up straighter, worried by the solemnity behind that statement while quite aware that Mythan had called him *my son* and not *den-son* or *Dephithus.*

"Don't fret," Mythan moved over and sank down beside him as though some great weight bore him down, "you have done nothing wrong. I just fear that you may not have an easy time ruling the kingdom when your turn comes to sit upon this throne."

"Because I'm different? A throwback to the Dragonkin?"

Mythan's grimace was full of guilt, but he nodded. "There's always your two half-sisters, and my brother in Cuvath has sons. If you don't want this, tell me now and I will not announce you as my chosen heir tonight. I know I should have brought this up sooner..."

Dephithus lifted a hand to stop him. "Den-father." He hesitated a moment, considering how he had been addressed. "Father, you may have only mentioned it now, but I've been thinking about this for a long time. If you will honor me by naming me your heir, I will gladly face any adversity to prove myself as worthy as any blood son."

Mythan's smile was full of relief, his eyes moistening with the depth of his gratitude. "Very well then. Be warned though, I will probably ask more of you than I would a blood son."

Dephithus grinned, showing himself ready for the challenge, and Mythan squeezed his shoulder once. They both rose in sync to move out into the greeting hall.

Avaline was already seated with Lornin on her left and Kent and his family below. When he looked at his blood-father, he was a little surprised to realize that Lornin shared some of the same darkly handsome traits that might have attracted Amahna to Rakas. Perhaps it was not so hard to image her being attracted to his father as well.

Dephithus pushed away those musings and took his place on his mother's right, his ornate throne, a fanciful piece embellished with bejeweled silver dragons on the arms and over the back, was pushed a few inches forward to distinguish him.

The throne was originally made for the Dragonkin Lady Verr ages ago and Mythan felt it was time to put it to use again. They agreed that it was better to acknowledge up front and celebrate that Dephithus was different rather than trying to gloss over the fact. The same effort went into his attire. His deep green coat and pants were embroidered in silver, proudly enhancing the strangeness of his eyes and scaling. He had long shared Mythan's concerns about how he would be accepted by the people as their ruler. He dressed this way tonight because he wanted everyone to remember that he was different now, not later when the day came for him to step into his den-father's shoes.

Mythan sat in his throne to the right of Dephithus and, with a subtle gesture, directed the doorman to begin the greeting ceremony.

Guests were escorted into the room in family groups and walked down the center in twos. Their names were called out by the usher as they entered, with Mythan's personal attendant whispering the names again before they stopped to bow or curtsy in front of the dais, ensuring that they could greet each one personally.

His blood-father, Lornin, scowled equally at everyone. He did not seem to harbor any dislike for anyone in particular, he was simply awkward in crowds and ill-at-ease with the formalities of the court. Dephithus could afford none of his blood-father's detachment. He greeted each guest by name with all the dignity he could muster in an effort to show himself worthy of Mythan's respect.

Their efforts to enhance his differences had the desired effect. Several guests hesitated before greeting him, their composure momentarily disrupted, as they met his strange eyes. The younger ladies giggled or blushed more often than not, seeming even more delighted than usual at his appearance. He had never seen them so finely dressed as they were now that he would soon be of an age to choose a bride. The brilliant array of gowns turned the room into a vibrant garden of colors and styles.

Amahna and Rakas entered with the other guests. Amahna had been apart from the family far too long to be granted a place of honor and, to her credit, she did not seem to expect one. She greeted him with an appreciative smile and a kiss on one cheek. Rakas was gracious, managing for once not to look like he was ready to dine upon delectable Dragonkin. He bowed and moved on without any hint of his usual fascination and Dephithus was so relieved he almost thanked him on the spot, but he caught himself and merely nodded politely.

He had to remind himself not to do or say anything silly when Myara and her family came to be greeted. For all that she looked every bit the beautiful court lady in her gold gown, he could not help feeling the urge to fall into their usual teasing ways. If anything, how amazing she looked all decked out like that, her shape enhanced by the cut of the gown and her hair done up with green leaf-shaped gems that reminded him of many a glorious afternoon in the Mother Tree, made it even harder to resist. But they both knew the importance of the occasion, so they simply smiled at each other with the agony of restrained mischief sparkling in their eyes.

When all the guests had been received and the greeting hall was filled with expectant faces, Dephithus stood, as had been rehearsed, and took a deep breath, borrowing confidence from the closeness of his family.

"I am grateful that you have all come to celebrate this special night with us. I hope that, in the years to come, I will prove myself worthy of the honor you do me by sharing this night with me. For now, I imagine the smell of the waiting banquet is clouding your mind as much as it is mine, so without further delay, I invite you all to join us in commencing the festivities with a grand feast."

Dephithus could feel the pride emanating from Avaline and Mythan as the gathering applauded him. Looking over at Lornin, he caught his blood-father shaking his head, his expression one of grim resignation. He appeared startled when he glanced up and caught Dephithus watching him, but Dephithus just smiled and Lornin broke a hesitant grin. Dephithus stood then and offered his mother his arm to lead the procession into the dining hall.

D ining was the part of the evening Dephithus had the least interest in. The food was of the finest quality and he was hungry, but there was much dancing to be done. He conversed politely with the nobles seated closest to him and his family while chewing at bits of perfectly prepared pheasant, savory meat pie, and a wide array of other delicious dishes. Myara's family was placed near them, but not quite close enough for them to talk without raising their voices more than was appropriate. Which they might have done under different circumstances, but not tonight. Every time he looked in her direction she had a smile ready for him and he began to wonder if she ever looked away.

The same number of chairs away in the opposite direction from Myara, Amahna was getting on quite pleasantly with Lord Davinar of Harkin and his family. Rakas had emerged from his silence and was engaged in an apparently fascinating discussion with Lord Davinar's eldest son Kuvin, He had not looked at Dephithus for the better part of an hour and Dephithus could almost make himself believe the other man's eerie obsession had all been in his head.

"I do hope you will be in the tournament at Dalynay next month. My daughter Larina is eager to cross lances with you."

Turning his attention back to the conversation at hand, Dephithus gave a polite smile to Larina, who blushed brightly and leaned back in her chair so that her mother, Lady Olisa of Dalynay, was solidly between them. "That's up to the commander of the Legion."

Lady Olisa leaned forward to address Mythan, foiling her daughter's attempts to hide. By the flush in Lady Olisa's cheeks it was evident that she had already indulged in plenty of wine. "I am certain Lord Mythan will be eager to put his den-son to the test. Surely there is no reason to doubt his ability."

Mythan grinned at the challenge. "I assure you, Lady Olisa, he will be up to the trial. Perhaps your daughter has not yet learned to lick her wounds, but she will."

Dephithus matched Mythan's eager grin. He would like to cross lances with Larina on the field. Despite her apparent shyness, she was the pride of Dalynay's fighting force. She was undefeated among the local lordships. However, at this moment, she was still blushing a furious red that almost matched her hair. She was also pretty, but he and Myara had decided several celebrations ago that her nose was a bit too bold.

"If it comes to that, Lord Mythan, perhaps Dephithus would be kind enough to lick them for her."

This time Dephithus blushed almost as bright as Larina before the laughter of everyone who had heard the exchange, but he joined in with a good-natured chuckle despite his embarrassment. His gaze was drawn to Amahna, who's vibrant laughter told him she had also overheard, only to find Rakas now gazing at him hungrily. Dephithus gave the man a brief curt nod that he hoped was polite enough while also being discouraging. Rakas smiled and nodded, raising his cup to Dephithus as he erased the desire from his features. Dephithus raised his cup as well, and his shockingly attentive guests up and down the tables raised their cups in response, falling quiet.

Dephithus was caught off guard this time and Rakas raised one brow archly, a little smirk turning his lips, but Mythan came to the rescue. He rose from his chair and addressed them all in a booming voice.

"I would like to take this opportunity to make an important announcement. This night, before the eyes of the people of Imperious, I wish to declare my den-son, Dephithus de NuTraven, heir to the throne of Imperious and all the lands and titles that go with that position." There was a haphazard chiming of glasses before everyone took a drink and raised their voices in a cheer. Mythan silenced them again with a patient gesture. "I turn the guests over to you, my son."

Dephithus glanced over at Lornin as he stood to make sure his blood-father had not been angered by Mythan's declaration. Everyone expected this day to come, but now it was official. He was surprised to find Lornin smiling at him, his eyes brimming over with pride and encouragement. Comforted, Dephithus regarded the throng of eyes that watched him expectantly.

"Lords and Ladies, I am honored and humbled by your acceptance of me. I will do all within my power to be the best king you could wish for when the time comes to accept that responsibility. Tonight, however, we are here to celebrate, and in the tradition of all great celebrations, it is time to dance."

The procession, now animated by drink, cheered Dephithus as he led them to the ballroom with Avaline again on his arm. Once in the ballroom the musician's struck up a lively tune and Dephithus picked a partner to start the dancing. He invited Dani, daughter of Lord and Lady Intraid, onto the floor. The tiny, wraithlike blond beamed like the summer sun as he led her out and began the dance. In a matter of moments, the dance floor was full.

Dephithus and Myara long ago agreed never to dance the first dance together for appearances sake. He almost stepped on Dani's foot when he looked over and saw that Myara had picked Rakas as her first partner. When the two pairs passed close on the dance floor, her wicked smile assured him that she had chosen her partner specifically to irritate him. Dephithus responded with the sweetest smile he could muster and swept Dani gracefully away. Before the dance ended, Dani slipped a fine little braid of her hair into his hand, decorated with assorted colors and shapes of beads. She smiled sweetly, her delicate little eyes glowing up at him in a soft, sultry gaze before she curtsied gracefully and floated from the floor.

Dephithus watched after her for a moment. This was something he knew to expect, but he simply was not prepared to receive offers so quickly. The braids expressed the giver's desire to be considered as a possible future partner for the recipient. The colors of the beads told him the giver's family, their age, if they were married, and if they had children. The shapes of the beads could tell additional information such as the giver's gender, how many spouses they had if they were wed, and the ages and genders of their children when applicable.

Dephithus glanced up from this first braid to find his mother watching him. Her smile was so big he worried it might split her face in two. As was expected of him, he tied the braid to his belt.

By the time he broke from the dancing to seek out the refreshment table Dephithus already had twelve tiny braids at his waist. Myara had given him one. It was expected of her and, judging by the jesting manner with which she had given it to him, that was the only reason she had given it. Dephithus had time to do little more than wet his throat with a large gulp of wine he had mistaken for something else before Avaline led him sputtering back out to the floor.

"I have a gift for you, my son."

He glanced over at the towering stack of gifts that adorned a table and much of the floor in one corner of the refreshment area.

Avaline shook her head. "No, this gift waits for you in the stables."

Excitement brought him a fresh burst of energy. "Fit for a soldier of the Imperious Legion?"

"And a king. It was not easy to find a war-horse that you would not be too handsome for, but Mythan helped. I think you will like him. He is called Hydra."

Dephithus started to pull away and she held on to him.

"You can wait until the dancing is done."

He itched to go meet this new horse, but she was right. He could not disappear yet. He was the guest of honor. "Shall we ride tomorrow then?"

"I would love to. Now, go add to your collection." She tugged teasingly at some of the braids as they parted.

Dephithus swatted playfully at her hand as he turned to scout out his next partner, struggling to keep his mind on the dance and not what waited for him in the stables. He decided to dance first with Amahna before following his mother's advice and seeking out some of the young ladies he had yet to dance with.

Amahna flicked the braids with one finger as they came together on the floor. "Quite the popular one, aren't you? Do you think it's the power, the charm, or the good looks?"

"I think that's my business to worry about and not yours," he answered a little more sharply than intended.

Amahna only smiled, her cheeks pleasantly flushed, her dark eyes piercing into him. "For me, I think it's the Dragonkin markings and those amazing eyes. I'd give you a braid myself if we weren't related."

He almost laughed at that, but her serious look

stopped the sound in his throat. Rather than respond, he took them to a more open spot and took her through numerous spins and complicated dance moves to discourage more conversation until the dance was done.

Dephithus danced out of that fire into a hotter one. When he turned away from Amahna, trying to ignore the smattering of applause their elaborate dance earned them, he found Larina standing so close he almost fell over backwards to avoid running into her. Gone was her earlier embarrassment. She smiled, somehow both sweet and bold, and offered her hands to dance.

He regained his composure quickly, executing an elegant bow. Larina appeared alarmed and she dropped into a hasty curtsy in response. It was his turn to look smug then. She danced with passion, almost as if they were already facing each other over lances. Dephithus had to fight to keep the lead and he tried not to let it fluster him more when he spotted Myara laughing at him from along the wall. At the end of the dance he bowed again and Larina was ready with a much more elegant curtsy this time.

"I do look forward to jousting with you, Lady Larina. It should be most exciting."

Her smile was confident and her eyes fierce as she handed him a small braid, slipping her hand around to caress the back of his as she drew away. "As do I, Lord Dephithus."

Once she was out of earshot he released a heavy exhale. He felt as if he had been sparring for a couple of hours with no breaks. It made him long for a partner he could relax around. Someone like Myara.

Almost as if aware she had entered his thoughts, Myara slipped in to steal the next dance and he rejoiced in the fact that he had nothing to prove with her. It was a refreshing dance, one of many they managed to scatter throughout the evening.

Just when he began to think his feet would never stop hurting, the guests finally began to depart. When the only ones left were those who wished to speak to Mythan or Avaline, he was finally able to retire for the evening.

He took the time to escort a stumbling and exhausted Myara, who may have imbibed a share of wine herself given her flush, to her room. She wished him goodnight with a kiss on his cheek that made him wish for more. He stood staring at her closed door for several minutes before he went to discard his fine clothes in his own room and trade them for more common attire. He was still too charged by the evening to sleep yet. Once the halls were quiet, he crept out to sneak a peek at his new horse and enjoy the bracing night air.

Outside of the palace Dephithus grinned at his own cleverness in escaping unnoticed and strutted through the gardens. The night air was crisp enough to be refreshing after spending such a long evening in the overcrowded palace. There was only a sliver of a moon, but every star shone bright and Dephithus picked out familiar constellations that watched from the sky like old friends. It was a welcome change from the hundreds of blindingly bright candelabras and chandeliers within the ballroom.

He chuckled to himself.

Thirty-two braids adorned his belt by the time the dancing was done. It was hard not to let that go to his head. Myara never seemed to find him all that dashing, and he had always assumed the young ladies who swooned over him were doing so mostly in jest. However, he was the heir to a powerful throne and that alone had to make him handsome enough for many. Six of the braids had been from young men. As a male heir to the throne he would be expected to marry a woman at some point to produce an heir, but outside of that there were no limitations.

Fortunately, most of the local lads knew his interests did not go that way. Many went so far as to tease that his interests did not go beyond Myara, though Dephithus had always corrected them, insisting that they were just friends.

He fondled the only braid he still carried with him. Myara's braid was nestled snuggly in his pants pocket, silky soft and reassuring somehow.

Only a few strides ahead of him, what his eyes had initially passed over as simply another shadow among many moved and a man stepped into his path. Seeming at home in the darkness, Rakas smiled at Dephithus with a deliberate suggestiveness. There was nothing truly threatening about the way the other man stood or his expression, but Dephithus swallowed against sudden dryness in his throat and his heart began to pound. There was no logical reason for the fear response that he could see. There was little doubt he could defeat the man in hand to hand combat if there were ever any need. Rakas was frail and a bit sickly looking. Still, the terror spread, making the hair rise on the back of his neck.

"I appreciate your interest, but I'm afraid I don't share it," Dephithus managed to keep his voice calm as he moved to casually step around the man.

Rakas shifted into his path again.

Dephithus considered turning back the way he had come rather than causing a scene, then a cold finger traced the back of his neck along the line of his collar. He could not stop a shiver as Amahna stepped close around him.

"You don't have a choice," she whispered, so close to his ear that her warm breath on his neck sent a chill through him. "We have a birthday present for you."

"Perhaps tomorrow would be a better time." He knew by Amahna's smile when she stepped around in front of him that she had heard the slight tremble in his voice.

Behind her Rakas placed a hand on a statue of Commander Parthak's predecessor to brace himself as a shudder wracked his body. In that brief fit Dephithus caught a glimpse of something like misery in the other man's face. Perhaps there was some way to use that misery to his advantage. Amahna, however, seemed unconcerned, casting Rakas a casual glance that was a touch annoyed if anything at all.

Turning back to Dephithus, she traced his jaw with one fingernail and laughed when he pulled away. "I really think you should get your present now."

Dephithus was glaring at Amahna one moment and the next he found himself stumbling into the dark, musty shed where the resident blacksmith stored his tools. Amahna shoved him forward roughly and, though she was not all that strong she had caught him off guard. He stumbled, landing hard on his knees. He tried to turn and curse at her only to discover that neither thing was within his power to do. Terror exploded inside of him.

He did not remember walking here. He could not move. He began to shake with fear and the fight to regain control. No sound passed his lips, but in his head, he was screaming.

Rakas helped Dephithus to his feet then he staggered forward again. Helpless, he ran into an old anvil that stood near the center of the crowded room. Without control of his body he fell forward so that his torso dropped over the anvil and his hands dangled uselessly before him. The stench of dust, metal, and oils was strong enough that it filled his nose, making it hard to breath. His head started to pound.

"What a wretched little room," Amahna grumbled. "It stinks in here. Let's get this over with quickly."

"Not like this," Rakas rasped, his voice strained.

"Give me more time with him. Perhaps he would come to this willingly."

"No. It has to be like this. It has to be tonight." Amahna's voice was strained, as if she wanted to yell at her companion, but was holding back out of the fear of drawing attention.

Dephithus realized what was happening and panic tightened his throat, a scream running up against whatever strange force held him silent.

"Then I refuse. I won't do this to him."

Hope sparked in his chest until Amahna laughed.

"That's adorable. And I just took away your ability to refuse. Do what we came here to do."

In his periphery, Dephithus saw Rakas unfastening his pants while Amahna did the same for Dephithus, pulling them down unceremoniously. The screams in his head turned to panicked shrieking, but he could not make a sound to express the tempest within.

Dephithus could neither fight nor speak. Silent. Helpless. Pain. Rage. Rakas forced himself inside. Bitter images of his family resting warm within the palace flashed through his mind as his body was shoved rhythmically against the cold, hard steel of the old anvil. The image he lingered on the most was that of Amahna's teasing while they danced not a more than a few hours gone. Humiliation and hatred he could not vent turned to bitter tears. Seconds stretched into eternities.

*

Amahna watched the coupling with a pleased little smirk. She had been afraid Rakas, who had started to want Dephithus in a more emotional way, would refuse at the last moment, so she had been prepared. It required her to use a lot more of the daenox within her, but at least Rakas had not expected it, so she had been able to take control of him almost as easily as she had Dephithus. The rest was simple. Rakas wanted the boy badly enough that she barely had to work at getting his body to behave the way she wanted.

Rakas had long harbored a misguided guilt for turning her to Theruses and had sworn off relationships with women as a result. She chuckled under her breath. Now what would he do?

She watched the torment twisting her companion's features, delighting in the tears that ran down his face. He suffered not because he did not physically enjoy what she was making him do, but because he did. Already, he had started to develop a sense of affection for the boy, much as she had, but she was better able to keep such things at a distance.

Even with the completeness of the control she had over his physical body, Dephithus was visibly shaking with pain and humiliation by the time Rakas climaxed. She relinquished control of her companion then and he withdrew immediately. He did not bother pulling up his trousers before he slid down along one wall and buried his head in his hands. His shoulders shook. It might be with the usual tremors, though she suspected it was with silent sobs. It did not matter now. The deed was done.

Amahna scowled at him and walked over to redress Dephithus. When she turned around again, Rakas was glaring at her. She could not remember when she had ever seen such hatred in her companion's eyes. There was little time for it now, though. The powers she was using to keep Dephithus controlled were draining her and the daenox could not be replenished at this distance.

Grabbing Dephithus by his shirt collar, she pulled him from the anvil, allowing him to crumple to the ground once he was clear of it. Tears streamed down his face unchecked and his pretty silver-green eyes glared death at her.

"Now, now Dephithus," she managed a thickly sweet tone, "you shouldn't carry on so. You might learn to like this someday."

His eyes flashed with fury and his body trembled more violently as he renewed his struggle against her controls. Amahna laughed when a shudder shook Rakas, whose gaze was locked on Dephithus as if he could not believe what had happened. Perhaps he did not. The man looked almost as broken as their victim.

There would be time later though to savor such things.

"Pull yourself together by the time I get back," she snapped.

She dazed Dephithus as she had done to bring him to the shed and they moved cautiously back to his room in the palace. With a touch of extra power here and there, they avoided being seen and Amahna managed a bit more to put Dephithus to sleep.

She smiled with false sweetness upon the sleeping dragon-child.

"Within you is great power. You are the hope of Theruses now. Of all of us," she whispered so as not to disturb the fragile sleep. So young and already he promised to be a great leader. What they had done to him would destroy that. The way they had done it, the physical and emotional trauma they had inflicted upon him, would make it that much easier for the seed to take hold and begin to change him. She smiled at Dephithus, watching his brow furrow in troubled sleep. "We have given you a special gift for your birthday. In you has been placed a daemon-seed. May it grow strong within you and free the daenox back into world."

The last of the daenox induced sleep wore off fast, leaving Dephithus to lie awake and search his mind for some way to make sense of what had happened. He curled about himself, but no matter how he twisted his body the only part that physically pained him felt exposed. For a time, he tried to convince himself he had suffered a nightmare, but the raw pain ultimately denied him that illusion. That effort having failed, he curled around a pillow, muffling his sobs in it. When the sobbing subsided, he realized that he should rise now if he wanted to avoid Myara and his family. They would sleep perhaps till noon after such a late night and he had no desire to see any of them.

Despite the lethargy that tried to pin him to the bed, Dephithus forced himself to rise. He ripped off the clothes he was wearing, kicking them into a corner to be dealt with later.

Had he done something wrong that he deserved such punishment?

He could think of no time when he had mistreated anyone or anything. No time when he had lied or deceived anyone out of pure meanness. He shook himself, trying to toss away his thoughts with the force of the motion.

Would Amahna and Rakas still be here?

A violent tremor shook him and he fell onto knees already bruised from the prior night's events, emptying his stomach on his discarded clothes.

For a time, he stayed there on all fours, trembling. Then the sour stench struck him, and he rose on shaky legs to dress himself in a simple shirt and breeches. Breathing deeply to slow his shaking, he took hold of the cold, smooth door handle and stepped out of his room. A serving man was passing at that moment and stopped to bow to the now official heir to the throne. Dephithus could not look at the man. He nodded recognition in his vague direction. The man either did not notice the avoidance or pretended not to. The latter was more likely considering his station.

"Some bath water has been warmed, my lord. Would you like your tub filled?"

Dephithus hesitated. A bath would mean staying in the palace longer, but now nothing seemed as important as a bath to scrub away the filth. He caught the serving man's patient gaze out of the corner of his eye. "Yes, please. Have the water brought, but I do not want an attendant."

"As my Lord wishes." The serving man bowed deep again and departed to his duties.

Dephithus let out his breath, though he had not realized until then that he had scarcely been able to breathe in the serving man's presence. The need to weep filled him again and he fought it back fiercely, digging his fingernails into his palms to keep it at bay. He could not break down in the middle of the hall like a child with a skinned knee.

He lingered like a thief in the shadows of a side-hall where he would be unlikely to encounter anyone until he figured it had been long enough. Then he went to the washroom adjacent to his bedchamber. The three young serving women were still there adding the last water to the tub. Their talking ceased and turned to giggling when he entered. Before finishing with the water, they acknowledged him with exaggerated curtsies and more giggling.

Suppressing her giggles one flushed blond girl stepped forward. "Is it to your liking, my Lord?"

He scowled and something in the expression made all three go suddenly silent, bowing their heads to hide their new uncertainty. "Leave me," he growled.

Their high spirits dampened by apparent failure, the girls curtsied again and shrunk from the room. Confused and frustrated, Dephithus simply stared at the tub, wishing there were some way he could go back and undo what he had just done. There was no reason for him to take his misery out on them. The worst thing was that he had been thinking that even before he snapped at the girls, but he did it anyway.

Finding no comfort in his own deliberations he sighed and slipped out of his clothes.

Dephithus scrubbed himself with a violent fervor until his skin was bright pink, though he knew that no amount of cleaning would ever be enough.

Maybe he had wanted what they had done to him. Why else would he have been unable to fight back? Neither Amahna nor Rakas had tied him in any way or threatened his life. So why had he been so helpless, like he could not do anything to stop them? Could he have drunk more than he realized? He did not remember returning to his room, so perhaps he had been drunk enough to pass out. Otherwise, there was simply no way that they could have had the power over him that they seemed to have last night. It was not possible. But he did not remember feeling drunk. So, it led to reason that he must not have wanted to fight. Or perhaps he was too much of a coward.

Dephithus closed his eyes, letting the steam of the

tub wash over his face as he tried to clear his mind. Turmoil filled him, and the ongoing pain would not let him escape it. Revulsion, confusion, and rage all vied for his attention, but he could not decide how he should feel. Angry with himself for not knowing what to think or do, he rose abruptly, spilling no small amount of water on the floor. Stepping out he scrubbed dry and dressed himself, then took a few deep breaths before leaving the solace of his chambers.

Somehow, the architecture of the palace made him uncomfortable as he hastened through its halls. Rather than encouraging and comforting him, the elegance mocked him with its attentions. The walls swept in around him, calling out to any who might see, *Here is Dephithus, see his shame.* He broke into a run down the last two hallways and burst out one of the back doors. Cool, moist morning air nipped at him ominously with the promise of a spring rain. Ignoring that promise, he ran from the palace toward the refuge of the woods. It was early still, so the grounds between were empty of anyone who might be inclined to question him.

His route took him close enough to the stables that he heard the blacksmith shaping a shoe against his anvil. The sound brought up a barrage of memories of the dark storage shed so vivid he gagged again on the overwhelming stench of oils, metal, and dust. He stumbled, the sense of helpless horror coming back in a debilitating wave, and hit the ground with enough force that the impact sent a shot of pain through his neck. His limbs went weak, refusing to support him, and he fell again almost before he had finished standing. Resting on one bruised knee, Dephithus dug his fingers into the soft ground and waited for his breathing to slow. As soon as he could stand, he took off again, though he had to keep his pace down to an easy lope to avoid another fall.

Once he entered the cover of the forest, he slowed to an exhausted walk. He was different somehow. It was not just the horror and confusion of what had happened, not just the lingering pain, but an unfamiliar bitterness. A welling of directionless anger he could not remember ever feeling before. Certainly, there were others who had endured such unspeakable things, but the problem was exactly that. They were unspeakable, and nobles did not talk of such things. Did anyone? Who was he supposed to turn to? Or was he supposed to keep it inside and hope it got easier with time?

The latter option seemed the most sensible. Such things did not happen to someone of his standing and no one would believe that the pride of the Imperious Legion had been used in such a way by a court lady and her frail companion.

The first drops of rain found Dephithus sitting high up in a tree deep in the woods. Not the Mother Tree. Someone might think to look for him there. This was far away from that tree.

He figured it to be about noon, but the cloud cover made it hard to be sure. For a time, the tree branches offered some shelter, then the rain increased, and the soon saturated trees dropped almost as much water on him as the open sky would have. When evening drifted in he was soaked to the bone and his muscles had grown fatigued from prolonged shivering. Some time ago he had begun to feel weak and nauseous. Even so, he still did not go back to the palace. He could think of no way to face his family and Myara. Somehow, they would know, and they would give him pity and sympathy, but their eyes would ask the questions he could not answer. How could this have happened to him? Why did he let it happen?

He stayed in the tree in the rain.

It was not until dark had settled in and he was shivering so violently from the cold and wet that he could barely keep his perch that Dephithus finally dropped from the tree. Upon landing he slipped in the mud and slammed down hard on his side. His drenched hair clung to his face in thick wet strands. He curled up under the tree until he could control his shaking enough to get up again then began walking toward home.

He stumbled along in the dark, vision blurred by rain and a new dizziness that had come along with the nausea. Not far from the tree he had perched in, he tripped over an exposed root and landed amidst a cluster of berry brambles. The thorns took hold of him and the mere possibility of being trapped made him thrash in panic. For a short time, he flailed about violently until a sane thought finally broke through the panic and he made himself stop moving. Though the spinning of the world around him and his wretched trembling made it hard to think, he finally worked an arm down to his belt and pulled out his knife. He cut at the vines until he was free, but one snagged his hand as he stood ripping the knife from his hand.

Dephithus growled in distracted frustration and left the knife in the brambles.

The Elysium palace seemed much further away now that he was cold and drenched and feeling sick. He emerged from the trees and tried to focus on the lights of the grand structure. Through the rain and dark he peered, but his eyes would not focus. The world was spinning faster than before. The fever that now rushed through him dissolved his thoughts faster than he could form them. He was shaking so badly that he stumbled again, and his arms crumpled under his own weight, leaving him to land face down on the cold wet grass. The rain pelted him with the same stinging force that it did the ground around him. Struggling, he managed to get up to his hands and knees before his stomach turned against him. His body heaved so hard it felt like his very guts might come up. Nothing came though, for, despite the best efforts of his body, he hadn't eaten or drank all day and there was simply nothing there.

After several minutes of dry heaving the revolt stopped and Dephithus fell to the side, resting his face against the cool ground. His arms lay limp before him, rivulets of water running along the lines of tensed shaking muscles. The shirt he wore was ripped in many places and blood from his battle with the thorny brambles mingled with the water where several deep gouges marked him. Even though it had happened only moments ago he remembered stumbling into the thorny brambles in the woods as if it had been a dream. Unable to face the dark blurry landscape without feeling nauseous he gave up and closed his eyes. Water splashed up from the impact of the rain on the saturated ground hitting his eyelids and lips.

Dephithus lay there for some time, wondering where he was and where he might be going. Was anyone looking for him?

After a time, those thoughts became too disjointed to follow and he simply lay there shivering until someone did find him. He struggled for the strength to open his eyes while someone rolled him onto his back and slipped their arms under his armpits. Another pair of arms lifted his legs. His eyes finally opened and through the blur of rain and fever he saw Myara.

No, it was Amahna.

Terror added a violent jerk to his shivering and the person at his legs lost their hold. His legs smacked to the ground and the person behind him fell to their knees but managed to keep hold of him. The hold was both gentle and firm. Myara bent down to lift his legs again and it looked like she was crying, or maybe it was just the rain. His eyes slipped shut and Dephithus drifted off.

He did not really wake for some time. He was aware of being dry and warm, and also conscious of the tremors that still ran through him. He knew Myara and Avaline were with him much of the time as he sometimes heard their voices, but he could not concentrate on what they were saying. All the food that had been spooned into him had come back up, leaving him weaker still. Yet, emotionally he was more at peace. His physical misery was such that he could not hold a thought for long, which meant he could not dwell on Amahna or Rakas and what they had done to him. What he must have wanted them to do to him. The freedom from such thoughts allowed him to drift in a disconnected peace that moved beyond his body's trials.

Then his body gave in to the daenox seed and the tremors subsided along with the fever. Completely drained of energy, Dephithus fell into a deep and very sound sleep then. He was only faintly aware of a gentle hand feeling his forehead as he drifted into delicious oblivion.

Amahna could remember how Rakas had been once, when she first met him. His long black hair the very image of dark elegance and his eyes pools of seductive midnight, promising the secret pleasures of the daenox. His body had been lithe and muscular then, his skin warm and smooth. They had been energetic lovers for a time. Every moment filled with some teasing glance or hidden caress. Their energy for one another without limits.

It was not that he had really changed that much, though his body's growing intolerance to the heavy concentration of daenox in the cave had left shadows in his cheeks and under his eyes and given a strange coolness to his now pallid skin. He looked tired much of the time because the trembling was often bad enough to keep him awake at night.

People responded to the presence of so much daenox in one of two ways. Some got very sick for a short period, as she had. Then they would die or suddenly recover and be fine. Others had no immediate reaction, as with Rakas, but the daenox would begin to affect them more and more adversely over many years. Despite the changes the daenox had wrought in him, Rakas was still very pleasant to look upon, but her desires had long ago turned to the intimidating and powerful lord of the daenox, Theruses.

If the truth were to be told, power had always aroused her, and the power she had been attracted to in Rakas was nothing compared to what Theruses had in him. She had not known such magnificence existed and she never doubted Theruses when he told her that one day he would be free of the cave. Several hundred years ago he had been imprisoned there with the daenox, at the same time the dragons had been trapped in their stone cells. It did seem ironic that two so opposite things, the daenox with Theruses its lord, and the dragons, should have the same desperate need, to be free. When Theruses was free, she would reap the rewards of her loyalty. She knew he would not give her everything she wanted simply for having the right smile and a pleasing body, but he did provide for those who served him well. Could anyone say they had served him better than she had?

Rakas rode quiet beside her now. After he took them the first part of the trip, from Imperious to Kuilen, using the dragon web, he no longer had the energy to cover the next leg of the journey. Amahna's abilities were also depleted because of the power she had used controlling him and Dephithus, so they made an unspoken agreement not to linger and continued the journey at the speed their mounts could take them. Rakas had been sullen and irritable most of the trip, choosing to keep his own council rather than converse with her. Judging by his inward gaze now he was deep in contemplation, deep enough that she could probably startle him with a word.

"Lovely hills," she said, a little louder than necessary, and Rakas snapped from his reverie with a jerk. Amahna smiled to herself. "Don't you agree?"

Rakas answered with a scowl that might scare a roving daemon, then turned to the front again to resume his sulking.

"Guilt does not become you, Rakas. You really

should give up all this sulking and rejoice in a job well done."

She stared at him as she spoke, fascinated by the contortions in his face as he struggled to control his temper. Almost every tortured emotion could be read clearly as it fought for control of his features. She was impressed when a cold, bitter glower finally won.

"You were taken with him yourself, Amahna." He spat her name as though it tasted vile upon his tongue.

She pretended not to notice. Patience would win this war. "Perhaps, but I remember my place. I must confess," she added with a light laugh, "I almost envied you that night."

Some sort of bad-tempered rebuttal had been expected, perhaps a few vulgarities tossed in her direction, but he managed to catch her off guard when he intercepted the tiny, but constant flow of daenox she had been using to control her mount instead. The mare started suddenly as if woken from sleep. Upon becoming fully aware that she was in a strange place with someone on her back and a steel bit in her mouth, the wild mare, predictably, panicked. She reared up then twisted and leapt sideways without her front hooves ever returning to the ground.

Amahna, moved with the animal, managing with skill and a healthy dose of luck, to stay in the saddle. She had never been one to tolerate bucking from a mount, but this type of fight was almost exhilarating. Still, she had no intention of letting Rakas get away with this simply because she got a thrill out of it. Reestablishing the flow of daenox, she got the mare back under control and wheeled her around to face him. He did not back down or attempt to apologize when she turned her rage on him, which surprised her some. In the last several years he had become easy to intimidate, wary of his weakened state. This was more like the Rakas of old. He did look a bit uncomfortable under her glare though, so she would be satisfied with what reaction she could get for now.

"If I had not given my dagger away you would be wearing it through your neck for that little trick," she snapped.

"And why *did* you give it away?"

His voice was so cold now it chilled her, though she hid the shiver by making a show of adjusting her seat in the saddle.

"Your guilt is extreme and Theruses will feel it. He might not like that you feel no pride in having served him well." She kept her voice soothing and calm, trying to sound more concerned than threatening now. She could not let him hate her completely or he might use that to focus his conflicted emotions.

"My service to Theruses is between him and me." Rakas turned toward the horizon, but not before she caught the uncertainty in his eyes. She allowed herself a little satisfied smile while he was looking away.

"That may be so, but you had best tend to it."

She let the silence linger, watching him for a moment, then followed his gaze to the horizon. The sun was setting. They would have to hurry if they wanted to reach the next town before full dark. She moved her mare over beside him and rested a hand on his shoulder. Rakas flinched, convincing her to rest her hand there for a few moments more until his tension eased a bit.

She pulled her hand away again suddenly and moved her mare a few steps forward. Rakas sat watching her as she sniffed the air like a wolf hunting. A slow smile eased across her face and he shuddered. Dealing with her frequently brought on his fits. She knew he feared her to some degree and unnerving him amused her.

After a minute or more, she nodded as if answering someone and nudged her mare up to a trot then a fast lope. Rakas followed her purposeful drive across the sloping hillsides until she pulled up abruptly at the peak of one hill. Dusk had come and was giving way to night, but the small town down below them seemed to have only just woken. Torches and two large bonfires lit the main road at the east end of the town. A band of lively musicians played a frisky tune from their seat in front of the inn and people already danced like wild beasts around the bonfires. They were celebrating something and Amahna could feel the lusty excitement of the revelers even from this far.

"This is what we need. To dance with abandon and delight in drink. Come along." She started down the hill then stopped to look back at her hesitant companion. "It will ease your suffering."

Rakas appeared almost afraid for a moment then he raised his head with forced confidence, looking, in the fading light of dusk, almost as he had when first she met him. He nodded brusquely. Amahna smiled and kicked her mount into a crazed sprint down the hillside. Without looking to see if he followed, she barreled boldly into the small town, pulling the mare up just before the inn. A stout, rough looking man caught hold of her reigns and grinned, showing off an incomplete set of yellowed teeth. Amahna swung down, tossing him some coins as she perused the festivities with her eyes.

"I can see by your wild countenance that you come to howl at the moon in Ithkan. You are both welcome here, especially on this night." He added, nodding to Rakas who now pulled his mount up beside them with a little more reserve.

"What do you celebrate?"

The man grinned. "A wedding, a birth, good crops or the color of the sky. Pick what you would and celebrate with us."

Rakas eyed Amahna and his guard faltered for a moment, allowing her to use daenox to see herself through his eyes. She did indeed look wild with her hair windblown and her eyes sparkling with fierce light. Something about her appearance in that moment must have moved him. When she switched back to her own perspective, old hunger lit his eyes and he nodded to the man, tossing him his reigns.

Amahna laughed and tossed her cloak onto her saddle. With a wild whoop, she danced into the crowd, her silken burgundy split skirts rippling fantastically around her legs with her movement. There was hatred in the eyes of many young women as she danced through them, though there were plenty of women who eyed her with desire. Amahna swirled among them, searching for just the right look and accepting drinks from those who hoped to bed her.

The bonfires blazed, defying the night sky with their brightness and adding their own music to the lively performance of the musicians. After the first few songs, she left the inner circle only to grab Rakas and drag him in, then she lost herself among the revelers again. Rakas loosened up once several drinks had dampened his throat so Amahna paid him no more attention until she found what she was looking for. She spotted a young man who was as handsome as he was beautiful. His green eyes gleamed bright with innocence, but something in his manner belied that look. Those pale eyes, glazed over with drink, sparkled like gems between his lovely dark hair and an open smile.

Ignoring the burning glare one young woman gave her, Amahna slipped in close to the young man she had chosen. She danced sensually to the wild music that filled the air. She was still beautiful enough to capture his interest. As she had hoped, the young woman he had been dancing with soon realized the futility of her efforts and ran off to sulk. Amahna lured the youth closer to one of the fires where the heat slicked her dress to her skin with sweat. Entranced, he ran his hands down her body and she threw her head back, allowing him to nuzzle her sweat-dampened neck. She kissed him with all the passion of the fire and the drink that coursed through her veins. When she pulled away he gasped and the hunger in his eyes matched her own.

Amahna laughed and led him over to where Rakas was dancing with several admirers of both sexes. When he saw the young man with her his face went pale and he stopped dancing. Her catch looked enough like Dephithus in his way that she worried Rakas might leave, but he hesitated, eyeing her levelly. Rakas was questioning her motives as his gaze moved between her and the handsome young man she had brought over. Those dancing around him, several of whom had lost articles of clothing at some point, coaxed him to rejoin them with sensual caresses. Rakas stepped through the ring they had formed and took the boy's hand drawing him back through the border of sweat-slicked bodies. Amahna danced into the circle as well, finding an eager dancing companion in one lovely young woman with flaxen hair and deep blue eyes. As the evening wore on she stayed sober enough to notice when Rakas and the young man disappeared into the inn.

As dawn neared there were still many revelers outside who slept where they had fallen, deep in drunken slumber. The moon had slipped down close to the horizon and those few who were not asleep on the cold ground had retired to nearby homes or rooms in the inn. The fires still burned, bright red with hot coals, but they were mere shadows of the blazing monsters they had been.

Amahna walked down the quiet streets towards the inn. She had found four companions to enjoy for

a while, yet she had not dallied long with them. There
was other business she wanted to attend to before the
dawn broke. The quiet that met her here on the now
mostly deserted streets was deeper than the normal
predawn voice of a small town. One cat crept stealthily
through the shadows on a search that no human would
ever witness. An old dog looked up at her from where
he had curled up next to his owner in the dry dirt road.
Amahna nodded to each in turn, recognizing that the
night did not belong to men and women.

The common room of the inn presented something
of a challenge. More people than she would have believed could fit in the whole town were curled up on the
floor or stretched out on benches. One or two even slept
on tabletops and the musicians, with their instruments
still clutched to them, had moved inside to sleep on the
small stage. She could feel faintly the daenox in Rakas
and she followed it up to the second floor, stepping carefully over soundly slumbering patrons. With an amused
smirk she wove her way around those that had not quite
made it to the second floor and settled for the stairs.
There would be many aching bodies come morning.

At the fourth door on the right she stopped and
pushed it open a crack. The faint moonlight that still
spilled in the room's one window illuminated two naked
bodies twined on the bed and dreaming. She waited a
moment, listening to them breathe, then slunk in, carefully shutting the door behind her. Neither one stirred
as she stood watching them in the moonlight. Rakas
looked peaceful with his arm draped over the young
man's shoulder. The young man simply looked quiet.
She did not think he would look much different dead.
Patiently, she sat in a chair in the corner and watched
them.

When the first light of dawn started to peek over
the horizon, Amahna knelt before the bed next to the

young man. With very gentle movements she leaned in to him and pressed her lips to his, using daenox to draw upon all of the untamed power of the numerous couplings that had occurred that night. He opened his pale green eyes, then opened his mouth to her and closed his eyes. Amahna breathed deeply of him as she kissed him, drawing away his breath, his heartbeat, his joy and his pain. She felt when the final silence took him and sat back, regarding his serene face for a moment before returning to her chair and closing her eyes to rest.

When she woke it was to the sound of soft weeping. Rakas lay cradling the dead boy's head against his chest with his lips pressed to his forehead. His face was twisted with anguish as he wept and slathered with unsightly secretions. He seemed unaware that she had woken. She watched as he rested the boy's head back on the bed, but he still did not look at her when he finally spoke.

"You gave that knife to Dephithus to torment him," his voice was so soft that she had to lean closer to hear. "Just as you torment me for wanting to love him."

Amahna considered denying his accusations and her part in this young man's death. She could blame it on excessive drink or some such thing, but she said nothing.

Rakas turned toward her, still not looking at her. "I suppose we should leave before the town wakes."

Such bitterness filled his tone, yet his words were so logical and ordinary. That distance made her cold, so she stood and moved away from the window as if it were the cause. Rakas leaned down and kissed the boy's forehead again before rising to dress himself. Waiting patiently by the door she feigned disinterest as he took the ring the boy had been wearing and dropped it into his shirt pocket. The gesture pleased her though. Keeping the ring would constantly remind him of this boy, of this night, and it would torment him more than anything she might think to do.

They went quietly and quickly to the stables and took their mounts, which had never been relieved of their equipment. At the edge of the town Rakas stopped and looked back at the inn. Amahna watched him in silence, waiting.

"Theruses gave you that dagger not long after I brought you to him." He looked at her then, seeming to be speaking more to himself than to her. "He always liked you because you have so much lust for power of your own." Rakas shook his head and turned away from the town. "We were a good pair once."

Amahna watched him kick his mount up to a canter, leaving her behind without a second glance. Patience, she reminded herself again. He had turned her away now, cutting her out of his future with his words. It could not take much more to drive him away from Theruses and the caves. Watching him a moment longer she considered finding her own path.

Perhaps he would simply get lost. A crooked little smile turned her lips. There was still more to do though.

Digging her heels into the mare's ribs she galloped off in the direction Rakas had gone.

ephithus woke with a start. Panic almost overtook him before he realized where he was. In the palace, in his own bed where he had spent the last sixteen years feeling safe. It did not feel safe anymore. The memories of how he had gotten here were vague and nightmarish. Shivering on the ground in the rain. A dark storage shed. The cold pressure of the anvil against his hips. Amahna's smile. She had been smiling.

He breathed deep to fight the sudden urge to throw up and stared at the ceiling high above his bed until the feeling had passed.

Looking around he saw two beds laid out on the floor, both empty now. An older gentleman he recognized as the palace healer sat in a chair between his bed and the door. The healer's head was tipped down as he read intently from a book, thinning brown hair slipping forward around his long face. A lengthy strand of hair fell in front of his eyes and they crossed as he focused on the intruder with an irritated scowl. After he brushed the strand away, his eyes refocused on Dephithus and he dropped the book in comical surprise. Trying to regain his composure, the healer brushed his hair back again, unnecessarily this time, and picked the book up, sweeping imagined dust from the cover before setting it down neatly beside him.

"My Lord Dephithus, it's good of you to return to us."

Dephithus shook his head at his company, not entirely sure he agreed with the statement, and pulled himself up to lean against the backboard of the bed. After spending a little time arranging his pillows and his covers for the sake of trying to get his composure about him, he regarded the healer. "From where do I return?"

"You have been sick, my lord. We feared you mortally ill. How are you feeling now?"

Dephithus ignored the question and looked again around his apparently shared chamber. "Who has been sleeping here?"

"The Lady Avaline and Legion hopeful, Myara. You appear much improved."

Dephithus smiled. There was a bitterness to it that made the expression feel unpleasant on his face. "Do I."

The healer drew back. He looked confused and perhaps a touch insulted.

Dephithus noticed a long slender box sitting on his bed-stand and reached for it. The healer started to say something as he pulled off the lid, but Dephithus was not listening. In the box was a dagger. The grip was smoothed wood stained glossy black. Below the grip two gold snakes wrapped around either side of the silver crossguard. Each snake had emerald eyes and a tail that dropped a good half-inch down the blade on either side. Above the wooden grip an emerald stone was embedded in each side of the silver pommel. Dephithus took a moment to admire the fine craftsmanship before he realized the healer was watching at him expectantly.

"Pardon, what were you saying?"

The healer smiled indulgently. "I said that your Aunt Amahna left that for you. They had to leave very early the day after your Dawning Day."

Dephithus growled at the dagger as he tossed it and the box carelessly back onto the bed-stand. The healer's brow furrowed when Dephithus threw off his covers and got out of bed.

The man stood and placed a gentle hand on his arm. "You seem agitated, Lord Dephithus."

Dephithus started to pull away, then he paused. The healer's name came to him then. Gvath. He was a kind and good-natured man, undeserving of the rude treatment he was getting. There was just so much anger in Dephtihus. Anger with no outlet. "I'm sorry, Gvath, I guess I'm just a bit confused and out of sorts right now."

Gvath's brow furrowed more deeply and Dephithus cringed with dread at the questions that he would certainly ask now. He mentally braced himself when Gvath opened his mouth to speak. Then the other man shut his mouth again and cocked his head slightly to one side, his expression softening.

"Perhaps a bath would soothe you."

Dephithus could not keep the gratitude from his face.

Gvath smiled and patted him affectionately on the back. "I will send for your water."

Avaline appeared as he was bathing to fret over his healing scratches from the brambles and worry over why he had left the palace when he was so obviously ill. When she finally gave him a chance to speak, he shooed her away, protesting that he was still too weary to talk of it and would rather put it behind him. Eyes downcast, she started to leave, but she stopped inside the door and looked back at him, her expression suddenly hopeful.

Dephithus blew out an impatient exhale.

Her eyes filled with hurt as she dropped her gaze to the floor again, but she still spoke. "Perhaps later, if you are up to it..."

She wanted to ride with him when he tried out his new horse. The horse he had been going to see that night. The night that…

"Maybe tomorrow," he snapped.

He pushed away a twinge of guilt in the silence that followed his abrupt response. Avaline stood in the doorway for a few seconds longer, regarding him as if she wanted to comfort him or slap him and could not decide which to do. Reluctantly, she nodded and left him alone to contemplate what he would do next.

Dephithus scowled at his feet, not sure how he expected them to be of any help. What would he do next? Who would he snap at or be rude to? Who else would he punish for what happened to him?

He glared at the water so viciously that he was almost disappointed when it did not start boiling.

After a bit he abandoned the warm bath and left the palace through a servant's entrance to avoid speaking to anyone. As he walked through the gardens he was greeted by several loungers who expressed their delight that he was feeling better. Somewhere within his aggravation and misery, he was able to muster up a smile or nod where appropriate, but he did not linger. Myara would be around, though she was most likely in training at this hour, for which he was grateful. He was supposed to have started his Legion practice today. Or was that today? How long had he been sick?

He walked for some time, a little surprised that his body did not quickly tire, as it should have after being so ill. By noon, he had found a comfortable perch in the Mother Tree. It had been a place of happiness and solace so many times in the past. It was disconcerting to sit and think of how much had changed in the short time since he had last been there. It seemed that his whole world had been overthrown and would never be the same again. He laid his arms on a branch in front of him and rested his forehead on them. Tears stung at his eyes, but he would not let himself weep endlessly like a child. There was no value in it.

"Dephithus."

That soft uncertain voice almost forced free the tears he was holding back. He did not respond to Myara right away. For a moment, he kept his head there and closed his eyes, breathing deep to calm himself and keep from breaking down blubbering like a baby. He listened to the rustle of leaves and the scrape of boots on bark as she climbed up into the tree and sat on another branch.

"How are you feeling?" Concern was thick in her voice and in her awkward distance.

"Not too bad." He leaned back against the branch behind him and glanced over in her direction, though he was careful not to make eye contact. Myara was not someone he could lie to easily.

She smiled, gentle and patient. "Do you want to go to riding with me?"

"No!" Her shocked recoil brought more guilt. "Sorry, I don't quite feel like myself yet."

The pain in her expression was sucked away into those dark eyes still brimming with concern. "Are you falling ill again? Maybe you shouldn't be out yet. Do you want to go back to the palace?"

"No. I just want to be left alone for a while."

A hint of moisture glossed her eyes at his rejection and the struggle to restrain herself from pressing was almost painful to watch. He turned his gaze to the rich green meadow below them. Myara dropped from the tree, her discouragement plain in the heavy thud of her landing. She stood there staring at the grass, prodding it for a perhaps a minute with her boot toe while silence stretched uncomfortably between them.

"They thought you might die. I've never known such fear as when I believed I might lose you." Her voice cracked, and silence reigned again.

He could think of nothing to say. Maybe it would have been better if he had died. This new world was stark and miserable. He hated it.

When she looked up at him, a single tear slipped down one cheek and she brushed it away. "When you are ready, I'll be here for you."

She expected some response from him, so he offered a solemn nod. Myara still watched him and he wondered what more she wanted, but then she lowered her gaze and walked away, looking ever so much like his mother had looked leaving the bath that morning. He lowered his head back down to the branch.

*Ride?*

Was that all they did in this place where evil could walk in and out with royal blessings?

His head snapped up.

That was where he had been going that night. He had been going to see his new horse. That was why this whole thing happened.

Rage boiled up in him. His hands shook with it and his vision turned red at the edges. He dropped from the tree and headed back towards the palace stables. The horse was the cause of all this. No matter how magnificent the animals was, he would never be able to appreciate it. It had to pay for the wrong done to him.

His fierce strides moved him along at a brisk pace, but the stables were some distance away and, when he reached them, his rage had simmered down. His violent crusade began to seem somewhat misguided. Regarding the dim interior of the barn, he began to feel an itch of uncertainty. It was only a horse. It was not as if it had sent a summons to draw him out into the night. Still, how could he have anything to do with an animal that triggered the memories and the hatred that crashed over him every time he thought about that night?

Perhaps it was time to find out. With refreshed resolve, if a somewhat altered sense of purpose, he entered
the stable.

He recognized most of the horses as he passed. Not
because he was especially fond of any of them, but because Mythan was always so eager to talk about and
share them, so he paid attention. It was plain before he
even saw the name plaque which horse was his. When he
was a few feet from the stall the stallion lunged forward
in a startling display of aggression, his hooves cracking
loudly against the wood of the door. Dephithus stopped
and regarded the stallion that was regarding him silently
in return, his muscles tense as though expecting danger.
Dequo ve la Hydra, the name plaque read. He was white
as snow with a pale silver dappling over his body. The
dappling darkened down his legs to his knees where it
turned a solid silvery-black and then lightened up again
towards the hoof. His tail started white and darkened
down to the same silvery-black as his legs. A fine elegant head topped his strong arched neck. His face was
almost pure white, beautifully contrasted by a silvery-
black mane.

Hydra was magnificent.

Dephithus stepped toward the stall and the horse
retreated several steps, delicate ears pulling part way
back. Eager for a distraction from himself, he flipped
up the bolt and slid it free, then stepped into the stall
and walked boldly up to Hydra. The stallion stood his
ground this time and Dephithus stopped beside his
head and growled. Hydra threw his head up, laying his
ears back the rest of the way and baring his teeth in a
very dog-like manner. Dephithus bared his own teeth in
response. The animal's fearlessness and aggression were
refreshing. The stallion stood still, his haunches bunch-
ing for quick action when Dephithus rested a hand on
his neck and began to stroke the silken coat. After a

minute or more, Hydra began to lower his head and his ears drifted forward. Grinning, Dephithus scratched his forehead under the thick black forelock.

When he finished acknowledging the magnificence of this animal he had come here intending to hate, Dephithus retrieved his personal tack and returned to the stall. The stallion's demeanor changed again when he saw all the gear being carried in. He tossed his head, nickering softly and pawing at the air with one foreleg impatiently. With a hint of an anticipatory grin tugging at his lips, Dephithus saddled and bridled the eager beast and led him out of the stall.

Only a few steps clear of the stall he mounted up, almost as impatient now as Hydra was. He reined the stallion around, feeling the animal tense beneath him at the sight of daylight beckoning beyond the stable doors. Hydra began to prance in place and Dephithus held him back, letting the stallion's excitement build and resonate through them. Perhaps it was dangerous, but the thrill of this immensely powerful animal dancing about, contained only by the discipline of superb training infected him. With subtle movements he eased his hold on the reins and squeezed Hydra's ribs gently. The stallion surged forward with the power and speed of a lightning strike.

Fortunately, no one was around the stable when Dephithus and Hydra burst through the doorway. Hydra stretched himself out and barreled down the main road with a single-minded focus, pent up energy driving him hard and fast. Dephithus leaned low on his neck, letting the stallion set their speed. The wild, dangerous abandon of their reckless gallop was exhilarating, freeing him, for a brief time, from his torment. They sped past a family in an open coach and a few startled cries faded quickly behind them.

Finally, Dephithus sat up, pressing his seat into the

saddle, and reined the stallion in. Hydra resisted for a moment, fighting the bit, then his training won out and he slowed to an easy lope. Dephithus allowed him to keep up that pace while he turned him in a wide circle to head back the way they had come. The stallion's sides heaved with exhaustion and excitement when Dephithus eased him down to a long cooling trot.

When he neared the coach he had dashed past earlier, they stopped, watching his approach with wary curiosity. Despite his urge to trot on by, he stopped Hydra alongside them and offered a polite nod.

"Lord Dephithus." The blond woman, dressed in the casual finery of local nobility out enjoying the sun, acknowledged him respectfully enough, yet her tone was tight with unease, her words cut off with a curt edge. "It's good to see you are well again."

He tried to focus on the words and not the cold look in her eyes. He tried and failed. "That would be an appreciated sentiment, if it sounded at all sincere." Both the woman and the man with her drew back at his response. They were shocked, though not nearly as much so as he was. Trying to keep the surprise from his face, he spoke quickly to intercept the anger he could see blossoming in their eyes. "Pardon, Lord and Lady, it seems I am not feeling as well as I thought. If you will excuse me."

Not waiting for their reply, he spun Hydra away from them and into a swift trot. There he went again, mistreating those who deserved no such abuse. Sure, the woman had seemed a bit artificial in her words, but the way he had startled them and risked upsetting their horses when he galloped by earlier was reason enough for that. The worst thing was that he did not feel nearly as bad about his rudeness as he knew he should. It was not like him to act that way and he should feel awful, yet some part of him did not care.

Dephithus touched his empty belt scabbard and sighed. Perhaps he should wear the dagger Amahna had given him. Maybe it would remind him where his hatred should be directed. With a solemn nod he decided that was what he would do. Reaching forward he rested a hand under Hydra's mane, feeling the muscles work as the stallion arched his neck to give to the bit. That strength was comforting. No matter the memories associated with that first attempted visit to the stallion, he suspected that more time with Hydra might do him some good.

Ignoring the healer's recommendations, Dephithus chose not to wait a few more days before attending his first official Legion practice. Physically he was much better and mentally he preferred it to tarrying around the palace with his parents and Myara watching him. He dressed in the same style blue and silver uniform that he had worn in Legion training, only now a royal crested falcon carrying a crown of ivy in its talons was embroidered on the breast of each practice uniform.

The royal crested falcon, a rare and majestic bird, was the symbol of Imperious. The crown of ivy was an aged symbol that bore little meaning for younger generations. It represented the Tuvoth family that ruled Imperious before Mythan's predecessors had taken control several centuries ago. It's presence on the Imperious crest was an effort to honor that fallen family's importance in the history of the region.

Dephithus sighed, staring blankly at his chamber mirror. It was rumored that so much happened back in the days when the Tuvoth's ruled. The books he had read in training barely hinted at the wars that occurred back then. The banishment of the dragons and a strange power referred to as daenox that took the daemons into exile with it—events that marked the beginning of their long peace—were only briefly touched upon in the histories available in the palace library. The swift vanishing of the traits of the Dragonkin after that was mentioned in some literature, but never with more than a vague sentence or two that offered no real insight. Perhaps, somewhere in the locked library archives, there was more.

Dephithus pondered those historical gaps and what filling them in might teach him about himself while he faced the mirror, which he had yet to really look at beyond staring into those silver-green eyes with their peculiar vertical pupils. A knock on his door snapped him from the reverie. He glimpsed his irritated expression in the mirror and forced a more pleasant look over his features before calling welcome to his company.

Avaline stepped into the room dressed in flowing violet riding skirts that appeared to be silk or some similarly clinging material. He had noticed a distinct increase of even more sensual daily clothing in her wardrobe since Amahna's visit. Perhaps she was jealous of her sister's more slender figure and sought to compensate.

He had to consciously stop himself from growling at the thought of his aunt.

"What is it, Mother?" He forced his memories aside and faced her, trying to at least appear attentive.

There was a hint of worry under her smile. "You rode Hydra yesterday. What did you think of him?"

Dephithus cracked a genuine smile for her with the memory of the stallion. "He was magnificent. I have never seen his equal."

Most of the worry vanished, though some unease lingered, making her reluctant to look at him. Instead, she wandered to a pile of clothes on a bench at the foot of the bed and began sorting through them, sniffing to see if they were clean enough before folding them. "I would like it very much if you would ride with me some afternoon. I know you have much to do these days, but you can let me know when is best. Also, the many gifts you received on your birthday are still awaiting your perusal."

He could not stop a scowl that made his mother smile falter. He disregarded her look of concern as he picked up Amahna's dagger, the serpent dagger, and slipped it into the sheath on his belt, trying to ignore the burst of revulsion at touching something she had touched. His birthday would give him no peace so long as those gifts sat untouched. "Yes, well, perhaps tonight I will attend to that. Thank you, Mother, I must go to practice now."

Her gaze followed him as he started to walk around her to the door, but she caught his arm when he was almost past.

Dephithus stopped, glaring down at the floor to hide his impatience.

"Are you well enough?"

"Well enough," he answered, pulling his arm away.

The moment he walked into the stable Hydra whinnied impatiently. The stallion was eager to be free of his stall again. Once he had finished saddling him Dephithus stood beside the stallion for a moment, considering his equipment. The saddle had a few smudges on it. Area Commander Parthak would be upset by that, but maybe Lance Commander Vicor would be more lenient. Outside the confines of his stall Hydra began to prance in place and Dephithus envied him the simplicity of his desires. Like Hydra, he longed to be careless and wild, but, unlike Hydra, the barriers that trapped him were not mere physical ones.

Swinging into the saddle Dephithus encountered the same little boost of confidence there that had greeted him the day before. Encouraged, he let Hydra out a little, allowing him to move into an extended trot out of the stable. The stallion fought for more, but Dephithus held him in until they reached the road then allowed him a collected canter.

"Dephithus!"

He clearly heard Myara call him. Not looking to see where she was, he held Hydra back for a few more strides, torn by the feeling that he ought to speak to her, then he let the stallion go. Hydra surged forward with such power that Dephithus nearly lost his seat. He barked a bitter laugh. Getting tossed would have so fittingly countered his attempt to avoid Myara. Perhaps the stallion had been intentionally rough to reprimand him for his cowardice, not that he believed the animal had that much awareness of such things. Leaning low over Hydra's neck, he aimed his mount at the Legion's outdoor arena, almost half a mile past the training academy's indoor facilities, and let him run.

Myara would be training in hand-to-hand combat today so she would not have a horse to catch him with. The actual Legion and the academy never did mounted work on the same day to ensure that they always had an adequate supply of fresh, healthy mounts available. Even among the nobility very few owned their own battle-trained horses. With no battles to fight most considered maintaining a personal war-horse an unnecessary expense.

Nearer to the Legion's assortment of practice facilities Dephithus had to bring Hydra down to a trot due to the increased traffic. Every Legion soldier was required to fit no less than two hours of some kind of combat practice into their day at least six days of the week. The only time this was excused was in the case of extended away duty, such as royal escorts traveling between territories. That was the kind of duty he would like to get stuck with right now. Anything that got him out of Elysium would be a good duty pull as far as he was concerned. However, such draws were typically reserved for soldiers with at least a year of Legion training behind them. Then again, the same was also true for the larger tournaments, and he already had a challenger lined up for the next big one.

Several soldiers, men and women of the Legion, acknowledged him with a nod or a wave, openly admiring Hydra as he passed. This was his first day as one of their ranks, but he was already far more well known to them than they were to him, though he recognized many of the faces. Dephithus nodded to each and distracted himself with trying to figure out where they were going by their attire and armaments.

A group of five younger soldiers who sat loafing against a building were the only ones he could not recall ever seeing around the practice grounds or palace. It was not often that the mere presence of the Imperious uniforms did not instill confidence and pride in him, but something about this group leached away that good feeling. One of the five, a particularly lean lad, tall and with the dark tan of someone who spent considerable time working fields in the sun on his off hours, sneered at him. Dephithus rested his off hand on Hydra's neck and responded with an uncharacteristic predatorial grin. It felt a bit strange on his face, but some part of him reveled in the unspoken challenge.

The tall lad nodded, not quite approving and obviously not concerned, then turned his attention back to the other four. There would always be those who did not appreciate how privileged they were to be a part of the Imperious Legion. Such dregs, if they did not get themselves expelled outright, rarely pulled the prized duties and never achieved honorable stations. They managed to skim by, always staying just within the limits that kept them from being expelled from the Legion.

The big outdoor arena was occupied by a number of soldiers, most older than Dephithus, who were warming up their borrowed mounts. Everyone from the veterans to the newly raised practiced in the same classes. It provided an opportunity for experience and new ideas to work together. As they neared the arena gate Hydra's ears perked straight up and his trot became more animated. Dephithus could not help wishing for a moment that his mount was not so attention-grabbing. However, Hydra was a proud beast and they needed to be a team. They could not afford to shame one another. Dephithus forced himself to sit tall in the saddle. His goal was not to appear arrogant, but to seem confident and strong as a future ruler should be. A lie he did not feel at all.

Since he was close to being late, Commander Vicor arrived on his heels and Dephithus managed to avoid having to converse with his fellow soldiers. Vicor, a lean gentleman with close cut black hair and a tidy moustache under his hawk-like nose, did a full equipment check before letting them move out in pairs to practice their mounted sword-fighting skills. He lingered longest on Dephithus and the two other newly raised soldiers, marking down the smudges on Hydra's saddle and a few barely noticeable tangles in the stallion's tail.

Dephithus caught himself glowering at the commander, cursing him silently for the negative marks and mentally reprimanded himself for it. He could not remember the last time he got negative marks in practice. Still, he had deserved them this time. His temper and attitude were lacking lately. He scowled and touched the hilt of the serpent dagger when Vicor gave him the signal to head out and begin practice.

His practice partner, Abron, was a burly redhead with a well-trimmed beard accentuating his angular features and a mild manner that contrasted his rugged appearance. The man did wield a strong sword, making Dephithus remember each hit with a rattle that went through his torso. Abron also liked to chat while fighting, which Dephithus found extremely annoying, though there was some compensation in that, most of the time, the man did not seem to desire any feedback. He rambled on about how the commander had been quite concerned when Dephithus fell ill and how good it was that he was well enough to join them today. As he feinted his mount agilely to one side or the other he bubbled over with his own excitement at being a part of the Imperious Legion. As they both began to break a sweat and a sheen of dampness started to show on the horses, Abron finally grew tired of listening to himself ramble.

"So, when do you marry?"

Taken aback by the question Dephithus faltered, failing his block, and took a solid blow to his shoulder. Even with the padded practice armor, the impact jarred down through his spine and a sharp pain flashed through the joint. Swallowing down an angry growl he parried the next attack.

"I haven't even considered a bride."

"Oh," Abron grinned knowingly as if they were sharing some special secret. Dephithus was almost surprised when he did not follow the grin up with a wink. "A number of us assumed you and Myara wouldn't wait."

Dephithus did growl then and Hydra lunged into the other mount in response to the sudden aggression, pinning Abron's leg for a moment. Dephithus caught Abron across the chest with a powerful swing as the man's mount leapt sideways to recover, sending him flying off the horse's back. A third horse lunged in between Hydra and Abron, who lay prone in the dirt wheezing to get his breath back, his face flushed crimson.

Commander Vicor regarded Dephithus with a stony expression until he lowered his dull practice sword and reined Hydra back. Another soldier was already helping

Abron up when Vicor turned to check on him.

"Just got the wind knocked out of him sir," the other soldier offered.

Commander Vicor nodded and turned his disapproval on Dephithus. This practice was for improving form and precision, and such an aggressive attack was inappropriate. Dephithus knew this, but he could not hold back a surge of rage at being singled out for his mistake and he did not feel any remorse for his gasping victim.

"Commander Parthak didn't tell me you were so forceful."

One of the others rode up then, a young woman Dephithus had known from academy training. She had moved up only four months earlier. "He has been sick, sir. I've sparred with Dephithus many..."

Vicor's angry glare silenced her defense.

She shrugged at Dephithus as if to say she had tried and backed her mount up a few steps.

"Your practice is done for today. I expect to see you at hand-to-hand tomorrow morning. I'll try to arrange a more appropriate partner."

Dephithus nodded. His temper raged inside him, irrational and untamed, but he managed a neutral expression as he inclined his head to the other soldiers and began to turn Hydra away.

"Dragonkin."

Despite his desire to get away from there before the red that edged his vision spread beyond his control, Dephithus stopped Hydra and turned to face the commander. He could not decide if he should be offended at the name, so he clung to his forced neutral expression.

"You will pull fifth watch at the second northeast guard tower. I'll see that Captain Laudon is made aware of the shift change."

Dephithus was afraid his irrational rage might burst

through his skin like some wild animal and attack the man. The woman who had come to his defense earlier started to speak again, trying to protest the midnight shift when he had been ill so recently. Dephithus stopped her with a very subtle shake of his head and she trailed off again, pursing her lips in frustration.

"Sir," he acknowledged, inclining his head somewhat stiffly this time.

Vicor nodded in turn and turned his back on Dephithus.

Swallowing down the growl that was rising in his throat as the rest of the soldiers were ordered to resume practice, Dephithus pranced Hydra from the arena with the same confident posture he had ridden in with. He almost wanted to hit himself. His temper had never been this quick and he would never risk unnecessarily injuring a fellow student like that. What was wrong with him?

Perhaps what had been done to him should bear some of the blame. Yet, was he not the one who controlled his reactions to the world? There could be no excuse for so thoroughly spoiling this day that he had waited all his young life for. This was his dream and he was making a mess of it.

Dephithus continued his mental reprimand as he rounded the side of the nearest building where the band of soldiers he had seen earlier were now standing.

The tall lad sneered at him. "I guess it doesn't help to be the royal heir, does it Dragonkin? You still have to follow the same rules as the rest of us."

Dephithus stopped Hydra, though the stallion pranced in place in response to the rising tension in his rider. "It hasn't helped yet, but I promise you'll be the first to know when that changes."

The other four youths tensed noticeably, as if preparing to defend their chosen leader. The tall lad only smiled, the expression slick with deception. He remained leaning casually against the wall, making a show of his lack of concern. "I look forward to it."

Dephithus moved Hydra out then, letting the horse's natural energy animate his trot. He did not look back, trusting that the stallion would let him know if anyone threatened them. For a very short distance he could hear them talking softly, though he could make out none of the words. Somehow, the encounter had served to soothe down his anger and frustration. Strange, but he felt much better for it. Perhaps a jaunt to the palace kitchens and then a long nap before his midnight post would be a good way to fill the afternoon.

Absently, Dephithus stroked the hilt of the serpent dagger as he urged Hydra to a canter.

CHAPTER TWELVE

Under a blanket of darkness, Dephithus struck out for the second northeast guard tower. The tower and wall were little more than a darker shadow among many in the night. The moon was again a sliver in the sky. Since the time he had fallen ill it had vanished and begun its growing cycle again. Fifth shift started at midnight and he was determined to start off on a better foot than he had with Legion practice. He was perhaps fifteen minutes early when he slowed Hydra next to the remote tower.

The tower was part of the inner wall that surrounded Elysium. There had been talk of taking both the inner and outer walls down, but Mythan and his predecessors had all turned down the idea for one reason or another. Mythan's father had kept them because of the labor involved in their removal. Mythan was a different sort of lord. He kept the walls because they were part of the history of Imperious, just as the Legion that he insisted on keeping strong and prepared despite the peaceful times.

The guard he would replace in the tower hailed Dephithus. There were two guards in each tower at all times, paired to keep each other awake. The guard that hailed him came down the inner stairs while Dephithus settled Hydra in the small shelter and paddock he would occupy for the next six hours. The guard did not have much to say, but he leaned close to Dephithus before mounting up to leave.

"Your duty partner is already here. Good luck," he said in a low voice before swinging up in the saddle and cantering away to leave Dephithus wondering after him.

After watching the guard disappear in the dark, Dephithus turned and walked into the tower. Flickering sconces lit the stairwell. The areas between the bright pools of candlelight were pitch black in contrast. At the top there was a window and archer slits on the side facing away from Elysium with a matching window facing into Elysium. On the other two walls were heavy wooden doors that opened out onto the top of the wall itself. The one candle burning in the far corner was almost out when Dephithus entered the small room.

"Look who it is. This must be where they send all the rejects."

The voice was unpleasantly familiar, though it took Dephithus a moment to make out the figure in the shadows. The tall lad from the practice grounds was leaning in the corner, his stance arrogant and careless. In the dark uniform, with his black hair and dark skin, it was hard to pick him out of the shadows. The silver accents gave him away, however, glinting in the light from the candle.

A sarcastic laugh escaped Dephithus as he turned his back on the lad and leaned out the small window for the breath of fresh air he suddenly needed. He heard the lad shifting behind him, but he stayed where he was, seeing if the easy target would tempt the other youth.

"I can't say I am excited about my draw of partners for this evening either. I suppose that doesn't surprise you much." He turned and leaned casually against the wall, scrutinizing the youth with his cat-like eyes, hoping their strangeness might unnerve the other a bit. "What are you called?"

"What do you care?"

Dephithus held his silence, waiting for a better answer. There was something about his hostility that was refreshing somehow.

The youth finally relented, grinning. "Darkin, by my friends."

"And what do the rest call you?"

His grin grew. "Any number of vulgarities. You're welcome to take your pick. Top marks for creativity."

"You seem to have an attitude problem."

Darkin barked a laugh. "Me. Have you listened to yourself, high and mighty Dephithus de NuTraven." His expression turned more serious as Dephithus touched the dagger at his belt. "You won't remain very popular if you finger that knife any time someone doesn't sing your praises."

Dephithus scoffed at him, trying to hide his distress when he realized he was indeed touching the hated weapon. He was only being bitter because he had not been prepared to deal with someone like Darkin, whose hand hovered just to the side of his waist where he undoubtedly hid his own blade. It was reasonable to be a little touchy under the circumstances. Wasn't it? "Popularity doesn't seem to concern you much."

Darkin's smile was a little too eager, his gaze vaguely hungry though his posture still gave the illusion of being relaxed. "You're certainly more entertaining than I expected you would be." Dephithus was unable to catch himself before confusion furrowed his brow, ruining his illusion of composure. "You know. They all say what a fine upstanding young man you are. I expected you to be more gracious and ethical, like a well-trained puppy. Pride of the Imperious Legion." Darkin offered the last in a mocking tone.

Dephithus turned his back on Darkin again, even though the lad had just pushed his jacket back to reveal the knife that rested there. He leaned out the window and closed his eyes to the night, refusing to let Darkin to see his torment.

It would serve him right if the other stabbed him in the back. There was nothing noble or good about the way he was acting. Pride of the Imperious Legion indeed. Dephithus forced down a bitter laugh. He tensed when he heard the other boy moving behind him. Then the light brightened as Darkin lit a new candle before he returned to his resting place against the wall. After that the room was silent for a time. When Dephithus finally turned around again he noticed Darkin watching him in contemplative silence.

Not sure he wanted to know what the other was thinking, Dephithus tried to ignore the look. "We are posted together, we ought to make the best of it."

"That's a weak thing to say. Why the sudden change of heart?"

"Don't push your luck." Dephithus half-growled the words, trying desperately to hold on to his calm. This was not like him. This was not him.

"Dephithus!"

He blew out a heavy breath, trying to expel his irritation. The last thing he needed was Myara confusing his emotions even more. He had not really spoken to her since his birthday and definitely was not ready to do so now. He brushed roughly past Darkin to the other window and peered down at her figure in the dark.

"I'm on duty," he called down.

"I need to talk to you. I'm sure your partner won't tell anyone if you come down for a couple of minutes"

Dephithus glanced back at Darkin, who merely shrugged, then he leaned back out the window. "I think you might have missed that call."

"What's the matter," Darkin whispered behind him, "isn't she good enough for you anymore? Maybe you wouldn't mind if I had a go at her."

The sudden torrent of rage was so strong that Dephithus feared it might split his skull. He swung around with his fist ready, but Darkin had already moved clear and he staggered forward with the force of his swing. Darkin kicked out, catching him across the chest as he struggled to catch his balance. Dephithus crumpled to the floor gasping for breath while Darkin leaned out the window over where Myara was.

"He's just dying to see you," Darkin called down, following it up with a sinister laugh.

Dephithus rose to a crouch and lunged, twisting to slam his shoulder into Darkin's back. Myara cried out below them as Darkin fell forward through the small window. He twisted like a cat in the air and barely caught the edge of the window with one hand. Dephithus regarded him, seething with blood-red rage. Below, Myara yelled for him to help, misreading their situation. Darkin stared up at him, his dark eyes blazing with a fierce inner fire despite his predicament.

"You won't let me fall." Darkin's voice trembled with the strain of holding on to the ledge.

Dephithus looked down at the helpless individual in front of him and realized, with horror spreading cold through his gut, that he very much wanted to see him fall. Myara screamed for him to help again and he grabbed hold of Darkin's wrist. Darkin swung his other hand up and Dephithus caught it, hauling him back into the tower as fast as he could, regardless of how painful it might be for Darkin. Darkin grunted as his shins hit the edge, but once he was inside he stood and backed away from Dephithus.

"You don't know yourself very well, do you?" The lanky youth accused him.

Dephithus said nothing. A week ago, he would have disagreed. A week ago, none of this would have happened. Now, there was nothing he could say.

Darkin turned away from him. "Go, talk to her. Get out."

He could see that Darkin wanted to recover from his fear and pain alone, so he took a couple of deep breaths to try and ease the lingering pain in his chest, then he started down the stairwell. He heard Darkin call down to Myara that everyone was fine, which was something of a lie, but it was a lie he appreciated. When Myara called back up to ask what had happened she was ignored. Wishing he had a mirror, Dephithus put on what he hoped was a calm and perhaps even welcoming expression and ran his fingers through his hair to settle it. When he stepped out, Myara trotted over, her lips drawn tight with worry and her moonlit eyes storming with a mixture of concern and suspicion.

"What happened up there?"

Dephithus took her hand then hesitated, not quite sure what he meant to do with it. Finally, he settled for a little squeeze then let it go. She looked a bit puzzled and plainly annoyed with his silence, so he tried to come up with some explanation. "Nothing. Just careless rough-housing. It was stupid and irresponsible really, but no one was hurt."

The night was cool and moist, but not unpleasantly so. He started to walk slowly away from the tower and Myara fell into step beside him. Her gaze was downcast, and it was obvious by her unusual silence that something was troubling her. He should say something, but he was not all that eager to talk, so he let her keep her quiet until she was ready.

"How did your first day of practice go?"

That was not among the questions he had expected. She was delaying and now he was going to lie to her.

Not the best way to start. "It was fine. I don't think Commander Vicor is all that impressed with me."

"He just needs time to get to know you." She smiled at him, but it was weak and soulless and faded too fast. "I saw you this morning. You were on Hydra and I called to you."

"Oh, I must not have heard you." He cringed inwardly with the building guilt of lies. If there was anyone he could be honest with, it had always been her. What was happening to them? What was happening to him? Was it all that one night? He gritted his teeth and pushed the thought away.

"I suppose."

Silence ruled over them for a bit and Dephithus gradually changed direction back toward the tower.

"Have you met someone?"

Dephithus knew what she meant, though he did not see how she could believe he had met someone who could take her place in so short a time. "No. I still have no prospective brides."

She laughed a bit nervously. "It's silly I suppose, but it seems like you've been avoiding me and I was sure you must have found someone special."

Dephithus sighed. Before he really considered what he was going to say, he blurted it out. "I have found someone special, and that someone is you, Myara."

She stepped around in front of him, forcing him to stop. Her expression was still uncertain, but there was something new in her eyes. Could it be hope that he saw there? "Do you really mean that?"

He shifted his feet and glanced at the ground. Did he? "I...yes, but..."

Myara leaned forward, her eyes closing and her lips moving toward him with obvious intent. Dephithus had a sudden powerful swell of desire and he imagined throwing her down in the grass and entering her right there. He hesitated, trying to bury the image under memories of racing through the fields and climbing the Mother Tree. Was that really him thinking those things? Stepping back, he placed a finger to her lips and shook his head when she opened her eyes suddenly.

Myara backed away, unable to meet his eyes. Even in the dark he could see the color of her cheeks darkening. "I am so sorry. I thought you meant—"

He interrupted her quickly. "You aren't wrong. I just have a few issues to work out."

"Issues?" Her face screwed up in a familiar puzzled expression, which he had expected, but he had not expected the way that adorable look suddenly changed, her eyes narrowing to angry slits. "I have been searching my mind for some reason why you would push me away like you have. I don't like it. It's not like you. Then I believed I had it all figured out." Dephithus considered interrupting again then decided against it when her eyes narrowed a little more. "I thought perhaps you had fallen for me too and that was why you were being distant, because you didn't know how I felt."

Dephithus leaned forward then, slipping a hand behind her neck almost before she finished speaking. There was no protest in her eyes as he pulled her to him and kissed her. He kissed her deep, his body responding with eager arousal. Slipping his tongue between her lips made him feel like a thief stealing a temple's treasures. He wanted desperately to press for more, but he did not trust himself not to hurt her, so he pulled away. For a moment she looked as stunned as he felt, then a slow smile curved her lips.

"Now..." he had to pause, finding himself a little short of breath. "Now will you have patience?"

"That depends," a sly little smile turned her lips. "Are there more of those at the end of the trail?"

Dephithus grinned then, feeling more like himself

than he had in days. He should have known she would have that power. "Many more."

When he returned to the tower he felt more at balance with himself, but the sense of wellbeing was tempered by a sudden rush of nausea since parting with Myara. Perhaps it was a result of being kicked in the chest. He looked up the stairwell. Like it or not, duty called. When he stepped into the tower room, Darkin was back in the corner, sitting this time, his knees pulled to his chest. He did not look up or acknowledge Dephithus in any way. There were dark stains on the shins of both of his pant legs and Dephithus suffered a pang of guilt.

"Are you all right?"

Darkin glanced up, his dark eyes cold with hatred. "I suppose this means I don't get a go at her."

Dephithus scowled. His good feeling vanished, but at least the nausea went with it. Leaning against the wall he stared out at the sliver moon and said nothing.

Amahna and Rakas did not speak at all the remainder of the long ride to the Dunues Mountain cave. Back in the cave the silence subsided, but they did not speak of their journey. Most of their conversations were casual and meaningless observations of this change in the flow of daenox or that individual having gained or lost favor with Theruses. She noticed Rakas fondling the ring from the young man in Ithkan much of the time, so she did not press him with talk of Dephithus. If he insisted on bathing himself in guilt, then it only made her job easier. Rakas was quiet and calm on the outside, but she recognized the misery in the language of his expressions and his movements.

Theruses was another matter. Since their return he had become increasingly agitated. It was not obvious at first, but now anyone could see it in the way he wandered through the cave's passages, restless and distracted, tail lashing. As Amahna and Rakas lounged in a small chamber, one of several with deep daenox illuminated pools in them, they could see him pacing through the adjoining room. They both watched him in wary silence, his tail switching viciously back and forth, until he passed from view. Amahna scowled after him, distressed that he should let his irritation show so plainly, but not certain how she might change it.

"He seems a little distracted," Rakas commented a little too flippantly.

Amahna nodded in response, too worried to bother reprimanding him for his inappropriate tone. She could not get out of her head how Theruses had been with her the last time they had been together. When she and Rakas returned from their trip to Imperious, Theruses had taken her like he meant to tear her apart. His violent passion had filled her with fear and pain to the point that she had not gotten any pleasure from it. She was still hurting. That had never happened before.

"Perhaps it seems too easy," she mused, more thinking aloud than seeking input from Rakas.

"Yes." A shudder forced Rakas to silence for several seconds. When it passed, he said, "I'm sure that's all it is." His tone said he was appeasing her. He did not believe it any more than she did.

"Well, he knows the dragons have only a fraction of the power now that they had when they were free." She hoped Theruses was listening so her words might reassure him. Sometimes he listened to them, sometimes he did not. There was no real way to know who held his attention at any given time.

With a thought, Amahna called Kara to her. The young woman had been moved to the cave before they returned. Theruses had known her pleasure with the young woman's services through the daenox that spilled over into the village and had given Kara as a reward for Amahna's fulfillment of his orders. Rakas had received no such gifts. Undoubtedly this was due to the guilt that he carried with him. Guilt that had grown significantly over the course of their journey. Theruses had no patience for such things. Amahna's gift, the Kithin shepherd woman, was a skilled server and, to her surprise, an eager sexual partner.

Kara stepped into the room and knelt before Amahna,

but not before she saw the fondness in Amahna's gaze
and a soft blush colored her cheeks. "How may I serve
you, my lady?"

"Wine. For two I think," she did not look to see if
Rakas shared her interest. "I trust you can pick a good
one."

"Thank you, my lady. It is my pleasure to serve."
Kara stood, curtsying gracefully before hastening to her
newest duty.

"Has Theruses tried her yet?"

Amahna ignored Rakas until the young woman
turned down a passage out of view. When she faced
him, he was turning the young man's ring on his finger
and gazing past it into nothingness. "No, she hasn't met
him yet. He wishes that she be mine for now."

"I suppose that's best. Once she meets him, you will
probably lose her. Skilled as she is, you might lose him
too."

Amahna laughed as if at a joke, but a chill swept
through her, bringing gooseflesh up on her arms. The
suggestion that he might choose Kara over her did not
concern her much. The impudence of the comment was
almost enough to anger her. Kara was still much too
young and inexperienced to have the drive and creativity
necessary to fulfill the demands of Theruses. It was the
implication that she somehow had a hold on Theruses
that upset her. It was not an idea that would appeal to
their lord much. If he were listening…

She turned away from Rakas as quickly as she dared
without alerting him to the panic he had caused. A
touch in her mind filled her with icy fear and the blood
drained from her face. She could feel Theruses throughout her body, like a thousand hands caressing her at
once. His voice in her mind told her she would come to
him later when he called, then he was gone.

Kara returned to the chamber then. Forcing herself

to breathe normally, she took the goblet Kara now offered her. With a nod to Rakas she gave the young woman permission to serve him as well.

When Kara left the chamber again, Amahna gazed through the crystal of the goblet at the deep red wine it held. Would Theruses caress her as he had if he were angry? No. There was no need for such deceptions between them. If he wanted to punish her, he would do so openly and no one would consider trying to stop him. Theruses was their lord and he would not see them harmed by anyone. At the same time, he would not hesitate to punish anyone he believed deserved it. This was his kingdom and he ruled absolute.

So Amahna waited. For a few minutes, she considered passing the time with Kara. That might annoy Theruses though, if he wanted her to himself today. Instead she waited in the chamber with Rakas who was immersed in his own contemplative silence. Then, perhaps an hour later, that familiar need tugged at her and she rose to follow the call of her lord. The need led her to a part of the cave system she did not recognize. Despite the years she had lived here, the system was vast. There were many areas she did not know well enough to find twice and some she had never seen at all. The path stayed dimly lit just in front of her while the area outside the light remained black as pitch, creating an eerie illusion of walking through nothing.

Finally, she stepped into a chamber that was lit using daenox to create an array of pale glowing orbs around the room that flickered in a candle-like fashion. The chamber was not big, but it was decorated from top to bottom with flowstone cascading down along the walls from the high ceiling and ornate shelfstone rimmed a deep aqua pool to one side of the room. A thick layer of blankets was laid over a naturally formed bed of sorts along one wall. Above the bed a wide fall of flowstone drapery created a canopy effect, adding a touch of natural elegance to the chamber.

The chamber itself was breathtaking, but Theruses was nowhere to be seen. She walked into the center, glancing down into the impossibly deep pool at the eerily lit stalagmites rising through its waters.

"We must celebrate."

His voice came from all around her and it took considerable will not to cry out in surprise. She bit the inside of her lip and tried to soothe her nerves, resisting the urge to turn and flee as memories of their last pairing touched off a black coil of fear in her gut. A phantom caress along her neck sent a chill down her spine.

"What are we celebrating?" She hoped her fear did not show in her voice.

"The presence of the growing seed of daemon power in the dragon-child has already created a powerful link to the outside world. The daenox can build on that link. As its power consumes and corrupts him, it will free itself a little at a time until the anchor in the outside world is strong enough that it can break out of this cave." There was silence for a moment, then he appeared before her. "I was too rough with you last time." He lifted her chin, regarding her through those chilling black eyes. "I will make it up to you now."

When he kissed her it was firm, though not rough as it had been last time. He was never gentle. Rather, he was erotically forceful, something she appreciated about him. Being taken by him aroused her to the point of intoxication. Her dress moved off her shoulders and slid down her body in a snake-like manner. It was fascinating that a touch of the daenox could make a simple thing like undressing so incredibly arousing. It was plain in mere seconds that he meant what he said. Every sensation was deliberately enhanced with the daemon power that surrounded them. Caresses coming at her from all angles. Touching and teasing. As her body trembled with an overwhelming array of sensations, Amahna began to forget all her fear and pain from last time. This pleasure left room for nothing else.

*

Vanuthan still clung to the wonder and joy she had experienced upon seeing Dephithus. Human though he might be, her essence was in him and she was connected to him no less than she would be to a true son. Despite the wrong that had been visited upon him since that moment, the Mother Dragon could focus on little other than his face in her mind, as clear as if he still stood before her. Her young Dephithus was handsome and perfect, or he had been when she saw him that day.

Amahna's very presence, saturated with daenox, had been enough to warn her that there was something unpleasant in the works. She had felt it coming long before seeing the woman. The disturbance had begun with Siniva and passed through Cylan and Tikat to her. All of their rage had passed through the web of dragons when Amahna and Rakas used it to travel to Imperious. When they had left, Vanuthan could do nothing to stop them. All she could do was wonder what evil they had worked upon her son.

Since the night of his sixteenth birthday, the echoes of some corruption came through her link to Dephithus, but there were so many limitations to the power of the dragons now. Somehow, Amahna and Rakas had poisoned him with the daenox. She knew their meddling in his conception had been a risk, as had all the dragons that had combined their limited power to make the child possible. The powers they had placed within him were almost more of a curse than a gift. Power that would make him attractive to those who were loyal to the daemon power. It had seemed a risk worth taking because the daenox was imprisoned like they were. Now they knew the daenox still had active servants, worshippers like in the days of old, and those servants had done something to him. Regardless, Dephithus was still their only hope.

It was not only the possible ruin of their plans that upset Vanuthan. Though she had assured the other dragons before they agreed to the plan that she could not love any child that was not a dragon in flesh, her distress now was almost entirely maternal.

She wanted so much to see him again. He was only a boy, a young man by human standards, but he was the most beautiful thing she had ever seen. From the start, he was destined to find hardship That was something she had easily accepted, up until the moment Avaline gave birth to their child.

Then it all changed.

Vanuthan was aware of his love for Myara, and she was aware of a new emotion. Something she had never felt from him before. Dephithus hated now. It was a hate she mirrored though she could not know the true depth of it without knowing what had been done to him. It might be easier to cope if she had a choice about helping him. Yet, here she was, one of the oldest of a once powerful race, and she could not help her own son. There was little more she wanted then to pin Amahna and Rakas beneath her lethal claws and make their very soft human flesh suffer for their deeds.

Doing her best to hide her love and anguish from the other dragons, Vanuthan reached out through the web with her mind and focused in on a distant point where the level of distress almost matched her own. It was Siniva. His presence boiled over with restlessness and irritation. She could picture the great fire-bronze dragon pacing, his long tail snapping back and forth with displeasure, claws digging into earth and stone effortlessly. Untouchably beautiful. He felt her touch and she instantly knew his turmoil. At the same moment, all the other dragons received his message and a mixture of rage and fear washed over the web. The effect across the link was nauseating and it took a moment for Vanuthan to truly digest this new information. When she did, her mind went as cold as the stone she was trapped in.

The daenox was starting to break free.

## CHAPTER FOURTEEN

Dephithus showed up at hand-to-hand combat practice early the next morning, hoping to make a better impression than he had on his first day. The floor of the combat stadium was well padded and looked comfortable enough to nap on. The idea appealed to him after the harsh schedule Commander Vicor had prescribed him for his first two days as a soldier of the Legion. After his duty in the guard tower he was tired, and his chest was bruised and aching from his confrontation with Darkin. He resented Vicor for the deliberate scheduling of this early practice.

Dephithus was very early, primarily because he had not seen much point in trying to get any sleep by the time he was done with tower duty, so he had come straight here. Even so, there were already several groups practicing around the floor. Vicor spotted him and approached from the far wall. By the sudden anticipation in his expression he had been waiting for Dephithus specifically. There was a small satisfaction in standing his ground and making the commander walk all the way across the stadium, though Vicor did not appear noticeably annoyed.

"Dephithus."

"Commander Vicor," he greeted with a slight bow of his head.

"I trust you had a pleasant shift in the guard tower. I do hope your partner was agreeable."

The smug grin told Dephithus that his draw of partners had been just as deliberate as this miserable practice time. Instead of sneering like he wanted to, he kept his face neutral and nodded abruptly. "Uneventful watch, Commander."

"Curious," Vicor muttered to himself then shrugged. "I have arranged a suitable partner for you today. Kota."

Dephithus hoped his stare was not too obvious. The man who approached them was a good head taller than Dephithus, who topped the commander by several inches himself. For all that Dephithus was solidly built and well-muscled, this giant Vicor called Kota was easily five or six inches broader across the chest and shoulders. Kota was bare-chested, perhaps for effect or perhaps they did not make shirts that big, and his skin was a dark bronze. Since neither Vicor or Kota were laughing, Dephithus figured that this was not the joke he briefly hoped it was.

"Kota is from Trylum. He is of the Fi'erthaga tribe. I think he might be more suited to your aggression level."

Dephithus mustered up a firm handshake. The Fi'erthaga, the Dragon Warriors, were a tribe as legendary in their land as the Legion was in Imperious.

Vicor sized them up together and nodded his approval. "I leave him in your capable hands, Kota."

The dark-skinned giant nodded, his gaze never moving from Dephithus as Vicor walked away to go coach the rest of his practice group.

*Cheerful sort.* Dephithus stepped back to ease the angle of his neck. "The reputation of your tribe precedes you."

"As it should," Kota responded abruptly, his voice adequately deep for his size.

"Perhaps you would care to back it up," Dephithus

snapped, his newly blossoming quick temper jumping in before a rational thought could stop the words.

Both moved into a fighting stance. Even before Kota advanced, Dephithus began to regret his words. Now he would most certainly get the beating his deteriorating manners deserved. Kota moved fast, distracting Dephithus with a bold right-handed jab and flipping him into the air with a sweep from his opposite leg. Dephithus landed on his back hard enough that it knocked the wind out of him and his sore chest protested with a painful spasm.

Embarrassment at being dropped so easily fueled his temper to a molten rage and he hopped to his feet before he fully had his breath back. The effortless and graceful upspring won him an approving grunt from his opponent.

Dephithus was ready for the next attack. Blocking quickly with his arms and legs he moved in aggressively on every opening that Kota left him. None of those rare openings gained him any ground and he hit the floor six more times in the first half-hour. After that, his lack of sleep began to wear on him and he hit the floor more frequently.

As Dephithus struggled to rise one more time Vicor finally returned to them. This time, he was more than a little relieved to see the commander. His rage had long since burned out and he had very little desire to go another round with the relentless giant. Breathing raggedly and dripping with sweat, Dephithus looked over Kota, who was now standing at attention. Kota's breathing was a little labored and a light sheen of sweat glossed his dark skin. Dephithus attempted a scowl of irritation, but gave it up before the more pressing need of catching his breath.

Kota grinned, watching him as his chest rose and fell rapidly. The commander dismissed Kota before Dephithus had regained his breath enough to act on his irritation. It was probably for the best. He knew it would be another of many mistakes to try and seek some sort of vengeance for his current humiliation.

"Feeling a bit humbler now, are we?"

Vicor's smug smile aggravated Dephithus more than Kota's grin had. A voice in the back of his mind wondered when he had developed such a problem with authority, but he smothered the thought. Such questions only frustrated him so perhaps the answer was to stop questioning.

"For now, perhaps."

Vicor scowled, but his eyes contradicted him with a glimmer of something like respect. Dephithus could only shake his head and wonder if he was not the only one suffering from inner crisis. A crooked little grin touched his lips and it was Vicor's turn to look momentarily puzzled. With a shake of his head much like Dephithus had just done, Vicor dismissed their enigmatic silent exchange.

"Very well," he grumbled as if they had come to some agreement. "You will pull night watch at the third northwest guard tower six days a week. I expect you to arrange your fill-in for the seventh night. You will attend mounted combat practice three days a week and fit in some alternative practice the other four days."

"Isn't that an unusually full schedule?" Dephithus objected.

Vicor regarded him silently for a moment. "It is," he finally agreed. The commander was quiet for a moment longer. Though he appeared to be struggling to keep it hidden, Dephithus could see doubt breaking free of the man's solemn expression. "So is attending an outside tournament this soon after being raised. I will not allow you to let Lord Commander Mythan down at Dalynay."

Dephithus scowled. "I don't intend to."

Commander Vicor nodded brusquely, but his look

remained skeptical when he turned to walk away.

A surge of longing hit Dephithus like a wall. He longed for Myara. He longed to have her as a practice partner. Someone he already knew. Someone he trusted and had no reason to hate. Then again, she too had been sound asleep that night. Comfortable in her bed while…

Annoyed with himself, Dephithus pushed those thoughts away. Myara was the best friend he had ever had. There was no way he was going to allow this awful thing to come between them. Putting determination on like an armor, he went in search of her. A few well-placed questions revealed that she was in training, and he gave up his pursuit with little regret. The resolve that had driven him all the way to the training grounds had worn thin. Failing in his original goal, he went in search of solace elsewhere.

The palace no longer seemed to mock him as it had for a time after his Dawning Day. He could almost make himself believe that Amahna and Rakas had drugged him somehow. Mostly, he tried not to think about it, forcing his thoughts in different directions every time they wandered that way. As the palace architecture wrapped around him, he wondered what other secrets those walls harbored. How many other nobles did it keep silent for? Like Hydra, the palace would never demand anything in exchange for its silence.

The day wore on and he eventually made his way to the library. It was a grand room. Consistent with the magnificent architecture of the rest of the palace, it catered to the ego of its occupants. Three stories of elegant shelves were lined with countless books. Even the grand staircase, that rose out of the center and split off to both sides halfway up, was lined with books. Books on nearly every subject waited to answer old questions and prompt new ones. Many fanciful stories lined two of the upper level walls and the two opposite walls were lined with books on the art of war, chivalry, and the ever-important royal etiquette. Nature, geography and numerous other subjects claimed most of the lower shelves.

The smallest section belonged to the histories. There were a great many parts of the history section that had been strategically omitted. Among them were books that dwelled on the Dragonkin and the religious orders of their time and many of the early wars. When he had questioned Avaline about the Dragonkin some said he resembled, she told him that information was in books stored away as relics of a time best forgotten. Mythan's great-grandfather had believed firmly in moving on and leaving the darker past behind.

Dephithus did not know what in those books was so awful that they felt it necessary to hide it away and forget it, but he meant to find out. It was the Dragonkin that interested him most. Perhaps, in learning of them, he could learn something of himself, maybe something that would help him understand what was happening to him now.

On both sides of the stairs a tapestry hung, concealing a passage that was periodically rediscovered by young children grown bored waiting upon their parents in the library. Outside of those rare occasions, it was ignored. Dephithus lit a candle on one of the wall sconces and stepped into this dark passage. Halfway through was a locked door that led to a room behind the back wall of the library. Dephithus pulled the key out of his pocket that he had taken from Mythan's bedchamber the day before. He had been told that the room had not been opened since Mythan's great-grandfather first locked it.

The lock was stiff at first. It felt as if the key might give before the door did. Then it shifted and the key turned until the lock clicked free. The door shifted out a fraction as he pulled the key from the lock. Slipping it back into his pocket, he stood staring at the door for a few minutes, a chill creeping along his spine and making the hair on the back of his neck stand up. Chiding himself for being paranoid, he pushed the door open. The shadows created by the candle seemed to rush at him and he jumped back, hitting the wall behind him as the air around him was sucked into the room, extinguishing his candle. He stood frozen in the silence that followed, afraid to breathe as he waited for whatever sinister thing might accost him in the cover of darkness.

When nothing happened, he dared a breath and then another. Leaving the door standing open he made himself turn his back on the unknown and walk away. Even on the other side of the tapestry he could not stop waiting for something to leap at him from under the stairs. Keeping his hand steady, he lit the candle and slipped back into the passage. The shadows wavered about eerily in the candlelight as he stepped into the room. Books were stacked in haphazard piles, some of which had long since toppled, at the base of half-filled shelves. It almost looked as if the process of storing them had been rushed for some reason, causing the movers to abandon order midway through the process. The ceiling was low, clearing his head by perhaps a foot. The room itself was smaller than his bathing chamber, though still large enough that the far corners vanished in darkness beyond the reach of the candlelight, and everything was covered over by a thick layer of dust.

Clearing the cobwebs off two wall sconces, he lit them with his candle. It was strange the way the added light was no better at pushing back the shadows then his single candle had been. He breathed in deep, trying to calm his dancing nerves. All he succeeded in doing was inhaling enough dust to make him sneeze several times. He grimaced at how loud the sneezes sounded in this abandoned space. Setting the candle base on a stack of books that looked stable enough, he closed the door and sat down amidst the menacing shadows.

Dephithus picked up the book closest to him and dusted it off, trying not to inhale the resulting cloud of dust. It was an old leather-bound book with the title branded in. *The Kin of the Dragon, an insight by the Prophet Landross of the Benevolent Order of the Gold Rose.* He had no idea what the Benevolent Order of the Gold Rose was, but this seemed as good a place to start as any. When he opened the book, the lights flickered, and he glanced around, one hand against the floor to boost him to his feet if anything looked amiss. Only silence greeted him. Scowling a warning at whatever might be there to see it, he settled again and turned his attention to the first page. He began to read.

> The origin of the Dragonkin is mysterious at best. We can only assume their nature to be of a relation to the dragons in some way, and therefore, also to the daenox. This, in itself, proves that their very existence is an ill tiding.

The uneasy feeling of being closed in upon compelled Dephithus to look around the room. If the shadows were any closer, he could not tell.

*The daenox?* What was it?

It was strange to hear the Dragonkin referred to in a tone that was plainly unfavorable. No one had ever let on that the line he resembled was looked upon in any truly negative way. Perhaps they meant to protect him from that truth. Puzzled, he turned his attention back to the book. Before he could continue reading the feeling of being watched intensified to the point that he had to look up again.

This time he was surprised to find more than oppres-

sive shadows peering at him. A cat with fur so black it was
almost blue, was sitting in the shadows beside one pile
of books, watching him. An uneasy shiver swept through
him. There had to be an explanation for the animal's presence. Perhaps it had come in through the door when he
had left it open to go re-light the candle. Still, that made
no sense. Cats were brought into the palace only when
rodents became a problem and they were gotten rid of
just as quickly once they had done their job. It had been
perhaps three years since there had been any need for cats
in the palace.

The cat regarded him serenely with its pale gray eyes.
*Gray eyes?*

Dephithus set aside the book and leaned forward onto
his hands to get a better look at the animal. The cat rose
up on its hind legs and pricked its claws into the third book
down from the top of the stack. It pulled back then, almost as if trying to remove the book. Wary of those claws,
Dephithus reached around the other side of the stack and
tugged at the book, freeing it from the cats grasp and
drawing it out. He sat down in his chosen spot and eyed
the cat one more time. It seemed preoccupied with cleaning its paws now, so he looked down at the book in his lap.

Like the other book, the title was branded into the
leather cover. *Dark Origins: Daemon Classifications and
Incantations.* As he opened the book the air shifted again,
causing the flames to flicker. The pages of the book, all of
them, were blank.

Dephithus shivered again and set the book aside. The
cat was no longer where he could see it. Eager to be away
from the mysteriously empty book, he went in search of his
furry visitor, to no avail. Feeling as shaky as he had right
after finishing a few hours in the combat ring, he retrieved
his candle and put out the two wall sconces. Maybe later,
when he was not so tired and given to hallucinations, he
would come back. As he shut the door behind him he

heard a faint sound from within the room, like purring. The moment it clicked shut, he hurriedly locked it.

Fiddling with the key in his pocket as he left the passage behind, he started wondering what other worlds might be unlocked within that room. What might he learn of the Dragonkin? Of the dragons that he knew only from his one visit to the stone dragon in the Imperious graveyard? What was it they said about curiosity and cats?

Halfway to the library doors, he turned around and headed back to the passage.

In the following weeks Dephithus had very little time to worry about the change in himself. Commander Vicor continued to give him late posts in the guard towers around Elysium, so he slept well into the morning. During the afternoons, Vicor kept him busy during his free hours by pairing him up against the best and brightest soldiers Imperious had to offer in each form of combat. They were good enough that, even with his natural advantages, Dephithus had to fight fast and furious and his recently quick temper had an excellent outlet in those sessions. He was exhausted and sore each evening by the time Vicor released him, but he still took an hour or so to sneak into the dark archive room and browse through the books. He did not see the cat again and the pages of the book on daemons remained blank. Every visit he opened the book, hoping vainly for some explanation.

The books he had taken time to read from were more confusing than helpful. He had trouble thinking of them as more than made up fancy like the romantic stories so popular with many nobles. The books spoke of a power called daenox, sometimes referred to as daemon power, that allowed people to alter the world around them. It had, according to these tomes, often been used to accomplish terrible things and was the source of daemons and undead visitors, neither of which he was inclined to believe ever existed.

One book, called *Practical Powers*, claimed that daenox did not deserve its dark reputation and that it was merely a tool that could be used to make everyday life easier. An alternate way of going about things. From what he read in other books, few seemed to agree with that assessment. Even among others who spoke in favor of the power, few seemed to view it so innocently. There was talk of cults devoted to its worship and use. Towns falling to plague because someone who could wield that power wanted revenge for some misdeed or other.

None of the books went into great depth on the subject or what had become of this odd power, which inclined him more toward the idea that most of it was made up. In addition, there was a second power spoken of that belonged to the dragons. The dragons were addressed as living, intelligent creatures. As of yet, he had come across no references to what had become of these sentient beings. The statues in city graveyards appeared to be the only remaining tribute. Having seen the one in the Imperious graveyard, he could hardly imagine such a magnificent and terrifying creature actually moving and breathing.

The first book he had started reading on the day he saw the cat, which he had now dismissed as an exhaustion induced hallucination, was very opinionated about the daenox and the dragons, as well as the Dragonkin. The author, Prophet Landross, insisted that the dragons were born of the same evil that made the daenox and that the Dragonkin were as much an offspring of this evil plague as the daemons. Toward the end of the book, he wrote very passionately of how the gods were deserting mankind for the sin of not only allowing these evils to exist but going so far as to honor an alliance with the dragons. The prophet was very adamant that all of these things must be banished.

Since no dragons or daenox or daemons existed now that he knew of, it was reasonable to assume that either the prophet's passion had been realized, or it was all a grand bit of storytelling. The notion of a human and dragon alliance was outlandish and the Orders of the Seventh House, which the prophet's order was a branch of, no longer seemed to exist either, at least not that he was aware of. Another strong argument for believing none of it, and yet all of it was written of as if it had been real and the information secreted away in here for some reason. The whole mess confused Dephithus and he resolved to continue his studies until he could make some sense of it.

The coming tournament in Dalynay did not concern him much. With Hydra's power and speed backing him, along with his own naturally boosted speed and strength, he was almost undefeatable at the level he would be competing. It was unlikely that he would be dropped from his mount. If, by some chance, he did get brought down, he was getting better every day at the ground combat. With opponents like Kota to challenge him, he had no choice but to excel.

Tower duty was a labor of sorts. It seemed his current partner wanted nothing more than to discuss the glory and honor of being in the Imperious Legion. It was a topic of conversation he found tedious of late. Darkin began to seem a pleasant companion comparatively. Dephithus did manage to engage with some semblance of the passion he had once had for the subject and Shianne did not seem to notice the distance in his eyes when they talked. Like many of the younger soldiers, most men and women in their teens and early twenties, she treated him like an old friend. It was an attitude that Dephithus could not seem to help being annoyed by. They did not know him. They did not understand who or what he was. He was a freak from birth and now he was tormented and twisted by what had been done to him. These strangers knew nothing of him.

Despite each of their efforts, Dephithus and Myara were unable to find time together in those weeks. Myara had a rigorous schedule of her own with her final training before her sixteenth birthday and Vicor kept Dephithus so busy that their schedules never permitted them to visit. He suspected that was for the best. Maybe, by the time they got some time together, he would have his temper and his moods back to something closer to what she was used to from him.

Before he knew it, the day came to set off for Dalynay and the tournament.

As he waited to depart with the rest of the royal party, his thoughts wandered to the archives and the time that he would lose from his research. The key was hidden away safely in his room, but what if a servant discovered it somehow? What if he lost access to the room before he had all his answers?

Hydra, who had muscled out even more with the heavy practice schedule, was showing remarkable discipline in his stillness, allowing Dephithus the luxury of dwelling on other things.

It was Mythan who delayed their departure. Commander Vicor had raised some fuss or another and the high lord of Imperious had led him off to the palace study to discuss it. Avaline passed the wait with a stream of endless chatter about how well Dephithus was doing and what a pair he and Hydra made. Dephithus made himself smile and nod when appropriate, but he was restless and itched to be away. There was no combat practice today to burn away his temper and his watch duty had been given to someone else, so he would be fresh for the journey. If they did not get moving soon he was bound to say something he should not.

Mythan finally emerged and mounted his courser,

then he sat there a moment scowling over the travel party. Finally, his scowl settled on Dephithus and he motioned him over with a sharp flick of his hand. His den-father's temper seemed as poor as his own today. Dephithus moved Hydra over and grimaced when Mythan leaned close to his ear, invasive in his nearness.

"I don't know what has occurred between you and Commander Vicor, but I do wish you would try to smooth things over. The commander insists that a sea-soned warrior accompany you to coach you. He says it is only because you are so newly raised, but his tone said much more."

Dephithus kept his tone even, at war internally with the desire to lash out. He was to be watched over like a Legion hopeful. None of the other entrants had to suffer such insult. "Who will attend me?"

"Kota?"

Dephithus scowled.

"Yes, that was the name he gave me. We will make the best of it and I will trust you to resolve this when we return."

Dephithus nodded. "I will, Lord Mythan."

Wonderful. He would have Kota watching over him like a child's keeper. He turned Hydra abruptly around and ended up facing the object of his irritation. Kota was trotting up on a large draft-like bay gelding. At least it was not another stallion. There were already two stallions in the party. More than enough to cause tension. Kota nodded to Dephithus as he slowed his mount to stop before Mythan.

"High Commander, I ask your leave to make a sug-gestion."

Dephithus glanced at Kota, trying to smooth the shock and apprehension from his face. That was the most he had ever heard the big man say in one sentence and, though he reluctantly admired the mighty voice, he doubted that any suggestion Kota had would be to his benefit.

"Go on," Mythan replied, his tone sharp with irritation at the departure from procedure. He was plainly as insulted by this whole affair as Dephithus was.

"I understand your displeasure with my presence and, if it would ease your mind, I would offer to partake in the tournament to disguise Vicor's purpose in sending me."

Mythan's anger melted and a slow appreciation brightened his features. "I understand your people scorn such contests."

Kota's nod was short and abrupt.

"I accept your most gracious offer and leave you free to choose your sport." Mythan looked satisfied for a moment and Dephithus thought they would finally leave when his den-father hesitated again. "Do you think this is necessary?"

"Given my station, my lord, and my lack of familiarity with your den-son outside of the training ring, I would prefer not to offer an unqualified judgement."

With an approving nod, Mythan marked the conversation finished and rode toward the front, falling in behind the first line of royal guard. Dephithus took his position among the tournament participants. The formal arrangement would be abandoned outside of the cities, but here there were protocols to follow and images to uphold. Kota lined up with the tournament participants, holding his mount back far enough to keep watch over Dephithus and still appear as merely one more entrant.

Although he had managed to drop Kota a few times in the last week of practice, the man remained a nagging reminder of how much Dephithus still had to learn. Vicor made the situation more frustrating by never acknowledging him for bringing the giant down.

Instead, the commander made a point of reprimanding Kota for dropping his guard on each occasion.

Riding through the city, Dephithus saw many familiar faces gathered to see the party off. Kathan was not present, probably kept away in training, but his family was there waving enthusiastically. Dephithus waved back, not really paying much attention to who he was waving at. He had learned a long time ago that, as long as he waved, most of them would assume they were the recipients of the attention. Though, in the past, he had made the effort to acknowledge as many as possible with a smile. His smile was not as ready today. A few of the resident minstrels, people he had met and whose music he had danced to at Kathan's parent's tavern, yelled out greetings and Dephithus nodded recognition, trying to ignore his lurking shadow.

Outside of the city proper, they moved up the pace to an easy canter. If they kept a reasonable speed, the party would reach Nunich around dusk. Then it would be no more than a half-day's ride to Dalynay.

*

The city of Nunich, smaller than Dalynay, but still big enough to class as a city, appeared amidst the trees as dusk began to set in. It sprouted along the side of a large lake and the tall lanterns that were being lit along the streets reflected serenely in the mirror-smooth surface. The blue and silver banners of Imperious hung from every other lantern, alternating with the red and beige of the local lordship.

It might be a perfect scene if he did not feel the heavy presence of Kota still flanking him when the group slowed their mounts to move back into a formal arrangement. The local lord's manor rested on the side of the lake at the far end of the town. It was large enough that he had offered to house everyone there, even the honor guard were given the option of staying in the military quarters that did not see much use these days. Nunich's lord was less convinced of the need to maintain a rigorous military program in these peaceful days. Anyone who wished to train moved to one of the larger neighboring cities to do so.

They were greeted by formal guards in ceremonial attire at the entrance to the manor grounds and Mythan and his family received a warm welcome. They were ushered inside right away, though Dephithus chose to stay back and tend Hydra himself. Kota bedded his large mount down alongside Hydra and Dephithus stopped what he was doing to watch the man for a moment. Kota turned and faced him; his large size had begun to seem less intimidating as Dephithus improved his combat skills. He wanted to respect the man. He knew he should and he knew Kota deserved it, but he could not find the right emotion within himself. All he felt was resentment.

Standing silently, Kota returned the scrutiny.

"Commander Parthak would never have felt such foolishness necessary." Dephithus stated, turning to resume Hydra's grooming.

"Perhaps," Kota replied, his tone even and calm enough to be irritating. "But then, perhaps you are not yourself lately."

That was true. Too true.

"That's absurd," Dephithus snapped. He was becoming practiced at lying to others. If only he could lie convincingly enough to himself.

Kota grunted in response and walked off to get food for his horse, passing Avaline on her way into the stable. She stopped near Dephithus and leaned against a post as she watched him in silence until he was almost done. Without a word, she went to get the hay for him.

Did she think he could not manage it himself?

As she tossed it over into the food bin Dephithus glanced up and managed a nod he hoped she would read as gratitude.

Avaline smiled at him.

"You have hay on your dress," he remarked to hide the threat of a scowl.

She looked down and picked at the offending hay. "I thought we might walk together. It is a lovely evening. The stars are out."

Dephithus cringed inwardly. Yes, those traitorous stars, so bright and beautiful, like on his Dawning Day. He remembered very well that night when he had taken a moment to look at the stars. It was an unpleasant memory at best.

Hiding his upset, he brushed at some imaginary spot of dirt on Hydra until he was more composed, then stepped out of the stall.

"Yes, that would be nice," he lied.

Avaline took his hand and they walked from the stable toward the lake. Dephithus let her keep the hand, though the contact made his skin crawl for some reason. Bats dove around in the pale evening light, feeding on the swarm of water loving insects that filled the air just above the lake. Dephithus admired the speed and agility of the winged rodents. Though, mostly, he longed for their ability to fly away. They walked in silence for a while, each watching the night as they saw it.

"My son, I am concerned for you."

Dephithus glanced over at her and shook his head, trying to banish the swell of frustration her words caused. He said nothing.

"You do not seem very happy of late."

"I have had a few problems with my studies. Nothing I can't work out."

A smile touched her lips then vanished as quickly

as it had appeared. She was obviously far from satisfied with his answer. "It seems you don't smile much of late and I have not seen you with Myara in some time. In fact, I haven't seen much of you at all."

A soft golden smile flickered in his mind and he was suddenly haunted by the taste of those lips and the desire they brought. Dephithus heaved a deep breath and Avaline's eyes softened with sympathy. "Commander Vicor has kept me very busy."

"Vicor thinks the upper nobility are too pampered and he has a tendency to try and overcompensate. Do you love her?"

*I am too broken to love.*

Dephithus pushed away the thought. He rolled his eyes at his mother and slipped an arm over her shoulders, knowing the contact would calm her. He remembered a time not so long ago when he had been too short to reach her shoulders. So much had changed since then. These days it was Avaline who had to settle for putting her arm around his waist. She leaned her head on his shoulder and sighed contentedly. Dephithus found a real grin slipping across his lips. Only his mother could make him feel this normal, free of the confusing emotions he experienced around Myara, and he liked the feeling.

Without warning, a jorycat lunged out of the brush and Dephithus turned, swinging Avaline out of the line of attack. The cat plowed into his back, throwing all three of them to the ground. Dephithus rolled onto his feet almost as fast as the cat did, pulling the serpent dagger from its sheath. The jorycat was smaller than the mountain cats that roamed closer to Imperious, but it was still very strong and a lethal hunter.

The cat hissed at him, it's eyes flashing a strange silvery color in the moonlight. Dephithus growled the way he had with the cat that threatened Myara. Undaunted, the cat lunged into him. Dephithus brought the knife around as the cat slammed into his chest, driving him into the ground and knocking the wind out of him.

"Dephithus!"

Avaline pushed at the still creature on his chest while Dephithus struggled to get his breath back. He helped shove the dead cat off and lay there, staring at the stars as the pain eased slowly and his lungs began to pull in air. The stars sparkled so bright he began to wonder if perhaps they were laughing at him. Then Avaline's face filled his vision, pale with tears sparkling on her cheeks like the stars above.

A man's voice broke through the sound of his strained breathing. "Is he all right?"

"Yes, Den-father," Dephithus answered, holding up his arm so that someone might help him to sit. The hand that took hold of him was too large for Mythan. As Avaline moved aside he saw Mythan standing behind her and Kota knelt to help Dephithus up. Once upright and able to breathe normally, Dephithus reached over and retrieved his knife from the neck of the jorycat. He wiped it off on the spotted pelt and sheathed it.

"What happened?" Mythan demanded.

"It lunged at us out of nowhere." Avaline's voice shook with the rush of panic that was still fading.

"That is odd. The smaller cats usually aren't that aggressive."

"There is something wrong with this one." Kota offered from where he had knelt next to the dead animal. He turned its head towards them so they could all see what he was talking about. "Its eyes are discolored."

Dephithus looked over at the dead cat's face. Two lifeless gray eyes stared back at him. With a shudder he looked away.

"Did either of you get bitten or scratched?" Mythan asked urgently, his voice thickened with fear.

Dephithus shook his head, not sure he could keep his voice level enough to speak.

Avaline looked at him, her eyes brimming over with gratitude and adoration. "It never touched me, thanks to my brave son."

Mythan nodded to Kota who hefted the cat onto his shoulder. "We will take it to be disposed of in case it's diseased. Will you be well for tomorrow?"

Dephithus met Mythan's even gaze. "Yes. I will be more than well."

Mythan nodded and took hold of Avaline's hand. She reached out to Dephithus with her other hand and he took it, letting Mythan lead them all back to the manor. For the rest of the night he could not get the image of the gray-eyed cat in the library out of his head.

## CHAPTER SIXTEEN

Dephithus sat upon his mount, watching with a removed patience while attendants cleaned up shards of wood from a lance broken in the last joust. Hydra was not so calm. Dephithus had to rein him in tight. The stallion half reared then fell to impatient prancing again. There was an undeniable excitement in the air and Hydra was extremely sensitive to it. Such was true of all tournaments, but both horse and rider were new to participating in this level of competition.

The earlier melee and archery tournaments had brought plenty of crowds, and Kota had only missed taking the melee by one opponent who had displayed an exceptional mastery in the sport. The joust always drew the largest crowds. Even many of the vendors left their shops to watch, knowing they would not have much patronage until the joust was over.

Dalynay boasted a grand outdoor stadium on the palace grounds that buzzed with activity between jousts. Though the city itself was much smaller than Imperious, there was more than enough ambition among its nobility to put up quite a grand spectacle. The glorious array of banners flying around the grounds showed that nearly every distinguished lordship in the region was in attendance. The vaguely offensive violet and orange banner alongside the banners of Dalynay and Imperious showed that even one lord from outside the region had attended. To encourage such interest, the foreign lord and his family had been given distinguished seats to one side of the royal family of Imperious.

Hydra reared up again and Dephithus gave the reins a sharp tug, popping the bit smartly down on the stallion's lower jaw. Hydra dropped down and tossed his head as he chewed at the offending piece of metal in irritation. Once he settled some, Dephithus slid a hand under his long, black mane and praised him with a firm pat. Hydra nodded his head in response and remained mostly still, though Dephithus could feel the tension in his muscles wound like massive springs.

There had been no more incidents after leaving Nunich. The attendants of the lord there had taken the jorycat out and burned it some distance away from the village. Dephithus still got a chill when he remembered those gray eyes, but he did not mention the archive cat to anyone. Especially since he was not even supposed to be going into the archives.

The horse at the other end of the list reared up then, challenging his rider with his impatience. Larina's stallion was a big dun colored creature as rough in appearance as Hydra was refined. The next joust was theirs. It was the contest that much of the audience had been waiting eagerly on all day. So far, Dephithus had come out on top in every joust he had fought, only getting unseated once. That pass had unseated them both, and he had taken the victory on the ground.

Larina's record for the day was nearly as spotless, making this truly the match to see. The stadium keepers were making the final passes with their draft beasts to smooth out the jousting field and ensure that no shards of the broken lance lay about to possibly injure one of the horses. As they cleared from the list the audience applauded, encouraging the tournament speaker to announce the next challengers while both stallions danced in anticipation.

"Check your straps."

Dephithus glanced down at his perpetual shadow in annoyance.

Kota reciprocated with a firm scowl.

With a sigh, Dephithus gave in and began to systematically check the straps and buckles of his armor for any weak points. When he finished Kota rechecked one of the leg straps then moved back to the side with a satisfied grunt. Dephithus heeled Hydra forward, lining him up along that end of the list and turning him to face Larina who was doing the same at her end.

"Now we enter our final jousting division." The applause died down. "We have a formal challenge between Lord Dephithus de Nu Traven of Imperious—" a heavy applause rose and Hydra showed off with a controlled rear so that Dephithus was forced to center him again before he could take his lance and settle it into position, "—and our own Lady Larina Moshvue of Dalynay." Even heavier applause greeted Larina's name, but Dephithus had expected that in her home stadium. "Let the contest begin!"

Dephithus heeled Hydra and the stallion burst forward with nearly enough force to leave his rider behind. Seconds before the lances crossed he was able to right himself. His lance slid harmlessly off Larina's chest plate. Her lance caught him more squarely and shoved him back and to the right. The left stirrup pulled free and the stadium went wild with shouts and applause. Dephithus was able to catch himself on the right stirrup and push back into the center of the saddle as he reined Hydra in. He spun the stallion around to the right, using the turn to help him gain his seat again. Larina had turned a bit faster and he could see her hungry eyes peering out of the helmet as she barreled back toward him.

The next two passes they both managed to keep their seats, and Dephithus knew the audience would be getting impatient. Focusing himself, he silently vowed to give the onlookers the show they wanted. On the fourth pass Larina's lance slid off, but his caught on her shoulder plate, throwing them both violently back. The lance splintered, then broke as Larina toppled off, bringing her mounts hindquarters down with her. Since he was already half out of the saddle, Dephithus swung his leg the rest of the way over and used the other stirrup to push himself away from Hydra. He landed with a grunt on his back and rolled up—not the easiest move in jousting armor—drawing his sword as he stood.

Larina wavered for a moment once free of the saddle and on her feet, yet her eyes were fierce when she pulled her sword. Her breastplate shifted oddly and Dephithus noticed that one of the leather straps holding it up was damaged. Then Larina lunged and Dephithus focused on blocking, striking, and blocking again. He planted several neatly calculated blows, watching with an eager fascination as the damaged strap gave a little more. Larina continued to fight ferociously, leaving her share of marks on his armor and moving in with a stunning aggression. The damaged strap finally gave under the weight of her armor. Dephithus parried her blow then thrust at his unsuspecting opponent, his blade scraping the edge of the breastplate as it fell away. The softer flesh beneath gave easily under the sharp steel point.

The blade trembled in his grip, grinding roughly against bone as it passed between her ribs. Larina's eyes widened with horror and pain as she stared at him, staggering back to pull free of the blade in her chest. Terror-stricken silence filed the stadium and she turned with a slow stagger to face her family's seats. Her hands clasped over the gushing wound as though trying to slow the thick red torrent.

Numbness spread through Dephithus. He tossed the sword away and stepped forward to catch Larina as she fell. Cries rose up all around them, but Dephithus could only hear Larina's mother, wailing as clearly as if she were the only other person there.

Larina's father reached them first, shoving Dephithus away. He knelt over his daughter. Dephithus stumbled back, staring in stunned silence at the blood on his hands. A choking sound came from Larina and he could see the blood coming from her mouth as she struggled to breathe.

But he had known. He had known exactly when the armor would fail. He should have declared it and stopped the match so it could be tended to.

Dephithus looked around, searching for some sense amidst the confusion. Faces surrounded him, full of distress as they watched the fallen warrior. She was still so young. Barely past her Dawning Day. Dephithus fell to his knees. He hung his head and closed his eyes to those many horrified faces. Still, the choking sounds Larina was making and the wailing of her mother resounded in his ears. A strong hand took hold of his upper arm, pulling him up with no little force.

"Come, you must leave this area."

Still numb, Dephithus nodded and let Kota lead him stumbling away from the stadium. For a brief moment, a glorious few seconds, the horrified numbness broke and he looked around in panic. Then he spotted one of his family's servants leading Hydra away from the stadium and the alarm faded, allowing the numbness to return.

*

The room Dephithus had been given in the palace of Dalynay was almost as large as the guestrooms in the

Elysium palace, if not nearly as ornate. Dalynay was only a lordship, after all, and should never display such wealth as that of the high lord of these lands. The bed was lavishly canopied with maroon and gold velvet, a traditional heavy style that the Elysium palace had stayed away from. It was a lovely piece with a frame of ornately carved wood, but his family's home was focused on elegance without the gaudiness.

Dephithus sat on the floor between the bed and the far wall under a large window. The elaborate baseboard pressed into his lower back painfully, but he could not bring himself to move away. Try as he might he could find in himself no sorrow, only guilt. Worse yet, guilt was more because of where it had happened, there in front of all those witnesses, than because it had happened.

What was wrong with him?

There were three slow taps on the door of the room, followed by a pause and two quick taps. Mythan was coming. Dephithus stood, his back groaning as he moved away from the uncomfortable baseboard. Kota had agreed to signal him with taps on the door when someone came. It was certain to be either Mythan or Avaline so they had arranged two different patterns. For once, the large man had shown a more understanding side that irritated Dephithus even more. It was easy to despise Kota the if he could convince himself the man was just a brute, but not so easy to despise Kota when he was being so supportive.

Dephithus sat on the edge of the bed, a somewhat more dignified spot then the floor. When Mythan entered he stood and bowed his head once respectfully, making quick note of the worry and tightness in his den-father's face.

"Dephithus, my son." He paused as if he could not bring himself to speak beyond that for several long seconds. "Lord Johan and Lady Olisa have demanded the life of the armorer. It has been determined that their daughter's death was an accident caused by the faulty craftsmanship of the bindings on her armor."

Dephithus cringed inwardly. Someone else would die for his evil deed. There was no doubt that the bindings had been poor, but he had known that before they gave. He had been watching, waiting for the binding to give. Keeping his voice even he spoke the words he knew Mythan was about to say. "And I must attend the execution to defend my honor and reputation."

"Yes. I know how hard this must be for you, but this is the way these things are handled. No one has ever died at your hands and you must believe that there was no way you could have prevented this. Nobody knew this was going to happen."

*I knew, Den-father, I knew.* He tried to swallow down the lump of guilt that was making it hard to breathe. Keeping the truth from Mythan only made it worse. "I should change."

Mythan nodded. "The dark green set you brought for tonight's dinner should be suitable. There will be no celebration this evening, so it won't be noticed."

Dephithus nodded to himself as Mythan stepped out. It was important to dress well out of respect for the deceased. Perhaps it was right that the armorer die. There was no way he could have killed her if the band on the breastplate had not been so weak. In a way the armorer was as guilty of her death as he was. Wasn't he?

Dephithus changed then moved to stand before the mirror. The man staring back at him looked older than he remembered.

*Why? What has happened to me?*

The reflection's silver-green eyes held no answer.

Maybe it was the Dragonkin. If they were related somehow to the sinister daenox, if they were evil, and he was a throwback to them? Could it be that such a curse might lay dormant for centuries then rise again for no apparent reason?

Dephithus frowned at his reflection and the reflection smiled.

Backing frantically away from the seditious image, he fell over the edge of the bed, landing on the floor with a heavy thud. Kota threw open the door and looked around the room warily, his hand on his sword hilt. Finally, his eyes settled on Dephithus who had gotten to his feet and was clasping his hands before him to try and hide their shaking.

"Is all well?"

"No, Kota," he snapped. His voice was shaking. "I just killed a girl not an hour gone. How do you think things are?"

Kota's stony features were softened by a hint of compassion. "You must be strong. You are Mythan's heir. Come, it is time you showed yourself."

"Yes," Dephithus muttered.

He glanced at the mirror as they walked from the room, but it reflected nothing out of the ordinary. Maybe he was going crazy. Taking a strange sort of comfort in that thought, he sped up a bit so that he was walking a few steps ahead of Kota. Regardless of the circumstances, it would not do for him to be seen moping along behind Kota like a scolded child.

Dephithus joined the rest of his and Larina's families on a balcony overlooking the courtyard. Lord Johan's face was twisted with misery and he looked away quickly when he saw Dephithus. Lady Olisa was still weeping. One of her ladies in waiting attended her, keeping her supplied with fresh kerchiefs and soothing words. The palace courtyard was packed full of Lord Johan's subjects shouting angrily at a figure that was being pulled through the midst of them by several guards. The goal of the party was a large scaffold with a guillotine on it.

They would behead him. At least it would be a quicker death than Larina's had been, though not by much.

The guards appeared to be making some attempt to protect the armorer from the onslaught of the angry crowd. However, when the burly man was pulled up the steps Dephithus could see blood on his face where the raging crowds had broken through. The man looked terrified, even from this distance, and he was shouting something that was lost under the din of the enraged crowd. By the top of the steps the man had begun to weep, and his body sagged so that his knees hit the wood of the scaffold with a loud crack before the guards could pull him up again.

When was the last time a public execution had occurred in one of Mythan's lordships? Certainly not since he could remember. Perhaps they had all been right. His birth marked a time of change, and maybe even a time when the daenox would return. His very existence, a child bearing the markings of the long extinct dragonkin, probably was the bad omen many had claimed it to be. Would it change anything if he had not been born? What if he were to die? Or was it perhaps too late to stop the changes his corrupted presence had set off?

Dephithus shook his head at his own wild thoughts. Then again, maybe he was just being ridiculously dramatic? It was crazy as well as arrogant to think that one person's life could be so critical.

The scrape of metal on metal as the guillotine blade dropped snapped him rudely back to the matter at hand. The burly man's body went limp and the dull thud of his head dropping into the wooden box resonated in the sudden silence. He did not recall hearing the man's name called out or the charges brought against him. Had anyone, outside of the condemned, protested the charges?

Lord Johan walked up to Dephithus and stood facing him as Lady Olisa was led past them into the palace. "Justice has been done and your honor and reputation have been restored."

Dephithus nodded, kept silent by the misery in the man's eyes.

Lord Johan's voice cracked when he continued and tears ran down his cheeks. "But my Larina is still dead, Lord Dephithus, she is still dead."

"If I could undo..."

Lord Johan interrupted Dephithus with a shake of his head. "I am deeply troubled that your blade did this, but it surely would have been some other if not you and your conduct has remained admirable throughout this trial. For that I thank you."

Admirable? Which imposter had Lord Johan been watching over the last several hours? Dephithus remained wisely silent and rested a hand on the man's shoulder as he passed. Johan stopped, laying his hand on top of Dephithus's, and nodded, accepting the gesture of comfort before continuing into the palace. Dephithus looked out over the courtyard for a few minutes longer, the guilt that had been fading blossomed up stronger than before. Mythan stepped up beside him, looking out beyond the courtyard and the city at the forest.

"Your silence there was very prudent," Mythan said, his eyes glossed over with sorrow for Dalynay's noble family. "In spite of these miserable events, I am proud of you."

Dephithus was again puzzled by this praise. Was there someone running around who looked a lot like him or was he better at deception than he realized. He could see how his reaction on the stadium field might have been mistaken for a gesture of respect and repentance. Still, it was hard for him to believe that he could do this terrible thing and come out looking not only innocent, but dignified as well.

"What happens now?"

"Now," Mythan sighed as if the weight of all the world bore down on his shoulders. "Now we go home and leave them to the mourning that only they have a right to. Your mother will come up with some token of our sympathy to send them. She is good at that."

Yes, someone else would lay the balm over the wounds he had opened. That was perhaps as it should be. Dephithus allowed his gaze to look beyond at the trees and the road home. With a solemn nod he led the way back into the palace.

## CHAPTER SEVENTEEN

Imperious held its own celebration in remembrance of the deceased Lady Larina. Wrought iron candelabras were placed about the ballroom and the guests danced in subdued lighting. Lovely night blue tapestries were hung on the walls and matching carpets were laid out on the floor to keep the dancing quiet and restrained. Everyone was dressed in dark, elegant colors and wore sedate masks, the same neutral mask for all the men and women, including the servants. Larina's face was to be the only face they should think of that night.

They drank as well, celebrating life with frequent toasts that all said the same thing in a variety of different ways. Dozens of speeches of remembrance all creatively reworded. Myara attended the celebration and she hovered near Dephithus, touching his arm or shoulder often in gestures of comfort. They barely spoke to one another, however. It was inappropriate to speak of personal things at a celebration such as this.

Practice the next day was conducted in the same somber mood and Dephithus began to feel suffocated by the delicate way others conducted their conversations around him, as if he were too fragile to handle the reality of what had happened. It was his day to practice ground fighting with a sword in one hand and a dagger in the other. His opponent, Culaine, who was far more

skilled with a sword than she was with a brush given the
wild disarray of her red hair, fought with reservation,
pulling her strikes and uncharacteristically leaving herself open to his attacks. Dephithus was more frustrated
than tired when the practice was over.

Wary of his own temper, he turned to leave the practice arena before he could say or do something he would
regret, only to find Vicor walking up behind him. Dread
created a hollow in his gut.

"Lord Dephithus."

Vicor hesitated a moment and Dephithus tried not
to fidget. It would do him no good to look as impatient
as he felt. The whole experience was making him feel
like a branch bent near to breaking.

"I... Perhaps I pushed you too hard. You may alter
your schedule as you see fit to maintain the required
practice levels. I will leave you on fifth watch in the guard
towers for now, but you may cut down to five nights if
you wish. Just be sure there is someone to cover."

Dephithus struggled not to let his confusion show.
Vicor's eyes shifted to the floor, then he made himself
meet his student's gaze with a visible effort. He looked
like he might throw up. Could it be that the commander believed he was somehow to blame for Larina's death?

Dephithus shook his head. Was he the only one who
would remain free of blame for a death he most certainly deserved it for? "Sir, I find this schedule challenging
in a good way. Might I request to maintain my current
partners and practice schedule for a while longer?"

Vicor started to shake his head. "It is an aggressive lineup. If you overextend yourself it will wear your
down over time and slow your reaction times. Accidents
are more apt to occur when you're not at your sharpest."

*He does blame himself!*

Dephithus had to control his reaction, knowing
it might draw questions if he allowed his jaw to drop

with the surprise he felt. Unless he was mistaken, Vicor believed the harsh schedule he had put Dephithus on made him too slow to stop that fatal strike when Larina's armor failed. He could think of nothing to say. Nothing at all.

Taking his silence for persistence, Vicor relented some. "If that is what you want, perhaps you can keep to that schedule, but only every other week. On off weeks you will have only five nights on guard duty and an extra free day from Legion practice."

Not quite what he had hoped for. The hard schedule kept him preoccupied so he did not dwell too much on those things that confused and angered him. It also kept his energy depleted, so his temper had less to fuel it. Still, if he argued too much, he might get even less out of their negotiation. However, if he showed that he could handle the schedule, Vicor might let him add more again in time.

He gave a nod. "Yes, Sir."

Vicor nodded as well. "Get some rest before watch tonight."

But rest was not what waited for him. Outside of the practice arena, Myara was pacing back and forth until she spotted him approaching. Then she stopped and stood, still as a statue, her expression as she watched him approach a very curious mixture of hope and reluctance. It was cute, in a vulnerable sort of way that was uncomfortably arousing.

Dephithus mustered up a reserved smile. It would not look good if he appeared too cheerful so soon after the tournament. Hope trumped reluctance and Myara responded with a much warmer smile.

"I'm due for training, but I had to see you. It seems that there is so little time for that lately." She attempted a lighthearted laugh, but it faltered, falling flat quickly.

Dephithus gave a nod to indicate a direction and

kept walking. He took hold of her hand as she fell into step alongside him. Myara gave his hand a little squeeze and made no effort to pull away. "I told you this would happen."

"Yes, well, I suppose you were right, though you said a woman would be the one to come between us. You haven't gotten married and had kids yet, have you?"

Dephithus chuckled. "Nope, not yet, and I don't expect to in the next couple of days either."

She stopped and faced him, giving his hand a tug to stop him with her. "I would like to spend some time together. When is your next free day?"

A creeping dread oozed through him at the thought. Could he try to be his old self for an entire day? Myara might not like the new short-tempered Dephithus that seemed to be controlling him these days. Still, looking down into her beautiful warm eyes, he was suddenly inclined to try. "Three more days of practice, then I have a day free."

"Wonderful. I can make that work. I better get going." She popped up on her toes and kissed him quickly on the lips before turning to go. After only two steps, she turned back to him, her expression suddenly serious, and he could see the shimmer of tears in her eyes. "I'm so sorry about what happened at the tournament. I know how horrible I would feel."

As she turned and walked away, the guilt began to burn through him again that he had believed himself free of. With a deep ache in his chest and a sudden miserable lump in his throat, he sought out the nearest quiet place he could find. It turned out to be behind one of the Legion stables near an empty paddock. With a massive sigh of frustration, he leaned back against the stable wall and slid down to sit cross-legged on the dirt. Not the most regal of positions, but with no one there to see, he could not muster up much concern.

How odd that a woman could make someone feel miserable simply by trying to make them feel better. Strangest thing was that, when women wanted to make someone feel bad, they could do that just fine too. Myara confounded him anyway. It was not so long ago that he was certain she only saw him as a friend. Now it seemed she wanted more than that, but how much and how fast? He wanted to couple with her. To touch her soft skin and join with her in passion. Yet, whenever those desires worked towards the surface he began to feel out of control. The same dark blaze that fed his new unpredictable temper sparked with his passion.

What if he hurt her?

Myara obviously did not blame him for Larina's death, but he knew better. He reminded himself over and over to make sure he never forgot who he had become. He could remember watching that weak point like a poor man would watch a bulging coin purse, hoping one coin might fall away unnoticed within his reach. If he could lose control of himself enough to take someone's life, then what might he do to her if his passion took control?

He heard footsteps coming around one side of the barn. They were too close for him to make himself scarce before they came around the corner, so he stayed where he was, hoping vainly to be overlooked. There was no such luck with him. Darkin led his group around the corner, stopping as soon as he spotted Dephithus. A crooked smile touched his lips and the other four stopped beside him, curious eyes homing in on the object of their leader's interest.

Dephithus realized what a precarious position he was in, especially if Darkin harbored any resentment for the incident in the guard tower.

"Careful my friends," Darkin piped up, his sarcastic grin growing wider, "it seems we have a killer in our midst."

Dephithus fought with himself, maintaining an outward calm despite the fast rise of his inner rage. It was a hypocritical rage anyhow. Darkin was the first person to call him out for what he knew he was, and he was going to get upset over it. This was what he deserved.

He regarded Darkin and his companions coolly. "If it makes you nervous, you're welcome to leave."

"But we aren't welcome to stay, are we?" By the time Darkin finished his sentence he had walked past Dephithus and hopped up to perch on the paddock fence alongside him.

The lone woman in the party, a lean blond with pale skin and cruel blue-gray eyes, sat on the fence beside Darkin. The remaining three stayed standing on the other side of Dephithus, perhaps ready to block his escape if Darkin wanted to try anything.

"This is my little band. Kip and Lanz." Darkin nodded to the two farthest lads in turn. Kip was a bit shorter and thinner than Lanz. They both had brown hair and eyes and pale skin, but their features were different enough to drastically reduce the odds that they were related. Darkin nodded to the third lad, a muscular youth with the same skin, hair and eyes as the girl. "That's Kovial and this is his twin sister Suva. Everyone," he gestured with a sweep of his arm toward Dephithus, "this is our future High Lord Dephithus, come here to wallow in the dirt with the dregs."

Dephithus scowled a warning at Darkin.

Suva smiled, though the expression did not touch her eyes. "So, I guess you won your first tournament challenge."

He turned his glare on Suva and she glared right back. Her eyes were hungry for conflict and he wondered if such corruption was reflected in his own expression. He understood it, that craving to start a fight and burn away some of the seething hatred within. His hand shifted a little closer to Amahna's dagger.

Kovial took a step closer to the fence and his sister. His eyes were not as unfriendly as hers, but they carried a warning. Judging by the way she moved and the fierce confidence in her expression, Suva was not likely to need or want his protection.

"No need to be so touchy." Kovial offered in defense of his sister and perhaps in the hopes of avoiding a scene. "How would you feel if it had been you instead of Larina?"

"Dead," Dephithus replied shortly.

The others laughed and Kovial sighed as though he was used to being the subject of their amusement.

Dephithus scowled at Darkin again, wishing they would go and leave him to his largely unproductive brooding.

Darkin managed to look suddenly serious, almost sympathetic. "It isn't like you could have prevented it."

"I knew it was going to happen." Dephithus realized as he said it that admitting such a thing to this bunch was probably the same as offering his neck to the headsman, but the words spilled out before he could stop them. He cursed himself silently for having half the wits of a cow. All he could do now was wait and see what they would do. Besides, it was liberating in a way to tell someone the truth. They would tell someone in charge and he would face the punishment he deserved.

Darkin grinned.

"Even better. Why don't you join us for a bite?" He jumped down from the fence and glanced over at Dephithus with an expectant look. No one moved. Darkin's companions looked as stunned as Dephithus was, though it was probably more from the invitation than his apparent approval of Larina's murder. Darkin spread his scowl around the five of them equally. "Are you all coming or am I eating alone today?"

Dephithus surprised himself, and probably the other four as well, by being the first to join Darkin. As soon as he was on his feet, he and Darkin began to walk away from the rest of the reluctant group. After a few more seconds of indecision, the others trotted to catch up.

Dephithus kept his pace even with Darkin's. He would not allow the other youth to get so much as a toe length ahead of him. "What did you mean?"

Darkin looked puzzled for a moment, then he realized what Dephithus was asking and smiled. "She had an ugly nose."

Dephithus fell into stunned silence. An ugly nose? How did that make any of this better? "Bold," he muttered, remembering his and Myara's critique of Larina's least appealing feature.

"What?" Darkin glanced over at him. There was none of the hostility in that look that Dephithus had come to expect, which made him very nervous.

"She had a bold nose."

Darkin shrugged. "It adds up to the same thing doesn't it?"

Dephithus could hardly believe he was having this conversation. "So, she deserved to die because she had an ugly nose?"

Darkin shrugged again, he looked vaguely bored with the subject. "If you must have a reason it's good enough for me."

Dephithus shook his head, trying to hold on to the sense of dismay that was fading too fast. He hesitated a moment, but a bit of twisted humor drove him to speak again. Keeping his voice level and very serious, he said, "I certainly hope my nose doesn't offend."

Darkin tripped, surprised by the comment, and the others chuckled when he turned to regard Dephithus with mock severity. After a moment there was a nod, accompanied by a satisfied grunt. "Can't find much to fault in that face. Suva?"

Suva grinned, baring her teeth like a wolf. No, she was not like a wolf. She was something much more violent than a wolf. Licking her lips hungrily she regarded Dephithus. "Nothing wrong with his looks at all. I guess we'll have to find another reason to kill him"

Dephithus could feel the other three behind him, but they did not concern him. Kovial did not seem the unreasonably violent type and the other two were followers. They would do nothing without a word from Darkin. Suva, on the other hand, had a passion for brutality that radiated off her, putting an edge on every word she spoke. Dephithus met her look with a challenging glare. With hardly any movement, Suva's stance turned aggressive and Dephithus moved his hand closer to the dagger again.

Before it could go any further Darkin stepped in, sliding one arm around Suva's shoulders. He directed a subtle shake of his head at the three behind Dephithus. Moving his hand away from the dagger Dephithus wondered how close he had come to getting attacked from behind.

Suva turned her glare on Darkin, but she did not pull away.

"Enough playing around for now. I'm hungry and I'm not in the habit of inviting people to eat with me just for the sake of a good brawl." Darkin waited, watching Dephithus expectantly.

Dephithus nodded after a moment. Whatever Darkin was up to, he was not going to find out if he walked away now. Darkin did not seem satisfied with just the nod though. He picked out Kovial with his gaze.

"Why don't you and the others go on ahead? I would like to talk to our young lord."

Dephithus remained silent as the other four went

on without them, their narrowed eyes making their displeasure at being sent on their way clear. Suva passed unnecessarily close to him in the process, her body brushing his arm, her feral grin up in his face. He and Darkin stood in silence, primarily ignoring each other until the rest of the group was out of earshot. Dephithus could not figure what Darkin might want with him that he would risk irritating his companions as he obviously had.

Darkin began to walk after them, keeping his pace slower. Dephithus, trying to fight the swell of rage at being expected to follow, trotted forward and made a point of falling into step just a hair ahead of Darkin.

"I don't like you any more now than I did last time we met," Darkin stated when the others were a little further ahead.

This did not come as a surprise at all so Dephithus held his silence and waited for more.

"Truth be told, I would love to let Suva have a go at you. However, I've watched you on that stallion of yours and you're practically unbeatable. Most of what I know I have learned from two of my companions. Suva is the most brutal and efficient fighter with a sword and dagger I have ever seen. Kovial is as good at unarmed hand to hand as you are at mounted combat. So, you see, my intentions are purely selfish. I am looking to improve my mounted skills and I expect you to help me."

*Expect.* A familiar rage began to boil within him. Still, there was little he could do. He had given Darkin the perfect tool for blackmail in being stupid enough to tell him the truth about Larina.

Darkin's smirk made it plain that the same thought was going through his head.

"I suppose you plan to use up more of my precious free time with this pursuit?"

Darkin's step was light. He was enjoying himself.

"Certainly. As much as I can. The others will get used to you. I might even get used to you eventually."

Dephithus sneered. "Don't expect the same."

The deeply satisfied grin on Darkin's face left a sour taste in Dephithus's mouth. "Come, we will eat and discuss our arrangement."

Arrangement indeed. Dephithus nodded, fidgeting with the hilt of the dagger as they walked. When the moment was right, he would make Darkin sorry for this.

When his next free day finally arrived, Dephithus lay in bed staring at the ceiling. Fully awake long before he needed to be. Was there really any reason to get up? He was supposed to meet with Myara in the afternoon. She had not been able to get the entire day free, but they would have some time to spend together later. It was probably better that way. Less time for him to mess something up, but the thought of finally spending time with her made him itchy with impatience and a little nauseous. Maybe he could try and go back to sleep until it was time. Then again, as eager as he was for the time to pass there was not much chance of him falling asleep again.

With a dramatic sigh, he threw back the covers and got up to dress. He had bathed the previous day to rid himself of the sweat of practice, so he wasted no time on such frivolities today. He tamed down his hair with a comb and stared long into the mirror, waiting for something. What he was waiting for was as much a mystery to him as it was to the mirror. He had long ago decided the mirror incident in Dalynay had been nothing more than stress playing tricks on his mind. After a bit he gave up and shrugged.

He stepped out of the room, shutting the door behind him, then he turned around and stepped back in.

After a quick glance around, he picked the serpent dagger up from the bed-stand, sheathing it at his waist, and left again.

Outside, a warm sun greeted him over the vibrant gardens. There had not been another heavy rain like the day after his birthday, but there was enough of a shower now and then to maintain the healthy color in the gardens. Purples, blues, reds and every other color flower imaginable adorned the statues and other stonework around the grounds, all mixed in tastefully with varying shades of lush green foliage. Some of the statues were drowning beneath a strangling sea of vines and blooms.

Dephithus strode out like a king with the flowers his robe and the sun his crown. A pleasant sort of confidence had come over him in the last several days. It seemed odd, after his encounter with Darkin, that he should start to feel so much better. Yet, was there really any reason to question such a positive change? Better to embrace and accept it, especially today.

He had not really decided what to do with his morning yet, but he drifted in the direction of the stables. It was as he was walking a path between the outer hedges that he overheard his name being spoken by someone on the other side. He stopped and moved through the nearest opening in the hedge wall. The speakers did not notice him. They leaned close as if sharing a secret though they spoke loud enough for him to hear clearly from several feet behind them. He recognized them. They were common visitors to the court, often dallying in the gardens with other nobles on lovely days such as this. Calt and Alexa were their names if he remembered right.

He crept closer as they spoke.

"Yes, well, all you had to do was look at his strange eyes to know he would go bad eventually." Calt was saying matter-of-factly. "I've heard that Commander

Vicor is having a great deal of trouble with him. I over-heard him arguing with Commander Parthak about the young lord's dangerous temper."

"He always seemed such a fine lad. So well-man-nered and kind, until recently. I do wonder what Lord Mythan intends to do. Especially after that horrible inci-dent at the tournament." Alexa sighed as if the thought troubled her, but her casual tone belied her.

Dephithus growled under his breath. The sound was loud enough to startle the two gossips.

"Pardon, my Lord Dephithus, we didn't see you there," Calt defended, his eyes shifting nervously to Alexa then to the ground.

Dephithus regarded them, an icy cold building in his gutting and spreading though him as they exchanged another nervous glance with one another, carefully avoiding his accusing gaze.

"Given your words, I see no reason to give you par-don." Turning abruptly the ball of his foot, he stalked away. They began to speak in hushed voices behind him, but he ignored them. Nothing they had to say was im-portant now. He knew their minds.

Stepping back through the hedge he discovered that he was not the only eavesdropper wandering the gar-dens. Darkin grinned and fell into step beside him as he continued along his original course. Of all the people he might want to overhear such things, Darkin had to be near the bottom of the list. Despite the numerous angry comments that his current boiling rage brought to mind, he managed to hold his tongue.

Showing unusual tact, Darkin did not speak until they had left the gardens behind and the stables loomed up in front of them.

"I thought you and Hydra might be up for a little exercise this morning."

Dephithus glanced over at the youth, making no

attempt to hide his annoyance. "That was my thought as well, though I had hoped for something less... social."

Darkin shook his head with an amused smile. "I will blackmail you into it if I must, my temperamental trainer, but I don't think it's necessary. Give it a chance. You might enjoy yourself."

Dephithus scowled, further irritated by the fact that Darkin was plainly enjoying his ruffled composure. "The fact that neither of us likes the other makes this arrangement a bit unconventional."

"I know." Darkin looked almost delighted by the observation. "I figure it might add a bit of authenticity to the fighting."

Dephithus hesitated at that. Maybe Darkin was on to something. There was little that eased his constant anger better than combat practice. Working without supervision with an opponent that he despised might provide exactly the kind of outlet he needed. A slow smile touched his lips. "That it might."

He forcefully reigned in his enthusiasm. He was the heir to the throne and he simply could not go around hacking people up at his own discretion. Although, recent events had proven that there were even exceptions to this rule.

Developing an increasingly positive outlook for the morning, he entered the stable with Darkin.

Dephithus immediately found some pleasure in picking out a mount for his pupil. In a matter of minutes, he was able to point out no less than ten flaws in the mount the other lad had intended to use. There was no challenge in defeating someone when your mount was distinctly superior to theirs. The gelding he redirected Darkin to was a good, sturdy bay with none of Hydra's flash, but plenty of noteworthy training as a war-horse. This was not a beauty contest. He remembered how ugly Larina's very capable mount had been.

Next to that beast, this gelding would look like a show horse. Darkin frowned once when he saw the gelding though he did himself credit as a student by not openly questioning the selection.

With mounts and weapons chosen, they headed out to a clearing in the woods. Unofficial practices like this were not forbidden, precisely, but they were discouraged because of the increased risk of injury without someone there to mediate. Darkin's group joined them, so there were four spectators who might keep Dephithus from trying to finish off his opponent if the bottomless pool of rage inside him ran too hot. He was not especially comfortable out in the woods alone with them when no one knew where he was, but so long as Darkin wanted something from Dephithus, the little band would probably leave him be. If that changed, who knew what might happen.

As they faced each other over the heads of their mounts, Dephithus swore to himself that he would find a way to even the score between them. Finding some way to permanently silence Darkin was unnecessary for the time being, but what if the other youth grew tired of their arrangement? Or what if he decided that exposing the truth about what happened to Larina was more fun than learning from Dephithus. Worse yet, any one of the others could decide to take that action for themselves at any time, which provided a greater threat given that he did not, to the best of his knowledge, have anything they wanted.

Dephithus shook his head slightly and focused on his opponent. He could try to figure those things out later. They began armed with sword and shield. It was a hard way to fight because it required you to be able to control your mount almost exclusively with leg signals. He and Hydra were a fluid team in this kind of fighting. The gelding he selected for his opponent he had watched in the practice ring enough to know the animal knew all the necessary leg commands. The question was whether Darkin did.

The answer was a resounding sort of.

They moved at one another and Dephithus took the offensive. He drove a hard jab at Darkin, who managed to deflect with his shield and spin his mount to give himself a better angle. They exchanged several blows, maneuvering their mounts to stay in as close as possible, each trying to gain the advantage and unbalance the other. Then Darkin put his power into a heavy swing and Dephithus signaled Hydra to pull back into a half-rear and spin away. Darkin, could have moved his mount into Hydra with the right leg command, but he had committed physically and mentally to the swing. His balance went with his blade and Dephithus lunged Hydra in at a different angle, catching Darkin with a blow to the side that sent him off his mount.

Dephithus managed to drop Darkin from his perch on the gelding several more times after that. While he was getting back on his feet and up into the saddle, Dephithus pointed out in detail the mistakes his opponent had made. At first, he took a sadistic kind of pleasure in watching Darkin hit the ground. Then, as they both started to break a sweat under the bright sun, he started to enjoy having someone to teach. His manner became more serious and he started taking the time to show Darkin not only what he had done wrong, but how he might correct the mistakes he was making.

Darkin was unexpectedly receptive to the criticism. Dephithus had always been told that people like Darkin who rebelled against society did so because they were insecure and unhappy. If that were true, he was not seeing it here. Darkin took each fall graciously despite the jeering comments from his companions, who seemed to take even more pleasure from his falls than Dephithus did. Darkin simply dusted off, rubbed out the sore spots and remounted. The lad listened intently to the advice he was given, often repeating things to be sure he had them right, and Dephithus watched with grudging admiration how fast he put his lessons to use. If Darkin was an outcast from society it was because he chose to be. Overall, it made Dephithus a bit more wary of having him as an enemy.

When they decided to stop for the day, Darkin still had not unseated Dephithus, but he was much closer to it than he had been when they started. Both horses were covered with a healthy sheen of sweat. Darkin's black hair was slicked down with the sweat that dripped down his face and Dephithus knew he looked the same. The exhaustion was strangely refreshing. There was no energy left for anger or frustration.

Darkin ran a hand through his damp hair and regarded Dephithus for a few silent seconds. A weary grin stole over his features and he gestured with his chin toward the trees on their right. Knowing what lay not far in that direction, he nodded agreement and they turned their mounts that way.

Not far from the clearing was a deep lake. They removed the equipment from the horses and rode them into the water. Hydra splashed at the water with one foreleg, sending up a deliciously cool spray that washed over Dephithus. He sat in the shower his stallion created for a minute, then he slipped off Hydra into the lake, leading the stallion in deeper. He and Darkin floated in the water next to their mounts while Darkin's companions engaged in a furious water fight closer to the edge of the lake, shouting insults at one another and laughing.

Eventually, Suva disengaged and swam over beside Dephithus. Seeing her predatory look, he began instantly to miss the dagger he had left on shore with Hydra's saddle.

"I could drown you right now and you would be too exhausted to stop me."

Her casual tone did not at all go with the threatening tenor of her words. A chill swept through him. He knew full well that she might be strong enough to hold him under after the workout he had already had. Before he could respond to the threat Darkin moved in close to her, displeasure apparent in his scowl.

"Even you have more honor than to attack someone who isn't your enemy when they are at a clear disadvantage, Suva."

She narrowed her eyes. "And who says he isn't my enemy?"

Darkin, who was just as tired as Dephithus and treading water with the rest of them, shifted closer still and somehow managed to make himself look intimidating. "I advise you to back off."

Suva snarled at them both, then turned and swam back to shore.

Dephithus gave Darkin a somber nod. It was the closest he ever planned to get to thanking him for anything. Darkin nodded back, an understanding in his eyes that brought back that ever-present irritation that plagued Dephithus of late.

"Have you ever lain with Myara?"

Dephithus scowled. Whatever reason Darkin had for asking, he did not like the other youth thinking about Myara in that way, or any way if he were to be honest. "Of course not. We both have our social standing to consider and she's not old enough yet."

"Soon though?" Darkin nodded without waiting for an answer. "If you asked nicely, I'm sure Suva would show you a few things."

Dephithus feared his jaw might drop off and become lost at the bottom of the lake.

Darkin shrugged off his shocked look, a gesture

mostly lost in the water. "I know she doesn't seem to like you, but she finds you attractive."

"I didn't get that impression." Dephithus protested, completely baffled and disturbed that the idea of her was suddenly arousing. "Besides, isn't she with you?"

Darkin laughed. "Suva is with Suva. Come on, let's head out. You can think about it."

They both swam back to shore and recovered their equipment. Dephithus had the uncomfortable feeling that he had somehow betrayed Myara simply by talking about Suva in that way. It was not at all unusual for someone to have many sexual partners before settling on one or more to marry. It was almost common. Still, something about the mere possibility that he might lay with someone like Suva when he had a lady like Myara, who would be with him because she loved and wanted him, made him feel unworthy of her.

"That's a fine dagger," Darkin commented as Dephithus donned his belt.

Sucking back on a surge of resentment for the giver of that gift, he turned to saddling Hydra. "I suppose so. It was a gift, of sorts."

"I told you that people wouldn't like it if you relied on your weapons to solve things for you." Rather than elaborate on the current relevance of that comment, Darkin continued, "I suppose you won't want to be seen with us if you are going to keep up proper appearances."

"I will do as I like," Dephithus snapped.

The two gossiping lovers in the garden were still fresh enough in his mind to make him angry again. He hauled on Hydra's girth and the stallion stamped the ground hard with one back leg in warning.

Was he anything more than a pawn on an elaborate chessboard? What was the point in keeping up all these foolish appearances anyhow? Perhaps he should be seen with the likes of Darkin and his companions. Had he not proven himself to be no better? Vicor certainly would not be surprised.

He finished cinching the saddle and glanced over his shoulder at Darkin. "Come on. I know where we can get some excellent refreshments. If your appetite is up to it, of course."

Darkin grinned. "Do you have to even ask?"

Dephithus shook his head and turned to swing up into the saddle.

"Hey, kids," Darkin called out to the three still in the lake. "Food, compliments of our lord. Hurry up."

They took the horses to the stable Hydra's stall was in, tethering the animals the others had borrowed outside while Dephithus took a moment to bed his stallion down. Darkin watched this with a puzzled expression, but he said nothing until they were walking around to the back door of the palace kitchens.

"Don't they have stable hands for that kind of work?"

Dephithus shrugged, "Hydra's touchy."

Darkin grinned, bumping Dephithus with his shoulder in a good-natured fashion. "I think Hydra suffers more from a touchy owner." Dephithus smiled and shrugged, drawing a chuckle from Darkin. "Does this mean we have to prepare our own food too?"

Dephithus shook his head as he opened the door for them. Everyone except for Suva accepted the habitual gesture graciously enough. Suva hesitated outside the door and scowled at Dephithus while the head cook on duty looked them all over. With a stern look the stocky woman set her flour-dusted hands on her broad hips and addressed him.

"Dephithus, my boy, bring them in or take them out, but don't stand there letting bugs into my kitchen."

Suva glanced up at the woman and Dephithus took advantage of her distraction. He met Darkin's eyes, hoping for backup, and gave Suva a firm shove through the door. Trying to stifle a laugh, Darkin caught hold of her arm before she could retaliate. Suva glared hatred at Dephithus, but he ignored her. The wonderful smells of the fine foods and the oppressive warmth of the ovens took hold of his senses. There were five other people at work under the head cook, all of whom looked away conspicuously when they saw who had entered.

Did they too believe he was turning bad? Did they believe his scales and strange eyes were dark omens now? Had they always believed that?

He suppressed the urge to glare at them all and turned back to the intimidating woman in front of them. "What culinary masterpiece might you spare us a bite of today?"

The woman's hard look disappeared and she shook her head at him. "Flatterer. Six of you? Usually you're not so demanding, but I think I can handle it."

ilence prevailed while the group satisfied their hunger lounging around one of the small garden pools. Suva even seemed to have forgotten her anger with Dephithus for pushing her through the door, at least for the moment. He caught his gaze wandering to her more often than he intended. Had Darkin really been serious about what he had said at the lake? From the scowl that crossed Suva's face when she saw him looking, it would take a lot more than asking nicely to get so much as a peck on the cheek. Not that he would want even that.

Dephithus adjusted his position to look out at the garden past Darkin, anywhere but at Suva.

Kovial lifted a fancy tea cake in toast to Dephithus, smiling appreciation. "Could you ever grow tired of eating like this? No wonder you rich kids never eat in the Legion dining hall. Where do they scrounge up the cooks down there anyway?"

Dephithus smiled and made to reply when a Darkin caught his attention with a wave of one hand and gestured past him with a jerk of his head. Dephithus looked in the direction Darkin gestured to see Myara walking up behind them. He knew her well enough to recognize the apprehension in her eyes when the others turned to scrutinize her, yet she kept her posture and her stride convincingly confident. He rose to greet her, spurred to

189

his feet by the realization that he was supposed to have
met up with her almost an hour ago.

She stopped in front of him, her gaze passing over
the others briefly before she spoke. "I thought we were
going to spend some time together today."

"I'm so sorry. I guess I forgot." He cringed inwardly
at how weak that sounded. How could he have forgotten the one thing he had woken up for?

Suva smiled a sultry smile. "It wasn't his fault. He
was a little distracted." She winked at Dephithus and
he fancied he could feel the heat rising off Myara in
response.

"Yes, well, do you remember now?" Myara's eyes
narrowed, bitterness putting a sharp edge on each word.
Her glare lingered on Suva for a moment then moved
back to settle on him.

"Of course I do. Shall we go?" He offered her his
arm, trying to keep his tone light and pointedly not
looking at Suva.

Myara hesitated and he wondered if she might not
refuse his arm in front of everyone. Finally, she nodded
to herself and slipped her arm through his, giving Suva
a hard look once more as they started to turn away.

"Dephithus, aren't you going to introduce us?"

Dephithus met Darkin's gaze. There was something
sinister in his smirk that reflected in the dark pools of
his eyes. "No, I don't believe I am."

"Well enough," Darkin gave Myara a nod. "I'm sure
our paths will all cross again."

Dephithus nodded. He was not going to explain
his sudden protectiveness to Darkin. To any of them.
He wanted Myara and Darkin's bunch of troublemak-
ers kept exclusively apart. Myara looked surprised at
his curtness, but Darkin did not seem to be offended,
though the other four, who probably had no real desire
to meet her, did look insulted. Darkin waved him on his

way, as though he needed permission, and Dephithus turned his back on them, leaving them to do as they wished in the palace gardens. He expected that they would probably not stay long. They did not seem the types to lounge around and chat in elegant gardens.

As they were passing the stables Myara freed her arm and bent down, picking a clover that she began spinning back and forth between her thumb and forefinger. Dephithus reached over, using his quick reflexes to playfully pluck one of the leaves as she spun them around. Myara frowned and dropped the damaged clover, gracefully slipping her leg out to trip him when she bent back down for another without missing a stride. He stumbled over it and caught himself, then chuckled at her as she smiled smugly down at her new clover.

"Not much of a lady are you," Dephithus teased.

"Not much of a gentleman. You didn't even introduce me to your new friends, shady though they were. It seems my little rebel is branching out on his own."

Dephithus rolled his eyes. "They're not friends, just..." He faltered, trying to decide what they were.

Her brow pinched with a dubious look. "Political connections? What?"

Dephithus scowled at her and she laughed. What a lovely laugh, even with that slight edge of tension beneath it. There was so much he wanted to do with her. So much he was afraid to try. He could not believe that she could be so perfectly beautiful and so enchanting. She deserved so much better. If she knew that Larina's death had been no accident she would shun him or worse. Dephithus kicked at the ground with his boot toe, scowling more deeply. Why had he been so foolish as to tell Darkin about Larina? Not only Darkin, but all of his pack as well. Then again, who would believe those five over the heir to the kingdom and pride of Imperious?

Myara's fingertips touched his cheek briefly, surprising him. Dephithus looked up and mustered a smile to wash away the concern in her eyes. She continued watching him a moment longer then glanced down the hill they were topping and her eyes sparkled to life.

"Race you to the bottom."

His long dueling with Darkin still weighed his limbs down. He shook his head. "No, I'm much too tired."

Not one to be dissuaded, Myara shoved him knocking him off his feet and dropped next to him. Pulling him with her, she started them rolling down the hill. Dephithus rolled with her, laughing at how absurd they must look. When they reached the bottom, he was lying partially under her. Seeing the mischievous mirth in her eyes he looked down to see that his foot was the furthest down the hill.

She followed his gaze. "Looks like you won again."

They both laughed and she rolled off to lie on her back beside him. Together they lay in the cool grass and stared up at a beautiful blue sky.

"I suppose you have even more issues to work out since the tournament," she said, taking them back to their conversation the night at the tower. That was the first time they had kissed. It was also the last time.

Dephithus remained carefully silent.

"I just want you to know that I'm here for you."

Still not speaking, he reached over and squeezed her hand. After a bit, she raised her arm, pointing at a particular cloud.

"Look, a swan."

Dephithus tilted his head to the side and frowned. "Looks more like a snake with a swollen stomach."

"Gross." Myara shoved him playfully.

"There," Dephithus pointed out another cloud, "a horse head."

"Oh, now I understand."

Puzzled, Dephithus rolled onto his side and propped up on his elbow so he could look at her. "What?"

"All this time I thought you found a special lady, but now I realize you're just infatuated with that horse your mother gave you."

Dephithus rolled his eyes and pinched her side. She let out a squeal of surprise and squirmed away. With impressive agility, she twisted up onto her hands and knees and lunged at him, knocking him onto his back again. She sat on him then, pinning his hands over his head with hers and leaning down so her hair fell around his face, the bright sun streaming through it, making it glow.

"What? Aren't you going to struggle?"

Dephithus shook his head, gazing deep into her golden eyes. "I was hoping you would take me prisoner."

Myara smiled, then leaned down and kissed him. Her kiss was as demanding as his had been the first time, claiming his mouth with hers like it belonged to her. He kissed her with equal fervor, too absorbed with the taste of her lips to worry about how awkward his arousal was given her current position. When she pulled away, her beautiful gold toned skin was flushed, her eyes burning with a hunger he shared. She dropped down alongside him like she had run a marathon, then snuggled up close and lay her head on his shoulder.

Dephithus wrapped his arm around her, making his squeeze gentle, fighting down the raging desire that made him want to demand more of her. He again had an image of forcing her down and making her give herself to him. As strong as she was, he was still stronger with his dragonkin advantages. The image in his head was violent, and arousing, which only served to frustrate him more. Would she fight him if he tried for more or did she want him to try? Would he stop if she did fight?

The last question was the one that held him back. He was not sure he knew the answer.

"Dephithus, I don't like those people you were with today."

Dephithus shook his head. "Suva was just trying to get to you. She enjoys being unpleasant."

"Not her. I didn't take her seriously." Myara chewed at a fingernail a few seconds before continuing, a habit she did not engage in unless she was very uncomfortable about something. "It was the one who asked you if you would introduce them to me. He looked at me in a way that made me feel... like a victim I guess."

Every muscle in his body tightened with sudden anger. He had tried not to notice Darkin looking at her at the time. He was too worried about her taking Suva seriously to pay attention to the one who was more apt to be a threat. They had almost killed one another on the tower. A day of training together did not make the other youth any less dangerous, especially given that Darkin had blackmailed him into the training in the first place.

The angle was a bit awkward, but he managed to twist his neck around so he could kiss her forehead and gave her another gentle squeeze. "Don't worry about him. He won't ever lay a finger on you."

She shifted closer, pressing the length of her body against him, and closed her eyes.

\*

They spent the rest of the afternoon together, chatting and picking on each other playfully, almost as if life had not changed. That evening they dined with his family. A tedious event primarily dominated by Mythan's discussion of the Legion and an unending barrage of questions for Dephithus about practice and such things. Topics chosen because Mythan, like many others, was still trying to reconcile what had happened in Dalynay.

For Dephithus the meal was redeemed only by Myara's presence. After dining they retired to their separate rooms within the palace, but sleep evaded him. He lay in bed for perhaps an hour then dug the key to the library archive out of a drawer and crept through the palace halls to the dark library.

Lighting a candle in the hall outside the library, Dephithus went into the big room and made his way to the back and under the stairs. The archive was no more welcoming now than it had been on his first visit, but he was getting used to the feeling of foreboding that met him in that dark space. He lit the candles in the room and sat in his usual spot that he had made more comfortable with a few cushions that had inexplicably disappeared from one of the palace sitting rooms. His mother had very solemnly announced that there was a thief in the palace the very day they disappeared. Mythan sent servants all over the palace searching for the missing cushions to no avail while Dephithus watched the entire drama with a bubbling of mirth that was hard to hide. Finally, Mythan had shrugged it off with a puzzled expression and ordered new cushions made.

Out of habit, Dephithus reached over and picked up the empty book of daemons. It put him ill at ease to see all of those empty pages in the book every time he looked at it, but he kept checking all the same. He did not really expect it to change, but he hoped that eventually he would discover some reason why this carefully bound and titled tome with no content had been hidden away in this room.

Opening the book to a random page he discovered it was now filled with neatly scribed words and almost dropped it in surprise. Dumbfounded he stared at the enigma in his hands. How could this be real? Books did not suddenly write themselves. Already on edge from the discovery, Dephithus nearly jumped out of his skin when something soft brushed against his arm. He looked down to see the black cat curling up on the edge of the cushion as though it had been expected there.

He set the book down, careful not to let it close in case the words were tempted to disappear again, and eyed his unexpected companion. Once it had settled in, the cat returned his regard with its odd gray eyes. There was no doubt about it when he looked into those eyes. They were the same color as those of the jorycat that had attacked them in Nunich.

"Sorry about your big brother, but he didn't give me much choice." Dephithus's voice was unsteady, but he could not imagine that the cat cared.

The cat closed its gray eyes and a soft purring filled the room. Dephithus reached down then hesitated, his hand hovering just above the cat's head. Should he touch it? Would it even let him? There was only one way to find out. Dephithus touched the black fur with his fingertips. The cat did not move, and the purring got a little louder. He stroked his hand along the cat's back, delighting in the silken softness of its black coat. Perhaps there was something wrong with it that made its eyes gray, but it seemed harmless enough. He stroked the fur a few more times and waited to see if it would leave. The cat opened it eyes to look at him once more then let them drift closed again.

Setting the heavy book of daemons on his lap, Dephithus turned to the front page, holding the first page he had looked at open in case it was the only part with writing. Finding writing in the front as well, he let the later pages fall closed.

I would like to open this by acknowledging the courage of my four late colleagues who dared to join me in this field of study. I have overseen the burial of each as they met their deaths at the mercy of their subjects. I begin this final writing before the study is complete, as I fear my own grave will soon welcome me in its embrace. I think we all realized that pursuing the origins of the daemons and the power that spawns them, the daenox, was dangerous, yet we were also quite naive of the powers we faced when we began this quest. Over time, we learned that even the lesser-most daemons are capable of storing memories and, as we move up the scale, the greater daemons have the ability to use this information to form most ingenious traps for their prey.

The implications in the words of this nameless author sent a chill through Dephithus. He fell to absently stroking the cat as he read on, appreciating the soothing effect of its presence.

But then, I get ahead of myself. We must begin at the start of this journey even at the risk of never reaching the end. Our purpose for this study was the hope of finding a way to exterminate the daemons roaming our lands. At one point, we speculated that these creatures were created by the cults worshiping the daenox, but it appears they are simply a manifestation of that power that needs no assistance in their formation. For this text, I will summarize each daemon form and then follow with actual journals from the study period given to that form.

Our first subject is the lowest form of daemon. This daemon form is much like a virus. It can be passed through contact with any infected substance, though humans seem to have some peculiar immunity to this form. Indeed, in our studies we were unable to infect a creature of mass any greater than a large dog.

Our theory is that this virus has a limited reproduction and may be able to infect larger creatures, but not thoroughly enough for the effects to be noticed. The primary symptom of this daemon virus form seems to be a drastically increased aggression. However, among the infected test subjects, no animal would attack another that was similarly infected, even in typical predator–prey type setups. For example, an infected cat would not harm an infected mouse or bird. Some of the other symptoms include a darkening of the skin and coat and discoloration of the eyes, often to a dark matte gray.

A violent chill swept through Dephithus, making the hair on his neck and arms stand up. His hand stopped midway down the cat's back. The cat was watching him when he looked down at it. The purring had stopped, and there was a feeling of expectation crackling in the air around them. Those gray eyes, a dark matte gray, held an unnerving intelligence. He was like an infant floundering in his protective enclosure. Every book he had read so far agreed that the daemons were born of a sinister power called daenox, though some argued that the power itself was not ominous and only those who used it in foul ways gave it such a reputation.

Might this creature next to him be one of these daemon-infected beasts? Was this somehow because of him? He had heard often enough the rumors that his strange appearance was an ill-omen of dark days ahead. Might they have been implying that his strangeness was a sign of the daenox returning?

Dephithus pulled his hand away from the animal and stared at it with a horrified fascination. If the daenox were returning was this how it would do it? Appearing a little at a time, starting with the lesser daemons and moving up to...to what?

He turned back to the book to find out more when one of the earlier lines of text caught his eye. It said that infected creatures, such as this cat if it were such, were extremely aggressive except toward other infected creatures. If this cat was truly infected with the daemon virus form, why did it not attack him?

Dephithus stared at the cat again and the animal rose up on its front legs enough to rub its cheek against his arm. He did not find the gesture at all comforting.

In the weeks that passed the daenox seeped out more and more, bringing with it many lesser daemon forms. Periodically, when Amahna would go to Kithin to indulge Kara with a visit to her family and friends, they would get news of strange attacks in the neighboring towns and villages. Kithin itself suffered no attacks because of the alliance with Theruses, but, elsewhere, it would continue to get worse as the weeks wore on and the daenox-seed in Dephithus grew stronger.

Amahna might have taken pleasure in the progress if it were not for Theruses. His pleasant temper had vanished of late and had been replaced by ceaseless irritation and more restless pacing. Servants darted from rooms in the cave when they knew he was coming and even his more valued minions were becoming wary of his presence. Almost no one dared to speak of it aloud, though Rakas, who seemed to have lost a bit of his good sense over the last few months, would make occasional comments about it. What angered Amahna the most when he brought it up was how he expressed mock sympathy for her position. He appeared to take some sick pleasure out of reminding her of how Theruses favored her and how she would probably suffer from his moods the worst because of it.

Today, Amahna had gone to Kithin, giving in again

to Kara's persistent pleading that they pay a visit on her family. Kara always wanted Amahna to go to the village with her. The young woman was proud of her position within the cave and loved to show off to the other less fortunate villagers how she had been chosen by someone so close to Theruses himself. She was the current envy of the town. Amahna, with Theruses in his mood and Rakas tormenting her when he was not sulking, enjoyed the trips to the village. She was almost reluctant to return to the cave this time, but she could not allow any such hesitation to show in front of Kara, so she returned to the cave with the same confidence in her stride that she left it with.

"It must be wonderful to be his favorite." Kara said, her tone reverent as they entered the mouth of the cave.

"It is a great honor, but don't envy me my position. You must always remember that being close to him means I suffer his turns just as you do mine."

Kara smiled, adoration plain in her young face. She was much too young and naïve for the deceptions of this twisted world she had been brought into. "Your temper is as beautiful as your smile, my lady. I think Theruses is much more frightening when he is upset than you could ever be."

Amahna stopped, taking hold of the youth's chin gently and placing a soft kiss on her lips. Kara pressed into the kiss and a shiver passed through her. Anticipation of more perhaps. Stepping back, Amahna smiled. "I could not have found a better attendant if I had searched the world over. Go now."

Her face beaming like a proud beacon in the dimness of the cave, Kara curtsied and trotted off down the first passage on the right. Amahna watched her leave, waiting with forced patience for the presence she had sensed to show itself. Rakas stepped out of another, darker passage, his hands clasped before him to hide the faint shaking that plagued him constantly now. He looked so weary she almost pitied him. Almost.

"Theruses was looking for you."

What was left of her better mood melted away like ice dropped in a fire. "He should have known when I left. He can feel that."

"He should have, yes." There was a certain unnerving warning in the faint tremor of his voice. "Still, he was looking."

The usual indifference and hatred he had displayed toward her of late was gone. He sounded fearful at best, like someone who had narrowly escaped death and wanted nothing more than to put it as far behind them as possible. Was the shaking in his hands worse today? His unease weighted down the air around them so much that she almost expected him to bolt for the exit. It would not have surprised her much. However, Rakas displayed remarkable willpower, standing patiently to wait on her.

Did he have orders perhaps? She was not going to let him get to her. "Is there something else?"

"Theruses expects you in your bedchamber immediately."

"Are you here to escort me?" She could not keep the venom from her tone. Did Theruses dare imply that he could not trust her? She stamped down on that thought quickly, chastising herself for her own impudence. Theruses dared whatever he wished.

"No. Nothing would appeal to me less. I simply intend to see that you go the right direction. We both know the daenox will kill me eventually; I don't think Theruses would hesitate to speed up that process in his current mood."

Amahna gave a curt nod. He was right, not that it mattered much to her. Donning a mantle of false confidence, she strode off down the appropriate passage with Rakas shadowing her. Despite his denying the intent to escort her, he remained a few steps behind up until the last branch to her chamber, then he vanished through a narrow opening in the opposite wall.

Her resolve weakened quickly once she had no one to put on airs for so she had to take the last several steps on force of will alone with a heavy lump of dread in her gut dragging her down.

In her bedchamber, or what passed for one in the cave, Theruses stood with his back to the entrance. All his muscles were taut like a predator about to spring, and she could not bring herself to speak lest she should startle and enrage him. It seemed that whatever was bothering him had upset him to the point that it was affecting his awareness. Never, in all her years in the caves, had she gotten this close to him without him noticing her presence. She knew that the longer she held her silence the more his wait would irritate him.

"My lord." She bowed her head as she spoke, sinking to her knees.

Theruses turned, growling as he did so, his tail lashing out behind him like a whip. "You make me wait."

He turned away from her again and she searched her mind frantically for something that might please him. Would it anger him if she rose without awaiting his leave? What would please him? He expected something from her.

Her insides trembling to mush with the rattling of her nerves, she stood and walked up behind him. She spoke slow to keep her voice steady. "Many of the lesser daemons have gone free, my lord. It cannot be long before you can leave here too."

"A while yet, for me."

There was a hint of a growl in his voice and she hesitated, running her words back in her mind to search for something in them that would have upset him more. She could think of nothing she had said wrong. He should be pleased with the progress they were making toward freeing the daenox completely. "Is something not right, my lord?"

Theruses turned to face her and she flinched before his cold black stare. "Why do you ask?"

Was he baiting her? Trying to get her to say something she would regret?

"You seem... agitated." Afraid, she thought, now that she could see his face. Amahna glanced quickly away, terrified that her thoughts might show through. No one accused their lord of being afraid, not even in their own head.

Theruses grabbed hold of her jaw and turned her face to him. As he stared down into her eyes, his grip began to slowly tighten, creating a painful pressure. Her instincts screamed at her to fight and run, but there was no escaping Theruses. She could only hope to avoid his wrath by submitting. One of his pointed nails began to cut into her cheek, squeezing tears of pain from her eyes.

Finally, he snarled, deep and full of rage. "I fear nothing!"

With a look of disgust, he tossed her across the room.

Amahna could not help crying out when her hip struck the cold stone floor. At least she was further away from him for now. For several seconds, as she lay on the knot that was already forming in her hip, the edges of her vision turned red and she wanted nothing more than to turn on him. To attack him with teeth and claws like some savage beast. Then she got control again and rage was replaced by horror at the realization of how such defiance would end. She shoved those thoughts away, pushing them down deep, and searched her mind for any way to appease him before she got more than a bruised hip out of the encounter.

"It is I who fear, my lord. I fear not being able to please you. I fear failing you." She dared to look up through the hair that had fallen over her face.

Theruses still looked irritable, but already a touch calmer than seconds ago. He stared sullenly out the doorway into the dark chambers and passages beyond.

"Something has been overlooked." His voice was soft, almost inaudible, but she could hear him clearly in her mind. He wanted her to hear. Only her. *There is more to the dragons' plan than this dragon-child. Their prisons have not been weakened at all by his mere existence. There must be something else they need. Another piece to the puzzle.*

"Then we will find out what it is." She sat up to speak and her voice was a surprise even to her. Strong. Determined.

Theruses looked down at her. For the first time since they had come together he looked uncertain. It was almost as if he did question her loyalty now. She had seen a hint of weakness in him, of vulnerability. Could he still trust her?

Even she was not sure how to answer that question in that moment. She held her silence and met his gaze, almost daring him to show his wrath again.

Theruses smiled. It was a bitter expression. "Your strength is what has always drawn me to you. You will find out what the dragons are doing, what they need, and you will return to me as soon as you know the answer. Take that slinking worm with you, I don't want him here."

"Rakas?"

His snort was answer enough.

She stood as smoothly as she could, grimacing at the resistance in her hip. "Might I take Kara as well?"

Theruses shook his head. "No. Your pet stays with me. I will watch over her."

Amahna longed to argue with him, to curse him for denying her this. What might he do to the young woman in her absence? Would she come back to a broken creature?

She gave a reluctant nod. There was nothing she could do about it. He had made his decision. Perhaps he sought to guarantee her return by keeping Kara here. If so, he sorely misjudged her. Everyone was expendable if they got in her way. For Amahna there was only one thing that guaranteed her return now. It was something she had only just discovered. In some way, she had power over Theruses, for she was the only one who could bring him to show his emotions, good or bad, so completely. Something in her intrigued him and that gave her some of the control in their strange relationship. That was all she needed to know. If he could be unbalanced by her then he was vulnerable, if only a little, and vulnerability could be exploited.

Amahna watched him as she waited to be dismissed. She refused to kneel this time. Perhaps he would assume her injury hindered her. Or he might at least tell himself that to make himself feel better about not making her kneel.

She regarded him in the silence that hung heavy between them. He was every bit as magnificent as she remembered him being the first time they met. Knowing that he had emotions she could perhaps use to her advantage did not change the fact that he could kill her with a touch and would probably feel no significant remorse.

Almost as if it were an afterthought, he walked up to her and kissed her. A deep, suffocating kiss full of hatred and desire. Despite her anger with him, she melted into the kiss and was reminded of her own weaknesses.

Even before he moved away she knew that he would not satisfy the desire he had set to burning. Turning his back on her, he ordered her to go.

Would he use Kara to sate his desire when she was gone?

Amahna inclined her head in a slight bow and strode from the room, keeping her steps swift but graceful and proud. Ignoring her pain.

Rakas was easy to find. He often wandered to a chamber they called The Sentinel Room when he was upset, as she knew he was. A single towering stalagmite in the center gave the chamber its name. Rakas sat at the foot of the tower staring into the floor. When Amahna entered the room with purpose in her stride he stood and waited for her next to the massive tower. She walked right up to him and redirected all the desire and rage Theruses had ignited in her into kissing him. Rakas gave into the kiss easily as she had known he would, but his eyes brimmed over with suspicion when she pulled away.

"Come along, we are leaving now."

"You're angry."

She barked out a laugh. "Yes, well, I probably would not have kissed you otherwise."

Rather than reacting with offense as she had expected him to, Rakas cracked a grin. Perhaps the most genuine grin she had seen on his face in years. "I know. You should get angry like that more often."

He waited a moment, watching her to see if she would respond.

Amahna only shook her head and smiled faintly before turning back the way she had come.

Rakas followed dutifully. "We're being sent on another quest? I believe that hired heroes used to make a substantial profit for fulfilling their missions. Maybe we should start charging him."

Amahna glanced back at him, eyes wide with warning, though she could not hide the hint of a smile. "Watch yourself, Rakas. I do wish to leave here alive. It makes these trips so much easier."

While they turned to gathering the few supplies they needed, she noticed that the boy's ring that Rakas had worn since that night in Ithkan was nowhere to be seen. It was not on the band around his neck or on his finger. She stopped what she was doing. "Your ring, did you lose it?"

Rakas scowled and she could see in his eyes that the emotion waiting to be unleashed on that subject was deep and dark. "Theruses apparently got weary of my messing with it. He made it a little more permanent." Rakas opened his shirt to reveal a ring-shaped scar over his heart with a small circular lump underneath. "He used daenox to burn it through my skin and said I would have to dig it out if I wanted to touch it again."

Amahna shivered. Perhaps there still were some advantages to being in favor with Theruses. She would have to fall a long way before their lord would inflict such a torture on her. Rakas tried to fasten his shirt, but the shake in his hands caused him to fumble several times. After a few failed attempts, she walked over and pushed his hands aside, doing up the shirt for him.

"Thank you." He placed his cool, trembling hands on hers and squeezed them gently. "I won't be coming back here with you when you return."

She looked deep into the black pits of his eyes and he lowered his gaze. She knew that part of him hated her, just as much as part of her hated him. Freeing one hand, she wrapped her arm around his shoulders and pulled him to her and he returned the embrace.

Then there was the other part of each of them.

"I know," she whispered.

## CHAPTER TWENTY ONE

Dephithus contemplated the daemons and the daenox often. Every time he went to the archives now, the daemon-cat was there. He took to calling it Prophet since one prophet or another wrote so many of the books in there. The cat took little interest in its name, but it did not object either. It seemed content, much like any other cat, with the simple pursuits of frequent bathing and lying next to him to take advantage of his warmth while he read. It was allowed many opportunities to engage in the latter pursuit as Dephithus spent an ever-increasing amount of time in the once forbidding room. The more time he spent there, the more he began to take comfort in its seclusion and the odd companionship of the daemon-cat.

In the book of daemons, he read that the second level of daemon was very similar to the first. It took a maggot-like form and burrowed into the ears of its victims. Once inside it would infect the mind and cause some physical changes including darkened fur, matte gray eyes, and occasional physical deformation. This level also amplified aggression more than the viral form did in the creatures it infected. Like the viral form, this form also seemed unable to affect larger animals and humans. If not for that, he might wonder if he had been infected. Instead, it seemed he was just broken. Broken

because he was not strong enough to fight his aunt
and her feeble companion. Broken because he was not
strong enough to cope with what they had done to him.
Perhaps it was inevitable. His birth, his markings, had
been considered an ill omen by many. The good life he
had known was destined to fall apart.

News trickled in from surrounding areas of incidents
involving other attacks by diseased animals with gray
eyes since the one that had lunged at him and Avaline
in Nunich. Only three days past, a rat had been found
attacking an infant in a nearby village. The creature
had gray eyes and a fifth leg protruding from its side.
It would not be long before the next stage of daemon
would show itself. Still, he said nothing to anyone about
the things he read in the archives, especially since he
was not supposed to be in there in the first place, and
the occurrences were attributed to an outbreak of some
illness, which was not entirely incorrect. The daenox
spoken of in the books was never mentioned in these
incidents, but Dephithus saw fear behind people's eyes
and heard the nervous edge in their laughs. The more
he read, the more he believed that the daenox was real
and it was returning to the world they knew. These
minor daemons were only the beginning.

He was starting to accept that he was somehow a part
of the bad things happening in the region. The cat in the
library, Prophet, had convinced him of that. At first it had
been upsetting, but it was out of his control. Now he was
almost fascinated to find out what would come next. It
was like a study of the people he lived among. To see how
they lied to themselves and pretended nothing was wrong.
Before long, his position here would be in jeopardy, if it
was not already, but he could not get that upset over it.
He was a curse.

People talked about him more frequently. They spoke
of how his presence was causing things to go wrong and

how he was succumbing to his corrupt nature. Larina's death and his recent disinterest in the Legion were brought out repeatedly as proof of his decline. People needed someone to blame. It only made sense that they should blame the guilty.

The more they talked about him, the less he cared.

It was a cool morning. A hint of drizzle misted the air as he walked toward the distant practice arena. He hoped that the exertion and calm of the walk would burn away some of his energy and help him keep his anger in check. As much as he loved riding Hydra, it got him too charged up. His energy and the stallion's energy worked to build each other up and he needed calm if he was going to get through a full practice without losing his fragile temper.

He had missed part or all of practice too often of late, finding ways to avoid people so he did not have to worry about his fits of temper. He had even been late for guard tower duty numerous times in the past several weeks. The only thing he made a point of showing up for consistently was his training sessions with Darkin—that release of pent up anger was the only thing that kept him from lashing out constantly at everyone else.

If he was not in the archives, it was often because he was out wandering the woods on Hydra or practicing with Darkin. He felt safe around the other youth because it was all right to hate him and occasionally try to kill him in their duels. Though he always held back. If he succeeded in killing Darkin, his outlet would be gone.

His poor attendance was already drawing attention. Commander Vicor had threatened only yesterday to put him on stall cleaning duty if he did not improve his attitude.

By the time Dephithus entered the practice arena, he was chilled with the damp and ready to warm up

with Kota. The big man beat him less often the more
they practiced, which meant he was getting better at
balancing his agility and speed against the senior soldier's experience and size.

"Look who decided to grace us with his presence.
On time even."

His anger ignited like dry hay put to flame. Dephithus
turned to face the commander who was walking into the
arena behind him. He ground his teeth and clenched his
fists by his sides. This, this constant rage he lived with
now that was always a comment away from bursting
into a wildfire, was why he had not been showing up at
practice on time of late. Sometimes not at all. The rage
simmering always beneath the surface had too much
power over him. He was its victim. Just like he had been
Rakas and Amahna's victim that night.

*You wanted it. How else could they have done that to
you?*

His fingernails dug into his palms.

Vicor sneered. "Feeling all right, young lord?"

To say that the commander appeared to be taking a
disliking to him would have been grossly understating
the situation. Vicor took every missed minute of
practice as a personal affront and, no matter how
Dephithus tried to convince himself to do better next
time, whenever he was there he rose to the occasion in
all the wrongs ways, fueling Vicor's loathing of him
with snide comments and callous disrespect for the
man's station. He knew he should fix things, but the
part of him that wanted to try was crushed beneath
his own self-loathing and the self-destructive spiral it
swept him into. He could see it happening time and
time again but could not seem to stop it. Sometimes
he did not want to stop it. Sometimes he exalted in the
chaos he caused. Other times he hated himself more
for it and wanted it to stop. Today he had gone out

with the intention of doing better, but today would not be any different. The hatred was unleashed.

He put his hand on the hilt of the dagger at his belt and smirked. "I was hoping I could spar with you today, Commander." He managed to spit out the title like it was the vilest of insults.

Vicor's eyes narrowed, the heat of anger reddening his neck, and one hand drifted closer to the sword he wore. Dephithus tensed, hoping the man would finally snap and come at him, give him someplace to release the toxic hate. Then Vicor clenched his teeth and moved his hand away from the weapon.

"Kota is on a special training project for me today. Working with another soldier who is worthy of his time. I hope you can keep your temper in check well enough to spar with someone more suited to your novice skills."

"I'm well past novice," Dephithus growled.

"Battering someone over with your freakish strength and speed isn't a skill," Vicor countered.

Perhaps it was time to leave, before someone got hurt. Dephithus shifted his weight, ready to turn and walk away. Except…if he walked away now he would be giving Vicor exactly what he wanted. To drive his problem student away and focus on the others, giving them all the training and attention. Dephithus was not going to let the man win that easily.

He stood his ground and met the commander's hard gaze.

Vicor gave a curt nod. "Fine. You can spar with Jath."

He walked away and Dephithus shifted his gaze, focusing in on a lanky youth standing near the edge of the arena. Jath was tall and lean. He had good reach and good speed, but he was a decidedly mediocre fighter. What did Vicor hope to accomplish by pairing them up? Was this some kind of veiled insult?

Jath gave him a nod that he did not return and they both walked over to retrieve practice swords. They moved to an open spot in the arena and squared off. Jath lunged and Dephithus evaded him easily. He smacked away the attack that followed and lunged into the opening, striking Jath a solid blow to the shoulder that made him cry out. The other youth backed off, rubbing his shoulder, sulking for a few seconds.

This was not a veiled insult. It was a bold, glaring affront.

Pure rage flooded Dephithus, bringing with it the reckless urge to teach Vicor a lesson. He would learn not to match one of his most skilled students with such an unworthy opponent.

Mustering his confidence, Jath readied his stance again and lunged, his swing coming in high and fast. Dephithus embraced his "freakish" strength and speed, dodging in under the swing and spinning around with a full power strike to the back of Jath's elbow. He aimed well, striking where there was an opening for the movement of the joint in the practice armor. The force of the blow was enough to break bone. A loud crack resounded through the arena. There was a second of silence when everyone stopped what they were doing to look, then Jath hit the ground, howling in pain and grabbing for the destroyed appendage.

Dephithus backed away, horror at what he had done seeping in around the edges of his anger. Vicor was there in seconds, he looked at Dephithus once with murder in his eyes, then knelt next to the wounded youth. Dephithus did not wait to find out what came next. In the midst of the sudden bustle of soldiers moving in to try to help or gape, he backed away, discarding his practice sword in the dirt and sprinting from the arena the moment he was clear of the crowd.

He had not quite reached the cover of the trees

when someone came rushing up behind him. He spun, grabbing for his dagger and Darkin sprang back out of range, putting his hands up.

"Easy boy. I have no interest in joining the ranks falling at your feet."

Dephithus gave a snort and turned away, sheathing the dagger while he continued his retreat into the woods. He could hear Darkin following him.

"Don't you have something better to do?"

Darkin chuckled. "That is as fun as tormenting you? Not at the moment."

He could outright kill the other youth. They spent a lot of time out in the woods practicing. An accident could happen. He would get in trouble for engaging in unsupervised practice as a newly raised Legion soldier, but that was not a big deal given how much trouble he was already getting himself into lately. Of course, another soldier falling at his feet, even one as delinquent as Darkin was in his own duties, would force them to start questioning the incident at Dalynay. Then it would not matter if Darkin was silenced. Even worse, he would lose the outlet for his increasing rage.

When did killing someone become an acceptable way to solve problems?

Even someone like Darkin had a right to live. Dephithus himself might be less deserving. In the time he had known the other boy, he had not witnessed him doing anything all that deplorable. In that same span of time, he had killed Larina, broken Jath's arm, and committed countless smaller infractions against many of the people of Imperious, including his mother and Myara.

"Have you decided whether or not to try and kill me today?"

He gave the dark youth a sideways glance. "Stay out of my head."

Darkin merely shrugged and kept pace with him.

Once they were well into the cover of the trees, Dephithus slowed his pace. "What do you want?"

"I was walking by when you pulled your little move in the arena. I thought maybe you could use a better sparring partner to burn off some of that destructive energy."

Dephithus glanced at him again, a grudging respect creeping to the surface. "You would put yourself in my path after what I just did."

Darkin shrugged again. He seemed to do that a lot. As far as Dephithus could tell, the other boy did not get his hackles up very easily. Even when he was acting the aggressor, there was a strange calm to him. He envied that calm.

"Life is full of risks," Darkin offered when Dephithus said nothing else. "I never learned anything from avoiding them."

Dephithus cracked a grin. "You don't learn much if you get killed in the process either."

Darkin grinned back. "I'd rather die young with a life full of experiences than grow old never having tried anything."

Dephithus shook his head, chuckling softly. "One might argue that some risks aren't worth taking."

There was that shrug again. "I've always been terrible at telling the difference."

"All right. Let's spar, then." Dephithus was still shaking a bit with the rush from what he had done to Jarth. He needed some kind of outlet and hiding out reading in the archives was not going to help with this.

They went to their usual clearing in the woods and, for a time, it was just the two of them casually trying to kill one another and inflicting the occasional superficial wound. Then Darkin's crew showed up. As the day passed, they went from sparring, to sharing a sparse meal the others had scavenged. Then they sparred some more, rinsed in the nearby lake, and Dephithus found himself heading into the village to carouse and drink with his unlikely companions. When he staggered back home to the palace, it was well after dark and his head was spinning, the world around him lurching uncomfortably. He was somewhat surprised, as he slunk through the gardens, to find others there. He heard their voices and clumsily staggered to a stop just before rounding the hedge to listen.

"How do you think it got in there?" A man asked.

"Who knows, but they said it was diseased like some of the creatures that have been attacking people in other villages around the area." This voice was a woman's.

"In the palace library?"

Another man asked the question and a spike of panic sobered Dephithus slightly. He stepped around the hedge, surprising the three palace servants. They all averted their eyes, refusing to meet his gaze.

"My lord," the woman greeted.

The other two mumbling similar greetings.

"What was in the palace library?" He heard the demand in his tone and saw how they flinched in response. It did not matter. He needed an answer.

"A cat, my lord," the woman answered. "It attacked Lord Mythan in the library."

*Prophet.*

His chest tightened. "What happened to the cat?"

One of the men recoiled slightly and the woman's brow furrowed. He should have been asking if Mythan was all right, not worrying over the fate of the cat. It was too late to backtrack now, however, and the dread in his gut demanded an answer.

"They killed it, of course."

*No.*

In a less inebriated state he might have tried to cover

up his error and ask after Mythan then, but the truth was that if the high lord had been injured in any significant way they would have already said as much. He did not care about his den-father being upset or suffering a few scratches, and he could not bring himself to pretend he did. He stormed away, loss twisting its way through his chest and moistening his eyes. He had lost one of the only companions who demanded nothing of him. He was alone again in this fight against himself.

## CHAPTER TWENTY TWO

Dephithus stared at the ceiling of his room, his head resting on the book of daemons he had taken from the archive the night before and hidden under his pillow.

The cat was gone, his head felt like someone was hitting it with a hammer from the inside, and Myara's birthday was only a week away. Avaline was helping Myara's mother plan a celebration in the palace since she had grown up so close to his family. He did not want to hurt Myara so close to her Dawning Day, but he had been avoiding her of late. His desire for her was a thing he did not know how to handle. When he thought of her, he thought of touching her, of kissing her, and, in his head, it always went too far. There was force and struggle and the images in his head set his blood on fire with dark hunger. His passion was accompanied always by an inexplicable aggression that was only made worse by the suggestive looks he kept receiving from Suva. Perhaps Darkin had told her about their conversation regarding her, brief as it was. Suva did not seem friendlier toward him, but she did not necessarily have to like him to find him attractive or even desirable. The longer his desire for Myara went unsatisfied, the more he wondered if Suva really would be willing to couple with him.

With everything that had gone wrong of late, there were only two things that disturbed him to any great degree, outside of the death of the cat. The first was the matching looks of distress he saw on Mythan and Avaline every time he was around them. The second was a broad number of things all revolving around Myara. The sexual tension was minor compared to his other concerns. He wondered how she felt about all the talk that was going around. Did she believe he was a curse upon them? Did she think he was becoming corrupt? How he would ever make her happy if things kept on the way they were? How would he get her to couple with him?

Dephithus gave himself a mental kick for that last question. He was running late yet again because he had overslept. His adventure into the village with Darkin and his group the night before left him foggy and miserable, his stomach roiling. They besotted themselves with ale and behaved in a generally loud and obnoxious manner as best he could recall. They had agreed to do the same again in a couple of nights when none of them had guard duty. Right now, he was regretting that decision as the throbbing in his skull intensified with every movement. He managed to get up and dressed despite the headache and the nausea, but he was dreading practice. Today was close combat with daggers. It was probably his weakest area in melee combat skills. He planned to talk to Darkin again about convincing Suva to work with him on dagger fighting, but that would not help today.

His bedroom door opened.

"Dephithus."

Mythan entered his room without waiting for any acknowledgement and shut the door behind him. Dephithus eyed the door opportunistically as Mythan stepped away from it and his den-father scowled discouragement.

"I see you are going to be late to practice again."

"I overslept," Dephithus said, the throbbing in his head growing worse when he spoke.

"I have been out talking with Lance Commander Vicor this morning. I understand there was an incident at the practice arena yesterday."

"Yes."

Mythan's expression darkened, his brow furrowing. "That's all you have to say? You shattered that boy's elbow."

*You killed my cat.* "Accidents happen."

"According to others who were watching, it didn't look like much of an accident. They said it looked like you were trying to injure him."

Dephithus held his tongue, fighting the urge to point out that his sparring partner had not been a proper match for his ability, as if that excused something.

"As heir to this throne I think it is important for you to realize that your reputation among the people you would lead has gone from polished gold to rusted iron in the last several weeks. There is no excuse for your negligent and dangerous behavior or for your poor attitude. Since you seem to have lost interest in your tower duty, I managed to convince Commander Vicor to move you to gate guard instead of stall duty. You will take mid-afternoon watch six days a week with Kota, starting today."

Dephithus walked over and picked the serpent dagger up off the table near the bed, drawing Mythan further into the room and away from the door as he tried to get Dephithus to look at him when he was talking.

"Your blood father was traveling, but I have sent a missive out that I hope will reach him soon. I feel that it is only appropriate to keep him informed of the situation. And your cousins are going to come stay with us for a while."

The pain in his head flared with his temper. Dephithus spun to face him, a sneer curling his lip. "Are you training my replacement?"

Mythan met his gaze levelly. "Not yet."

With a growl Dephithus hurried past him and threw open the door. He stopped in the doorway and glanced back in Mythan's direction.

"The archive key is in my top dresser drawer." With that, he turned and stalked out down the hall.

Mythan made no move to stop or follow him. Dephithus could hardly believe what was happening to him and around him. He had known this was a risk of his recent behavior and yet he could not seem to stop doing things wrong. If Mythan sought to make a king out of one of his sniveling cousins, then the lord of Imperious would get what he deserved. However, where did that leave him? It was wrong to be lazy about his responsibilities as a member of the Legion. It was also wrong to be short-tempered and snappish to all of those people who had once admired him. Since Larina's death, he had done nothing else so deeply awful, though his stunt with Jath had been pushing it, but he could not bring himself to care about the smaller evils he was committing daily.

As Dephithus threw his shambled thoughts about in his head he slowed his walk, increasingly reluctant to show his face at practice. Anger was building, binding his muscles like springs of rage, waiting to be unleashed. He would lose his temper again and that could only mean more trouble. Though no such announcements had been made, he knew inside that he had lost the throne of Imperious. Worse yet, he had lost the respect of his den-father. Thinking about it made blind rage boil up within him to the point that he might go mad if he did not release it somehow.

He did not make it all the way out of the palace

gardens before he was intercepted, though not by any-one he would have expected. Suva, her short blond hair hanging straight and uneven after another inadequate trim from her father, stepped into his path. He stared at her for a minute, wary and curious. Somehow, the less-than-perfect haircut along with her pale blue eyes gave her a look that was both motley and arousing.

Realizing something was missing, he glanced around for her companions. Darkin at least should be nearby.

"I came alone."

He made no effort to hide his mistrust, shifting into a stance that would allow for quicker defense if necessary. "Why?"

"Darkin told me you needed some help with your dagger fighting."

Dephithus nodded, though he maintained the cautious distance between them. "That was considerate of him. What does he want?"

Suva blew out a heavy exhale, impatience surfacing in her stormy eyes. "He's already getting what he wants."

Dephithus mentally scolded himself for being so paranoid. Easing his stance a fraction, he asked, "Then what do you want?"

She shrugged, feigning innocence, much like a cat pretending disinterest until its prey was close enough to pounce on. "A little thrill perhaps."

Dephithus deepened his scowl. Suva was more trouble than one person had a right to be. Then again, he did not want to go to practice this morning so maybe she would prove to be a worthy diversion as someone he did not have to worry so much about offending. He gestured toward a garden exit. "Shall we?"

Suva grinned and Dephithus could almost feel teeth closing around his throat.

No. He refused to believe that she was any more dangerous than he could be.

But how dangerous was that?

Slipping into his thoughts, he walked silently off the path, veering toward the woods. Suva was long and lean and, now that he really looked at her, she was not at all unattractive. However, her appeal was more of a feral, sexual attractiveness, where Myara possessed of an inner beauty the equal of that on the surface. Through time spent with the group, he had come to see that Darkin's words were very true. Suva was with Suva and no one else. She liked who she liked when she wanted to like them and changed her mind often.

They did not go to the same meadow he and Darkin practiced in. Some unspoken accord to find a place of their own brought them to a smaller clearing a little further out. Without speaking, they discarded any loose clothing that might get in the way and faced each other with daggers bared. Real daggers. Neither had said anything about getting practice weapons. For him, that choice was intentional and, given the hungry gleam in her eyes, he suspected it was the same for her.

Suva lunged at him with her arms close to her body then blocked his strike with her one arm and stabbed swiftly with the other. Her attack left a line of blood on the forearm he had used to try and block her. The wound was shallow, but it got his attention.

After that they fought with equal ferocity and neither could get in a good attack, though Suva came closer than he did several times. Since they were wearing none of the usual practice armor the fight had an almost desperate viciousness to it. Dephithus did manage to leave a mark on her shoulder, but he paid for the effort with a deeper cut in his side. He lunged and she dodged his attack then swept her leg around and caught his legs, dropping him on his back in the same manner Kota often had. Before he could roll, she pounced down on him, pinning him with a knee hovering above his groin and her knife at his throat. His knife hand she pulled down and pinned roughly under her other knee.

Was this how he was going to die? He did not doubt that Suva was more than capable of finishing what they had started. She leaned down over him, lowering her face close to his, and licked his lips quickly and teasingly. Pent up desire surged to the surface like a fire gone wild and out of control. Then she kissed him, but when he opened his mouth to her tongue she pulled back just out of reach, her dagger still resting at his throat.

"Kiss or kill? What do you think?"

Dephithus watched the cruel smile spread to her eyes, and the pressure of the dagger lessened a little. Taking advantage of her pause and driven by the desire that was burning him up inside, he brought his free hand up and shoved her sideways. Suva toppled off him and he rolled quickly over on top of her, switching their positions. Her head came up and she met his kiss demandingly, her empty hand coming up to rub at his hardening erection through his trousers. Giving into hunger and the always-present rage he began to roughly pull at the fastenings of her trousers and she did the same to his. They did not bother with upper garments. Her breasts were smallish. He could see that through her clothes. This was not about appreciating one another.

He shoved into her and pain seared through him. Not physical pain. This was emotional. A violent wave of hatred and self-loathing that swept through every fiber of his being. He pounded the torment into her again and again. Hating himself more with each thrust.

She bit his lip. He tasted blood.

He wished she would bite him harder. Wished she had cut him deeper with her blade. Wished she would hit him. Fight to get him off her. He wished she were someone else. Wished she were Myara.

He drove harder into her, wanting to hurt her, but she only opened up to him. Taking him in deeper. Kissing him harder.

Then it was over.

He shuddered with release and collapsed on top of her for exactly long enough to finish. Then he forced himself to get to his feet despite the trembling in his legs. She got up as well, smirking as she pulled her trousers up.

"Seems like we both needed that."

He shook his head, disgusted. He hated that she did not feel his torment. His guilt. "Wouldn't you rather make love with someone you care about?"

Suva barked a bitter laugh. "I don't believe in making love. This is the only way I do it."

"Why?" As he asked the question he suddenly knew how to hurt her. He was not going to suffer alone. "Because this is how your father does it to you?"

Something broke behind her eyes, shattering her shield of indifference. For a split second, she was a scared, vulnerable girl. Then her fist hit his jaw and he was on the ground, staring up at a mocking blue sky. He lunged to his feet, fearing another attack, only to see her disappearing at a run into the woods. His head spun and he sank to his knees. She had quite the fist. At least she had not come after him with a dagger while he was down. He would not have blamed her.

He stayed there for a time, still trembling with his release. He could not remember anything else in his life feeling as amazing as it had felt to come inside her. The memory of that pleasure only served to torment him more. There could be no deeper wrong than what he had just done. He loved Myara. Perhaps he and Suva had used each other, but the fact that it was mutual did not make it right. He could never have that first time again. Never do it the way he had always wanted to, with someone he loved. Never make it something special.

He got to his feet and stood for a moment, staring in the direction Suva had gone. Perhaps she was not as bad as she made herself out to be. Or perhaps she was. Either way, he was ruined both for what they had done and for what he had said. Then again, he suspected he was ruined long before today.

Rubbing at his aching jaw, Dephithus started out toward the stables where he could saddle Hydra and ride to the gate for duty.

## CHAPTER TWENTY THREE

Dephithus was not more than a few minutes late for guard duty. Kota's scowl when he rode up, however, was worthy of several hours' tardiness. He directed Dephithus to his post with a curt gesture and said nothing, which was typical of Kota, though the big man's eyes did linger a few telling seconds on the bruising swell along his jaw. Dephithus simply turned the tables, giving Kota a smile he did not feel and a nod of greeting as if nothing were amiss. The other two guards on duty at the gate avoided looking at either of them, pretending to be absorbed in other pursuits. One stared out over the rolling hills as if the gradual green slopes were truly the most exciting thing he had ever seen and the other studied a parchment that had far too few words upon it to be taking up that much of his time.

Dephithus shook his head and walked over to where he would spend the next six hours. He was posted on the ground level of one tower. In good weather, the ground level guards tended to linger outside of the tower door where they could enjoy the sun and fresh air. The upper lever guards stood on the wall over the gate where they could also enjoy the sun and still have a good vantage to see anyone coming or going. Today, Kota sent the other two up top and stayed on the ground level with Dephithus.

"Rider approaching fast from the palace side," one of the upper guards shouted only a few minutes later.

Dephithus cast a look of annoyance at the guard for the startling pitch he had achieved, the sound still bouncing painfully around his head with the fresh headache Suva's punch had given him. Then he stepped away from the tower door to peer at the approaching figure. Whoever it was, they were coming up at a full gallop. It was only a few moments before he recognized the rider and his gut began to feel as though it had been weighted down with lead.

Commander Vicor pulled up fast from a hard run, his mount locking its front legs and skidding a few feet to stop. Vicor's face was flushed red with anger that he had obviously held on to for the full ride out. The twisted, enraged expression was quite showy and impressive combined with the dramatic entrance. When their eyes locked, there was no doubt for whom Vicor was here. Swinging down from the saddle, the commander dropped the reins, trusting his mount to ground tie, and walked up to Dephithus.

"You couldn't be bothered to come to practice again. You mock the entire Legion with your apathy and shame it with your temper. You're a disgrace to the halls of Elysium."

Dephithus hated Vicor. He hated all of them. Bitterness rose up sour on his tongue. He threw up his hands in feigned dismay. "I feel quite contrite now. Thank you, Vicor."

The commander looked as if he might attack right then or risk bursting his skin with the rage that made his hands shake. He appeared taller somehow in that moment. Then he stepped in closer, so their faces were only a few inches apart, and lowered his voice. "Dephithus de NuTraven, I challenge you to a duel. You will not make a mockery of everything I have worked my whole life for.

If you can defeat me, I will only suspend you from the Legion for a month or two. If not, you will be expelled permanently."

Kota took a step toward them, the disapproval on his face making it clear that he had overheard the challenge. Commander Vicor held up a hand to keep him back and watched Dephithus expectantly, his gaze burning with the fire that brought him out here.

A flutter of panic spread in his chest. For him, to be expelled from the Legion was only a small step away from being denied the throne. Vicor meant to deny him his future, a future that he had probably already denied himself. He let his loathing come through in a cruel smirk. "I accept your challenge."

"Very well." Vicor appeared to shrink back to his former height then. "Tonight, when your guard shift is over, we will meet in the outdoor training arena and settle this."

Dephithus leaned forward, now close enough to Vicor that his breath would be warm on the commander's ear. "I will understand," he said, his voice soft and a hint sensual as he caressed the hilt of the serpent dagger, "if you don't show."

Vicor jerked away and stepped back, his eyes glaring death upon Dephithus. Without another word, he stalked back to his mount and swung up. He did not look at any of them before he spun the animal and galloped away. Next to Dephithus, Kota simply shook his head and returned to his post. It was not proper to accept such a duel. In fact, it was against the law to settle such matters outside of a regulated tournament. If Vicor was willing to risk his reputation and several months of his freedom for this, Dephithus was not going to worry about his own hide. His life was already going to ruin and Vicor deserved to be put in his place.

Gate guard duty dragged on endlessly after Vicor

left, the minutes creeping by like battle-weary soldiers marching to war. The only activity through the gate was the typical run of nobles and Legion soldiers wandering to and from the surrounding city and the farms beyond it. On a typical day, gate duty was almost as dull as the guard towers.

Dephithus itched with impatience, finding it hard to stand still. Now that the challenge was offered and accepted, he was eager to test his sword against the commander. The man needed to be put in his place. Vicor had disrespected his status and insulted his skill one too many times.

*Don't I deserve it? Haven't I proven myself to be worthy of little more?*

Dephithus ground his teeth. Trying not to think of the many things he had done wrong in the last several months. Trying not to think of how it all started. His thoughts wandered to his encounter with Suva then and he pushed her away only to have Myara take her place in his mind. He tried to push those thoughts away as well, trying not to think of either of them and, most especially, not to think of both at the same time.

As dusk began to settle, an excited tension filled him, and Hydra started to pace restlessly around his enclosure in response. Minutes before he was scheduled to depart, Kota walked over to him.

"I encourage you to forgo this madness, Lord Dephithus. You and Vicor will both be punished severely. Remember, you are still heir to this throne."

Dephithus looked deep into Kota's eyes and saw the lie there. "You know better than to believe that." As he spoke he realized the truth of it and his own words fell heavy on his chest. A sense of remorse began spreading through him like some fast-acting poison. He swallowed hard. "Mythan is too good a leader to let Imperious fall into my hands."

Kota lowered his gaze and stepped back, making no further efforts to discourage him or deny his words.

Dephithus sighed. Somewhere inside he realized that all the things that had gone wrong had finally taken him past the point of no return. This was not the way his life was supposed to go. He was supposed to take the throne with Myara by his side. He was supposed to be the next great ruler of Imperious. He was supposed to be happy. Fate had gotten confused.

He could remember laughing and dreaming with Myara, before that night. He could remember how wonderful it was to race with her and spar with her and simply be with her. He could remember how good it felt when his mother and den-father were proud of him. What happened to the satisfaction he got out of making a stranger smile or helping a fellow Legion hopeful improve their skill? A thousand smiles and laughs he had been privileged enough to be a part of played through his mind. Parthak beaming at him for his accomplishments. Kathan grinning ear to ear as they made jokes and listened to music at his family's inn. The love in his mother's eyes when she mussed his hair.

Something inside him recoiled from those memories and he shook them away. Dark anger swelled up in their place. He retrieved Hydra and mounted up. In the saddle, with Hydra prancing impatiently, he felt stronger again. Touching the serpent dagger once for the reassurance the habit gave him, Dephithus kicked his mount and they charged toward the training grounds in the rapidly falling dark.

He could see the ring from some distance even with the darkness falling. The tall fire poles circling the training arena had been lit and an eerie light flickered about, cutting strange shapes into the shadows around them. This was a small practice arena with no seating for observers and it was set a little closer to the forest than the others, away from most of the more crowded buildings. Still, the torches and the sounds of clashing steel would undoubtedly bring a crowd of some size if the fight lasted more than a few minutes. Vicor apparently had no intentions of keeping their confrontation private. He had issued a challenge and he was going to stand behind it.

Dephithus tied Hydra and strode into the arena. He made his movement both predatory and bold, stopping a step out of reach of Vicor's already drawn sword. They would waste no time on pointless formalities. This kind of dueling was forbidden, so there was no approved protocol for it.

Dephithus drew his own weapons as Kota galloped up and dismounted outside of the arena along with one of the other two gate guards who had been there to witness the challenge. They had their first couple of observers even before their blades touched.

Without a word to one another, they both attacked, neither hesitating to play for an early upper hand. Each swing of a sword was followed immediately by the jab of a dagger or another swing. The same hatred and self-loathing that had driven him when he was with Suva returned to him now, pushing him to fight fiercer. He would show them how terrible he was. How undeserving of the throne and of Myara's love.

Several indirect blows glanced off about his arms and he was not sure, with the speed of the fight, if he had made good contact on Vicor yet or not. In a short time, their audience expanded, growing with every loud clash of the blades, but there was no time to pay attention to such distractions. Lance Commander Vicor earned his rank with skill and experience. Even as one of the best in his age group, and with the extra physical abilities granted by his dragonkin blood, Dephithus soon began to feel the strain in his muscles.

He was holding his own, but Vicor struck hard and fast, not missing a single opportunity. When Vicor's sword cut into the still raw wound Suva had left in his side, Dephithus staggered, sloppily blocking the blade from cutting in any deeper. The commander took advantage of the falter and lunged in close, slamming their crossguards together and using his momentary advantage to twist the blade out of Dephithus's grasp. Dephithus glanced after his sword only enough to spot and remember where it landed, then he turned to Vicor and growled. Red filled in the edges of his vision, the pain of his wound fueling his hatred.

He had been disarmed, but he was far from finished. He managed to parry several sword swings with his dagger while he dodged Vicor's dagger. Still, without a sword against someone with Vicor's skill, he would not hold out long. It was strange, looking into his opponent's snarling face, to realize that Vicor truly hated him. He was sure none of the onlookers were overflowing with love for him, but no one had ever hated him as openly as Vicor did. It was refreshing somehow.

He deserved this.

Cries of alarm rose up on one side of the arena. Dephithus, locked together in a match to the death with Vicor, tried to ignore them. A powerful sword strike caught upon the dagger and Dephithus staggered back, his wrist twisting painfully, his balance and focus suddenly broken. Vicor swept his blade back, the intensity of his glare making it clear he meant to strike a fatal blow. Several people screamed and the now sizeable crowd nearest them parted. Something burst from edge of his vision and slammed into the commander, barreling him over.

For a moment, Dephithus thought it simply a dog that had attacked his opponent. Then, as they hit the ground with Vicor on the bottom, his struggles stopping within seconds of impact, Dephithus saw two rows of large spines down the animals back. They looked like overgrown porcupine quills. The animal's body bulged with grossly oversized muscles. He did not have to see its eyes to know it was one of the third level of daemons he read of in the book.

The daemon-dog growled, it's strange spines growing more erect as it turned its gray-eyed gaze on Dephithus. Beneath the dog, Vicor lay still, his throat ripped open. Blood pumped forth in a gushing stream. Dephithus stepped toward the beast and growled. It cowered, its spines falling flat to its back, and snarled defensively. Another soldier, taking advantage of the beast's distraction, rushed in and brought their sword down in a swift arch, severing the daemon-dog's head. Dephithus looked up and a wave of shock turned him cold. Suva stepped back from the beast, her blade dripping blood. She gave him a slight nod; her hard gaze made him realize that he was lucky she had gone for the dog instead of him.

Another figure entered the arena then. Mythan shoved Dephithus aside and looked down at the two bodies that lay there. A sharp intake of breath was the only evidence of his upset.

When he spoke, his voice was commanding and steady. "Duels are illegal. You know that Dephithus, as did Commander Vicor. However, it's clear that you did not strike the killing blow. I will need some time to figure out what happened here and determine an appropriate punishment."

Dephithus shrugged. He was numb. Being saved by the daemon-dog may have been a worse fate than the death that would have found him otherwise.

"We will return to the palace. Someone summon the Silent Watch to take care of the Commander." His eyes swept the crowd. "Someone also tend to their horses."

Dephithus started to lift his lip in a snarl of warning for whoever might be inclined to touch Hydra until he saw that Kovial had taken hold of the stallion. For whatever reason, Suva's brother inspired trust in him. Kovial spotted him looking and nodded recognition before leading the restless stallion toward the stables. Dephithus followed Mythan out of the arena, adrift in the chaos of his cluttered thoughts until he saw her.

Myara was walking away amongst the dispersing crowd, her shoulders hunched with her arms wrapped around herself. There was nothing more important than her. He loved her, and that love was the one good thing left in him. He sprinted after her.

"Myara!"

She stopped and turned to face him, though she took a step back when he got close, refusing to meet his eyes. Her avoidance pierced through him with a pain greater than any wound he had ever suffered.

Behind him, Mythan was yelling at him to come back, but he had no interest in his den-father now.

"Myara." He started to raise a hand to her face then hesitated, warned off by the fear in her eyes. "I love you, Myara."

Tears started spilling down her cheeks and she took another step back from him, shaking her head. "Dephithus." Her voice cracked and she swallowed hard before continuing. "I'm afraid to love you."

Anger and torment swirled up like a storm inside him, bringing back the hatred, the self-loathing, the red at the edges of his vision. He held his silence long enough to contain some of the anger, struggling against the powerful desire to strike out at her. "What do you mean?"

"That…" she glanced in the direction of the arena, her gaze touching upon the bodies there and jumping quickly away again. "That thing was afraid of you. It tore Commander Vicor's throat out. That's not normal behavior for a timid creature, but it cowered when *you* stepped close to it. Why was it afraid of you? What's happened to you?"

Her voice fell to almost a whisper at the last. The anguish that twisted her features and the tears that spilled unchecked from her eyes tore at him like the claws of a wild animal. There was a violent twisting in his chest and his throat was painfully tight. So tight he was not sure he could speak.

Myara was afraid of him. Without her, what was left for him to try for?

Before he could come up with something to say, someone touched his arm. He prepared to unleash his rage on Darkin, but the other youth brushed aside his glare, disarming it with an unsettling frown and a discreet shake of his head.

"Your father is sending a guard to escort you. Save face and go with him now."

Dephithus needed to speak to Myara, but he glanced over his shoulder and saw the grim expression on the three soldiers who were approaching them. Darkin was right. He nodded his reluctant gratitude to Darkin then looked back at Myara. She quickly looked down, avoiding his gaze. Dephithus scowled, grabbing hold of his anger because it was the easiest to deal with of the many emotions raging through him, and turned to head out after Mythan. The three soldiers stopped to watch him pass, then followed a short distance back as he headed towards the palace.

He dared one more glance back at Myara. She was turning away. One of the other soldiers slipped his arms around her shoulders and hugged her much too firmly to his chest. If she was afraid to love him then who would she love? Jealous rage scalded him, burning away the remorse. Now was not the time, however, for any more confrontations. He stayed to his course, etching the soldier's face in his mind as he walked away.

The next evening a death celebration was held for Vicor, but Dephithus attended only briefly, vanishing at the first opportunity. His punishment for the duel was decided quickly and had been announced prior to the celebration. It was the final excuse Mythan needed in order to officially renounce Dephithus as his heir. On top of that, he suspended him indefinitely from the Legion. Dephithus was, of course, still part of the family and expected to stay in the palace as he always had, but this disgrace was not a title he could wear with pride. Once the announcement was made, Dephithus spent the next several nights outside of the palace in one tavern or another with some or all of Darkin's band for company. He came back at dawn for a change of clothes and a quick nap in a comfortable bed.

Another announcement was made the night of Vicor's death celebration. Mythan informed the court that he had sent summons to several scholars around the region requesting their relocation to the palace. When they arrived, he would officially open the archives for study.

There were changes in the region and beyond, and Mythan was wisely looking to the past for advice. Dephithus no longer had the archive key, but he had the book of daemons in his room. There was much more to discover in that dark room under the stairs, and he dreaded that he would not be the one to discover it. There were answers to many things in those books; of that he was certain. Answers he might never get now.

According to the book of daemons, things would continue to get worse and worse. The unknown author had lost his first colleague to a level four daemon. Level four differed from the level three only in its increased ability to change the physical form of its host. After that the daemons became more diversified in their forms. The next several levels needed no host body. They could roam the land in whatever grotesque form came naturally to them. Above this, there were daemons that could raise the dead and roam the earth using those bodies, at least until the connective tissue decomposed beyond a point of structural integrity.

Even higher, and thankfully more uncommon than most, was a daemon the author had discovered after the rest of his colleagues were killed by lower levels. This daemon form chose to possess primarily human hosts and was intelligent enough that it could destroy the mind of its host and still pass for human. It was this type of daemon that the author was being hunted by when he stopped writing. The book ended abruptly with this form, not indicating what, if anything, might be beyond that.

During the remainder of the week, Dephithus faithfully courted the jealous rage that had developed the night of Vicor's death and the hatred within him thrived on it. He did not know who the other soldier was to Myara, but he could not shake the certainty that she had betrayed him somehow.

The day before Myara's Dawning Day celebration, he returned to his palace bedchamber to find a note on his bed from his mother requesting that he attend her before the noon meal. He knew he should go, but anger and a desire to hurt someone steamed and bubbled inside him like a stew left too long on the fire. Instead, he donned a light jacket and went to the stables to disappear into the woods on Hydra. He had barely left the stable when five riders came galloping up from the lower stable, Darkin in the lead.

Irritation flared up. He stamped it down again. For all that he would prefer to be alone, there was something to be said in support of having an opportunity to blow off steam training with Darkin. The activity was becoming less effective at burning off his temper, perhaps because he had developed a grudging admiration for the other youth, but a little release was better than nothing at all.

He waited for them and they turned into the woods toward their favorite practice meadow in unspoken accord.

A few hours later they were rinsing off the sweat in the lake. He submerged himself a few times to rinse the worst of the salty sweat from his hair, then pulled himself back up on Hydra, who was himself halfway submerged. Darkin was doing the same only a few feet away with the mount he had been using for their sessions. He and the gelding had begun to form a solid bond through their practice together and that bond was helping him become a more effective opponent.

The other four were sitting on some old logs they had pulled out of the trees to use as seating around an unlit fire pit they had made. From what he could hear of their conversation, they were discussing the shapes of the fluffy scattered clouds above and laughing at their own foolishness. It sounded so normal and ordinary. Having burned off a great deal of energy, he almost felt normal enough to join them, except for that something deep inside him that wanted to mock them for acting like children.

Dephithus glanced down at the water and released a heavy exhale. His reflection stared up at him, the eyes narrowed, the nose and brow wrinkling in, the lip curling in an ugly grimace. Startled, he kicked the water to distort the twisted image.

"Everything all right? You looked like you saw a monster in the water for a moment there."

*I did.* He glanced up at Darkin. No. Everything was not all right.

"I'm well enough," he lied and turned Hydra to the shore.

The day was beautiful and warm, the sun going right to work on drying their clothes on their bodies as they sat with the other four around the silent fire pit. Dephithus listened to their bantering and joking in silence, mostly because every comment that came to mind was somehow cruel or insulting. They did not deserve that. They were not that bad, really. Except Kip and Lanz perhaps, but Darkin kept them around because they were strong, simple, and immoral enough to get their hands dirty for him if he asked it of them.

"You coming into town with us again tonight?" Kovial asked.

Dephithus glanced up, a little surprised to find them looking at him. "Me?"

"No, your horse," Kovial laughed.

Anger flared up, hot and irrational. "Not even my horse would stoop low enough to spend more time in your company."

The others scowled, but Suva laughed. "There you are. I was wondering when your childish temper was going to pay a visit."

His hand went to his dagger and the four other boys mirrored the movement, tensing for action. Suva did not bother. She trusted her speed to save her if he attacked and he did not think her confidence misplaced. Even with his dragonkin speed, he would be hard pressed to match her swiftness with a blade. He would have to be a fool to attack against these odds anyhow, though his *childish* temper urged him to do so regardless.

The sound of a rider approaching broke the tension and they turned to watch Myara ride into the clearing. She glanced around the group calmly, looking every bit as though she had expected to find all of them there. Perhaps she had. Her gaze homed in on him quickly enough and she stopped her mount by the edge of their ring of seats.

"Care to join us," Darkin offered.

Dephithus opened his mouth to protest the idea, not sure if he did it for her benefit or his own, but she spoke over him.

"No. Thank you for the offer though." She gave Darkin a polite nod before turning back to Dephithus. Her gaze held him captive. "I was hoping we go for a little ride. Just the two of us."

Dephithus responded with a curt nod and walked over to swing up on Hydra's back. The stallion tossed his head and pranced a few steps, responding to his rider's temper. Dephithus jerked back hard on the reins and the stallion kicked one back foot in irritation.

"You sure it's safe to be alone with him?"

It was Darkin who asked the question and there was a tone of sincerity to it. Concern even. It made Dephithus's vision turn red at the betrayal even as his chest flooded with guilt at the realization that the other youth was probably right to be concerned.

Myara hesitated. She stared at Darkin for several silent seconds, considering his words. Then she tore her gaze away and nodded, not quite looking at Dephithus now.

"I'll be fine."

She began to ride away and Dephithus struggled with the fact that she apparently expected him to follow. The nerve. And yet... he did need to talk to her. They needed to talk about the young man who had comforted her the night Vicor died. He needed her to tell him the truth. He would make her tell him the truth.

He kicked Hydra after her.

They rode through the woods in silence, her destination obvious from the direction. She was heading to the Mother Tree. He did not want to go there, but he did not know how to explain that to her. There was too much confusion there. The good memories and all the bad things that had happened over the last few months got mixed together there and it made it hard to think. It made the frustration stronger and, as a result, the anger too.

She dismounted a short distance from the tree and walked the rest of the way on foot. He left Hydra near her mount and stalked after her, the image of her in the other soldier's arms burned in his mind. When she stopped and turned he grabbed her arms, hatred buzzing in his ears like a million bees.

"Have you kissed him?" He demanded, squeezing her arms. Trying to hurt her. "Have you done more than that?"

Myara's expression turned dark and she twisted her arms around his, breaking his grip. Then she punched him in the jaw, hard enough to stun him a bit, though not hard enough to do damage.

Violent hatred exploded through him. He would make her pay.

Myara must have seen it in his face. She drew the dagger she wore and he paused, wary of the weapon in her well-trained hands.

"What is wrong with you? You aren't the same person I used to know. Where is my best friend? Where is the man I fell in love with?" Her eyes were bright with unshed tears, but her stance and the pain in his jaw told him she was willing to fight him.

He looked at her then. This was Myara. His best

friend. The woman he loved, ready to defend herself with a weapon if necessary, from him.

"I don't know." His voice cracked. His chest felt like it had split open, a gaping wound, spilling out all his suffering and anguish into this excruciating moment. "I don't know what's happening to me."

She sheathed the dagger and stepped closer, placing one hand on his arm and the other against his face. "Do you love me?"

He wanted to rip her clothes off. He wanted to throw her on the ground and force her to give herself to him. He stayed still and nodded. "I do."

"Then let me help you figure it out. We can beat this."

She kissed him then. It hurt. It hurt to feel her love and know he did not deserve it. It hurt to know she deserved someone better, but she still chose him. It hurt not to hurt her.

He kissed her back, urgently, a kiss full of needing and wanting. She started to meet his urgency, kissing him harder. He felt himself growing aroused and pushed her away, battling that darkness that wanted him to take her hard and make her know she was his. That darkness that wanted to punish her for letting anyone else touch her.

She searched his eyes. "What is it?"

"I don't deserve you."

She smiled softly. "I love you. I want you."

*I want... I want to hurt you. No!*

He shook himself slightly and she gently touched his jaw where she had punched him. "Sorry about that."

"I deserved it." He brought his lips closer to hers again. "I love you too," he whispered.

He kept repeating the words in his head, over and over, to drown out the dark thoughts while she kissed him again and began to unlace his shirt. They disrobed each other slowly, deliberately. Every second ticked by, anger screaming in his head, trying to drown out the words he kept repeating.

*I love you. I love you.*

They lay down beneath the Mother Tree and he entered her slowly. Gently. Something inside him urged him to drive into her. He wanted to be as rough with her as he had been with Suva and more. He fought it. At first it made his skin itch and crawl denying the dark urges. Then it began to hurt like a thousand blades cutting slow into his flesh, but he fought it. He fought it. This was Myara. He loved her.

He listening to her moans and gasps, moving with her. Responding to her changes in pace and intensity. Watching her expression for cues. The pain continued to cut into him making his stomach turn. Despite it, he could feel pleasure building. He could feel their shared love rising between them.

Then, suddenly, he could feel the pain of Rakas forcing into him. The pleasure of being inside her was overshadowed by the agony of that memory. He squeezed his eyes shut. Remembered Rakas pounding into him. Hatred became his heartbeat, pulsing darkest anger through him until he started to tremble. Then a hand touched his face.

"Dephithus?"

He opened his eyes.

Myara was there, gazing up at him, her face full of love and concern. She brushed a thumb across his cheek. "You're crying."

Was she worth this much pain?

She deserved to be loved. She deserved love from someone better than him, but she had chosen to be here with him. He would give her the love she deserved, no matter what it cost.

"I love you," he whispered.

She met his kiss with warmth and passion and love she did not need to voice for him to feel it. She gasped, breaking the contact of their lips when he pushed deeper into her. He met her eyes, fighting through the pain and the memories, though it felt like it might break him. He touched her and kissed her and moved with her, pleasure and pain growing together. She touched and kissed him in return, murmuring soft words at all the right moments, helping him fight the darkness inside. He was shaking with exhaustion from the inner battle long before he shuddered with release. The very ground beneath them seemed to tremble in that moment, as if some great power had been disturbed with their love making.

For several minutes he lay there, still inside her, shuddering with release and with pain, sweat coating his skin from his inner battle as much as from their exertions. She kissed him, his cheek, his neck, his shoulder. Finally, he moved off her and collapsed next to her, one hand still resting on the damp skin below her throat. A few inches up, just a few inches, and he could wrap her throat and squeeze. She would struggle, but then she would be still and the pain would go away. The pain would...

Dephithus felt the soft skin of her throat as his hand slid up into place. Then he jerked his hand away and rushed to his feet.

Myara sat up. "Dephithus? What's wrong?"

He hastily began to pull his clothes on, trying to block the thoughts that urged him to not just hurt her now, but to end her. The pleasure of release was gone now, leaving only pain that pulsed through him with the pounding of his blood. Pain that fed the anger and the cruelty that was trying to surface.

Looking confused, Myara pulled on her shirt to cover herself some.

"What's going on?"

He looked at her, trying to stop his eyes from wandering to her tender throat. Trying to stop his fingers from wandering to his dagger. "I'm sorry. I love you."

He made himself kiss her gently, though it made him want to scream with agony. It felt like something was breaking within him. Some last thread of sanity. The last lingering piece of all that had ever been good in him imploding upon itself. Everything that was rising in its place was a culmination of the anger and hatred that had driven him to do so many terrible things.

"I have to go."

He sprinted to Hydra and leapt up, kicking the animal toward the trees in whatever direction he was facing. Anything to get away from the one person he did not want to hurt before he did something he could never undo. He heard her call after him once before he vanished in the trees.

He did not go far. It was not about going far away, just far enough to stop and breathe and let the pain of loving her ease. He dismounted and punched a tree, grimacing with the hurt of skin splitting against the hard bark. He wanted to hurt someone. Needed to. Someone who deserved it. They all deserved it. The need was like lighting under his skin, crackling and thrashing about in search of release. It was frantic. He hated everything. Every leaf, every blade of grass, every...

A twig snapped and he turned.

Kip and Lanz were walking through the trees toward him, grinning like dogs who had found a savory bone to chew on.

"That was so sweet," Kip taunted. "You two making love under the tree."

"Oh, yes. I think I let a load off twice just watching it," Lanz added.

Kip laughed. "I was hoping we could have a turn

now that you're done. I think she's still back there crying under the tree."

The need to hurt someone was no longer manic.
It was crisp and clear and focused. Dephithus smiled,
letting them get a little closer, then he lunged at Kip,
the serpent dagger in hand, and buried it in the other
youth's throat before he slammed into him with the full
force of his weight. They both hit the ground, but Kip
did not move. He stared up wide-eyed at the canopy of
the trees. For a few seconds, the only sounds were the
chirps of birds and the crackling of underbrush coming from Hydra and from another direction where some
animal crept through the trees. Dephithus grabbed the
dagger and stood up.

Lanz looked down at Kip, the color draining from
his face, then he turned and began to run. Dephithus
ran after him, his dragonkin strength and speed letting him close the distance quickly. When he was close
enough, he leapt, bringing his knee up so that it jammed
into the other youth's spine when they slammed to the
ground together. Something cracked beneath his knee
and Lanz let out a hideous cry, muffled by the dirt he
had landed face down in. Lanz did not struggle, perhaps he could not. Dephithus took the serpent dagger
and shoved it in through the back of the neck until the
crossguard hit flesh.

He drew his dagger and stood. When he turned,
he saw a jorycat, one with three tails and strange spikes
that looked like claws growing out of its front legs like
thorns on a rose bush, already tearing at the flesh of
Kip's lacerated throat. He growled and sprinted away
into the trees.

**D**ephithus did not return home that night. He slept in the woods, curled beneath some trees. He was not sure where he had left Hydra. He could not think clearly enough to remember. What he had done with Myara beneath the trees was a blur of pain and pleasure. Somehow, she had hurt him. He could not figure out how or why. He could not focus past the hatred burning under his skin. He needed to make it better somehow. Needed to hurt someone again.

It was her Dawning Day today and he knew he was supposed to be there. He did not go. He lurked in the shadows of the forest, pacing and waiting. The dancing would start mid-afternoon and taper off around dusk. When evening neared, and he was certain the dancing was well underway, Dephithus returned to the palace.

The palace ballroom was full of cheerful laughter and dancing. All that joviality turned his stomach. Staying close against a pillar in the entry he peered out among the dancers, searching for the guest of honor. Spotting Myara, he watched as she danced. The young soldier who had hugged her so firmly the other night was dancing with her, smiling down into her eyes. She was smiling back at him, though now and then her gaze would sweep the room and her smile would falter. Dephithus could see those warm golden eyes as clearly as if he were the one holding her so gently. She swayed like rye grass in a soft wind, her dark-golden hair waving down her back thick and sweet as honey. There was pain in his groin and chest, and his throat constricted as though her slender hands were squeezing it.

"You!" Avaline's soft snarl surprised him. "You destroyed her by not being here earlier. How dare you show up now?"

Dephithus sneered at his mother, keeping his voice equally low when he spoke. "She doesn't appear so upset right now."

"Myara has appearances to keep up, and she cares enough about the people around her to do so."

*Unlike me.* Dephithus regarded his mother, her unspoken words resounding in his head, feeding the anger. Despite her the fury in her tone, she looked very unstable. The slightest push might drop her into a crumpled, weeping mass on the floor.

"Get out," she hissed.

Out of the corner of his eye, Dephithus saw Mythan approaching, managing a polite smile and quick excuse for anyone who tried to detain him. The cold look in his den-father's eyes warned Dephithus that it was time to leave. Touching his mother's cheek with gentle fingertips he smiled false sweetness upon her. "Anything for you, Mother."

Dephithus departed swiftly, looking back once to see that Mythan had arrived just in time to catch Avaline as she began her transformation into that crumpled, weeping mass he had expected. Outside he walked rather casually down to the lower garden and waited. Eventually, much of the gathering would move outside to enjoy the perfect atmosphere of a mild night in the well-lit gardens. Here he might just have another opportunity to ease his own pain.

As the last rays of sun faded away over the horizon

and the air began to cool, revelers started drifting out into the gardens as expected. Uninvited guests drifted up from below the palace as well. Among them Dephithus found his new companions, minus two of the usual members. Darkin hailed him as they wandered up to where he was sitting. Dephithus nodded in response and gestured to the unoccupied space around him. As they picked seats, Suva greeted him with a more than friendly kiss that Dephithus returned willingly. Darkin looked undisturbed by the gesture.

"Where are Kip and Lanz?" He asked, his nerves dancing with some strange blend of apprehension and anticipation.

Darkin shrugged. "Haven't seen them since yesterday. They do their own thing sometimes."

Dephithus almost laughed with the giddy burn of his hidden guilt.

As Suva moved to take a seat, Darkin leaned towards Dephithus. "Looks like someone is moving in on your territory."

Myara had entered the garden and was standing among some others just a short distance away. The young soldier she had been dancing with noticed her and smiled as he began to work his way in her direction. Myara smiled and nodded back, blushing lightly. Dephithus's tenuous control snapped, and he relented completely to the dark anger that infected him. Eager to be unleashed, red rage swept through him, giving full rein to the dark influence driving him to hurt and to punish another. She was his. They had consummated their love only yesterday amidst much suffering. No one was going to move in on that raw ground.

He was much closer to Myara than the other soldier and it only took a few long swift strides to put him next to her. With the momentum of one last long stride, he backhanded her across the cheek. The force of the blow and the surprise of it knocked Myara off her feet into one of the hedges.

"Whore," he accused as she stared up at him, her eyes brimming over with tears, her hand touching her bruised face in disbelief.

For a second, he stared down at her.

*I love her.* The thought made his head hurt with such agony that he grabbed it for fear it might explode. He had to banish that thought. Had to chase it away to the dark, tormented depths of his mind. He surrendered whatever was left of him to the daemon-seed within.

A roar of anger alerted Dephithus as the young soldier who had been dancing with Myara came to her defense. Dephithus swung around and twisted to the side in time to dodge the soldier's lunge. Turning fast, he dove into the back of the young man who was already off-balanced by his failed charge. The soldier toppled over, landing hard on his side, and rolled onto his back. Dephithus pinned him there, little more than an animal now in his fury, and drew the serpent dagger. With one slash he split the soldier's face from ear to nose.

In an instant the nature of the struggle had changed as the soldier, no longer concerned with Myara, fought desperately to free himself. He tried to grab Dephithus by the arm only to have his palm slashed open. Dephithus slashed madly, lost completely in blind rage. Several other soldiers came to their comrade's aid, straining to pull him off. When they finally wrenched him away, Dephithus was covered in blood and his victim had stopped moving. Myara, still backed against the hedge, reached a shaking hand toward the fallen soldier. Dephithus lunged against his captors and Myara pulled back with a cry of alarm.

"Arrest him!"

The hands holding him tightened in response to Mythan's order. With a surge of panicked energy, he thrashed wildly, breaking free, and bolted. He could hear the soldiers he had escaped shouting for help and giving chase as he leapt over several benches and decorative plants, shoving anyone who blocked his path roughly aside. Many of the soldiers coming up from duty or practice to partake of the festivities had tethered their horses outside the gardens. Dephithus wasted no time being picky. He grabbed the reins of the first mount and leapt up, kicking the animal to a full run. There were towers in the palace for relaying messages to the gate guards, but not all of those were staffed these days, so Mythan had no way to pass word to stop him from escaping the palace grounds.

When he neared the first gate he slowed his mount enough for the guard to recognize him. He began to feel a hint of apprehension as he neared, then the gates swung slowly open. Once the gates were opened enough for his mount to fit, Dephithus kicked the animal faster again and bolted through. The second gate was usually kept open from sunrise to sunset, staying open later during celebrations. They had only started closing it when Dephithus passed through. One of the startled guards called after him in anger at his speed, but he was busy making good his escape.

In the city, he slowed his mount to a trot and wound his way through the streets in a senseless spectrum of twists and turns to keep the route unpredictable. The people of the city had gone mostly indoors except for the odd individual traveling to or from a tavern or inn. Outside of one inn, Dephithus waited for the street to be empty then he traded his winded, lathered mount for another one tethered at the hitching post. With a fresh mount, he headed out of the main part of the city toward the surrounding farmland. He had a destination in mind and once he was near, he discarded this mount as well, sending it off in the direction of the city with a firm smack on the hindquarters.

Dephithus stood in the roadway for a moment amidst the stand of trees that spread out for some distance in every direction from the point he had chosen. It was nearing full dark and he hoped Darkin would choose to travel home that night. He usually did with the logic that being home to do a few chores in the mornings kept him supplied with a warm bed and a ready meal when he needed either. Dephithus peered down the dark road for a moment then climbed up into a tree that hung over the way and waited.

While he sat there, he tried to wipe the blood on his hands off on the tree bark. Myara's fear and her tears plagued him. Hate still burned in him, so strong now that he could hardly think past it. Somewhere beneath that was the guilt and the self-loathing. Somewhere deeper still, he wanted to die. He deserved to die for the things he had done. Of course, Myara had found someone else. He was ruined, and she knew it. They all knew it. He knew it. She had made love to him out of pity. He was sure of it now. The daemon-seed blazed in him. It had taken on a life of its own and it was stronger than he was. It seared his blood and jumbled his thoughts. He needed to leave this place. To take himself far away from here.

He turned his head, feeling a call in that direction, something beckoning him. He should go. And yet…

*I love her.*

Myara face, tears streaming down her cheeks, filled his mind. He punched the trunk of the tree, the already torn skin on his knuckles tearing more with the force.

*She was supposed to be mine. For a brief moment, she was mine.*

The moon was up full and bright enough that Darkin did not need to hold a lantern over his mount as he came down the roadway. His mount was a worn old farm beast that was probably the best his family had to offer to get him to and from Elysium palace grounds each day. When Darkin was almost under him Dephithus dropped from the tree in their path. The tired animal tossed its head and stopped walking but was otherwise undisturbed by the new arrival. If anything, the horse seemed grateful for a chance to stop. Darkin, on the other hand, looked less than happy to see him.

"What are you doing here?" Darkin hissed under his breath as if he feared someone else might be listening.

"If there were any soldiers nearby we would already know." Dephithus stepped up beside the horse, placing a hand on the animal's neck near the rein so he could grab it if his quarry tried to escape. "I find myself in need of a place to stay."

Darkin scowled and started to shake his head.

The moonlight was bright enough that Darkin would be able to see the threat behind the look Dephithus gave him then. He touched a hand to the serpent dagger for added effect.

Darkin had seen what he did to the soldier and, after a moment's hesitation, seemed to decide against pushing his luck. Not for the moment anyway. "You can sleep in the hay loft, but in the morning, you will leave when I tell you to and not return until I say."

Dephithus nodded. "Fair enough."

Darkin's displeasure was plain in his moonlit glower. "Not really. If they find you, my whole family will be held accountable."

Dephithus shrugged, revenge was sweet. "Did he die?"

"The soldier you attacked?"

Dephithus responded with a sour look. "Who else?"

"Eventually. They tried to save him, but he had lost too much blood. You certainly ruined Myara's…"

"Enough!"

Darkin fell silent and Dephithus walked along beside his horse without speaking again. Perhaps Darkin realized how little the truth about Larina was worth now, or maybe he simply feared his unpredictable companion. Regardless of which it was, he did not say anything at all after that. When they arrived at his home, Darkin showed Dephithus where he could sleep and gave him some worn blankets to use for his bed. There was mistrust in his eyes that Dephithus could see, but Darkin was not one to hide such things. No words were necessary. Both of them knew where they stood with the other. Darkin could turn Dephithus in tomorrow if he wished and Dephithus could turn his wrath on Darkin and his family at any moment tonight. For now, they would both keep their peace.

"Sleep well and think what you will do come tomorrow," Darkin sounded uncharacteristically weary when he spoke, but there was a determination in his eyes that promised Dephithus this would not be his haven for long.

"Do the same, my enemy."

Darkin's forced smile had a faint edge of sarcasm to it before he left the loft to Dephithus and his torment. By morning, he had sprinted out into the woods outside of Elysium, running from something inside him. The daemon-seed pulled him toward the caves far away. Myara kept him close. Together, the two made him a crazed beast who barely resembled the youth he had been.

\*

Amahna and Rakas decided to travel to Colvan, the Storm Dragon in Whay.

Colvan was one of the eldest of the dragons and his location put them only one dragon away from Imperious. Returning to Imperious for their research would have been foolish knowing that Dephithus would certainly seek his revenge upon them if they dared to go there. When they reached Colvan, Amahna and Rakas stopped at an inn in Whay and coupled passionately. The next morning, he was gone, taking with him nothing more than the clothes he was wearing. After several days Amahna knew she had finally won. He would not be coming back. Somehow the victory was hollow, but at least his absence would allow her to focus her full attention on the task she had been given.

Theruses had not been entirely correct when he said the dragons were no closer to freedom. There was definitely more power in the web of dragons then there had been the last time she tapped into it. Over the past several months it seemed they had somehow pooled together more of the power they had been locked away from. It was nowhere near enough for them to free themselves, but there was no telling how much more they might pull in.

Every day, Amahna sat just out of sight of Colvan and probed gently into the power of the dragons, searching for some indication of what this power they had amassed was going to be used for and how they were accumulating it. Was it through Dephithus as the daenox was? What were they planning to do if not free themselves? It would take a long time to do so at this rate of accumulation, though they had been waiting for ages already. She had to touch the web gently with the daenox and move slowly to keep from having her meddling noticed by the dragons. There was really no way for them to keep her out, yet, they might have some way of hiding their actions from her if they knew she was there.

One morning she sat again behind the same group of bushes and faced the stone dragon in the cemetery. Sighing with the weariness of boredom, she closed her eyes and reached out toward the dragon web on a tendril of daenox. The web was, in her mind, configured much like a spider web of pale green strands. The daenox she used was a deep purple, barely discernible from the blackness around her vision of the web.

Amahna sent her tendril of daenox out toward the center of the web when the whole structure suddenly pulsed a blinding white. The power in the strands began to move rapidly to one point, leaving the thinnest threads of power to hold the web together. Amahna knew where the focal point was immediately. The power was being pooled in Imperious with Vanuthan. Without hesitation, she pulled on more of the daenox within herself and prepared to travel to Imperious. She cursed Rakas now for his absence. It would take at least two full days to make the trip alone.

## CHAPTER TWENTY SIX

Amahna was not at all prepared for the chaos that had befallen Imperious since her last visit. The inner and outer walls were heavily patrolled with foot soldiers pacing between the towers on top of the wall and several mounted soldiers making circuits around the ground level perimeter. She was forced to use much more of the daenox than she had hoped to get from the graveyard out through the walls and around to the front gates of the Elysium palace grounds so she could arrive from the appropriate direction. A tall, dark-skinned man who was broader through the chest than her horse stopped Amahna at the front gate.

"What business?"

Amahna was taken aback by his abruptness, but judging by the other guard's slight cringe it was simply this man's way. "I am here to visit with my sister, Avaline de NuTraven."

"Dismount please."

Amahna did as requested, watching with curious surprise as the large man searched her packs.

When he finished with a satisfied grunt, he faced her, his gaze dropping to her belt. "Do you have any weapons other than that dagger?"

"Certainly not. Might I inquire as to why you are treating me like a common thief?"

The large man scowled and the other guard stepped in to intercede. "Pardon Kota," he offered an apologetic nod to the large man—Kota apparently—as he interrupted. "We mean no disrespect, my lady, but there have been some—" his eyes drifted uneasily to Kota and back to her again, "—incidents. We are just trying to keep everyone safe."

Amahna narrowed her eyes. "What kind of incidents?"

Kota took over again, waving the other soldier back to his post. "The Lady Avaline will tell you what she wants you to know. You will be escorted to the second gate and from there we insist that you head directly to the palace and make no stops until you have arrived."

Amahna mounted up again and passed through the first gate. She made no attempt to question her escort, as the woman looked almost as friendly as Kota. At the second gate the woman hailed the guards and gave them leave to let Amahna pass, reminding her once more that she was not to stop until she reached the palace. Could so much have happened that Imperious was already regressing to the war wary ways of times almost forgotten? She could now feel the strong center of daemon power that was the seed they had planted in Dephithus somewhere outside the city. It had grown considerably. She was tempted to go in search of it, but the suspicion she would face at the gates for turning back so soon was not worth the trouble. They had expected Dephithus to give in to the pull of the daenox and leave Imperious long before now. Something within these walls must have a strong hold over him if he was still so near and she had a feeling she knew what—or rather, who—it was.

At the palace Avaline greeted her with tear-stained cheeks and puffy red eyes.

She hugged Amahna desperately and wept for several minutes before collecting herself again. The damp spot of tears left on her shoulder vaguely annoyed Amahna, but she was much too curious to learn what had happened to waste any energy on it. With Amahna to release her sorrow upon, Avaline proceeded to go over all the terrible events that had occurred with Dephithus, starting with his sickness the day after his birthday. Amahna hung on every enticing detail, knowing when Avaline told her about it that Larina's death was certainly no accident. She knew also that the daemon-dog that killed Vicor was undoubtedly protecting Dephithus because they were kin, in a way. The brutality of the young soldier's murder in the garden only four days past surprised her some. Then again, the seed of daemon power should have driven him mad long before now. She could only assume the dragon power within him had helped him fight it as long as he had.

"There has been no sign of Dephithus since he killed Garen." She choked on a sob and shook her head, brushing away more tears. "I guess our times have taken a dark turn. Poor Myara found a couple of lads torn apart by some animal in the woods the day after Dephithus killed young Garen in front of her. The poor girl is a mess. She has hardly spoken to anyone since."

Amahna waited patiently while Avaline fought down some more sobs, making a few soothing sounds and placing a hand on her shoulder. She had a feeling the bodies in the woods might also have something to do with Dephithus, given his disappearance and the state of things, but she was not going to suggest as much to Avaline. The fact that Dephithus had not fled the area long ago said volumes for the power of his bond with Myara.

Eventually, she calmed and Amahna could speak.

"Can I see Myara?"

Avaline looked puzzled then she shook her head, though the gesture was uncertain. "I don't think Myara will want to be bothered. We have been trying to give her time until she is ready to talk about it."

"Give me a chance. The poor child can't work through this trauma with only her memories for company. I had some hard experiences after I left here. Perhaps I can help." Amahna assumed the most concerned expression she could manage, nodding encouragement while Avaline considered her request.

"Well, I don't see how it could hurt. It is kind of you to want to help, sister."

Amahna was forced to endure another adoring hug before she could go. Squeezing Avaline's hand once to reassure her, Amahna excused herself and followed the directions she was given to the room Myara occupied. A knock on the door brought no response so she opened it enough to put her head in. Myara looked up from where she sat, curled in a blanket in the far corner. Seeing Amahna, she attempted to make her pathetic position a little more dignified by sitting up some. With her face swollen from crying and her clothes disheveled, the effort failed miserably. Amahna felt a bit sorry for the pale, shaky looking creature.

With slow movements, as though approaching a frightened animal, Amahna entered the room and closed the door behind her. Myara appeared a bit confused as she watched her pass by the chairs in the room to sit a few feet away on the floor. When Amahna reached for Myara's hand the girl pulled away so she settled for keeping her hands in her lap.

"I won't pretend to know all that has happened, Myara, but I need your help." Myara pressed back further into the corner. Amahna pressed on, hoping to profit from the young woman's unbalanced state. "Dephithus is very sick. You know that don't you?"

Tears began to spill silently down Myara's cheeks as she nodded. How much did she know? What had happened between them?

"I believe I know where he is and I know someone I think can help him, but he does not know me that well. I don't think he will trust me in his current state, so I need you to come with me to convince him."

Even before Amahna was finished Myara had begun to shake her head frantically and her hands were trembling now. "I can't. I can't see him after—"

Interesting. The girl was afraid of Dephithus now. That made things a little trickier.

"I will be with you," Amahna added a soothing flow of daenox to increase the persuasion in her words. Soothe her. Draw her in. This young woman was going to help her find out what the dragons were doing. "He needs help. I can tell you have loved him."

"I still love him." More tears spilled over with the statement.

"Then you must remember how he was before he became sick."

Finally, Myara wiped away her tears and nodded, and Amahna had to fight back a smile.

*

In the late afternoon they rode out, leaving Elysium behind only after a long delay at the outer gates. They told everyone that Amahna was taking Myara to get a sip of good ale and listen to a bit of lively music to help her feel better. The lie slowed them down several times simply because everyone had recommendations on where to go. The delay at the outer gates involved several such recommendations as well as a dispute over whether they needed an armed escort.

Once free of the outer wall they rode through part of the city and promptly back out toward the forest. Amahna could easily focus in on the daenox in Dephithus now because it was so strong and so completely out of

control. The lesser power of smaller daemons roaming
the area in surprisingly large numbers was only mildly
distracting. Amahna smiled at the amount of daemon
power that had accumulated here, drawn out through
Dephithus.

"What is it?"

Myara's suspicious tone alerted her to how inappropriate her smile was in that moment. "I'm sorry. I know
this doesn't seem like a time for smiling, but I am certain we will succeed. You must be confident."

Myara did not look confident at all and the longer
they rode, the more often she cast glances back in the
direction of Elysium. If this took too long, the young
woman might bolt, but Dephithus was moving and that
made him a bit harder to track. A hint of unease began
to make her mount restless. They had to find him before
Myara turned back and, judging by the young woman's
wide eyes and the death grip she had on the reins, it was
starting to look unlikely. The strong concentration of
daenox was very close now, but she could not quite pin-
point the location clearly. It seemed to be coming from
all around them.

Her nerves started to crackle with unease. The underbrush here was thick and the canopy cast dark shadows on the forest floor. There were many places to hide.
If Dephithus had been driven so far past the brink that
he had attacked and killed a young man in the palace
gardens, he would be a dangerous enemy, especially
given how much reason he had to hate her. Perhaps they
should turn back.

A loud growl made them both start. Dephithus
burst from the bushes, his eyes wild, charging directly
at Amahna. Her mount panicked, twisting sideways
and slamming into Myara's horse. Amahna's horse
went down as the other mount reared up, tossing his
already terrified rider. Amahna was able to roll clear of

her mount and draw her dagger. He was undoubtedly the better fighter when he was thinking clearly. Now was not that time. He had myriad small scrapes and cuts from wandering through the thick underbrush and he was hunched and snarling like some kind of feral animal.

He charged her again and she slashed at him as she leapt agilely out of his path, drawing a line of red across the back of his arm. Dephithus turned on her once more, seeming unaware of his injury, and charged with the serpent dagger bared. The rage in his eyes was colored with the blood he hoped to spill. None of the elegant young man she had met the first time was left in those silver-green cat eyes.

Realizing she was going to need a lot more than a silver tongue to escape with her life, Amahna dodged the second charge and grabbed hold of Myara who had backed up against a tree. A cry of terror escaped the girl when Amahna twisted her arm behind her back and held her between them with the dagger at her throat. Dephithus hesitated, his eyes focusing on Myara for a moment, clarity changing his expression for a second. Anguish flickered across his features, then, with another growl, he locked eyes with Amahna and bared his teeth in a very animal gesture.

Amahna no longer cared about Dephithus. A delighted laugh escaped her lips as she tightened her hold on Myara's arm. There, in the young woman's pulse, was power and more. Myara was pregnant and the dragons had placed their pool of power within that new spark of life along with the power that had passed to it from Dephithus. He must have raped her. Given how mad he was now, it could not have been anything else. No wonder the young woman was such a mess.

Myara was only a few days pregnant, but the unborn child harbored more dragon power in it than Dephithus had. It made perfect sense now. Because of how they were imprisoned, the dragons could pull a limited amount of power to place in Dephithus, much weaker than the concentration of daenox in the daemon-seed. Their link to the outside world through Dephithus allowed them to pull in more power, which they now placed inside another child. His child. This child would be the one to free them, Dephithus had been nothing more than a necessary stepping stone.

Myara's elbow caught Amahna in the ribs and she grunted in pain, almost losing hold of her. Realizing she could not fight them both, she sent a surge of daenox into Myara, using it to drop her into a sudden sleep, and let her fall limp to the ground. Now that Dephithus did not matter, her reluctance to harm him vanished in a surge of blood lust. Enough of the daenox was free now that it would continue to work free even without the daemon-seed in him as an anchor. Dephithus was no use to them or to the dragons anymore, unfortunately for him.

Pulling on the power of the daemon-seed in her opponent, Amahna sapped at his strength, using it to boost her own. Dephithus heaved a deep breath and his grip tightened on the dagger. He looked confused, but it did not stop him from attacking again, but without as much power this time. Amahna dodged him easily and brought her weight around, driving the dagger into his back with the force of all the power she had stolen and sinking it through into his heart.

Dephithus staggered and fell to his knees. He wavered there for a moment, kneeling like a repentant child, then fell forward trying to catch himself on his arms and failing. He landed near Myara. With his face against the cold ground he stared at her sleeping form and tears ran from his eyes. One arm began to reach out for the sleeping girl. Amahna stepped over him and pulled her knife from his back, letting the blood run free and fast from the wound. Dropping that dagger in front of his face, she took the serpent dagger from under his other hand and sheathed it at her belt. His right hand fell still only a few inches away from Myara. Dephithus stopped moving and drew in his last breath.

...and the stone dragon in the graveyard beyond Imperious became flesh.

*

There was natural power in a great many things. Two of the strongest accumulations of this power occurred at the moment of birth, when the first breath of air was drawn in to newborn lungs, and death, when the last breath passed the lips. It was this power that Vanuthan used, the power in her son's death, to free herself from her stone prison. It was a forbidden thing to use these natural powers because they were recycled back into nature and used again, a non-renewable resource. However, breaking the web of dragons was so much worse that the Mother Dragon thought very little of this violation. There was no time for her to deliberate over her actions or seek the council of the others. The natural powers would right themselves before long, taking back the power she had stolen, and she could not be sure what effect that would have on her.

Vanuthan knew exactly where Dephithus was and she flew there fast spreading her massive wings to the sky. The feel of wind under her wings, a sensation so terribly missed, only added to her misery. It was a sensation that nothing else could compare to and one that would soon be lost again. Where Dephithus lay there was no longer any sign of his killer or anyone else. The sight of him made the massive dragon cringe inwardly, her heart twisting in her chest as she sensed the daemon-seed still within him. Her pain at the loss of her human son clouded any good sense that might have sent her back to the web of dragons and she picked Dephithus up gently in her jaws. Rising into the sky again she turned to the north where she hoped to find safety, if the structure still stood.

There was a temple, construction began on it not long before the dragons and the daenox were imprisoned, that had been built utilizing power from the dragon web. It was originally designed as a place of protection for the dragons when it became apparent that religions rallying against them intended to see them destroyed, but the temple had not been completed in time. It was finished later by the Alcatith, a nature-driven religious group who believed the dragons were good, necessary creatures and hoped to find a way to free them someday. Most religious groups had since disbanded after discovering that their powers had been drawn from the power of the dragon web and the daenox which they no longer had sufficient access to after imprisoning both sources.

Uncertain how long she would be in the temple and even if what she planned to try would work, Vanuthan snatched up a few meat beasts from a farmer's herd. With the two beasts dangling in her murderous claws and Dephithus in her mouth, the smell of death was nearly overwhelming. It was Dephithus, his body so lifeless in her jaws and his blood in her mouth, that drove her to fly faster and stronger still. The temple was nearly invisible in amidst the mammoth trees of the old forest, but Vanuthan knew where to look. She dropped the meat beasts in front of the entrance, its structure overgrown with massive vines and moss, and landed.

Laying Dephithus in front of the temple entrance, a massive granite archway designed to allow a dragon to enter, Vanuthan consumed the meat beasts quickly. That done, she lifted him gently again, wishing as she did that he would stir and save her the agony of what she planned. Folding her wings in close she passed through the massive halls of the temple until she reached the large central chamber. A small statue of a dragon served as an altar to one end of an elaborate granite floor. Using the finest craftsmen, the floor had been engraved with an elegant pattern depicting all sixteen of the original dragons of the web. Those sixteen dragons had created the web many ages ago. With the dragons imprisoned as they were, the strands of the web could not be moved in any way, leaving Vanuthan no method for contacting the others after breaking free.

What she hoped to do was restore the natural power that had left Dephithus upon his death. It would take much power to restore that natural power to him and heal his wounds, and that was only the beginning of the challenges she faced. Because she did not have access to that kind of power all at once, it would take considerable time to gather it in. They would have to enter a hibernation state, requiring her to delegate some of her limited power to keeping them alive during the sleep. Lastly, she would have to delegate more power to suppressing the daemon-seed and keeping it that way while she worked. There was no way to be rid of it now. The daemon-seed was part of his body, made as essential as his heart by its design.

Vanuthan laid his still body in the middle of the carving of the web and curled her massive form around him. Careful of her deadly teeth and the power of her size, the Mother Dragon moved his head up to pillow it on her leg. For a moment she lay her head out on her own likeness carved into the floor. Another of the original sixteen dragons had broken from the web. Only one other had done so, before their imprisonment, and that had been the Death dragon, Theruses.

Change was upon the world again, and it would suffer

the daenox until the dragons could be freed to restore the balance. With the child of Dephithus taken by servants of the daenox, that balance might never return.

How long would it take to bring him back? Curving her head in and lying it next to Dephithus, Vanuthan closed her eyes to all the questions she could not answer.

She used her own power and the power in the temple to draw his life out of herself and wrapped it around her mental image of him. In her mind he was a dragon with silver scales and ever-lovely silver-green eyes. It did not matter what she saw him as, the part of herself she had placed in him at his conception connected them and would guide her power. Layering over it with her own powers she forced his life back into him.

Dephithus screamed in mental and physical anguish, and the daemon-seed pulsed in response. Suppressing the daenox with another layer of power and drawing Dephithus into her hibernation state so that his body would not shut down again, Vanuthan started to heal her son.

## CHAPTER TWENTY SEVEN

It took Amahna most of a month to get back to the Dunues Mountains with her captive.

Something had changed.

The dragon web was inaccessible, so they had to make their journey by the speed of horses and her captive insisted on stopping regularly to tend her needs or rest their mounts. Amahna had not been able to even look upon the web using the daenox since the day she killed Dephithus. It made her nervous, not knowing why the web had seemingly vanished from her sight, but she had the unborn dragon-child. She had to believe that was the most important thing.

Myara was not as difficult a travelling companion as Amahna might have expected given her situation. The young woman wept sometimes, curling forward as much as she could on horseback while her body shook with endless sobs, and she was sick many times, which might have been nerves or early morning sickness from the unusual child she carried. A couple of times she tried to run, and she tried to kill Amahna in her sleep three times only to be thwarted by daemons drawn to the daenox in Amahna. The rest of the time it seemed that she receded completely into herself, glaring silently at the world in general and Amahna in particular. Perhaps she had simply gone away to hide away from a world that had dealt her more than she could handle.

Myara had given up asking why she had been taken. Amahna refused to answer. As far as she could tell, Myara did not know she was with child. Knowing she had an unborn child to protect might make her fight harder and give her hope. That would only make things more difficult. The only question she did not hesitate to answer was when Myara asked if Dephithus were dead, which Amahna responded to with a pleased and enthusiastic affirmative.

For a time, she considered killing the young woman and the child, but it occurred to her that Theruses might prefer to do the honors of vanquishing the dragons' last hope himself, so she was patient.

For whatever reason, she often caught herself caressing the hilt of the serpent dagger she had taken back from Dephithus. His silver-green cat-like eyes visited her in her dreams. One dream sequence haunted her over and over in the night, sometimes so vividly that she would wake and be unable to return to sleep anymore. In the sequence she would be standing in the midst of a perfectly black landscape facing Dephithus. She would place her hands on either side of his face and lean forward, closing her eyes and kissing his lips with the softness of a lover. When she leaned back and opened her eyes, she would be holding a clay mask of his face that would crumble to dust in her hands. Then the sequence would end with her standing alone in the darkness next to the pile of dust from the clay mask.

The dream should not torment her so, but there was something in that empty darkness that terrified her. Dephithus was dead. She had killed him with her own hands; she just wished he would stay that way when she fell asleep.

Myara spoke his name in her sleep, which Amahna suspected might be the catalyst of her own relentless dreams. Sometimes the girl would call Dephithus with longing, other times her voice would crack with fear and she would thrash as though trying to escape something. It had taken very few nights of the latter for Amahna to decide that Dephithus must have acted out their cruelty to him upon his beloved Myara. Undoubtedly, this was not what the dragons had in mind for the conception of their savior. It was very likely that his love for Myara, the very thing that kept him from fleeing Imperious, was also what had driven him to succumb so completely to the influence of the daenox. When they fought, it was plain that Dephithus was no longer in control of himself and had given in to the daemon power that thrived off his destruction.

When the mouth of the cave revealed itself before them at the end of their journey, the daenox that hid it responding to her nearness, Amahna dismounted and watched her companion for some reaction. Myara, however, stared straight at the cave while not seeming to see it, as had been the case with most everything her haunted gaze fell upon toward the end of their journey. To see the person you loved turn bad, to watch them slaughter someone you considered a friend before your eyes would be hard enough. To be subsequently raped by that person and kidnapped by his aunt was probably more than anyone could be expected to handle. The whole series of events was delightfully horrible. Getting to confirm that Dephithus was dead was simply a nice bonus to make it worse, but Myara had apparently been too devastated already to have much of a reaction to the news.

Myara dismounted when Amahna told her to and walked up to the cave with her, responding like a creature in a trance. Amahna watched her for several seconds then she let her curiosity tempt her. Would the girl respond to anything at this point?

"We have reached the end of our journey, my dear. Your death waits in these dark passages."

Though her expression did not change, Myara's gaze focused on the blackness that dared them to enter. Apparently unconcerned with the lack of lighting, she started into the cave. Amahna walked in as well, keeping close to the girl and creating the necessary light to traverse this very dangerous section of the cave. Though she manipulated the daenox to make them visible, Myara did not move to go around the first of the deep pits that blocked their path. If Amahna had not taken hold of her arm at the last moment she did not doubt that the girl would have stepped off the edge. Taking firm hold of Myara's arm, Amahna guided her safely past the remaining pits. If she believed the girl would scream dramatically she might have been tempted to let her fall, but she suspected there would not be a sound until she hit the bottom.

"Who is she?"

It took Amahna a moment to place the voice. Never before had she heard such a bitter tone from Kara. The village girl stepped into view, her skin pallid and drawn tight over her bones. She looked nervous and very afraid, and the way she eyed Myara could be described as nothing less than jealous hatred. Theruses had plainly used her and he had not been kind. Now, her illusion of their glamourous world shattered, she appeared to think Amahna had replaced her.

"The girl is a gift for Theruses." As she spoke Amahna twisted Myara's arm for leverage and forced her to sit on the cold stone floor. She did not try to fight it.

Kara stared at Myara for a moment, mouthing Amahna's words several times over. Then she smiled. It was a sickly expression that drew a touch of pity and possessive anger to the surface. Amahna opened her arms and Kara ran into them burying her face against her master's breasts as she began to sob. Theruses would grant her exclusive rights to Kara after he saw what she had brought him. He would not use her pet again.

Amahna stroked Kara's hair and murmured to her. "I am sorry I left you, my sweet one. I would have taken you with me had I been given the choice." Kara continued to weep, and Myara watched them more intently now as Amahna lowered herself and her attendant to sit on the floor. Forcing Kara to arm's length she looked deep into those dark tear-filled eyes. "You know I would have taken you."

Kara nodded and wiped at a fresh tear on her cheek. She glanced around then. "Rakas didn't return? Is he dead?" she asked around a sniffle.

Amahna smiled. There were many reasons to rejoice after this journey. No more Rakas. No more Dephithus. No more threat from the dragons. "He is dead to us, child. Go now. Wait in my chamber for me. I must take this girl to Theruses."

Kara really looked at Myara this time, giving her a brief once over before gazing directly into those haunted eyes. To Amahna's surprise, Kara leaned forward and touched Myara's cheek with gentle fingertips.

"Be grateful you are already gone," she murmured. "Theruses can do you no harm."

Kara kissed Myara on the forehead then turned back to Amahna and kissed her softly on the lips before departing.

Amahna watched her go, then she looked at Myara again and wondered if Kara was right. Was the girl too far gone for Theruses to harm?

Taking hold of the girl's arm, she stood and led her deeper into the cave. They did not get far before a new, far more powerful presence joined them. Theruses appeared before them, his tail swishing methodically, revealing nothing of his present temper to help her navigate their reunion. Myara stiffened slightly when he reached out to her with his sharp-clawed fingertips. He touched Myara's slender neck then pulled abruptly back, his gaze sinking to her abdomen.

"She is with child," Amahna confirmed.

"Another dragon-child?"

"Yes," Amahna replied, eager to show off her success. "This child will be much stronger. It carries the power passed down from Dephithus as well as that placed in it by the dragons upon its conception. This is the child the dragons have been waiting for. I brought the mother here so that you might be the one to destroy the dragons' hopes and kill the child."

Somewhere during the brief exchange Myara had rejoined them. Her hands went to her abdomen, covering it protectively. Her gaze riveted upon Theruses with open fear.

"I'm pregnant." Disbelief was plain in her face. At Amahna's brusque nod, she leaned back from them and lifted her chin in a puzzling display of defiance. "Then you did not kill Dephithus. He lives on in me."

Amahna snarled and stepped closer to Myara, her hand dropping to the serpent dagger. "That can be corrected."

Theruses grabbed her arm, his claws digging into her flesh. "This child will not die today. I want it born here, in the caves."

"No, not here." Myara's protest drew his attention back to her and she shrunk away from his cruel black eyes.

Theruses lifted her from the floor with the daenox so that he would not have to inconvenience himself with looking down at her and, without a doubt, to try and intimidate her into behaving. His molten black eyes bored into hers. "You belong to me now, as does your unborn child."

Myara trembled, though defiance remained in the stubborn set of her jaw.

Amahna yearned to demand an explanation, but it was not her place to demand. Instead, she sank to her knees, trying to keep her confusion and irritation hidden behind a show of reverence.

What reason could he have for wanting the child alive? There was no sensible motive she could think of for letting the child be born and risking the chance of the dragons going free. No matter what it took, she meant to find out why he would make such a choice. There was something more going on.

## CHAPTER TWENTY EIGHT

Cries of anguish echoed through the passages. Between the cries, the loudest sound was that of water dripping inexorably—eternally—forming new cave with its perpetual movement. In the chamber, there was ragged breathing and murmured words of encouragement from Kara, who had helped bring a child into the world before. Kara brushed Myara's hair back from her forehead. She let the young woman grip her hand so tight Amahna knew it had to hurt, but she did not pull away. The world felt strange as though time outside this chamber had stopped. Dread filled Amahna, squirming through her gut and lifting the hairs on the back of her neck. Beside her, Theruses stood perfectly still, a statue, watching the struggle to bring forth new life.

Myara cried out again, tears leaking from eyes squeezed shut against the pain. Or perhaps she closed her eyes so she would not see the dark, damp chamber that was her prison. It would be her child's prison as well. Were the tears from physical pain or from the suffering the child would be brought into. Would Theruses kill the child? End the hope of the dragons the moment it drew breath? Or would he wait a while and observe the curious creature the dragons had made with their meddling.

When the creature finally came, there was much blood and other fluid that came with it. The cave itself trembled then was still. The infant drew in a breath and Amahna braced for the squalling. It was quiet though, as Kara cut the cord and cleaned the child. Then she handed the baby to Myara.

"It's a girl."

Myara took the child in shaking arms and gazed down at her. "A girl," she murmured. She held the tiny human close to her chest. "I will call you Raine for the tears that fell the day you were created and the water that falls here where you were born. One day, you will be free of this place and the world will learn to love you. Until then, know that I love you and that you were conceived in love."

Theruses remained statue still and Amahna stepped back into the shadows, shocked by Myara's words. Could it be that Dephithus had not raped the young woman? It was hard to believe, but there was something sincere in Myara's voice when she spoke those words.

Disconcerted, Amahna strode swiftly from the room. The child's silence followed her through the cave.

*

The child had come earlier than expected.

Theruses sent Amahna away a few months after Myara's daughter was born. Kara was put in charge of seeing to the essential needs of mother and child, and Amahna was given a more dignified task, for which she was grateful. In the months that had passed since her return to the caves, the daenox had begun to make its presence known more throughout the land. Daemons were wreaking havoc in many villages and towns and driving terror into the hearts of those who lived outside of the cities. Now rumors had come to the cave of some young upstart who was building an army of daemons.

Theruses did not seemed concerned. In fact, he appeared to have interest in little other than the abomination recently born in their midst, but he sent Amahna to investigate as much to get a break from her constant questions about the child, she suspected, as anything. When given her choice of companions for her journey, she opted to go alone. They had already come to an agreement about her exclusive rights to Kara, so the girl would be safe enough tending to Myara and the child without her. Since she had never traveled from the caves with anyone other than Rakas, she saw no reason to change that now.

It was disappointing, once she emerged from the caves, to discover how many rumors and bits of gossip never reached them. Upon passing through the vast city of Vorticade, she was delighted by the tidbits of "news" she picked up. Imperious had recently held a loss celebration for Myara and herself, not even a full year after their disappearance. Amahna was almost hysterical with the thought that she was "lost" and wondered giddily where she might find herself. Oddly, no one had discovered the body of Dephithus and he was now wanted for their disappearances as well as for the murder of a young soldier. Perhaps scavengers or roving daemons had consumed his body. Regardless, he was a convenient scapegoat for her crimes. With no word of any of them reaching Imperious, Dephithus was the obvious malefactor.

The lords and ladies of Vorticade overflowed with exciting gossip coming from the Elysium palace. The Lady Avaline had gotten herself reinstated into the Imperious Legion and was out fighting daemon bands with the other soldiers. Mythan, with Dephithus a wanted man and his wife gone away to battle, had announced that he would step down and pass the throne to his brother's oldest son, Allondis. Allondis was not a favored choice.

Many whispered that he was cowardly and weak and that such traits, under the pressure of kingship, would turn him bitter and cruel. Mythan's more charismatic nephew, Favrin, was too young to be offered the kingship that Mythan was now so eager to escape. It seemed that all the populace could say in response to the situation was that it was a shame Dephithus had turned bad.

Imperious troops went out several times a month to fight the ever-increasing population of daemons that were ravaging the lands. Vorticade sent troops of its own out to help the Legion soldiers, but the smaller lordships hoarded what fighters they had to protect their own lands. With the lack of organization and the unpredictability of the daemons, there was no way to face them down in adequate numbers. Small troops were forced to run scattered all around the land and this disordered warfare was taking its toll on the ranks.

All of this was delightful news for Amahna. As she headed northeast, toward where the rumors of the daemon army stemmed from, she was thrilled to see the chaos that the daenox was causing all around her. Over the land she saw more changes then just the presence of the daemons. Religious orders, disbanded when the dragons and daenox were imprisoned, were reappearing everywhere. People needed hope, and the gods that had been long ago abandoned were being looked to again for protection and salvation. Prophets and priests came out of nowhere, using daemon power with careless abandon to amaze their followers.

Another less substantial part of history had been reborn amidst the chaos of these times. The hired heroes were returning. Amahna had already run across three of these wandering hunters. They were all energetic and brave and two of the three were barely old enough to marry. It was impressive how quickly the young could enterprise upon their times while the old struggled to adapt.

As she moved into the high desert areas southeast of Dalynay, talk of daenox priests and the daemon army became almost common. Despite her previous misgivings, it was beginning to seem that finding just one man among thousands might not be so hard. In the village of Scamper, several miles southeast of Dalynay, she found what she was looking for.

The oddly pastel colors of the high desert were peaceful in the same way the calm before a storm was peaceful. When she rode into the town that rose like a weary beacon from the flats she was almost overwhelmed with the eerie sensation of waiting that had come with venturing out into this rough, dry region. Waiting for what, she was not sure. Something dangerous yet subtle rested near here. It was like being drawn in by someone's eyes and finding yourself at their mercy before even saying hello.

Amahna stopped at the first inn and instantly she could sense the daenox nearby. Not a strong presence, but someone within those walls was using it for something. With confidence boosted by the always-ready power of the daenox within her, she walked into the nameless inn. Perhaps the plaque of wood over the door had boasted some title once, but it was long faded.

The door creaked conspicuously as she stepped through, so she moved inside brusquely to avoid seeming timid. At the feet of a young woman seated in the corner lay a daemon-dog, resting peacefully as any normal canine companion. The woman had been lazily using daenox to spin her dagger in the air over the table. It was a sign of her inexperience that she reached up and plucked the dagger from the air rather than sending it down to her hand. The daemon-dog lifted its head, gray eyes alert, and regarded Amahna with interest. Other than this odd pair, there was no one in the common room except the innkeeper and two ragtag serving girls. The innkeeper regarded Amahna from behind the bar with less interest than the daemon-dog had shown.

Drawing on a touch of daenox, Amahna focused her intent at the daemon-dog. The massive animal rose abruptly and paced over to her, lying down again with his head at her feet. The woman he had abandoned, a lean creature with dusty blond hair cut short enough to give her a masculine edge, scowled and narrowed her eyes. Dropping her feet off the table she sat up and leaned a touch forward as though she might stand, though she stopped and held her position at the ready.

"What do you want?"

Amahna regarded the woman with cold calm. "I am searching for the man who claims to be raising an army for the daenox."

"He does not just claim it," she snapped. "And what makes you think I know him?" Amahna said nothing and the woman realized after a moment that she had already professed to more knowledge than she wanted to give. Her eyes darted around the room like a cornered animal and she jumped to her feet, approaching Amahna with wary steps, as though expecting an attack any second. "What do you want with him?"

"I only want to see."

"That's all?"

"Yes. Shall we go?" Amahna led the woman, whose name she had no interest in, out to where her horse was tethered. The daemon-dog followed devotedly along after Amahna. It was all too easy to influence low-level daemons, though the control would be lost if anything managed to distract the creature thoroughly enough.

The woman led Amahna out the other end of the small town under the sedately curious eyes of the few people along the roadway being bathed in the dust of their passage. Once past the edge of town, Amahna discovered that she needed no more guidance. She sensed daenox in large concentration not far away and to the northeast of where they were. Confirming the direction, the daemon-dog veered off that way, Amahna's influence vanishing before the power of this greater presence.

Amahna followed the daemon-dog, leaving the woman to do as she wished.

The other woman turned her mount with them, scowling. "I can take you to the temple."

Amahna's lip lifted in a silent snarl as she kicked her mount faster to keep up with the daemon-dog who was now loping away from them. "He's not in the temple, and I will not go there to wait for him."

With an angry glower set on her face the other woman focused on spurring her horse viciously to pass Amahna. If she hoped to beat Amahna to their destination it was not to be. She kept her mount up beside the other horse. Someone very skilled was using a great deal of daemon power for something. She needed to know what.

When she spotted the one rider in the distance, seated atop his bay gelding as still as a statue, she knew this was the man she was seeking. He did not turn his attention towards them until they were stopping beside him.

"Kyouin, I could not stop her."

The man, Kyouin, glanced at them, his gaze drifting over the other woman with insulting disregard before settling on Amahna. He offered an unexpected and friendly smile.

Amahna tried not to gape. He looked so young. She would be surprised if he was even sixteen yet. Younger than Dephithus had been when she killed him. Kyouin was not overly handsome, but his face was smooth and soft, almost more pretty than anything. His eyes were blue like a warm summer sky under a head of dusty blond hair that was just enough out of place to hint at distraction. He wore a dusty gray cloak and clothes the color of the surrounding desert and his almost childish smile was disarming.

"Are you an admirer or a critic of my army, my lady?"

Amahna said nothing, noting the proud way he scanned the surrounding valley. Looking around she pulled on more daenox and saw through his illusion. On both sides of the area in front of them, masked by the illusion he had created, were perhaps forty or more waiting predator daemons of varying sizes and perhaps three times that many foot soldiers. They were plainly prepared to ambush someone.

Amahna looked at Kyouin again. Could this boy really be the priest raising an army?

She focused on him for a moment, using daenox to know him on a different level. The amount of daemon power coursing through him was all the answer she needed.

"I am neither. I have only come to learn what I can about you."

Kyouin raised an eyebrow in question, his smile devoid of concern. "For whom?"

"Someone you had best not make an enemy of. Who are you setting this trap for?"

Kyouin said nothing. Still smiling, he turned his attention forward. Amahna did the same and was surprised to see an approaching troop that appeared out of a cloud of dust still some distance away from the ambush. They were Imperious Legion by their uniforms, and they were arranging into a defensive formation as they approached, perhaps sensing something in the air. Kyouin appeared undisturbed by their preparation.

As the riders moved into the area of attack Amahna recognized one of the lead soldiers. Avaline, her face set in grim determination, was flanking the leading officer. For the briefest of moments, she was tempted to call out a warning. Then the urge passed, and she moved her mount closer to Kyouin to get a better view.

A soldier toward the back of the troop appeared to be breaking down under the stress, the anticipation in the air undoing his resolve. He let out a strangled cry and spun his horse, spurring it to a gallop. Some of the other soldiers around him stopped their mounts and lost their formation in the sudden confusion. The bolting soldier did not get far. Within only a few full strides a twisted daemon burst from the earth under the horse's chest, throwing both mount and rider over sideways. The horse surged back to its feet, but one leg dangled uselessly as it struggled to get away. The soldier lay still, crushed by the weight of his mount.

The rest of Kyouin's mixed army attacked while the Legion troops were watching this horror unfold in their ranks. With the illusion dropped, Amahna saw Avaline focus in on them. Narrowing her eyes, the High Lady of Imperious drew her sword and charged. The action caused a massive change in the forward portion of the Legion troop. The front Legion soldiers turned and followed Avaline, creating a wall of fighters to either side of her as she charged the small daemon army. The daemons and their allied soldiers attacked this stream of warriors, trying to break the line around Avaline. More Legion soldiers moved into position alongside her the instant one fell.

Avaline did not slow her charge and Amahna began to clutch her reins tighter, ready to spin her mount and bolt. She did not know if Avaline would target her, but with only a few yards left to find out Amahna and the woman from the inn began to back their mounts behind Kyouin. Before she got there, the woman from the inn was taken down with a crossbow bolt in her forehead. Amahna backed her mount further as a daemon-cat took down the last soldier close to Avaline. Kyouin still did not move and his lips curved into an eager smile.

Avaline brought her sword around in an arc as she closed the space between them. Her blade was well aimed, but her swing was broken by a daemon-dog that lunged into her mount from underneath the priest's horse. Even Amahna had not known the beast was there. As Avaline's horse started to fall underneath her, taking her alongside Kyouin, he caught hold of her sword arm, lifting her from the saddle. Using the momentum of her mount's final forward lunge to his advantage, Kyouin brought her up in front of him and slammed her upper spine down on the horn of his saddle then shoved her back off to the ground. He was stronger than he looked. Perhaps he used daenox to add to his power.

Avaline landed hard, tumbling a short distance before coming to rest on her back. Amahna moved in closer, spotting the blood welling up between her sister's lips as Avaline stared dazed at the man who had downed her. Kyouin was no longer smiling. With a pitying shake of his head he turned his mount and left her there. Amahna could see terror in her sister's eyes when she opened her mouth to speak, but she simply choked on the blood. Avaline closed her eyes then, not once looking at Amahna.

Amahna, not sure what to do or if she should do anything at all, stared down at her sister. Avaline choked a few more times and then was still. Kyouin seemed to have forgotten her. The massacre that had taken down the Legion troop—for that was all it could be called—was over quickly, and he was done for now.

Amahna did not want to face him again. This daenox priest was a foolish young upstart, who, though plainly skilled with the daemon power, would probably get himself killed out of arrogance before long. Theruses would be happy enough with that. There was no need to follow him.

The daemons, most of which were already feeding off their kills, did not disturb Amahna. Nor did the daenox-allied soldiers linger to loot the bodies. She suspected they did not want to fight the daemons for access to the spoils. Some of the soldiers glanced her way as they followed after Kyouin, but they let the daemons judge and left her alone. With one more puzzled frown down at Avaline, Amahna turned back toward home.

## CHAPTER TWENTY NINE

When the healing had progressed far enough, Vanuthan pulled them both out of the timeless hibernation and allowed Dephithus to return to a more natural sleep while he finished recovering. He partially woke several times after that but remained in a state of semiconscious delirium while his mind and body tried to cope with the reversal of his death and the suppression of the daemon-seed. High fevers sapped his limited strength as the daemon-seed fought her efforts to put it into a permanent remission.

For Dephithus, there was little to remember of this time. The only thoughts that stuck with him were disjointed memories of how terribly he had treated Myara. How he had violated her trust and the love he had for her. Often, he lay curled into a fetal position and shivered, moaning with mental and physical agony while tears burned at his tightly closed eyes. At these times some massive presence would wrap its length around him, the warmth bringing with it a brief period of peace and he would slip into a calmer sleep again.

Dephithus had met death with little grace and he came into his new life with even less. After several weeks of fevers and delirium he finally woke to a strange place and an even stranger companion. The beast looked ever so much like the stone dragon in the graveyard, only flesh. Her massive form was covered in burnished red scaling and two spiraled horns swept back from the top of her head above her strangely delicate, pointed ears. There was little doubt that her long slender jaw housed the sharp teeth of a killing beast. Her clawed feet ended in large bird-like talons that he had no desire to dally near and her muscular build and large wings warned of her efficiency as a predator.

Dephithus rose quietly so as not to wake her and started to back away on shaky legs.

His confusion and weakness made him clumsy, and he fell over her long tail, landing hard on his backside. He was stunned for a moment by a sharp pain through his back and chest. When he recovered from that shock, he discovered that the dragon had raised its head and was now regarding him with shimmering reddish eyes. Reaching for the serpent dagger, he was surprised to find himself unarmed. A faint ache remained in his back and, remembering his very last moment with a start, he looked down at the dark red stains on his clothes.

"I am Vanuthan, the Mother Dragon. You did not fear me in the graveyard. You need not fear me now. You know I did not cause you this pain you feel."

Her deep voice was comforting somehow, but he resisted the unnatural urge to trust her.

"You were stone then," he replied as he was struck again with a memory of weakness, of Amahna dodging his clumsy lunge. After that came pain. He remembered so much pain. How could that have been real? Never had he fought so poorly. He remembered also a blood-soaked dagger being dropped in front of his face. He had been reaching out for something. What had he been reaching for? "This seems more nightmare than reality."

The dragon waited in patient silence as he pulled off his shirt and studied the scar of the tiny exit wound. Reaching around his back his fingers felt the much larger scar where the dagger had entered. There was a certain detachment to his exploration, as though he studied someone else's wounds.

"You were not quite yourself when you fought her," the dragon reassured.

"How could I have survived such a wound?"

Vanuthan regarded him for a long moment with her reddish eyes. Regardless of her apparent lack of aggression toward him, he could not help feeling uncomfortable under her scrutiny. At least she remained lying so that her great size was a little less intimidating. Her expression appeared somewhat sorrowful, though he could not be sure given his distinct lack of experience with dragons.

"You did not survive, Dephithus. I restored your life to you."

He opened his mouth to dispute the possibility of such a thing when more of his memory returned.

*Myara.*

He had been reaching for Myara where she lay, knocked unconscious by Amahna. Memories of all the horrid things he had done washed back through him like a storm driven wave. It was his betrayal of Myara's love that caused him to cry out with the agony of the truth. He had been so angry. He had hated everyone, even her, even while he loved her. He had been mad with rage and it had hurt so much to fight it. Wrapping his arms around his legs, Dephithus bowed his head to his knees and rocked himself in a vain effort to ease the mental anguish. The dragon made a distressed sound, but he ignored her trying to make sense of the things he had done.

"I can do nothing for this pain. I am sorry." The dragon was silent for a few minutes, allowing him some time to struggle with his conscience, but she did not let him dwell for long. "Dephithus, there are things you must know."

"Leave me, beast!"

Vanuthan growled as she rose, looming over him.

He glared up at her with a bitter sneer. "I can growl too. You don't impress me."

The dragon lowered her head so that her face was in front of his, baring tapered teeth that were as big as his forearm. "You cannot back it up against me. There is no time for self-pity if you are to save your child."

Dephithus had a rebuttal ready, but it disintegrated with her words. Almost as if it had happened only a moment ago, he could picture Myara beneath him. Her eyes full of love. Love that had given him the strength to fight the daemon-seed long enough to be with her.

Terrified of the answer yet needing to know for certain he forced himself to ask. "What child?"

"Amahna took your life. Then she took Myara and your unborn child. You must go after her. You must save the child. But there are things you need to know before you leave this temple."

The misery of his awakening had left Dephithus feeling drained, but this new information rejuvenated him. He was a father. His last act of love before he gave into the madness had created a life. One that he was responsible for. Myara and that child were in danger and there was nothing in the world that was going to keep him from the woman he loved and the life they had created. Despite all the wrong he had done, he had a family waiting for him. He had people to rescue and protect.

The dragon nodded as if satisfied by something in his expression and laid back down on the carved floor before speaking again.

"Do you know what the daenox is?"

He nodded, remembering with a confusing twinge of regret the archive key he had stolen and the daemon cat. "I read about it some in the archives."

Vanuthan nodded again. "Back in our days, when both the dragons and the daenox were free, it was the role of the dragons to maintain the balance of nature and keep the daenox from becoming too powerful. Our power was ours alone, though some people were able to tap into it and use it. The daenox could be channeled and used by all humankind if they chose to learn how. Numerous religions developed around worshipping the daenox. But the power of the daenox drove many mad and led to the committing of great atrocities that we were unable to prevent. Other religions gained power, following powerful priests who began to speak lies to their congregations, claiming that the dragons and the daenox were all evil and must be cleansed from the world. Amongst their many sects they began to convince people of this at an alarming rate. Certainly, keeping all of the power and the contributions of their many worshippers to themselves had no influence in all of this dogma."

Dephithus smiled faintly at the very human roll of her eyes.

"Those priests eventually combined their power to imprison the daenox in a cave deep in the Dunues Mountains. The dragons they turned to stone statues. They only discovered after those forces were imprisoned that they had never had any real power of their own. All the powers they had been using had been pulled from the raw power of the daenox and the virile power of the dragons. Their followers decided that if dragons and the daenox were evil because of the powers they had, then so must be the priests who had used those powers. Helpless without the power they relied upon, the priests were run from their temples and put to death. And so, we have waited since then, both the dragons and the daenox, all searching for some escape from our prisons."

Vanuthan's uncertain pause indicated that this was where he came into the story. With a nod of understanding, he encouraged her to continue.

Returning the nod solemnly she resumed. "The dragons are connected by a web of power, as is shown in this carving on the floor. The power in that web is limited by our imprisonment. Over many years we gathered together what power we could collect and placed it in you when you were conceived. In the years since your birth, using you as our link to freedom, we gathered even more power and placed it in your child when it was conceived."

"Conceived in evil," Dephithus growled. "Will it... will the daemon-seed have an effect on the child?"

Vanuthan's massive shoulders lifted in a shrug, but her eyes brimmed over with uncertainty and fear.

"The dragonkin? Is this how they were created?"

Vanuthan shook her head. "The Dragonkin came about when a number of the dragons used a power that allows our kind to take on the form of humans. In the night they traveled to different areas and seduced numerous lovers. The children of their brief trysts in this form were the first Dragonkin. From that time on, every twenty years the dragons would do this again and mate with humans to create more Dragonkin and keep the bloodlines strong. When the dragons were turned to stone, the Dragonkin were eventually bred out of society."

This was everything he had wanted to learn in the archives before his fascination with the daemons had drawn him astray and more. There was still more he needed to know, more he was reluctant to bring up.

"Am I to blame for the daenox..." He struggled, trying for the right words and failing.

Vanuthan shook her head, her eyes blazing to life with pent up rage. "We could not protect you. Your aunt, Amahna, and her companion, Rakas, are allied to the daenox. They placed within you a seed of daemon power that you could never have fought. Just as we used you to pull in more power to secure our freedom, they used the seed in you to free the daenox. You were driven to the evils you committed by that seed."

He wanted to feel relieved, but there was no absolution in her words. Whether or not he had been a victim of this daemon-seed, the actions were his own to remember. They were still his fault.

"Is it gone now? The daemon-seed?" Even as he said the words he knew that it was not. There was something deep inside him. A well of black hatred yearning to break free. "Will it affect my child?"

The magnificent dragon before him seemed to droop. Even her burnished scales looked suddenly duller.

"I could not rid you of this daemon-seed. It is part of you now. To rip it free would be to kill you. I did drive it into remission, but I don't know how long that will last. Nor can I tell you if it had any effect on your child. For all my grand appearance, I'm afraid my powers are limited. I cannot leave this place because the power that allowed me to come here is gone now. It is only the enchantment of this temple that keeps me from turning back to stone. This place is my prison now. You must stop Amahna, for she has taken something of great importance. Your child, the future of my kind, is beyond our help so long as it is held by those who ally with the daenox."

"Why didn't you save Myara and the child instead of saving me?"

She lowered her burning gaze to him. "A part of me is in you, Dephithus. You are my son. I should have saved them, but my child was dying. I could think of nothing else."

He wanted to scream at her then. He could not

though. There was something in her demeanor that
made him believe she saw him as her son and something
in him that made him believe she was, in some part, his
mother.

He stared at the floor of the temple, at the dragons
carved there, connected by a web of lines. He had known
from the moment she mentioned the child that life was
not going to be any easier this time around. There was
much he had done that he could not undo. He could only
try to make it right. "How will I find them?"

"You must go to the Dunues Mountains. The cave
system the daenox was driven into is east of a village
called Kithin. You will find the child there. I can offer
no more than that."

Unarmed and barely dressed as he was, the whole
thing sounded rather hopeless. Yet, was there any other
way to redeem himself of his wrongs? A child needed
him. His child. "How long have I been here in this
temple?"

Vanuthan sighed. "I had no way to track the passing of time. I would guess a few years have passed at
least."

His mouth went dry. There were too many powers
at work here that he could not begin to comprehend.
His child already born and being raised as a captive to
his enemies? Setting his jaw, he stood before Vanuthan.
"Is the child even alive?"

"Of that I am certain."

"And Myara?" He steeled himself for the worst possible answer.

"I cannot say. Without the child in her, I have no
connection to her."

It was not a no. "I owe you much it seems. All I can
offer in return is my promise that I will find my child."

Vanuthan nodded, eyes glistening with tears. "That
is all I ask. Be strong, my son."

Already knowing where he would go first, Dephithus bowed to the dragon and left her there. Everything he remembered from his sixteenth birthday on was like something out of a nightmare. As he stepped out into the mixed light of a cloudy day, he wondered what might have changed in the uncertain amount of time he had been gone. Regardless, having already died once, he had experienced more than many twice his age. He had to hope he had learned enough to do what needed to be done.

The dull throb of the closed wound in his back kept time to his steps as he began his journey.

Amahna might not have despised the child as much if Theruses were not so fascinated with her. Within a month of returning to the cave, Amahna became accustomed to finding him in the balcony chamber above the child's prison whenever she went searching for him. He stood up on the balcony and watched the child for hours on end, and sometimes the child would sit below and watch him in return. Perhaps he was watching her grow, which was a distinct possibility.

Not long after the child stopped nursing, which was itself unnaturally fast, they took her away from Myara. Theruses put her into Amahna's full time care, a duty Amahna immediately delegated down to Kara. The girl was given very little attention, though Kara sometimes lingered with her and had taken to calling her Raine, the name Myara had given her, when she brought food and other such necessities to her. Despite the solitude they forced upon her, Raine flourished.

Myara, on the other hand, had not done so well alone, especially after Amahna told her they had killed her daughter. A week later, they found her dead at the bottom of one of many deep pits in the cave. She suspected Theruses may have compelled the young woman since he no longer needed her. Whether she had ended up there through her own efforts or had been assisted by someone did not matter much. It was one less mouth to feed.

Raine grew at a terrifying speed, maturing both physically and mentally much faster than a normal child. According to Theruses, she matured at the speed of a dragon. By two years, at which time she had the appearance and intelligence of a six or seven-year-old child, Raine had taught herself how to create an orb of light using the daenox that surrounded her. From then on, she never had to sit in darkness, though she did so quite often anyway, perhaps because she was used to it. Within a few days of this discovery she began to build upon it and soon could entertain herself for hours with increasingly complex light shows using daenox. The shows became so elaborate that some of the mid-level daemons were often lured in to watch in senseless fascination. Amahna wondered how long it would be before Raine started to figure out the power that was keeping her imprisoned.

Now, at around four and a half years of age Raine was the physical equivalent of a girl of about fourteen or fifteen, and her intellect would convince any skeptics that she was at least that age. Her long hair and piercing catlike eyes were brassy black in color. The scaling that appeared on areas of her arms, legs, and back was also black with a light brassy sheen. The same scaling could be seen at her temples and running down behind her ears when she brushed back her long hair. Her features were delicate and refined, but the strength of the dragons was concealed behind that illusion. What troubled Amahna most deeply was that the whites of her eyes were no darker now than when she was born despite living her life practically inundated in the daemon power.

Amahna sat cross-legged in the dark at the edge of the balcony opening. She had been sitting that way for some considerable time before a light appeared in the chambers below. Raine rose from the few blankets they allowed her to use for a bed and pulled her shabby cloak around her. Standing quietly, she angled her head a bit as if listening for something and peered into the darkness. After a still moment, she turned her gaze up toward the balcony.

"I know you're there, Amahna." Raine's voice, already starting to get fuller and more mature, penetrated the dark like a candy-coated dagger. She smiled then, and it might have seemed sweet if their relationship were different. "You are not alone."

Amahna started, discovering with a quick glance over her shoulder that she was not alone. At some point, Theruses had joined her on the balcony. Pondering their captive had so absorbed her awareness that she had not noticed her lord's approach.

Her lord? In that she bent knee to him she supposed he was her lord, though she now knew that much he had told her was not true.

"She has grown so quickly," Amahna murmured, though she was not sure why she lowered her voice. Raine knew they were talking about her. The gleam in her eyes and that little sideways smirk made that much clear.

Theruses moved up beside her now, his voice also kept low. "And I have told you before, dragons mature very quickly."

"Dragons," Amahna mused in the same soft voice. Raine's orb of light had moved up higher in the chamber, close enough now to create a silhouette of light around each of them. "I think she is more dragon than human."

"Do you think she knows that?" Theruses growled, plainly annoyed with the familiar direction of the conversation.

Amahna could not help her fears. They were greatly underestimating the potential this child possessed. She was sure of that. The bars that kept Raine in her designated prison were reinforced with daenox, but Amahna did not think they would hold her much longer. Eventually, Raine would realize her own power and figure out how to break free.

Another fear tormented her as well. The fear that Theruses would act upon his obvious desire for the child that grew as she did. That would open up a whole new chamber full of possible disasters. Though, there was always the welcome possibility that it would result in the girl's death.

"No, I don't think she knows that, yet. I do think she will figure it out on her own. The daenox is free. We should kill her."

"No!"

Amahna startled at the ferocity of his negation and the child below looked up at them directly now. Staring down into those brassy black eyes, anger welled in Amahna. Anger at knowing that Theruses had been lying to her for so long. She was sure of it now and her anger drove her past her fear of him. "It's because your freedom hinges upon this child. You can't leave this place until she is free, can you?"

Amahna could feel his gaze on her, but his temper remained hidden. Even his tail was still. When she dared a glance his way, he had turned to look at Raine again. Together they watched the child in silence as she sat in the chamber below them and began to work her light shows. For someone who had never seen the world outside, she created a surprising array of color in her lights. Perhaps it was that which lured the twisted daemon forms from other parts of the cave. They seemed to have some sense that drew them to her when she was playing like this and Raine appeared to enjoy their audience. The child was not at all put off by their grotesque appearance.

"You're perceptive," he finally answered. "I should have expected as much from you. You realize the extent of my dilemma then?"

"I realize that you don't want the other dragons free and yet the key to your freedom is the key to their freedom. Perhaps you believed freeing the daenox would convince that power to return the favor?"

There was no response from Theruses. He was unusually tolerant of her anymore. He had allowed her more and more boldness of manner over the last several years, especially around the child.

"Is there not some other way you can escape this prison? Maybe even some way to change the child so her freedom doesn't bring about theirs?"

Theruses nodded in unexpected approval. "These are things I considered. I have tried many works of daemon power upon her from up here. She is oddly resistant to it."

Troubled, Amahna watched the child below them. Raine appeared so very simple at a glance. Elegant and quiet. The child seemed almost peaceful despite having been captive from birth. Then, maybe that was because she had never known anything else.

"Do you think that resistance will weaken?"

"It might," Theruses replied simply.

"But it might not. That is why you have called upon Kyouin." Amahna thought she heard him growl, but the sound was too soft for her to be sure. The young daenox priest had continued to grow in power and reputation despite Amahna's certainty that he would not last. Over the last several years he had increased his army tenfold and kept up his battles, but always with a deliberateness and patience that hinted at some greater plan.

As if mentioning the subject were some sort of summons, Kara entered the balcony chamber with the messenger Theruses had sent to Kyouin. Both Kara and the messenger—who was an alluring sort, but sadly interested only in men—knelt and bowed their heads in respect. Theruses dismissed Kara with a thought and bade the messenger speak as soon as she was gone. Amahna was given a great privilege by being allowed to stay.

"My lord." The messenger's voice trembled, promising unfavorable news and the knowledge that such was likely to bring punishment. He licked his lips and began again. "My Lord, the High Priest Kyouin has refused your request. He insists that any meeting between you must be held outside of your lair."

Now Theruses did growl, very loudly, and Amahna trembled, though not as visibly as the messenger.

Below them, Raine looked up, smiling that child-sweet smile. Sweat beaded instantly on the messenger's forehead when Theruses stepped up to him with rage rippling through his muscles. The man looked pitiful next to the powerful mass of Theruses.

"He dared refuse?"

The response came out as a whimper.

"You will return to him. By the time you arrive he will have witnessed a demonstration of my power and you will again lay my request before him, this time as a command. He has only one month to present himself once you have given my message."

"Yes, my lord." The messenger's voice cracked with fear. Upon his dismissal he ran stumbling from the room.

Amahna watched Theruses in silence as he turned and looked down on the child below them again. Raine looked up at him for a moment, her face suddenly devoid of expression, then she returned her attention to entertaining her audience of daemons with just a hint of a smile turning her lips once more. Her insolence enraged Amahna, but Theruses seemed almost amused by it.

"Doesn't her manner infuriate you?"

Theruses shook his head. "She has learned much of that manner from watching you."

He said nothing else then, only walked from the room with his tail switching once or twice lazily as if he had not been fuming over Kyouin only a mere minute before.

Amahna left the balcony behind him.

If Theruses was fond of Raine partially because the girl reminded him of her then Amahna was justified in her concerns. Would he dare forget who this child was? At the rate she was maturing, she would look like a young woman all too soon. It seemed much too likely that he might ignore her obvious powers simply to indulge his own desires.

Going down into the area where Raine was kept put Amahna's nerves on edge. Kara entered here several times a day to bring the child food and cart away her waste. It seemed that Kara had enough maternal drive that she never complained once about caring for the child. Indeed, the only complaint she had made was about not being allowed to stay and visit with her longer. Amahna suspected Raine shared Kara's longing, but the only indication of this was the irritation in her eyes every time Kara hurried away to avoid displeasing her masters.

When Amahna entered the chamber Raine ceased her light show and drove the daemons away with little more than a stern look. That done, the girl stood and clasped her hands before her, managing to look innocent and unassuming even with the odd color of her hair and eyes. Raine was already lovely and every part of her promised that she would be an exotic beauty of a woman. That alone was enough to make Amahna feel bitter toward her. In the outside world, she would be wanted by many a man. Still, the child knew very little of the world outside and would be a social outcast if she ever did escape. Though that fact brought very little comfort.

"Why have you come to me?"

The phrasing of the question was almost insulting, but she dismissed it as due to a distinct lack of etiquette training. "I am troubled by you, Raine."

"In several ways, I imagine. Of which do you speak?"

Amahna had not exchanged more than a few words with the child in some time and she was astonished by the refinement of her speech. The boldness was as much because of her innocence as anything. Could someone be born with such word skills? Amahna refocused herself. "You are quite lovely, and many of the men here might start noticing this as you develop more womanly traits."

"I do not think Theruses will try anything. Though no one here could stop him if he did."

Amahna was speechless. The child's perceptiveness filled her with fear and made her want to slap it out of her. Her eyes, with the brass amidst the black, seemed perpetually in motion, constantly gathering information even as she gazed at Amahna with an insulting lack of concern.

"You knew my father."

Amahna shrugged roughly, her irritation starting to break away from her. "I killed your father."

Raine shook her head. "I'm not interested in that. He was very handsome. I have a picture of him in my mind. Did you find him attractive?"

"Why do you say that? You've never seen your father."

Raine maintained her patient silence, waiting for an answer.

How could she know what Dephithus looked like? "Yes, he was quite attractive, especially his blue eyes."

Raine responded with another shake of her head,

her tone edged with a touch of reproach. "Silver and green eyes. Do you think I do him justice?"

A shiver of unease swept through Amahna and she scowled at this enigma standing before her. "Why would you want to? He raped your mother."

"No. He did not, but you can continue to believe he did if it makes you feel better." Raine created a violet light and began to swirl it through a myriad of patterns in the air between them. "Why should that make me want to be any less attractive?"

Amahna stared at the child with a swiftly expanding sense of dread. Nothing about Raine gave any indication to her lack of years. Her speech was the equal of a well-born lady and her questions were not those of a child. What disturbed Amahna the most was her inexplicable knowledge of things she should not know. How did she know the color of her father's eyes and whether her mother was raped by him? How did she even know what rape was? Could she have somehow inherited knowledge from her parents? Was that also a dragon thing?

Amahna's forehead wrinkled down with the weight of her concerns. "If looks were the only factor here, I would couple with you as willingly as I would have with Dephithus."

A hint of a smile touched Raine's lips as she peered past the violet light into Amahna's eyes. Amahna turned from that gaze and moved to leave, stopping with her back to Raine when the child spoke again.

"We are related you know. I think you should visit more."

Amahna did not respond. She hurried from the chamber so the child would not see the shudder of foreboding that wracked her.

## CHAPTER THIRTY ONE

An orange cast tinted the storm-gray evening sky. The warm, slightly humid air was as still as glass, promising a strong and wet storm. From his vantage point in a large tree that had not yet begun to lose its browning leaves, Dephithus could see the outer gates of Elysium. Obviously, he could not saunter on up to the gates and expect to be greeted with warm smiles and open arms. Considering his actions before leaving, something he was trying not to consider too often, he would probably be welcomed right in and escorted to the palace in shackles. He had picked this spot where he could watch the comings and goings without being noticed and wait for his opportunity.

The journey to Imperious from the temple where Vanuthan was had not been overly difficult. Aside from trying to avoid the occasional travelers and alarmingly common daemons, the trip had been uneventful. The last two evenings he had held this vantage point and listened to his stomach complain about the berries and roots he had sustained himself on.

As he waited, Dephithus wondered about the dae-mon-seed within him and if it would stay dormant or begin changing him again. No matter who or what was at fault, the things he had done with its influence had certainly changed him forever. The constant bitterness and sorrow he could not seem to shake were proof of that.

A troop of thirty well-armored and polished looking soldiers rode out as the storm continued to threaten above. Not more than a few minutes later, a different troop rode in. This battered and bloodied troop, consisting of only eleven weary soldiers, led behind them seven rider-less horses and a wagon holding few bloodstained, misshapen bags that Dephithus could only assume carried bodies. These passing troops were disturbingly common, and he was itching to know what battle they were fighting. Such small troops could not be facing an organized army, but whatever they were facing was obviously a deadly opponent. As this sad looking band passed through the gate, three more soldiers rode out. Dephithus perked up, his ears and eyes alert as he watched them move down the hillside toward his perch.

"You're coming up for a troop again soon, aren't you Darkin?"

Dephithus recognized Kovial's voice. His nerves began to dance about with anticipation. Darkin's group was not the most promising given that they had no reason to want to help him, but they were the only chance he really had at getting inside the walls. And he had to get inside. There was no way he was going to make good progress stuck out here with no clothes, weapons, food, or coin to buy them with.

Suva was the third rider. Forcing back the emotional torment of that memory, Dephithus climbed down the tree, carefully staying out of sight. As the three riders began to pass him, he stepped out, though he kept the trees between him and the distant gate towers. Suva's horse was the first to notice him, turning its head and blowing at Dephithus with irritation at being surprised. The animal was most definitely a war trained mount, which was new for this crowd. The rest glanced his way casually then some variation of hatred, fear, or shock touched each one's face as they abruptly pulled up their mounts.

"Speak of evil things and they shall come to you," Suva muttered under her breath.

Dephithus forced himself to ignore her comment as he stepped closer to Darkin's mount. Darkin tensed and his horse backed a step in response to its rider's unease.

"You are a fool to show your face here. There is a standing bounty on your head, and it's a good one."

Dephithus grimaced. This would be even harder than he had dared imagine. Darkin looked more than ready to claim that bounty. Suva's expression remained wary, but not all that aggressive, which was almost odd. Kovial had started to move around behind Dephithus, perhaps to help Darkin take him down. If they tried, Dephithus did not think he could put up much of a fight as he stood, still weak and unarmed.

"For the soldier in the garden? I suppose I should have expected that." Dephithus tried to keep his tone conversational, though with a tightness of remorse that did not require much acting. Displaying his frustration and impatience now might set off the wrong chain of events.

"Also, for the kidnapping and murder of Myara and Amahna," Suva added.

*Amahna.* There was someone who needed murdering. To be blamed for her kidnapping of Myara was almost more than he could calmly take, however. "I am not guilty on either count, but I can't blame you if you don't believe that. I need help and you three are my best chance."

Darkin gave a derisive snort. "Doesn't bode well for you, does it?"

"Daemon's blood! Have you seen the scar on your back?" Kovial's outburst startled all of them and, for a tense moment, Darkin's hand closed on his sword hilt.

Trying to break the tension of the moment Dephithus rolled his eyes with a show of mock exasperation. "I find it extremely difficult to turn my head at that angle actually."

He glanced back at Kovial who shrugged and grinned sheepishly. A little nervous laugh escaped Suva, plainly against her will given the sour look she followed it up with.

Darkin sighed, his hand leaving his sword hilt after a few more tense seconds. "We'll hear you out, but we still might find that bounty more appealing than your story."

Dephithus locked eyes with Darkin. Strangely enough, he was confident in that moment that this man would not betray his trust. "That's all I can ask."

"Kovial, let him ride with you. There is an old abandoned house in the woods. We can talk there."

Dephithus turned to Kovial, noticing his wide-eyed look and the way his horse bunched as though ready for attack.

"I can walk," he offered.

Suva grinned and moved her mount up beside him. Her eyes were no less predatory than he remembered, but he was less wary of her than he had once been. She offered down her arm.

"C'mon, you can ride with me. If I am going to get no bounty out of this I should at least get a warm back."

Dephithus relented to a smile as he put his foot in the stirrup she left open for him, took hold of her arm, and swung up behind her. The whole movement caused a mild complaint in his back, but the smile felt good enough that he barely noticed. It was hard to feel good when he knew that Myara and his child were being held as prisoners. Still, if he drove himself mad with guilt he would never have a chance of helping them and he suspected the negative emotions would only strengthen the daemon-seed. Wrapping his arms around Suva's waist, he closed his eyes and allowed himself to enjoy the motion of the horse.

They told him the cabin they rode to had been left abandoned after a pack of daemon-dogs came through the windows in the night and killed the family who had lived there. The bodies had long since been removed and burned and the few valuables stolen even before that.

The three of them told Dephithus many things that were almost too horrible to believe. The daemons had increased dramatically in number throughout the region and people were coming up dead from such attacks almost daily. Kip and Lanz had been two of the first found dead within the walls of Elysium from such an attack.

Faced with this mass mutilation of his people, High Lord Mythan had begun sending out troops to hunt down and destroy what daemons they could find. Mythan had since stepped down from the throne, passing his empire over to his brother's son, Allondis. None of them would go into detail on why Mythan had stepped down, or who and how many had died in these daemon hunts. All they would say was that it was not getting better and that people had started siding with the daenox as priests and soldiers more and more often.

"Now, what do you have to say that will convince us not to take you in for that handsome bounty?"

Before responding Dephithus looked askance at the several medals on Darkin's uniform. Darkin only shrugged in response and waited for him to begin. Dephithus considered all three of them as they faced each other over a table belonging to a now dead family. Looking at the new age in their eyes and the patient expressions he began to feel a bit more hopeful.

"There is a lot that has happened that I think you would have trouble believing so I will try to keep it brief. My aunt, Amahna, is like one of those daenox priests you mentioned. She is the one who left this scar on my back. She left me for dead and took Myara. I don't know why," Dephithus deflected quickly when Darkin opened his mouth to ask. "What I do know is that I must go after her, but I can't do it half-naked, starving, and unarmed."

"So, you want us to get you into the palace for supplies."

Dephithus nodded while Darkin eyed him somewhat skeptically.

"Where have you been the last four and a half years?"

Dephithus's chest tightened so much he could hardly breathe for a few minutes. "Four and a half years!"

They all looked puzzled by his reaction, but he could not help himself. A lot had happened since he had been gone, but he never dreamed it could have been that long.

"I almost died," he said finally. "A stranger took me in and healed me, but I was unconscious for a long time. Longer than I realized."

Darkin glanced at the other two and they shrugged, willing to take his explanation at face value for now.

"What makes you think Myara is still alive?"

"She has to be."

All three were silent for a long moment. True to form, it was Darkin who finally spoke, the other two deferring to his leadership. "There is a lot you're not telling us. In fact, I would venture that you've barely skimmed the surface."

Dephithus shifted uncomfortably. What else could he really tell them without sounding crazed?

Darkin chewed at his lower lip for a few seconds, then his eyes narrowed a hint. "Last time we spoke there was madness in your eyes. Where did that go?"

Dephithus met Darkin's gaze and took a deep breath before answering. "That is still here, it's just sleeping."

Darkin looked pensive. He was clearly working something over in his head. After a few minutes he turned to Kovial and eyed him critically. "We'll need your uniform. You're closer to his size."

Suva shoved back from the table, showing her first protest to the situation with a touch of drama. "This is madness. We'll be caught and imprisoned."

"No, *we* won't."

Dephithus nodded his agreement as Darkin spoke. There was no reason to involve all of them.

"I will get him in and out alone. All I need is Kovial's uniform." He focused on Dephithus now. "I will get you in as far as the stables, from that point, you're on your own until you meet me back there. If you get caught, none of us ever saw you."

"Friends appear in the strangest places," Dephithus mused as Kovial tossed a glare around to each of them before stomping into the tiny bedroom to strip off his uniform.

Darkin gave Dephithus a calculated look. "Don't push it. If I had any sense I would be turning you in and I still might if you aren't careful."

"Then why don't you?" Suva snapped.

For the briefest of moments Dephithus saw a hint of sorrow in Darkin's eyes, then he shrugged and offered up a crooked grin. "It's more exciting this way."

Suva looked doubtful, but she said nothing.

"Go kill something, Suva, we need some blood."

Suva grinned then and left them, pleased to have a purpose. A crash of thunder shook the floor as she slammed the door behind her. Darkin looked up and smiled after her then stepped around the corner into the bedroom.

"You're going to ruin my uniform," Kovial lamented from the other room, though his tone was resigned.

"It won't be the first one you've lost. Just have them fit a new one." Stepping back out into the main room Darkin threw the uniform to Dephithus. "We'll rip it up a bit and rub some blood on it. The gates open for the dead without question these days. It happens too often for them to get suspicious and with this storm rolling in they probably won't even stop us long enough to recognize me."

Dephithus shook his head at the misery of the world he had returned to. Before he left it this chaos had just been starting. At least he knew now that the world would always keep on without him, though it did not seem to fare well in his absence. A flash of lightening reflected off the broken glass in and around the windows as Dephithus began to change. Before he was finished dressing Darkin pulled his knife and started some tears in the fabric. Dephithus was a touch broader through the chest than Kovial, so Darkin made a point of ripping down from his right shoulder to the bottom of his ribcage.

Stepping back, Darkin grinned. "Dashing. Now for a little blood."

Almost as though cued, Suva burst through the door with a rabbit dangling from one hand. Dephithus grimaced as the creature twitched weakly. The blood they needed was draining out fast.

Darkin scowled as he took the animal from her. "Could you have wasted any more blood?"

Suva narrowed her eyes at him. "It isn't as if they are easy to find in the middle of a storm. Next time you can hunt and I'll help with the undressing. As it is, I missed all the fun." She gestured towards Dephithus as she finished.

Darkin rolled his eyes at her before approaching Dephithus with his bloody rabbit. While he helped Darkin spread the blood, Dephithus eyed Suva who was scowling at the window. Kovial had still not emerged from the bedroom, even though Darkin had given him the pants Dephithus was wearing.

"Do you three get along this well all of the time?"

Darkin grinned. "It's love."

A sarcastic laugh escaped from the back room and Suva snorted derisively. Dephithus and Darkin shared an amused glance and resumed their work. Help did come in strange forms sometimes and Dephithus could not keep from wondering when luck had turned his way. More importantly, how long would it stay around?

"Perfect." Darkin tossed the mangled rabbit to Suva who caught it with a scowl. "Let's go."

Darkin was right about getting through the gates.

Both the guards passed them on with weary directions to take the body to the stables and report it in the morning. Dephithus was appalled when Darkin described it to the guards as "just another daemon attack" and assured them he would bring a replacement out within the hour. At first Dephithus expected a harsh reaction to this callous manner, but the first guard seemed too tired to care and the second responded with disinterest. Were they losing soldiers so quickly that one more was just another nameless body among the masses? For an instant, at the inner gates Dephithus almost forgot he was supposed to be dead and caught himself as he opened his mouth to speak. Luckily the small movement went unnoticed.

Getting to the palace was likely to be just as easy. Darkin said that no one wandered outside if they did not have to at night because of the daemon attacks. He warned Dephithus to be careful and gave him his boot knife for some small degree of defense.

Dephithus gave the inadequate weapon a dubious look. "Better than nothing I suppose."

As he turned to leave from their spot in the shadows near the show stables, Darkin stopped him. "One more warning. If you get caught, don't come this way for help. Dead men can't point fingers, and I won't give you the chance to implicate me in your pleas for a merciful sentence."

Dephithus nodded. If there was any one place he could not fault Darkin it was in his frankness. Not once had he failed to call a thing for what it was.

G etting in to the palace unseen was a challenge he and Myara had taken on hundreds of times throughout their childhood. There was an old stairwell obscured by some bushes that lead from outside into the cold storage under the kitchen. The kitchen itself was usually busy well into the night hours and often the first to start up again when morning drew near. This made things a little riskier, but rarely was there a reason to enter the cold storage once the evening meal was done.

At some point someone had placed a lock on the slanted door, but the old boards gave way easily to the prying of the dagger. Whether or not he had any other purpose for it, Dephithus reminded himself to thank Darkin for the little weapon. Once inside he walked to the top of the stairs on the other side of the storage room and listened at the door into the kitchen for some time, counting the voices and searching for patterns in their movements. Time began to tick away, grating his nerves while he stood there alone with no one to help make a game of it. Only two people were speaking, and sound of movement came from over near the big sinks along the far wall. Drawing in a shaky breath—there was so much more to fear than a slap on the hand this time—Dephithus opened the door a crack.

Two younger serving girls were cleaning up evening

317

dishes and gossiping. Their manner was more subdued than one might expect of young ladies in their station, but they appeared engrossed none-the-less. Dephithus pushed open the door only as much as he had to and slipped out, darting into the shadows after easing it shut behind him. From then on it was easy. Simple patience while waiting in the shadows got him past the patrolling guards to his room. As he bolted to the door he experienced a moment of panic. What if it had been locked up or someone else was using it?

The handle clicked down and the door opened. Dephithus entered and stood in the dark, listening until he was sure no one was sleeping there. Carefully, he pulled a candle out of one of the sconces and lit it off the one outside his door then closed himself into the familiar space. Nothing had been moved. It was almost like he was returning after a day rather than several years. It was tempting to linger and remember how good things had been once. Still, there was no time. He changed into a clean, properly fitted uniform and stuffed the torn and bloodied one into a pack. In a separate pack he stuffed some other clothes and then donned his belt and a standard Legion issue dagger. Lastly, he dug out his stash of coin for visits to town and pushed the pouch it was in down into his clothes.

From his room, Dephithus made his way to the library. There was one more thing he needed. If he was to go to the Dunues Mountains he needed to know how to get there and there were map books in the library. If he was fortunate, one might even have a map showing the location of this cave system near Kithin that Vanuthan spoke of. Any information at all would be better than what he currently had to go on.

There were two candles burning in the library when he entered, set within a circle of high-backed chairs. The candles were down to almost nothing, and their light was minimal. He was reasonably sure after listening for a few minutes that no one else was in the big room now. Next to all the chairs in the circle were stacks of books. Dephithus stopped at the edge and knelt by one of these stacks. They were all books from the archives. It must have been Mythan's research group and, judging by the dust on the books, the group had not met here in some time. Odd that they should leave it setup in this manner almost as if the research and the library itself had been forgotten. And yet... there were lit candles.

Dephithus stepped into the circle, moving cautiously towards the table in the center.

"Dephithus."

He jumped, turning to face the figure hidden in the shadows of the chair he had just stepped past.

"You're late for practice again."

He was taken back by his den-fathers words. Late for practice? That was a considerable understatement of the situation. When Mythan leaned forward into the candlelight, Dephithus was caught by surprise again. The proud ruler looked haggard and there were dark circles under his unfocused brown eyes. Kneeling before him, Dephithus took hold of Mythan's hands and bowed his head, afraid to meet that haunted gaze.

Mythan pulled a hand free and mussed his hair affectionately.

Swallowing down the lump in his throat, Dephithus forced himself to look into those eyes. "Where is Mother?"

Mythan looked puzzled by the question. "In the garden with her ladies undoubtedly."

Dephithus dropped his head again, fighting back tears. Mythan was speaking madness. What had done this to his den-father? How much of this was his fault?

The scar ached in protest of his inner turmoil and he started to feel nauseated. With a deep breath he

squeezed Mythan's hand and searched for the strength
to walk away, as he knew he must. His hesitation was
apparently too long, for it was not strength, but the icy
touch of a steel point against his neck that forced him
to rise.

Standing, Dephithus turned to face his aggressor.
Kaydina, Myara's aunt, stood at the controlling end of
the sword touching his neck. She did not quite stand, actually, for a heavy crutch supported most of her weight.
One leg was bandaged from the knee down to the ankle
where the leg ended prematurely. Dephithus cringed
with the pain of her injury. Was nothing he had known
left unmarred by this misery? Still, her arm was steady as
she scrutinized him down the length of the ornate blade
that was waiting on her command.

"Kayd," he breathed, pleading with his eyes for her
to lower the sword.

She hesitated and he brought his hand up, taking
a chance and slowly pushing the blade away from his
throat. Conceding, Kayd lowered the weapon until the
point came to rest on the marble floor.

"Your mother was taken down in one of the earliest
battles against the daemon army."

"What do you mean? Mother left the Legion long
before I was born. She fought no battles."

With frustratingly slow movements, Kayd made her
way to the closest chair and sat. Mythan had leaned back
in his chair and was facing them, but his eyes were empty.
Dephithus was much too distressed to sit and time was
slipping away from him. He had to get a mount and get
out of Elysium within the hour Darkin had given him,
or he was on his own.

"Avaline had herself reinstated into the Legion not
long after you disappeared. Everyone in her troop was
killed, even Area Commander Parthak."

The tightness in his throat made it hard to get words

out, but he forced them through. "And Lord Mythan, what has happened to him?"

Kayd shook her head, sorrow lowering her gaze. "This is how he copes with his losses. After Avaline died, he stepped down and raised Allondis to the throne so that he might be free to recede into himself without taking his kingdom with him. I have assigned myself the duty of keeping him presentable and happy since this injury took me out of the Legion, but he does not care much for impressing anyone these days. All he ever wants to do is talk about you and Avaline. That is the only reason I didn't kill you, that and one other thing."

Dephithus tried to appear interested in her reason, but the loss of his mother weighed on him, making him feel suffocated and trapped. He had to get out of this place, if for no other reason than to escape the memories bombarding him.

"Where is Myara?"

"She was taken by someone allied with the daenox. I'm going after her."

Kayd nodded as though she had expected this, which Dephithus found vaguely puzzling. "I don't understand what is happening. I don't know why you come here now, after so many years, but I know she would not have loved you so dearly if you were not worthy of it in some way. This sword," she tilted the ornate weapon so that the candle reflected brilliantly on the polished blade, "was given to Myara on her sixteenth birthday. I want you to take it to her."

Speechless, Dephithus took the sword belt she handed him and fastened it around his waist. He was reluctant to accept the blade as she turned it over and offered him the hilt. Kayd's expression waned towards impatience so he finally took it. The weight was divinely balanced, and he let the beauty of the jewels inlaid in the pommel and crossguard of the hilt entrap him for a moment.

"You might wish to make a cover for the hilt or you could find yourself fighting bandits for it at every turn."

Dephithus nodded, sheathing the sword. "I need a horse."

"Hydra is yours." Both Dephithus and Kayd turned toward Mythan, each mirroring the others surprise at the sudden focus in his eyes. Mythan's gaze blazed through Dephithus with determination. "You will take Hydra. Allondis can have any other horse in the kingdom."

Dephithus stepped over to Mythan and squeezed his hand again. "Thank you, Father."

"I can lure the stable guards out of the way as long as you don't rush over there too fast." She scowled at him when he glanced at her bandaged leg. "I move fine without that sword unbalancing me."

"I hope I can repay you for your help, Kayd."

Kayd gave a rough shake of her head. "Just get that sword to Myara and bring her back to us."

"I will."

Without another word she left the library. Dephithus waited behind a moment and lit fresh candles for Mythan before heading out toward the kitchen. He shook his head after Kayd as she disappeared down another hall. She had always been one to question the judgements of society and he was glad she was staying true to form in this. Or perhaps she was merely desperate enough to take a chance on him. Either way, he was grateful.

Keeping in the shadows, he slipped carefully from hall to hall. Once he bumped the sword on a marble column and the sound, though muffled by the sheath, was enough to send his heart pounding into his throat. When no one came he moved the weapon on to the other hip and hurried to the kitchen.

It was easy to slip back into the cold storage room, which seemed colder now than it had before despite the humid warmth outside. He climbed the far stairs and slipped quickly though the hole he had made in the door. A twig snapped behind him as he was crouching down to press the boards back into place. Standing, he turned to face whatever or whoever had found him.

Kathan stood there dressed in the attire of the palace guard. An accomplishment he might have congratulated the innkeepers' son on under different circumstances, but there was something different about his once-friend that Dephithus could not quite place. The grin itself was almost sinister, which was not at all like the Kathan he had known in training. It was not the grim look of a guard doing his duty, it was the look of crazed man.

"I could sense you a mile away," Kathan drew his blade and cocked his head to the side in a very dog-like fashion.

Dephithus raised his hands and smiled, hoping to win over his old friend, then he realized what was changed about him. Kathan had blue eyes, but the hostile eyes looking at him now were unmistakably gray. Regretting having moved his hands away from his weapons, Dephithus leapt to the side as Kathan's sword whistled through the air. The point of the blade nicked his back when Dephithus dropped to the ground and slipped under one of the bushes. As rain began to pour down on them Dephithus leapt to his feet and bolted toward the stables.

The daemon gave chase. Despite his dragon-enhanced strength, Dephithus was still weak and he could hear the daemon gaining on him. Each stride sent pain through the scar in his back. When they neared the stable Dephithus spotted Kayd and the stable watch off to the side. They appeared to be arguing, but he could make out very little of what was being said over the sudden downpour.

"Daemon!" Dephithus screamed the word then dove to one side.

The daemon continued several strides past him and the stable watch was charging it before it could correct itself. Another soldier appeared out of the dark and ran into the fight while Dephithus bolted for the stable under the cover of the confusion. Kayd had already gone into the stable and was pulling out a bridle for Dephithus. Grabbing the item as he passed, Dephithus ran down to the familiar stall. He would pick up a Legion saddle in the lower stable.

Hydra greeted him with ears back and teeth bared. Without hesitation Dephithus stepped into the stall and raised the bit to the stallion's lips. His intimidation attempt failing, Hydra put his ears back up and took the bit. With a small sense of satisfaction, he swung up on the big animal's back. Hydra tensed and Dephithus held him back, feeling as if he needed to say something more to Kayd.

"Go," she snapped.

He let Hydra go, and they charged out the smaller rear door of the barn into the pouring rain. At the lower stable they met with Darkin who scowled his disapproval at his choice of mounts, but he said nothing as they saddled him and headed out for the gates. Dephithus donned a cloak, the rain giving him an excellent excuse for keeping the hood up. With his eyes and scaling hidden from view, they passed the gate guard easily enough. It helped that the guards were more concerned with keeping dry in the gate tower than with delaying a couple of uniformed soldiers on their way to fill a post that had stood empty for too long already.

Once they were out of sight of the gate Darkin pulled up his mount and Dephithus stopped Hydra with a subtle leg cue, finding satisfaction in the stallion's quick response. The briefest of smiles touched his lips thinking of how furious Allondis would be when he discovered that Hydra was gone. The good feeling vanished when he noticed Darkin regarding him soberly.

"Why did you help me?"

Darkin turned his face to the sky for a moment and closed his eyes to the warm rain. The downpour began to ease off some, but they were both already too soaked for it to matter much.

He lowered his gaze then and regarded the horizon thoughtfully. "We are losing more soldiers every day since the daenox priests gave our enemy a sense of organization. I go out with a troop in three days. What did I have to lose? Anyhow, in spite of the things you've done, I think there is a part of you that is better than most of us. Though I can't say much good about the other parts," he added with a tired grin. "Maybe I'm just trying to win favor with some higher power."

"I think you feel guilty for trying to blackmail me before," Dephithus offered, finding it easier to smile now that he was reunited with his trusted mount.

Darkin rolled his eyes. "Don't insult me. If I were a nicer sort, I might offer to go with you. Lucky for me, I'm not. As it is, I think you're crazy for even trying after this much time."

That passage of time was like a vice closing on his spirit. "I have to try." He drew a shaky breath. "She was pregnant."

Darkin nodded and had the tact not to ask any of the questions that passed behind his eyes. "Good luck to you then."

"The same to you."

With nothing left to say, they parted and Dephithus resumed his quest, but this time he did not have to continue alone.

## CHAPTER THIRTY THREE

Amahna waited with Theruses for the daenox priest, Kyouin.

Once his messenger had located the priest again, Theruses channeled a surge of daenox through the messenger, destroying a plethora of lesser daemons and the messenger himself in a chaotic wave of power. The show of power apparently impressed the ambitious young man, who had now drawn in thousands of daemons and human fighters to his army. A high-level daemon served as Kyouin's messenger to precede his arrival. A counter show of power. The simple act of luring such a daemon into service was impressive enough to put Amahna on edge.

Kyouin, whoever he had been before, had risen to power quickly amidst the chaos the daemons were creating. Amahna had not expected him to last, but, as if born to it, he had taken hold of the daemon powers now coursing through the land and begun turning them to his purpose. That was one of the many things that still had her mystified. What was his purpose? Driving across the land fighting the legions of Imperious and other kingdoms that dared to try and stop this wave of changes. Why was he doing all this?

Theruses looked up, his gaze moving to the entrance suddenly. His eyes narrowed and his lip curled in a snarl that revealed slightly pointed teeth. He appeared, for that moment, like a predator waiting to ambush its prey.

"He is here, and there are other *priests* with him."

Amahna wished he would not sneer so at the title they had chosen. How much untapped power might Kyouin and his followers possess? "How many?"

"Two, and one other. A servant probably."

Amahna assumed a calm and confident exterior, which was far from genuine. Having Raine around was beginning to leave her feeling constantly strung out and exhausted. The child's intelligence and beauty captivated Theruses, though he still had not tried to act upon his fascination in any way. For now, he channeled much of his desire into his couplings with Amahna, something she did not mind, but he would not always be satisfied with that. When he watched Raine with eyes full of curiosity and passion, Raine returned the scrutiny with eyes full of hate. The child had learned little about human emotions from them, but hate was born very naturally out of her imprisonment.

It was hard to maintain her serene facade when Kyouin and the other three entered the room. Kyouin still looked so very young. Not more than eighteen, maybe twenty at most, but certainly not three years older than last time she had seen him. He was definitely much younger than the two grizzled men flanking him and still more childishly pretty than handsome. The fourth, a boy no older than nine or ten, flanked the three with his head bowed in apparent subservience.

All three men wore cloaks of a dusty gray, but that was the extent of their similarities. The two men flanking Kyouin were near opposites. On his right was a tall, slender man with pale skin and long gray hair. This man wore black pants, shirt, and high boots under his cloak. On his left, nearer the young boy, was a stocky, muscular man with sun-darkened skin and short, graying red hair and beard. He was obviously a warrior of sorts, with the hilts of a few daggers peeking out from under his cloak, but his tan and brown clothes and leather armor suggested the discretion of a thief. Kyouin wore a silver shirt with a dark charcoal vest, pants, and boots. The shirt was of a silk-like material and there was minimal, but elegant silver embroidery done along the border of the vest. Just a touch fancier than what he had been wearing the first time she saw him.

Both men flanking Kyouin tensed and glanced around them uneasily once they saw Theruses, perhaps cataloging escape opportunities. The small boy darted up to stand near Kyouin who placed a hand on his head absently as one might do to a child they cared for. She logged that information for later. Kyouin kept any reaction to Theruses well-hidden. He glanced once at Amahna with a flash of recognition in his eyes and offered a quick nod of acknowledgement. Then he inclined his head towards Theruses in the slightest semblance of a bow. A hint of inadequate respect.

"I found your second request for a meeting much more intriguing than the first." He glanced at Amahna again and a hint of a smile touched his lips before he looked away.

Theruses regarded the group for a moment in silence, which Kyouin bore patiently despite the shifting of his companions. He was probably cooling his temper and using the time to see how easily they could be unnerved.

"I suspected you might. You have given me good reason to dislike you, primarily by directing my minions about as if you were born to the right." Kyouin met this accusation with a slight nod of acceptance, which Theruses either did not notice or chose to ignore. "Most of your actions otherwise have been entertaining, even pleasing, but you push my patience with your arrogance.

I would have destroyed you if you had dared refuse me a second time."

"Undoubtedly, Lord Theruses, but I will dare to be bold and skip to the ultimate point. You want something of me and I believe you have a fair trade in mind."

Amahna watched curiously as Kyouin removed his hand from the younger boy's head only to have the child snatch hold of it with both of his small hands, preventing whatever gesture the daenox priest intended to make. Again, Kyouin appeared undisturbed by this behavior and allowed the young boy to keep his hand without ever losing his intense focus on Theruses. He was an ambitious individual for certain, but one with a potentially devastating weakness in this youth beside him. Perhaps reading the boy's manner as subservience initially was an error. She was beginning to suspect their relationship was more familial.

Theruses was silent again and Amahna had no doubt that he was soothing his temper this time. The lord of the daenox did not like having to ask for assistance from this self-proclaimed daenox priest, and she suspected he liked it even less after meeting Kyouin. Still, daemon power coursed through Kyouin as if it had found a haven within him. She wondered if that power had made him sick at all as it did to so many people. If so, he did not show it.

Kyouin glanced at Amahna as if he had heard her thoughts. It was then that she noticed the ring hanging on a fine silver chain around his neck. Any hesitation at approaching him vanished and she stepped up next to Theruses.

"Where did you get that ring?"

Kyouin looked surprised for a moment then he fingered the ring and smiled. "One of the daemons brought it to me off a woman I killed. I believe you where there. She turned out to be the Lady Avaline of Imperious. It was almost a shame to kill her. She was rather lovely and remarkably courageous."

Theruses grinned, but Amahna stumbled over a confusing swell of emotions. There had never been any real sadness in her for her sister's death, yet a powerful resentment filled her toward this man who had killed her. She hated that he wore Avaline's ring. Still, demanding it and causing an unnecessary scene would make Theruses question her loyalty.

"I knew I recognized it. Pardon my interruption." Amahna stepped back again, though her eyes lingered on the ring a moment longer.

Kyouin looked curious, but he forced his attention back to Theruses who had endured her interruption with more patience than she deserved.

"I have captive within these passages the child whose freedom would free the dragons. Her freedom would also get me out of this cave. I could easily let her go."

For the first time, Kyouin's composure cracked. His brow furrowed, his eyes clouding with alarm. He cleared his throat softly to indicate his need to speak, though he did not wait for acknowledgement before doing so. "I think that would work against both of us. We both represent a power that the dragons would not tolerate."

"Yes." Theruses was contemplative as he regarded Kyouin with feigned patience, his tail twitching behind him where only Amahna could see. "If you can find a way to free me from this cave, I will teach you to master the daemon power you play with. Otherwise, the child will go free."

Kyouin shifted, perhaps due to the insulting tone in which Theruses had just spoken of his powers. That was his only reaction to those words, however, though his companions both sneered and moved their hands closer to their weapons, looking ready to draw blood.

Kyouin held his free hand out in a placating gesture to the other two who relaxed only a fraction. "Don't you worry that I might turn your teachings against you?"

Theruses grinned. "You will never be that strong."

A touch of a growl rolled out with his words and Kyouin narrowed his eyes at this challenge. Amahna began to wonder if she could slip out in the tense silence that followed. She wanted Theruses to kill him so that she might take Avaline's ring, but that was unlikely under the circumstances. Theruses had lost his long-held patience around leaving the cave. He wanted out of these dark chambers and passages and he did not want to wait any longer. Any chance that Kyouin might be able to help would be one more thing keeping the young man alive.

"I wish to see this child." In response to this request the young boy looked askance up at Kyouin who did not seem to notice the gesture, though it fueled Amahna's curiosity more.

Theruses nodded. "Alone, you may see her."

Kyouin nodded to his companions but made no move to detach himself from the boy. Kara entered the room then, apparently summoned by Theruses and was directed to guide the other two priests to one of the outer chambers to wait. Kyouin, with his small attachment still clinging to his hand, followed Theruses from the chamber. Having received no opposing instructions, Amahna joined them. Letting Kyouin, as powerful as he was, anywhere near Raine seemed a bad idea to her. What purpose could it serve?

When they got to the edge of Raine's prison chambers there were no lights. Amahna dared to hope that she might be sleeping, but when they neared the blue tinted steel bars that bordered her small section of the cave their light brought her out of the shadows. Raine was standing there waiting for them, which only increased Amahna's unease at allowing the daenox priest to meet her.

Her brassy black eyes fell instantly upon Kyouin.

With a rather rapt expression Kyouin stepped up to the bars and took hold of one with his free hand, stopping with his nose just shy of the perceived perimeter between two bars. The bar he was holding began to glow a dim blue. Amahna saw Theruses tense as Raine approached him, perhaps only now realizing the potential volatility of the situation. The girl paused a few inches out of reach and focused on the ring dangling from the chain around Kyouin's neck. Cocking her head in a manner that was endearing yet somehow ominous, she refocused on his face.

"That ring."

Kyouin touched the ring with the hand he had, at some point, freed from the boy's grasp. "Fancy this, do you?"

Raine shook her head to indicate his lack of understanding. "It belongs to me."

Kyouin grinned, plainly amused. "Perhaps you are thinking of a different ring, but I might give it to you eventually anyhow. Maybe when you get out of here."

Raine's eyes narrowed with irritation at his taunting grin as he held up the ring so she could see it better. Amahna wondered why she would seek to claim a ring she had never seen before. It was just one more mystery of this child.

"I will leave this place. The silver dragon will come here and then I will be freed." Her tone was solemn as death and she stepped closer to the bars, close enough that there was no more distance between them than that of the thickness of the bars. "Then I will come and take it from you."

Amahna's pulse raced with the flare of desire in Kyouin's expression. His stance wavered a touch as though he might lean in to try to kiss her, but Raine turned and began to walk away before any such disaster could occur. She turned back when the young boy spoke, seeming to notice him for the first time.

"She is not yours to keep," the child stated with firm conviction.

Theruses, irritated by the entire confrontation, stepped closer to the boy and sneered. "And who is going to take her from me? You?"

Kyouin drew the boy in closer to him, placing a protective arm around his shoulders.

Comforted by the daenox priest's presence, the boy faced Theruses. "Someone will."

Amahna stepped in. She did not care to see bloodshed in the presence of the dragon-child. Not because she feared for Raine, but because she feared Raine might be able to use the natural power released with such shedding of blood. "I think, my lord, we might be wise to discuss this agreement elsewhere now that he has met her."

Theruses started just a touch, distracted from his violent inclinations. He nodded reluctantly, his gaze following after Raine who had retreated deeper into the darkness. "Yes, I think that would be for the best. Who is this boy you are mothering?"

Kyouin glowered at Theruses, but he managed to sensibly restrain his anger. "My younger brother, Vaneye, he is learning the ways of the Daenox Priesthood."

"He has much to learn," Theruses muttered. He turned away then, leading them from the chamber.

Amahna lingered behind, waiting until they had turned out of sight to approach the bars. Raine had moved forward again and stood gazing past her in the direction the others had gone.

"No dragons will go free child, as long as you are in here, so no dragons can save you. Perhaps your time alone has led you to flights of foolish fancy."

Raine's expression did not change. She pointedly ignored Amahna's presence.

"Say something," Amahna hissed.

Raine smiled softly to herself. Amahna could only stop herself from lashing out at the child with the sobering realization that Theruses and Kyouin were not far away and only a few choice words from unleashing their own tempers. With a cold scowl she spun and stormed from the chamber, her blood raven hair whipping around in an outer display of her anger.

## CHAPTER THIRTY FOUR

D ephithus rode a wide circle around the main body of Imperious. Once he was comfortable with his distance from the city he stopped long enough to change into more common clothes under his cloak and stuffed the uniform away into his packs. The crests and signets of the Legion he tore and cut away from the saddle carelessly to bury along with the hair from thinning and shortening Hydra's mane and tail. It pained him to cut away some of Hydra's beautiful hair, but the animal drew enough attention without the added flash of his long, thick mane and tail.

There was little choice for them but to continue through the dark storm-riddled night. It would be much too dangerous to shop for provisions in Imperious. They needed a town where his appearance and history were not so well known. He stopped the next day in the first remote town, a place small enough that he forgot the name almost as soon as he read it on an aged wood sign at the border. The main street was the only one worth noticing and that was little more than a wagon track with weeds growing up between the ruts. Any supplies to be found here would undoubtedly be minimal, but so was the chance of being arrested.

Dephithus approached an old covered storefront leading Hydra along and keeping the hood of his cloak pulled well forward to hide his face. The suspicious way he stayed within the shadows of the hood did nothing to endear him to the shopkeeper, but his eyes were too distinctive to risk a more open approach. As soon as he started to peruse the scant selection of provisions, focusing on foods that would last a long time, the shopkeeper pushed up in front of him asking his business.

"I wish no more than a few provisions for my travels, good sir." He kept his voice level and his hands away from the shopkeeper's wares.

"There is no room for beggars or thieves in this town and I'll judge you as the latter from the looks of your mount." The shopkeeper folded his arms and set his jaw to add stubborn weight to his words.

Dephithus sighed inwardly. Small towns suffered the most in times of chaos leaving little warmth for strangers. It would have been much easier if he could have stopped in Imperious. Pulling a picture of Myara up in his mind to remind him of his purpose, he managed to maintain his calm manner.

"I assure you that am neither of those two. I simply need a few provisions and I will pay honestly for them. This is a shop, is it not?"

The shopkeeper looked a bit unbalanced by the question though his nod was still gruff.

"Then, as a customer, I would appreciate a bit of service for my coin."

When the man remained hesitant Dephithus bumped his coin pouch, producing a jingle that reverberated as a glimmer in the shopkeeper's eyes.

As expected, the selection was not impressive, and the price they finally settled on was a bit steep, but Dephithus was wary of wasting time. Though the food was a far cry from a palace meal it would keep him going for a long way, perhaps all the way to the cave itself if he rationed carefully. He kept his purchase down to

the barest necessities while always remembering that the
end of his journey promised only an even greater struggle than the journey itself. It would do him no good to
be weakened and sick when he faced Amahna again.

The shopkeeper had warmed to him some, or at
least to his coin. As he turned to move on, the man
called after him. "There's a tavern just a short way down
the road. They don't have any rooms, but they'll rent
you a stall where you can bed down with your mount."

Dephithus peered down the nearly vacant roadway
through the gray drizzle that had started up after the
storm died down. "Thank you, but I think I'll continue
on. A good tree will provide ample shelter when I must
rest."

The shopkeeper's expression was solemn when
Dephithus glanced at him again. "These lands are lovely
boy, but death in beauty's shadow waits."

It was an elegant warning, and there was a cadence
to it that hinted at frequent usage. Dephithus nodded
his thanks again and moved Hydra out so that he could
mount. Back up on his proud companion, he turned
toward the shop one last time. The shopkeeper was
looking at him, but he could tell by the sorrow in those
eyes that he was already dead to that man. Putting his
heels softly to Hydra's sides he trotted toward his goal,
leaving others and their ill tidings behind him.

The drizzle finally tapered off toward late afternoon
and Dephithus found a place well off the main road to
stop. He could have napped and eaten on horseback,
but he also had need to make a cover for the sword hilt.
That was a much more complicated process to attempt
while riding. While enjoying the rare kiss of sunlight
that escaped the clouds, he made a slip cover and fastened it into place by winding a thin strip of leather
down the grip. It was not an attractive job and he was
very pleased with it. The less attractive it looked the less

likely he was to run into trouble over it.

He nibbled a bite of dried meat and leaned up against a tree. Close by, Hydra snorted as he munched contentedly at the grass. It was easy enough to be lulled by the smells of the damp forest. The light breeze that chilled his wet body had faded away and he was now warm by comparison. The constant tension of the ride since leaving Elysium was soothed away by the quiet sounds of birds and the brush of Hydra's hooves on the ground as he shifted about, seeking that perfect bunch of grass. Dephithus closed his eyes, just for a moment.

He was jolted awake by something hard bumping his thigh. Opening his eyes to the near blackness of night he was forced to feel beside him for the offending object. Reaching out, his hand met Hydra's leg. Considering the source, the bump had been rather gentle, though there would be a tender bruise there for a few days. A soft blowing well above his head indicated that Hydra was standing very alert. Something had the large war-horse on edge. Moving slow so as not to draw unwanted attention he slipped around to the stirrup, his eyes gradually adjusting to the darkness. He had been a fool to fall asleep, but at least he had left his mount geared up.

As he reached his foot to the stirrup a small growl rose up behind him. Carefully resting his foot back on the ground, he turned slowly and backed up against Hydra, hoping to draw the beast out of the darker shadows. Falling victim to his lure, a cat, no bigger than Prophet from the archives, moved out of the shadows. Its back was arched and its brown striped fur stood on end while it hissed as ferociously as possible for such a small creature. The moonlight revealed the gray eyes of a daemon-infected animal.

Dephithus drew his dagger with every intention of dispatching the beast, then paused. He remembered

Prophet, who had been drawn to him by the daenox they were both victims of. Regardless of the reasons for their rapport, he had taken great comfort from the cat's presence for a time. This animal did not appear to sense the daemon-seed in him since Vanuthan had weakened it, so there would be no common ground. Still, he could not find in himself the desire to kill this creature that the daenox would soon dispose of without his help.

Sheathing the dagger, he turned to Hydra. The cat's ears laid back even further and it hissed as he moved, but it came no closer. Mounting up, he moved Hydra back from the small aggressor and rode away, giving the cat a wide berth. Even though he did not think the daemon infecting such a small animal could be passed to Hydra, he was not going to take chances. He saw no reason to worry much about himself though. With the daemon-seed and the power of the dragons vying for control of him, he doubted either would let a mere daemon move into the competition.

Using the quarter moon for a guide they traveled back to the main road and resumed their journey at a fast trot. The route he had chosen was considerably less traveled than the one passing through Kuilen and Derg. About thirty miles northeast of Derg, and around seventy miles southeast of Kuilen, was Vorticade, the second largest city in the region, second only to Imperious herself. This road, which loosely paralleled to the west of the other, passed through no city bigger than Corbent Calid, which was about the size of Dalynay. If he traveled at a good speed and took no more unplanned naps off horseback he would reach Corbent Calid in perhaps two and a half or three more days.

Hydra was able to keep up the trot until dusk the next day. They had given a wide berth to other travelers as much to be polite as to avoid scrutiny. One traveling merchant had called after Dephithus to survey his wares, but had not persisted once they passed quickly by his wagon. As dusk was setting in Dephithus began to slow their pace and search around for a promising area to lay camp. To the east lay rolling hills and grasslands, to the west it was much the same for some distance then it turned to the deep forest and steep climbs of the Gmuir Mountian range. The same range that ran past Imperious and housed the temple Vanuthan waited in. Beyond those mountains lay the Illtide coast. Dephithus longed to travel that way some day and see the rocky shores that had earned that name. Maybe he could take his child there someday.

The encounter with the cat long faded from his mind and exhaustion causing his focus to falter, Dephithus's thoughts turned to Myara. The love he still had for her made him cringe again with the horribleness of the things he had done. Would she ever forgive him for what he had done on her Dawning Day?

To ease the pain of these contemplations, he tried to imagine what their child would look like. He could imagine a handsome little boy or an elegant, but feisty girl. It would have dark hair and probably some pattern of scaling because of all the dragon power in it. Somehow, it was easier to picture the girl and the image renewed in him an aching guilt.

Hydra had settled quickly into the slower pace. It had been long enough since their last stop that the stallion was probably sleepwalking, lured on with the promise of grain in his dreams. With a weary smile Dephithus patted Hydra's neck. Any horse in Elysium would have been less risky to steal, but he could imagine no other horse working so hard for him without complaint. He brought Hydra down to a slow walk as he peered out toward a stand of weeping trees that would make an excellent camp if it were not already taken.

Without any cue from his rider Hydra suddenly

stopped. Turning to see what the problem was, Dephithus nearly jumped out of his seat in surprise at finding
a slender woman standing before them. Her hair was
the color of dry prairie grass and her skin glowed a pale
cream even in the dark. In the fading light her eyes were
emerald fire, brilliant enough to tie his tongue in knots.
In contrast to those striking eyes, her dress was a plain
brown piece with a braided rope for a belt and worn
brown sandals peeking out at the hem.

"Pardon, I didn't—can I help you? I mean, I'd rather
not." Dephithus stopped trying and glanced down at
the dirt, appalled his pathetic fumbling. "Blasted green
eyes," he snarled under his breath.

A light, melodic laugh recaptured his attention.
"Thank you. I need no help. However, a little evening
companionship might do fine."

The seductive lilt in her lovely voice distressed him.
His body responded to the mere possibility of what
companionship could mean and Myara surged to the
fore of his thoughts, countering any interest he might
have had. "My apologies. I have no time to…"

"Don't lie. You just picked out your campsite, did
you not, Dephithus de NuTraven?"

Dephithus started again. How could she know his
name?

The woman walked up to Hydra's side and held her
hand up to him. "Come, we will talk and…whatever."

Wary and curious now, Dephithus lifted her up behind
the saddle and turned out toward the stand of trees. They
said nothing as she leaned into his back and rested her
head against his shoulder blade. When one hand slipped
below his waistline Dephithus bumped Hydra up to a
trot keeping her occupied with holding on. His hopes
that the stand would be taken, forcing him to move on,
were dashed as they slipped into the quiet group of trees.
The woman set up a small fire as Dephithus cared for

Hydra then she sat silent, watching him.

Seating himself across the fire from her, he reluctantly held out some food and was surprised when she declined. With a shrug Dephithus slipped the food back into his pack. "Who are you?"

"Daenox Priestess Jadean. Just a witch, I suppose." She smiled and Dephithus shivered. "The price on your head has gone up a great deal since you stole Lord Allondis's horse."

Dephithus scowled. Someone must have told Allondis that he had been there. Searching his mind, he settled on Suva as the most likely traitor. "Hydra was a birthday gift to me long before Allondis took the throne."

Jadean nodded agreeably. "My mule was wounded by a daemon-wolf some way back. The daemon was strong enough to drive her mad and I had to kill her. I have been walking since."

Dephithus did not want to seem unsympathetic. Still, his first concern was not for this woman's lack of a mount. Plenty of people traversed these roads on foot. "Could such a creature infect my stallion?"

"I would not worry about it. There is no death in his eyes for a long time. In your eyes I see death past seeking to take you back. Death past," her tone was bemused as she pondered her own words for a moment. "I don't quite see how that can be right, but that is what your eyes say to me."

"How did you know me?" He heard a defensive edge in his voice, undoubtedly due to the unease her words had brought. Would death be driven to reclaim him and right the wrong Vanuthan had done in defying it? He was assaulted by another cold shiver.

Jadean rose and stepped around the fire to him. She held out her hand in offering. "I am a Daenox Priestess. That power tells me some things. It works differently for different people."

Dephithus looked at her hand, long slender fingers with long nails too clean and well-shaped to be those of a traveling woman. He made no move to take it.

"If it will make it easier, I can work a bit of the daenox so that you will think I bewitched you into it."

Dephithus shook his head and took her hand. No one would look badly upon him for seeking pleasure with her even if anyone were there to see. As it was, only Hydra would witness their coupling. Dephithus himself could find no guilt in the want of her warmth and the comfort of another human body next to him. Whatever it took to keep him sane on his journey. Jadean's eyes promised that she wanted nothing more in return than that same warmth and comfort he was seeking.

With the fire flickering an enchanted light around them, they came together softly. Nothing of her manner indicated that she was more than a lonely woman. Even knowing that she was a daenox priestess, he could find no reason to dislike her in the gentle passion and tender caresses she divulged upon him. For the briefest of moments, he could almost imagine that she was his beloved Myara and that everything they had endured was a nightmare to be forgotten.

When they had finished, Jadean sat up and looked on him with sadness in her emerald eyes. Dephithus rolled onto his side and propped his head on his hand. This beautiful woman carried with her an ability for knowing that he could see now was eating away at her.

"What is it you see?"

"Dephithus, on the next moonless night you will find yourself in bad company. Take care when the moon does not travel with you. Also," she hesitated, looking as though her own thoughts were puzzling to her.

Dephithus touched her arm. "You don't have to tell me anything more. I know my journey will not be easy."

Jadean shook her head. "I want to. You might seek help from an objectionable source, but it will make your journey easier if you do." In her silence she seemed to be struggling with something. After a moment she took hold of his hand and stared at it as though to avoid his eyes. It seemed odd, when she had shown no such timidity before. "I don't think you should continue on with this journey you are making. You could leave this place and go overseas perhaps."

Dephithus shook his head. "I have to go on. I will never know peace if I don't. Will you stay with me this night?"

Looking slightly pained she nodded and placed a soft kiss on his lips. "Until you leave," she whispered, "I will stay."

## CHAPTER THIRTY FIVE

*I wander in the darkness,*
*Like you I roam the night,*
*But I do not wander with you,*
*For above you, I am the Moon.*

*On the nights you do not see me,*
*In darkness will you weep.*
*On the nights you do not see me,*
*Bad company you will keep.*

Dawn found Dephithus alone again.

He had suspected it would be so, though her spot next to him was still warm in remembrance of her shape. If she was not long departed, he hoped she at least traveled in a different direction than he did. After the evening they had spent together it might be awkward if they crossed paths again. The words retreated to the back of his mind as memories of Myara drove him back to his journey. She was so clear in his mind this crisp morning that he fancied he could smell her. The sweet almost floral scent of her when she was dressed up for a formal gathering. The delicious salty tang of her sweat when they had been sparring. He would give anything to have her at his side.

Once they were on the road again, Dephithus pushed Hydra to an extended trot. By noon, the morning dew had dried from his clothes and the sun baked down on them, countered nicely by a soft breeze. Such a beautiful day must be a good omen. It lifted his spirits. At their current pace they would reach Corbent Calid by dark, sooner than expected, and that would be a strong start on his journey to find Myara. Hydra responded to his positive mood as well, his stride picking up in strength and animation.

As dusk neared, however, the sky began to cloud over and their road angled east enough that they were now traveling amidst the trees. Unease crept through him, making his skin crawl as he watched the sky vanish, and his good mood faltered. Some part of him lifted with the passing of his cheerful mood and he wondered if that were the daemon-seed waking up within him. He scowled. The last thing he needed was to have his thoughts and actions twisted by that evil influence. What good would he be to Myara then?

The fall of dark found him without the comfort of stars or moon. He took some solace from the certainty that Corbent Calid should be close enough that music from the taverns would soon reach his ears. Many narrow tracks branching off the main road, almost certainly leading to homes, promised of increased civilization. Despite this, Jadean's words returned to him, playing over and over in his head and haunting him more with each moment. On the next moonless night, you will find yourself in bad company, she had said. Looking up at the thick black of the sky he urged Hydra onward, though he knew the stallion was weary.

As he expected, he could soon hear the music from inns and taverns and he caught glimpses of light through the thicket. He was beginning to feel confident again when Hydra laid his ears back.

A man stepped into their path, and the stallion lunged forward unchecked by Dephithus, who trusted the animal's combat instincts. Caught by surprise, the man was unable to dodge the attack and Hydra plowed into him sending him spinning to the ground with a cry of pain. A second and third bandit dropped from the trees above them, pulling Dephithus from the saddle.

Before they hit the ground, Dephithus had his dagger free and lashed out at the one who landed next to him, cutting the man across the back as he rolled to stand. The other bandit had ended up under Dephithus with an arm around his neck, seeking to choke him. Hydra was quick to react, rearing up and bringing both front hooves down with crushing force on the leg of the bandit that had hold of Dephithus. The shriek that followed the strike was unmistakably feminine.

In the seconds it took Dephithus to recover from the pain in his scar and suck in air through his abused windpipe, the woman drew a dagger and lashed out at Hydra. Before any of the wounded bandits could lay hand to him again, Dephithus was mounted and they bolted from the scene toward the waiting city. After rounding a few more bends in the road they could see Corbent Calid stretching out before them. Dephithus could feel a break in Hydra's stride. He was favoring his right foreleg rather significantly, but he continued to run toward the city at his rider's urging.

Despite his concern for the stallion, Dephithus did not slow them. To slow now would only put them in danger of injury or death at the hands of other opportunistic bandits or daemons drawn by the conflict and the smell of blood. They did not slow until they were in front of the first inn, then Dephithus leapt from the saddle almost before Hydra was stopped and knelt next to the favored leg. The woman bandit had left a deep gash in the stallion's upper foreleg and blood was streaming freely, making a thick trail of dirty reddish brown down Hydra's leg.

Dephithus pulled up his hood and led Hydra into the stable. The stable boy on duty there jumped down off a bale of hay and trotted over to them. His practiced eyes trained in on the wound even before Dephithus spoke.

"You need a dressing, and you gotta pay for it."

Dephithus scowled and grabbed hold of the boy's arm when he moved to step back from them. "I will pay. Get my horse the help he needs now and I will see that an extra bit of coin crosses your palm instead of the lashing you will get otherwise."

The boy pulled away angrily and glared at him, but the worry in his eyes and the quick trot that he broke into leaving the stable was enough to assure Dephithus that his threat was taken seriously. Alone with the stallion, Dephithus pulled the saddle and packs off to give him a break from the weight. A few minutes later, a lanky, scholarly-looking gentleman entered the stable with the boy in tow carrying an assortment of packs. Dephithus eyed the tall, narrow character with skepticism. He did not look like the type to doctor horses, but he was not going to turn away any help he could get for Hydra.

The man with his graying brown hair and moustache on a long almost comical countenance frowned at Dephithus with a skepticism that undoubtedly mirrored his own. They both knelt next to the wounded leg and the man snatched a pack from the boy with a hint of impatience.

"You can pay for this?" The man asked as he rinsed the wound with some clean water, then after a quick examination, pulled out some bandages and began to snuggly dress the injury.

Dephithus soothed Hydra before responding, though the well-trained animal did not really need it. He could not help admiring that the man had started tending to his patient before getting any guarantee of payment. "Yes sir. Whatever it takes. Just see that he is treated as well as any king's mount and I will see that you are well paid for it."

The older man chuckled to himself then turned a

more serious expression on the stable boy. "Leave us. Don't you have other duties?"

The boy hesitated, eyeing Dephithus expectantly. With a sigh Dephithus, drew a coin out of his pouch and tossed it to the lad. Grinning at his newfound wealth, the stable boy darted off to attend some other intense chore, like lounging on hay bales. Dephithus turned his curious gaze on the old man then. His tone said there was more to sending the boy away then just keeping him on task.

The older man glanced up suddenly, catching a good look up into the hood of the cloak before Dephithus could draw back out of the light. With no more than a hint of a smile he returned to tending Hydra's wound. "Now then, he is a king's mount, isn't he?"

Dephithus said nothing. He focused on soothing the stallion, more to quiet his own nerves than anything and keep out of the way so the elder could finish his work and be off.

"Don't expect to keep such a secret from everyone. You will only fool the fools. The rest of us know you, but we aren't much interested in turning you in."

The man's words surprised Dephithus a little. "Suppose I were who you think I am, why would you not wish to turn me in and get a good pocketful of coin for your trouble?"

"Imperious has soldiers here, but they are here in pursuit of a daemon army. With the daemons and daenox allies in the area, we need much more help than a pocketful of coin can offer."

Finished with dressing the wound, the man stood, perhaps a half-inch taller than Dephithus, and held out his hand. With only a slight hesitation Dephithus took the offered hand and shook it firmly.

"I am Endre. If you need more dressing on this before you move on again just ask for me. That wound won't be very sound for a bit. I would wait a few days perhaps before I would risk putting much strain on it."

*A few days! With Imperious soldiers crawling about!*

The weight of defeat pressed down on him. "I can't stay that long. Is there any way to speed the healing?"

The man looked almost sympathetic, which was not exceptionally comforting. "Only if you can use the daemon powers. This inn would be a good one for you to hide out at. No one here is interested in much more than a lonely drink and a place to lay their head for a night. Nobody looking for trouble stops here and nobody looking for friends does either. Maybe because it is too close to the edge of town and only the weariest of wanderers settles for the first offering."

Dephithus nodded, still focused on the problem of healing Hydra. Daemon powers? For the purpose of healing, it seemed odd to mention the daenox. Where would Jadean be now?

"Thank you." Digging into his coin he settled with Endre and bedded Hydra down in one of the stalls.

The odds of finding Jadean were slim, though he was sure she would help him if he could find her. This army of daemons was the most likely place to find her, but he could no more march into the midst of such an army than he could expect to find help among the Legion soldiers. The only fast option seemed to be finding a new mount and he liked that alternative almost less than any of the others.

With a growl of frustration, he kicked the stall wall and received a painful protest from his scar for his efforts. Hydra snorted as he sniffed at his bandages then leaned his head over the side to find out what ailed Dephithus. Rubbing between the stallion's eyes Dephithus sighed. Hydra made him much more obvious wherever he traveled, and he would be much better off without such attention. Still, regardless of the wisdom behind getting rid of him, he could not bring himself to humor the idea for more than a moment.

"Rest and heal," Dephithus murmured, leaning close to Hydra's head and slipping his fingers into the black forelock. "We will finish this together."

Dephithus hoped this inn was everything Endre said it was. Slinging his packs over one shoulder, which further irritated his scar, he left the stable for the lights and low music of the common room. A somewhat comical sign hung over the door depicting a worried looking man holding a frayed piece of rope as he fell down the side of a cliff. Large letters in faded red paint introduced the building as The Drop Right Inn. He was a bit comforted by the sense of humor. It certainly did not seem an unfriendly place. The worn state of the building professed to oddly light patronage despite what would seem an opportune location.

Adjusting his hood to be sure his face was hidden, he stepped through the door. The first thing he noticed was that even the minstrel in one dark corner appeared to be contentedly alone with his music. A group of men and one woman sat around a table playing dice, but they said nothing to one another as they went about it and every one of them appeared lost within their own thoughts. He noted that each player was so protective of their solitude that they barely watched to see if any of the others were cheating. Nearly all the good shadowed spots were occupied with lone travelers as well as a few groups who were enjoying their silence together. The minstrel was perhaps the most active in the bunch as he moved with the mournful music he played on his lute.

The music was somehow more pleasant for coming from one instrument. In the palace and even the inns of Imperious where he had spent his young life there, were usually many players and singers melding their talents. This sound was a new and sweet change from the evening's events and the problems he had yet to face. As he walked toward the bar he peered about for the elusive innkeeper. The serving girls moved between the tables in a relaxed manner, free of the taunts and fondles they would receive in most inns. No one here could be bothered to notice them that much.

Dephithus opened his mouth to call one over when he spotted the gentleman behind the counter leaning back in the shadows with his eyes closed.

Gentleman was a good description. The innkeeper, if he indeed were such, was a trim, well-built man perhaps as tall as Dephithus or at least very close to the same height. His chocolate brown hair and moustache were neatly trimmed and his clothes were clean and tidy, not worn at all. In general, he would have looked more at home in a palace garden entertaining a group of ladies.

He stared at the resting man for a few seconds, trying to decide how best to draw his attention, when one of the girls walked up and poked the sleeping fellow in the ribs rather unceremoniously.

"Random, you have a customer," she hissed in his ear as she tipped her crown of blond hair to Dephithus.

The innkeeper started awake and shook his sleep off quickly. Locking his warm brown-eyed gaze on Dephithus, he smiled and strode over. "Welcome to my inn," he offered with an accented voice that was deep enough to be clearly heard but pleasant enough not to annoy the patrons. "I'm Random Mayby. What can I do for you?"

It took a few seconds to fight off the urge to ask if that were the man's real name. Ultimately, it did not matter, so he moved on. "You own this inn?"

Random's smile did not falter. "Yes, sir, unless you want it."

Dephithus grinned. This man was no mercenary, that was certain. "No, thank you. I think I would settle for some real food and a room."

"I've got a fine boar steak if you're game for it?"

Dephithus nodded agreeably and Random's smile grew as he turned away and stepped through the door to the kitchen.

Within a few seconds he reemerged and nodded to Dephithus, offering a most disarming grin. "It's cooking."

Dephithus nodded his thanks and turned to find a seat.

"One thing before you settle." Random motioned him closer and Dephithus leaned over the bar. "Just between us, my nephew mentioned that you've got a problem with your horse. There's a fellow who has been here for about two weeks. He usually comes down to the common room a little before daybreak and, unless I miss my guess, which I rarely do, I think he can help you."

Gratitude swelled in Dephithus and he cracked a smile. "I mean no insult, but your mother named you well. I thank you for the tip and will approach this fellow in the morning."

Random waved Dephithus away with a good-natured chuckle. Picking out the only remaining shadowed seat, one next to the minstrel's corner, Dephithus sat down to await the first—and probably the last—good meal he would have on this journey.

## CHAPTER THIRTY SIX

As dawn crept in Dephithus woke and lay in bed for a time watching the increasing light through the dingy window. It was a luxury he had forgotten the appeal of. With the daunting task of trying to speed up Hydra's healing ahead of him, it was extraordinarily hard to convince himself to get out of the bed. It was such a welcome break from sleeping on the ground or in the saddle. Still, if he was to catch this individual Random mentioned, he needed to get up and moving.

*Just one more minute.*

Dephithus stared at the ceiling. Worn wood planking and exposed beams stared back at him. Maybe two minutes. The sound of a horse trotting past in the street below acted as a spur, driving him up and into his boots. It would do him no good to miss his window of opportunity for approaching the stranger.

He gazed into the stained, cracked mirror. A change of clothes would be nice. Perhaps, if this person were able to help Hydra, he would have time to peruse the nearest clothier's wares for a suitable outfit. Perhaps he could even get a gift for Myara and their child. The child would be going on five by now.

*Has the daemon-seed effected the child?*

Dephithus scowled at his reflection and it betrayed him as it had once before, not smiling this time, but retaining his thoughtful expression of a moment before. A sudden wash of bitter anger coursed through him and he punched the reflection. The mirror shattered out from the existing crack and jagged fragments of glass cut into several knuckles. Cursing under his breath at his own reckless behavior, he rinsed the new wounds in the washbowl. The mirror was too broken now to offer much of a reflection, which was fine with him.

A strip of the soldier uniform made a passable bandage that he tied tight over the wound. Collecting his belongings, he made his way down to the common room. The last time his reflection had chosen to betray him it had been the work of the daemon-seed. That could indicate that the seed was getting stronger again. If there were anything he needed less than that, he could not think of what it might be. Would he be able to focus on his journey if the daemon-seed gained too much power? Regardless of the answer, it was plain that he had to get moving again quickly.

Dephithus stepped out into the common room with his packs slung over one shoulder and scanned the few patrons.

It was a matter of seconds before he locked eyes with the man seated midway down the near wall. Cold rage washed through him, numbing him to the rest of their surroundings.

Rakas, his face a perfect image from a loathsome memory, appeared frozen with shock himself, if only for a heartbeat, then his gaze shifted to the door. Letting his packs fall from his shoulder, Dephithus reached for the sword hilt. It was fitting that Myara's sword should kill this man.

Rakas shoved his chair back, the sound of the legs scraping on the wood floor coinciding with the loud thud of the packs hitting the floor. The sword sung free of its sheath and Dephithus lunged after Rakas who was already bolting for the door.

*He's going to get away.*

Dephithus grabbed the nearest chair and flung it after Rakas, catching his legs and making him fall. Ignoring the curses of alarm from the few other patrons as they scrambled clear, Dephithus sprinted over and swung out with desperate, brute force. The blade arched down towards his opponent's neck and Rakas threw out an arm to deflect it. Oddly, it stopped cold against the flesh as if he had swung it against an iron rod. Rakas did not get away unscathed, however. The force of his fall when the chair tangled in his legs had left him with a cut on his forehead and a bloodied nose.

Stunned by the fall, Rakas moved a little slower now, fumbling to get ahold of the nearest table to pull himself up. Dephithus placed the edge of the blade against the man's throat and hesitated there. His hatred was so great that, in this moment of reckoning, he faltered. His arm shook. His breath was harsh and loud in his ears.

Rakas looked up and swallowed. There was expectation in those black eyes. Expectation, sorrow, and acceptance. He wanted it to be over and Dephithus struggled between the desire for vengeance and a powerful revulsion at the thought of giving the man anything he wanted.

"I take it you know each other?" Random stalked over, stopping a few feet from Dephithus, a little out of easy sword range. Barely controlled anger made his voice tight and his presence more threatening. "The least you can do is finish this outside of my establishment. I thought he might be able to help you, lad, but apparently whatever assistance he could offer is much less important than your vengeance." He shook his head in disgust and pointed toward the door.

*You have no idea.*

Dephithus growled, his abhorrence for Rakas fueling similar feelings now for Random who had no concept of how deep this hate was rooted. Still, he hesitated. What had Jadean said?

*You might seek help from an objectionable source, but it will make your journey easier if you do.*

Rakas watched his internal struggle with a wary curiosity, though he stayed poised beneath the blade, apparently sensing that it was too soon to make any assumptions about his future.

Dephithus clenched his teeth so hard it made his head hurt. Hydra needed healing if he was going to get back on the road to go save Myara and their child anytime soon. He could always try to barter for another horse, but that route risked exposing himself to too many people and possibly getting stuck with a mount he could not rely on should he be attacked again. What if Rakas really could help them?

Fighting the violent rage still coursing through him, Dephithus forced himself to lower the blade. The light of a new day filtered in through the dirty windows and danced brilliantly along the polished steel. "First, you are going to help me."

Rakas did not move from his spot on the floor. "And then what?"

"Then I'm going to kill you."

Random heaved a sigh next to Dephithus.

Rakas narrowed his eyes. "Is that supposed to inspire me to help?" His gaze darted to the blade suddenly as if he had forgotten it was there.

Keeping the blade down took a monumental act of will. "Don't push me. I'm already past my limits. Do you have any idea how much suffering and death your actions caused? You destroyed my life and that of those I love. You would not dare claim that I don't have a right to seek justice in this."

Rakas grimaced and lowered his head, his long black hair falling forward around his face. Random moved away from them, perhaps realizing, when Rakas did not deny the accusations, that whatever history was between them was well beyond him.

Keeping his sword ready, Dephithus backed up a few steps to give Rakas room. "Get up," he snarled, "and don't try to fool me with your feigned remorse."

Rakas stood, wincing as he got to his feet. "Where are we going?"

"Stable," Dephithus replied curtly, gesturing to the door with his blade.

With all the forced composure of a man walking to his execution, Rakas led the way from the inn. Random took a few steps after them as if he were tempted to follow and supervise. No innkeeper wanted bloodshed on their property. Dephithus gave him a hard look and shook his head. Random stopped and returned the look with an expression of pleading as they stepped outside into the morning light and closed the door.

Dephithus was still shaking and now that he was alone with Rakas, he wondered how long he could hold back his rage.

The same stable boy from the evening before was reclined on a bale of hay near the door. When he saw them, he started to rise until he noticed the drawn blade and looked questioningly at them. Dephithus shook his head, indicating that he was not needed, and the boy slunk away, retreating deeper into the pile of bales. Hydra was already watching them approach with his head stretched well over the stall door.

Stopping in front of the stall, Dephithus scowled toward Rakas, though he did not look directly at him. "His leg is injured and I can't wait for it to heal. If you help, I might consider letting you live."

"Your tone and the white of your knuckles from your grip on that sword hilt tell me I'd be a fool to believe you," Rakas replied, glancing at Dephithus now with something that might have been longing.

His rage started boiling over again, something Rakas seemed to sense as well, prompting him to turn his attention to Hydra. Once they had the stallion out of the stall, Rakas knelt next to the injured leg as Endre had the night before. Hydra laid his ears back, showing his displeasure while Rakas removed the dressing and cleaned the wound so he could better see what he was dealing with. Dephithus grimaced at the deep gash, but Rakas appeared unconcerned.

"Why are you in Corbent Calid?" Rakas asked, poking around the wound until the stallion's tail swished about in irritation. "With all the Legion soldiers here, this seems like the kind of place you would be avoiding."

"Amahna took Myara and my child to some cave in the Dunues Mountains. I have to go after them." Dephithus stroked Hydra's neck, soothing the big animal. As satisfying as it might be to see, it would do them no good if the stallion threw a kick and killed Rakas before he could heal the wound.

Rakas drew in a quick breath. "That must be what the dragons were waiting for. Your child."

Dephithus was about to warn Rakas not to speak of his child when he noticed that the wound was starting to close up. Stunned into silence, he watched the flesh heal and knit together the same way it would in time naturally, only extremely accelerated. It stopped short of growing hair again, but it was still a massive improvement.

"How did you do that?"

"The daenox has become very workable since being freed. There are limits on such healing and it is tremendously draining, but it has obvious valuable applications." Rakas stared at the ground as he spoke, as though he could not bring himself to meet the eyes of the man who meant to kill him now.

"What happened to the tremors you had when you were in Imperious? Or were those just an act to put me off my guard?" Dephithus inquired as he ran a hand over the wound, expecting to find that the healing was an illusion. The skin was good and healthy and Hydra's ears had perked forward again.

"They continue to improve the longer I am away from the cave where the daenox is most heavily concentrated."

The realization of what he should do then made Dephithus suddenly nauseated. He leaned against Hydra for both physical and mental support as he regarded Rakas and swallowed against the growing urge to throw up. "Do you have a horse?"

Rakas shook his head. He started to look up, but caught himself and averted his gaze again.

"That's a problem, but not an insurmountable one." Dephithus took a deep breath and forced himself to continue. "We need to get one for you and I need to find a change of clothes."

Rakas did look up then. "You want my help?"

Dephithus stared at him, his voice getting stuck in his throat. This man was the one who caused it all. This man was the reason he had to fight every minute to keep the daemon-seed from taking control again. He was also the one who knew where the caves were and how to navigate within them. "It's the last thing I want, but you know this cave and how to find it. You're going to lead me to Myara."

Something brightened in other man's eyes.

Dephithus let out a low growl and Rakas flinched.

"No. There is no chance for redemption in this for you. You will never deserve forgiveness and you will never have it. You destroyed my life with your actions. I hurt and killed people. I hurt the people I love the most." *And I will never deserve forgiveness for what I did to her.* Tears stung his eyes and he looked away. "You will help me find her and then you will run as fast and as far as you can or I will kill you. And know that, if you touch me even once, even if it is an accident, I will kill you right then."

Rakas slowly stood, taking a step back from Dephithus, and nodded. "Fair enough."

*

Theruses charged Amahna with watching Kyouin for a time. It was an assignment she was happy to be engaged in. The most pleasing aspect was being sent away from the cave and the constant torment of Raine's presence. This left Theruses in a position, devoid of his primary outlet, where he might be more likely to try and force himself upon Raine. Amahna could only hope he was smart enough to realize the danger of the uncertain powers the dragon-child possessed. The relief of getting away from Raine aside, Amahna did not trust Kyouin and she hoped to learn something of his origins and his intentions, if he had any coherent plan at all.

For most of their journey toward Corbent Calid, where she would turn back, Amahna spent her time observing his motley collection of troops. Men and women filled the roles of everything from daenox priests and priestesses to laboring grunts, with warriors of assorted specialties and skill levels filling the ranks between. Those who had been with Kyouin the longest or who had won favor with their skills were dressed in dusty gray uniforms with black accents. The most common daemons in the army were daemon-dogs and daemon-wolves, such as the ones that flanked Kyouin's mount and those guarding his young brother, Vaneye, next to him. There were also some higher-level daemons who had established their own peculiar forms as well as daemon possessed humans and undead. None of these were uniformed in any way. They had their own distinct appearance to set them apart.

Kyouin claimed that more of his army waited outside Corbent Calid, amusing themselves with terrorizing the locals while he tended to business. That portion of his army was, he said, being overseen by an undead warrior on his undead horse, an uncommon daemon arrangement that Kyouin claimed to have manipulated himself. The things he claimed to have done simply with the influencing of daemons astounded her. It was not that these things were not possible, simply that the necessary skills had been all but forgotten over the last hundred years. How had this fool boy ever discovered them?

The cool, crisp morning air of a new day saw them passing outside of Ithkan. Kyouin opted to skirt the town since he had a destination and did not want to be delayed by frightened townsfolk enticing his army. Daemons were drawn to fear. It was one of the many challenges of controlling them. It seemed rather backward that he would choose to blame his army's blood and fear lust on the people who feared them, but Amahna said nothing. Instead, she regarded the distant town in tactful silence and wondered where Rakas was now.

"You have a memory living there?"

Amahna glanced at Kyouin, soothing her scowl into something more neutral. On the other side of his brother's horse, Vaneye watched her curiously. The boy was curious about everything and she suspected it would land him in an early grave. "Nothing of interest. What future do you have in mind for this army of yours?"

Kyouin glanced at the youth next to him. "Not much for light conversation, is she?"

Vaneye grinned at his older brother then schooled his features to regard Amahna again, eerily mimicking her rapid change in expression from a few seconds ago.

Kyouin faced forward again. "I considered taking Imperious before too much longer. My lethal bands have proven more than a match for the Legion soldiers so far. I think that would be a nice attainable goal to start with."

An itch of frustration gained power in the back of her mind. "No. You—I—" She stopped herself and took a deep breath, calming her recently irrational temper. "I am trying to understand *why* you are doing this? What is the point of it all?"

"It's Raine who has you so tense, isn't it?" Kyouin gracefully ignored her sudden glare. "Who is this silver dragon she spoke of?"

"Raine is just a foolish child. No dragons will go free as long as she remains in the cave." Amahna cut off the last word sharply, hoping he would drop the subject. She wanted nothing more than to forget about Raine for as long as possible.

"That child is no fool. She is a creature of power. Whoever or whatever this silver dragon is that she speaks of, I would not be looking for a literal representation of it."

Amahna eyed the surrounding scenery with a fresh scowl. Before them the rolling hills grew steadily smaller and flatter leading into the flatlands immediately outside of Corbent Calid. Behind them, those hills rolled down from the mountains like grass-covered waves. It was the same to the west where the Gmuir Mountains cut across the horizon, only those hills were heavily forested. Where the Gmuir range ran north to south, the Dunues range ran at a gradual angle from northeast to southwest until the two ranges met. Where they came together the mating resulted in a region full of shear canyons and jagged peaks, creating a large stretch of land that was not at all hospitable and rarely traveled.

Realizing that Kyouin had lost interest in her and

turned his attention to the front again, Amahna moved her mount a touch closer to his, ignoring the growling of the daemon-dog on that flank. The growl was enough to draw Kyouin's attention as well as win her an irritated glance from Vaneye. The small boy was almost as protective of his brother as Kyouin was of him.

"I have not failed to consider other meanings to Raine's words, but that doesn't have anything to do with what I asked you."

"Granted," Kyouin shrugged, giving a flippant roll of his eyes that earned a giggle from Vaneye.

There was a thought sprouting and gaining strength in the back of her mind that Raine, as unnerving as she was, might be more tolerable than this arrogant lad.

"Theruses is much less patient than I am," she warned, "and I'm about ready to throw you over my knee like the child you are."

Kyouin grinned, and Amahna instantly regretted her words. "Remind me to take you up on that later, but I think we should pick up the pace for now or we'll never get there."

**B**y noon Dephithus was set up with new clothes and a companion whose death he fantasized about in myriad creative ways. At least the fantasies brought a smile to his lips, albeit a rather grim one.

Shortly after Hydra was cared for he had sent Rakas out with a pocketful of coin to find a mount and some other things they needed to continue the journey, including a change of clothes for him.

He almost hoped the man would take the coin and disappear.

Still, he had no idea how to find this cave, and, if it were a small enough entrance he might never find it alone. If he did find the cave on his own, once inside he would be completely at the mercy of his enemies who lived there and knew the dark passages and the dangers that he might overlook. With Rakas as a guide, assuming he dared trust the man, the odds were more balanced. That was to say that it was no longer an impossible task. Unlikely, perhaps, but no longer impossible.

Rakas did return, to a mix of relief and displeasure, and he brought with him a handsome rust-colored gelding he must have bartered fiercely for to afford with the coin he had been given. The clothes he brought were also much finer than he should have been able to get at that price. Dephithus found himself dressed in a lightweight jacket and pants of a satiny forest green with sparse silver embroidery. The shirt was a light tan color with the same satiny feel. It was almost as if he was preparing for a casual family dinner in the Elysium palace.

Then he noticed Rakas standing watching him from the corner, his mouth slightly open and desire burning in his features. From that moment, on a roiling hatred filled Dephithus again and every word he spoke dripped with bitterness.

Even as they rode out of the city, in the dust of a Legion troop that had recently passed, Dephithus could not shake the foul undertone of bitterness that coated everything he thought and said like oil. There was an obvious problem pending with the unit of soldiers somewhere not far ahead of them, but he could not focus past his all-consuming hatred for the man beside him. Every minute that hatred boiled over in him it was making the daemon-seed stronger and that, in turn, would make rescuing Myara and his child much harder. Still, taking advantage of his unwanted companion's knowledge of the caves location and its passages could save him a great deal of time. Time that Myara and his child would otherwise spend suffering in those passages. He had to be stronger than his hate.

Eventually, it was Rakas who suggested the obvious.

"Perhaps we should ride away from the road, more in the cover of the trees."

Dephithus nodded, scowling despite himself and making no move to turn off the road. The suggestion, as sensible as it was, got churned in with the rest of his thoughts too quickly for him to internalize and respond to it. After a few more minutes, Rakas began to turn his gelding into Hydra, trying to herd them off the road. Hydra snorted and gave a warning kick at the other horse, jarring Dephithus from his ponderings.

Looking at the other animal encroaching on their space, Dephithus recalled what Rakas had said and turned Hydra away from the rust gelding. Rakas bumped his mount to a trot for a moment, moving ahead, then slowed again once Dephithus was behind him.

Glaring holes through the drab, dark clothes Rakas wore, Dephithus urged Hydra to catch up. With his intent focus on the other man's back, he noticed something unusual about the man's attire. His dark cloak moved with an unnatural elegance even in the slightest breeze. It rippled in a way that was more like fluid than fabric. Maybe there was some secret in that garment. Or maybe it was something else. He had blocked the sword with his arm and had somehow gotten far more value from the coin Dephithus had given him than he should have been able to.

He moved Hydra up next to Rakas, tempering violent hatred to a more passive loathing for the sake of curiosity. "How did you deflect my blade with your arm?"

Rakas glanced at him, looking puzzled for a moment before recognition flickered in his black eyes. "Oh, yes. When you tried to kill me at the inn. I was using a manipulation I figured out with the daenox over the last several years away from the cave. Now that the power is free in the world and not so concentrated, I find it easier to work with."

The shade dropped the temperature several degrees and Dephithus absently pushed back his hood once they were fully in the cover of the trees. He noticed, for the first time, that, in addition to losing his tremors, Rakas looked healthier than when he had last seen him in Imperious. The man had filled out some and regained a more natural color. He would be rather attractive if such refined masculinity and base evil appealed to Dephithus.

The toxic rage started seeping through his veins like lava, and he had to willfully tamp it down.

"Why did you leave the cave?"

"Theruses was growing tired of me, and he isn't known for tolerating unwanted things in his cave. My life had no value to him anymore. I decided to move on before he moved me on."

"Theruses?" As Dephithus spoke the unfamiliar name it slid, thick and vile, over his tongue. That could not be a good thing.

"He is the one Amahna bends knee to. The one I used to bend knee to. Theruses, Lord of the Daenox, or so he claims, but the daenox is free and he is still in that cave."

That was wonderful news. All he needed was a bigger, meaner enemy than Amahna to contend with. "What is he like, this Theruses?"

The name did not taste any less vile the second time.

Rakas regarded him in the most detached way, almost as one might look at someone who they expected to die. Despite the connotations, Dephithus found it more bearable than the desire and longing that usually accompanied his looks.

"Theruses is a little like you, only larger in build all around. Stronger. Much taller. He has scaling like yours, only gold and more of it, and a tail. His feet are clawed and his eyes and hair are as black as soot, much like mine, only they seem darker somehow. He is not at all forgiving, but he looks after those who ally to him and sees that they are provided for, so long as they don't displease him. Theruses is very powerful, and he is not likely to hand your loved ones over to you if they are his prisoners."

"Aren't you afraid he'll kill you if you go back there?" Dephithus forced a calm tone, though his mind raced with the complications this new information provided. Why hadn't Vanuthan mentioned this Theruses? Did she not know about him? Or perhaps she believed

Dephithus would give up before he started if he knew what he might face.

"I'm sure he will, right after he is done killing you."

Dephithus spared a glance for his odd, unwelcome companion. "Then why are you coming?"

"I gained a little more time by leaving the caves, but the daenox is still killing me. I would rather die doing something to right some of my wrongs than sit around and watch this chaos unfold while I waste away."

Dephithus shrugged. That was good enough if it was going to work to his benefit, though he got the feeling there was more Rakas was not telling him. With a nudge of his heels he picked the pace up to an easy trot. There was no point in delaying the inevitable.

If he could perhaps get Myara and their child free before Theruses knew they were in the cave, he would count that a success whether or not he lived through it. Still, living through it was the preferable option. Maybe Theruses would be angry enough with Rakas for bringing him there that he would kill him first. That might buy them some time. Then again, what if Rakas were seeking to win favor with Theruses by bringing Dephithus to him? There were simply too many unknowns.

As the day moved toward another cloud covered dusk, Dephithus began to feel uneasy again. Bad company was already with him, but there was more of that to go around nowadays than any one person could handle. He silently cursed the clouds, and Hydra sped up in response to his disquiet.

Perhaps it was the swift pace in the darkness or perhaps it was that they were each too lost in their own thoughts. Regardless of which, they came out of the trees at a controlled canter into a clearing filled with the soldiers they had been behind earlier. The troop had stopped to set up camp for the night, the lack of fires and noise making it clear that they were trying not to draw attention. Dephithus and Rakas pulled up fast in surprise and a stunned silence followed. Even in the deepening dark, his face was too well known, and the picture-perfect stillness was broken when one of the soldiers cried out.

"Arrest them!"

With panic swelling in his chest Dephithus drove Hydra from a dead stop to a full gallop with a powerful strike of his heels. In seconds, Rakas was rushing along on their heels. The soldiers around them broke for their own mounts and gave chase. At the far side of the clearing they barreled into the forest, dodging trees and risking jumping the fallen ones rather than wasting time to go around. Hydra was surefooted and Dephithus did not care if Rakas could keep up on his mount or not. It sounded like a whole herd of bad company was right on their heels.

Amahna's attention was constantly being drawn back to the abomination Kyouin had heading up the rest of his daemon army. There were grotesquely twisted higher level daemons all around them now, and they all seemed to be bound to the young daenox priest in some peculiar way that she had not figured out yet. Their smaller party coming down from the mountains had joined in with numerous human warriors as well at the camp near Corbent Calid, but Kyouin seemed less interested in these. He showed off his undead warrior with great pride, and Amahna began to feel a creeping dread as she realized the power of the army he was bringing together.

The undead warrior on his undead horse was an impressive achievement in daemon manipulation. In life, the beast had been a renowned warrior who fought in the last wars before the banishment of the daenox and the dragons. He had been known as Ryche. His true name had become lost in the great shadow cast by his achievements under that name. In battle he had brought down thousands of daemons, even daring to go and drive them out of their lairs into the swords of other warriors. Yet, when the fighting ended after the dragons and daenox were imprisoned, he was brushed aside, and his great deeds forgotten. So Ryche turned his formidable skills on those he had fought for, slaughtering hundreds of kingdom soldiers before they finally brought him down.

Legend spoke of Ryche as a boldly handsome man, but that did not bear true for the newly raised version of him. The warrior had been dead long enough that there should have been nothing more than bones.

Kyouin had somehow used the daenox to reverse the decaying process far enough that his prized warrior would not fall apart on impact. The muscles and other tissues were partially restored so the undead corruption could function as a fighter and his horse was similarly rebuilt. As grotesque as the pair was, Amahna found them fascinating. Ryche did not speak, which Kyouin said was probably due to the limits of his restoration, but the evil creation watched intently.

Amahna knew she was being watched now, as dusk set in, the deepening dark blurring the horror of Ryche's countenance. She and Kyouin and his ever-present young shadow, Vaneye, were on a slightly higher rise in the landscape looking over the impressive army. Their horses shifted nervously in response to the fourth member, the undead Ryche, who had ridden up to them, stopping back and to the side of Amahna.

She tried not to give in to her nerves, but that gaze, like a cold, viscous fluid washing over her made her want to scream. The beast clicked its teeth every now and then, perhaps longing to say something. While Kyouin seemed undisturbed by the sound, Amahna began to wonder if she could listen to it much longer without losing her mind.

She diverted her attention to the task Theruses had given her. "So, Kyouin, where do you and your army go from here?"

Below them the daemon-dogs wandered amongst the human soldiers rather than the other daemons.

Still tied more to people than to the power that infected them. The one that Amahna had been watching stopped moving and turned its head toward the forest as if it had heard something of interest. The reaction passed through the rest of the daemon animals in that part of the army.

"We might stay here long enough to inflict some losses on the ranks of the Legion. After that, I think we will move out to the east. There is a large village that way that I think we could take over with little disorder and perhaps use as a base for the human portion of our army. Then maybe I will think on what to do next."

"I don't buy that you are this disorganized. I think you know full well what you plan to do after that."

Kyouin started to grin when his attention was drawn to the sudden clamor coming from the edge of the forest below and to the right of their survey point in the direction the daemon-dogs had been looking. Amidst a chaos of barks, howls, and unnatural cries two riders had plunged into the camp. Riders and mounts were plainly shocked at what they had stumbled upon, but the speed of their recovery hinted that there was more to their unexpected arrival than a wrong turn. With impressive agility the first mount leapt the fire in front of him and dodged around the nearest warrior.

The second mount was not so willing and reared up, twisting around the fire and plowing over the two warriors in its way as it finally bolted after the first. There was something familiar about the second rider, but her scrutiny was interrupted by the sudden swarm of Legion soldiers that flowed out of the trees into the daemon army after them. Kyouin giggled in an almost girlish manner and his warriors, who had been swiping half-heartedly at the first two riders, turned their full attention on the soldiers of Imperious. Even Ryche surged to life, leaving them at a gallop to go join the slaughter.

Already frantic cries of retreat were spreading amongst the Legion ranks.

"That's him."

Kyouin's tone drew her attention and she turned to see him pointing after the two escaping riders.

"That is the silver dragon your dragon-child spoke of."

Amahna's heart seemed to skip several beats as she peered through the dusk and fire smoke and recognized the two riders.

Rakas was on the reluctant animal in the rear and on the magnificent white and black mount in the lead was someone she recognized too well. "Dephithus? It can't be. I killed him."

Next to her Kyouin broke into almost hysterical laughter and blurted out, "Well done."

It seemed that Rakas would betray them after all. Given their location and direction of travel, she had little doubt that he was taking Dephithus to the cave to rescue his missing love and their child. Amahna trembled with rage and a deeper feeling that she recognized, with a burst of self-loathing, as fear. The first dragon-child was dead. She had watched him die and there was no reversing that, not without great cost and greater power. Even as she tried to deny what her eyes told her was true, she knew that this was somehow the work of the dragons and Dephithus was indeed alive.

"I have to stop them."

Amahna kicked her mount hard in the ribs and spun the animal. The horse pulled up short from a forward lunge, slamming her up against the front of the saddle. Without her noticing, Ryche had returned to his master and placed his monstrosity of a mount in her path. Her own mount would go no closer to the undead creatures and the daemon-dogs that always flanked Kyouin and his brother had closed in on both sides of her.

"How impolite of you to try and leave so abruptly. Just like last time, if I recall correctly. Why would you leave now? The fun has only just started."

Carefully turning her mount enough to face Kyouin, Amahna fought down the swelling panic that threatened to burst from her chest. His eyes were not kind, not at all forgiving. There was no way she could destroy him and his pets before they got to her, especially with the undead Ryche there. "Don't you realize that the dragons go free if Raine escapes?"

"Don't worry. I'll protect you from the big lizards." He grinned.

Amahna noticed an unmistakable trace of madness in his smile then that reflected strong in his eyes. How could she not have acknowledged it before? It was unforgivable that she had not predicted as much. She had believed her status with Theruses would keep her safe, but nothing could protect against that which had no reason.

"If your arrogance doesn't kill you, the dragons will," she growled, suddenly more angry than afraid, though the anger was mostly with herself for allowing this to happen.

The daemon-dogs growled in response and Kyouin laughed, the sound rising up with the screams of Legion soldiers.

Long after the screams died down, Amahna could not fall asleep.

Dephithus and that traitorous bastard Rakas were riding toward the cave. Theruses needed to know. Better yet, she needed to stop them. But Kyouin's undead warrior had not gone far from her side since he decided he was not going to let her go. Now Kyouin was walking toward her where she stood gazing out over his army. Her hand dropped instinctively to her belt. It came upon emptiness there, for Kyouin now wore

the serpent dagger. That dagger had been a gift from
Theruses. She had given it to Dephithus to torment him
and took it back again when she killed him. She knew
Kyouin would notice her looking at it, but the dagger
was hers. He had no right to it.

Kyouin stopped in front of her, he fondled the hilt
of the dagger very intentionally and Amahna looked up,
making herself meet his haughty gaze. She gave him a
cold scowl.

He smirked. "I think I've had enough of you."

Amahna was suddenly confused. Was he tired of her
in general? If so, what did that mean for her? Did he
mean to let her go or kill her? His tone was not threatening, but rather matter of fact, offering no insight.
"What do you mean?"

"I mean you can leave. I have no more need of you
and I'm bored of your contrary behavior. You're a drain
on my energy. You may chase after your silver dragon."

Amahna searched his eyes for that familiar flicker of
amusement that would betray a hidden motive. She did
not find it there.

"You took my horse," she stated. Her gaze dropped
again to the dagger in a silent addition.

Kyouin fingered the serpents on the hilt while he
looked down his nose at her. A flicker of something
passed through his eyes, madness, but still no silent
laughter showed there. "You may have your horse back.
I suggest you accept your other losses."

Amahna lowered her gaze. She did not want to
appear defeated, yet the arrogance in his face mocked
her and her rage was almost unbearable. To show him
that would only encourage his cruelty. Without another
word, she walked around Kyouin and went to retrieve
her mount who stood with Vaneye at that moment.
Once mounted, she started toward the trees beyond the
edge of the camp. The eyes of the daemons were upon

her as she passed, but they did not move to intervene or follow. A chill passed through her as she stepped past the last daemon, a sort of implied barrier had been crossed. Still, she was not free of him. With every step she felt the daemons slipping further away, but Kyouin's gaze she could feel like a cold touch on her spine, no more distant and no less hateful.

Amahna longed for Theruses or even the despised Rakas to be there with her. Anyone who could glance behind and assure her that the daenox priest did not follow. She refused to give him the pleasure of looking back. Several yards ahead loomed a thick stand of dead trees. Once she was past that, maybe the sense of him would be gone. It was hard to keep her mounts pace calculated, but she would not run from Kyouin. That was the only vengeance she could hope for now. Later, when she told Theruses what had happened here, Kyouin would pay for his actions and for her mangled pride.

When the nearest tree was close enough to touch, Amahna could finally relax enough to take a normal breath. It turned out to be premature. The sound of pounding hooves coming up behind her drove her to turn around in the saddle. Ryche, on his partially de-cayed mount, burst from the edge of the camp behind a pack of daemon-wolves. Amahna spun back around and kicked her mount up to a gallop. She drew upon the daenox to press the animal for more speed, but she could already hear the hard breathing of the daemon-wolves.

Dodging through the trees, she searched her mind for some way to escape the death closing in on her. She had known she could not trust Kyouin, but here, in the dead forest, she at least had some small chance of getting away. A deep growl sounded almost along-side of her. The beast darted under her mounts legs and the animal tripped, going down on her knees.

The impact threw Amahna free of the saddle and she slammed hard into the dry ground. Getting up seemed to take much too long as she listened for the now absent sound of hoofbeats. Once on her feet she turned around just in time to see the daemon-wolf before it lunged into her.

She hit the ground again, this time exposed on her back. There was no time to move before the beast wheeled around and lunged again, its gray eyes focusing in on her throat. Frantic, she threw her arm up for protection and the daemon-infected animal's jaws closed on it, teeth ripping through the skin. Amahna pulled desperately on the daenox in the beast and used it to rip a hole in the animal's throat. Shoving the limp beast off with her good arm, she got to her feet, clutching the bleeding arm to her chest.

Pain made her head spin. She backed up against a tree, placing her good hand against it to ground herself, and closed her eyes to try and stop the dizziness. She had used too much daemon power too fast and the injury to her arm was bleeding profusely. The bark of the tree was dry and rough against her palm and it gave her something to focus on. The weakness lured her to rest for longer than she should.

A soft clicking sound jarred her back to reality. It was a sound she had feared for some time. The dreaded sound of the undead Ryche clicking his teeth together.

Her eyes snapped open and she scanned the dead forest around her. Where was he? Where had the daemon-wolves gone? There was not that much cover in the dead forest.

The clicking sound continued, but she could not pin down a direction with her blood pounding in her ears and pain muddying her thoughts.

Where was her horse?

She had to run.

Moving her leg forward felt like dragging weights. Even lifting her uninjured arm to brush a strand of hair out of her mouth was a challenge. The clicking was getting louder, and a despairing sob escaped Amahna. She vainly willed her body to move faster. The clicking sound moved up alongside of her. She turned her head to see Ryche there. The exposed muscle and sinew on his undead mount moved in a macabre dance of flesh as the beast cut around to stop in front of her.

Amahna stared up at Ryche, but there was not enough flesh on his face for her to read any expression there. He dismounted. Tears flowed freely down her face when he reached for her. At the last moment, her legs refused to hold her and she started to fall.

With uncanny speed, Ryche caught hold around her neck and lifted her up so that her face was level with his, her feet dangling several inches above the ground.

The regenerated muscle in Ryche's hand was warm and wet against her skin. Amahna realized she would slowly strangle to death. Yet, she was again wrong. Ryche did not intend to wait for her to strangle. He stopped clicking his teeth and lifted his free hand to her cheek as if to offer a caress, but his bone fingertip dug into her flesh, slowly cutting a long deep gash from below her eye to the corner of her lip.

The pain was like an unstoppable fire of agony. Amahna screamed, the sound broken by the hand still gripping her throat. That hand could crush her throat and now she wanted it to. Wanted him to end the agony.

He moved his free hand then and placed the fingertips against her abdomen right below the ribs and began to slowly press in. The skin started to split before the sharp fingertips and she screamed again, but the only sound was a pathetic croaking.

She squeezed her eyes shut, willing it to end.

"Ryche!"

The fingers pulled out of her flesh, and the hand around her throat released. She hit the ground and crumpled.

Kyouin rode up leading her mount and gazed down at her, a slight smirk curving his lip. "Sorry about that. I guess I forgot to tell him you could leave."

She opened her eyes and stared up at him, the pain too great for her to even find energy to hate him. "Please... help."

"That arm doesn't look so good. The face is an improvement though. You look good covered in blood. I'd be wary of those wounds infecting, especially the ones in your gut there. Looks painful." He turned his mount to leave and she spotted his younger brother, Vaneye, riding behind him, his youthful, grey-eyed gaze no more sympathetic than his brother's.

*Grey eyes?* When had his eyes turned grey?

"Come, Ryche, we've got other things to do."

"Don't leave me like this," she pleaded.

Kyouin smiled at her. "Don't make a scene, darling. What we had could never last."

He tossed her mount's reins to the ground and rode away. Vaneye and Ryche followed, the undead warrior still making that hideous clicking sound. Amahna lay back and closed her eyes, struggling to focus. She drew on the daenox flowing through the ground beneath her. There was no time to heal the wounds properly if she wanted to catch Dephithus. She used the power to cauterize them, hating that Kyouin would hear her screams.

A bitter, chill morning found the two riders moving across the gradually steepening landscape toward the mist shrouded Dunues Mountains that rose above them.

They had kept up a grueling pace for many days after their nocturnal encounter with the Legion and the daemon army, as much to put distance between themselves and the danger as to get Dephithus far enough away from Amahna that it was no longer practical to consider going after her. He had seen her on the hill when they broke from the trees into the daemon army, her image as clear as if she were standing before him in the light of day. Somehow seeing her again was worse than seeing Rakas had been. The way she had betrayed him was bad enough, but she had also taken Myara and his child.

She had also killed him, though it was so hard to believe that had actually happened that he did not include that among his counts against her. It had taken Rakas yelling Myara's name at him to remind him of his quest and keep him moving.

Rakas was on his bad side even worse than usual this morning. Sometime past midnight the previous night they had come upon the small town of Ithkan.

Dephithus wanted to stop and give the horses a rest, perhaps even get some real food at an inn, but Rakas had adamantly refused to enter the city. The impossible man had stopped his mount and stood his ground, even when Dephithus threatened to kill him. Rakas had stated, with maddening logic while rubbing his chest over the raised ring-shaped scar there as though it pained him, that if he were dead he would not be able to help Dephithus in the cave. As much as he resented it, Dephithus could not deny that it was a winning argument. He finally relented, and they continued around the village at an easy walk so the horses could at least take a break from the more demanding pace.

In the light of the misty morning Rakas was watching him, his brow furrowed with worry, as Dephithus scowled ahead, glaring at the mountains rising defiantly before them. One hand rested on his sword hilt and sometimes his fingers absently stroked the grip of the weapon. As the incline got more severe, Rakas turned them on to a narrow animal path that moved up the mountain in a series of switchbacks. Off to the east was a narrow, and somewhat precarious wagon road that led to a village called Kithin, but Rakas insisted that this was a little faster way to get there and no more dangerous.

"We could stop in Kithin and rest the horses there," Rakas offered, though he sounded reluctant.

"We will stop in Kithin." Dephithus turned his glare on Rakas and caught a hint of longing in the other man's eyes again. "You will lose the hand you ever dare to lay on me."

"Such is my punishment," Rakas murmured, turning to face ahead of them.

The desire to unleash his rage on Rakas swept up through Dephithus like a fast-moving storm, and he clenched his fists, twisting the leather reins in his hands. Perhaps he could break his arm or inflict some other injury that would cause long-term pain without entirely debilitating him. Once this whole journey was over, Rakas would be wise to make himself scarce. The temptation of revenge was almost more that he could handle, especially with the influence of the daemon-seed making his vengeance driven thoughts seem so pleasant.

With that daemon-seed in him, how good a father and husband could he make? Maybe Vanuthan could continue to help him once she was free.

"Don't you sense the daenox when you are near it or something?"

"Yes, in heavy concentrations," Rakas replied as he was forced to move in front of Dephithus to keep his mount on the safer footing of the animal trail.

"Then why did you allow us to ride into the middle of the daemon army the other night?"

"Because I was busy trying not to get killed by the Imperious soldiers you rode us into. You were in no more danger than I was. Amahna saw me, and she is not likely to take my helping you very lightly."

"Why was she there?"

Rakas shrugged. "I don't know. It's probably safe to assume Theruses has some interest in the daemon army." Rakas slowed his mount, forcing Hydra to move slower behind him on the narrow track. "That night—"

Dephithus growled under his breath.

Rakas hesitated a few seconds, then forged ahead. "I did not want to do it to you. I tried to refuse, but Amahna used the daenox to force me to go through with it."

*Amahna.*

He could remember her watching Rakas rape him as though it happened only yesterday, the coldness of her words. Rakas at least seemed torn with guilt. Guilt he deserved to rot in even if Amahna had compelled him with the daenox. Dephithus did not think Amahna even knew what remorse was. Did she know her sister was dead? Would she care if she did know?

His throat and chest tightened and he was suddenly thankful Rakas rode in the lead where the other man could not see his tears. If there was anything he could not handle right now, it was pity from Rakas.

"That's the only reason you were there though, isn't it? You didn't come to Elysium for the festivities and libations then decide to plant a daemon-seed in the heir to the throne as an afterthought. The heir who was, coincidentally, already a pawn for the dragons."

Rakas urged his mount a little faster again and said nothing.

As dusk neared, it brought with it a cloudless sky and the welcome crescent moon shone down brilliantly on them. The stars and moon were almost blindingly bright after the last several nights without them. They searched out a spot that was reasonably flat off the side of the animal trail. The light of the stars and moon was enough to eat by, so they did not bother with building a fire. There was no point in drawing the attention of anyone or anything that might be nearby. The exhaustion of the last several days riding with barely a break made it easy for them to fall asleep.

Sometime later, even before Hydra could wake him, Dephithus snapped awake, aware that they were no longer alone. The crescent moon hung a little lower in the sky, marking it as a little past midnight, and its light cast eerie shadows on the steep, rocky landscape. Careful not to make their visitor or visitors aware of his movements, he slid the arm under him to the sword he always kept close. On one side of them, Hydra made a low nickering sound in his throat, a warning, and Dephithus could hear the other horse shifting uneasily. Opposite the horses, he heard the soft clack of a rock slipping under the weight of something. Panting emitted softly from several different directions.

Dephithus waited.

Preceded by a growling bark, a daemon-dog leapt out of the dark toward Rakas. Dephithus lashed out with the sword and cut open the side of the beast's body from spine to sternum. The daemon-dog fell dead on top of Rakas and the blade, finishing the arch of his swing, hit the ground next to the other man's ear. Rakas, who was now very much awake, stared wide-eyed at the sword point next to his face, looking more alarmed by it than the by the dead daemon-dog on his chest. With a distrustful scowl for Dephithus, he shoved the dog off and sat up, peering calmly into the dark at the many pairs of eyes watching them from a wary distance now.

Dephithus swung his sword back around in time to decapitate another daemon-dog that lunged at him from behind. The entire pack, which appeared to be seven more as best he could see in the moonlit dark, closed in and tensed to lunge.

On the steep mountainside, this could be a most unpleasantly painful, if not fatal, battle. He drew his dagger with his free hand and tensed for the attack, but the daemon-dogs suddenly relaxed and began to back away. Their attention was riveted on Rakas now, at least until they backed far enough that Dephithus could no longer make out their forms in the dark. Keeping his blades ready, he watched around for whatever surprise attack might still be coming.

"You can relax. They won't be coming back. I sent them home."

"Sent them home," Dephithus hissed. "Is that supposed to be a joke?"

"I sent them back to the daemon army where they came from." Rakas responded patiently as he kicked the dead daemon-dog further away.

"They followed us this far?"

Rakas made a sound of confirmation.

"I didn't think the daenox would attack its own.

It may not be very apparent in me right now, but they should have sensed it in you." The irritation in his voice grew with each word while he watched Rakas lying back down as if nothing had happened.

"They can be manipulated to, but such manipulations have their limits."

Suddenly Dephithus understood. "You mean they were sent to kill us and you were targeted first because the sender knew you could stop them."

Rakas nodded and laid his head down on his pack.

"What if more come?"

He closed his eyes. "Then I am sure you will let me know in a hopefully less dramatic fashion next time."

It would be so very easy. All he had to do was swing the sword as he had to kill the daemon-dog, only a little further forward. Trembling with the effort of holding back his rage, Dephithus settled back down, but he did not sleep again that night. Through the rest of the night he listened to Rakas sleep. The other man's breathing was erratic, sometimes almost frenzied as though his sleep were plagued with nightmares. He hoped they were truly horrible ones.

Dephithus had them moving again before the sun cleared the horizon. A thick mist folded around them, dampening their clothes and skin faster than rain. It was almost like traveling through water. The mist obscured their surroundings enough to force a slow, careful pace along the steep winding path toward Kithin. Rakas sounded nervous when he warned Dephithus that the people of Kithin served Theruses. If Theruses knew they were coming, they might be in for a brutal welcome at the mountain village. Regardless of the danger, they needed some good, solid food for themselves and their mounts before covering the last few hours ride to the cave. It did not seem wise to arrive there depleted. He assured Rakas that, if the atmosphere seemed hostile or even unwelcoming, they would move on quickly.

"And what if they only pretend to be friendly with the intention of luring us in and killing us?" Rakas worried aloud.

Dephithus, riding in front today, grinned over one shoulder at his companion. "Then I am sure you will let me know."

Rakas looked ready to spit at him, and Dephithus turned his smug smile to the front.

Late in the afternoon, the animal path brought them up a little less than a mile west of Kithin. It would require some backtracking to stop at the village before going on to the cave, but Dephithus did not feel like they had much choice. They needed to reach the caves with some strength to spare. The obvious displeasure in the other man's manner delighted Dephithus and was more than enough to convince him that the stop was absolutely necessary.

If Kithin welcomed them, then Amahna had most likely not found a way to warn Theruses of their coming. No matter how he looked at it, their odds would be better if they only had Theruses to face without Amahna by his side. Even better if Theruses did not know they were coming. His vengeance on Amahna would simply have to wait for another day.

Upon first look, the village of Kithin appeared normal. If anything, it was more enchanting than most in some peculiar way. The sun had broken through the mist over the top of this place and the sound of laughter and children playing greeted them as they drew near. It was not until Dephithus began to get a good look at the people of Kithin that he started to feel uneasy with the place. All of them, children and adults, had black hair and blackened over eyes, just like Rakas. He stood out as different in most places with his hints of scaling and strange eyes, but here he might as well be wearing a brand on his forehead labeling him as an outsider. At least they were unlikely to have heard of him here given that Imperious was much too far to be useful for trading, which meant they would probably not know that there was a bounty on his head.

A group of villagers, moving together in a way that reminded him too much of a wolf pack closing in on its prey, began walking up to greet them, several children running ahead to be the first. He wondered if they might be just that eager to finish them off for Theruses, but Rakas slowed his mount to a gradual stop. Dephithus saw no weapons on them, and their smiles looked friendly enough, even when they glanced his way. Still, he kept his sword hand close to the hilt so that he could try to make an escape if necessary.

"Lord Rakas," a gruff, though well-trimmed fellow hailed, bowing his head respectfully. "It has been some time since you have passed this way. We are honored by your visit. How might we serve you?"

"A good meal for us and our mounts would be more than enough." Though his manner was curt, the words Rakas spoke came out as more of a request than order or demand.

"We would be honored to serve you, my lord. Dine and rest at your leisure."

Dephithus moved close to Rakas as the party escorted them into the village. "Is this normal?"

Rakas nodded. "Theruses has always protected them from the daemons in return for their service whenever it is needed."

In front of the inn, their horses were taken and they were escorted inside. Dephithus was reluctant to leave Hydra in their hands, but Rakas assured him the animal would be well cared for. There was no indication that they suspected anything amiss and Hydra was more than willing to go with them, so Dephithus opted to trust the stallion. The inn was more of a town gathering place, providing an area to relax together or hold meetings. Every available body within the inn catered to them, seeing that they had sufficient food and drink and providing pleasant music to dine by.

It was so intoxicating to be treated like royalty again that Dephithus longed for more time. Still, knowing that Amahna had seen them increased the already powerful need for urgency. Wasting time here might give Amahna the chance to reach the cave before them and warn Theruses, assuming she had not stayed back with the daemon army. After they had eaten and relaxed for a moment at the table Rakas reclined back and glanced at Dephithus with an oddly content expression.

"Shall we move on then?"

Dephithus hesitated. More powerful than his apprehension at facing this Theruses was his nauseating dread at the idea of facing Myara after the things he had done. "Aren't you in the least bit nervous?"

Rakas shook his head. "Regardless of what happens in the caves, this will probably be the only chance I get to make up for some of the wrong I inflicted upon you."

The reminder was like a hot iron under his feet. Scowling, Dephithus snapped to his feet and made for the door, rising so fast he startled one of the boys that had been attending them.

The boy bowed down to Rakas. "Have we done badly, my lord?"

Dephithus cringed at the dread in the boy's voice.

"No," Rakas reached out and ruffled the boy's hair, earning a joyous smile. "You have done very well; we are just in a hurry."

Dephithus shoved the door open. It irritated him that Rakas had the audacity to act like a decent human. That rage dissolved when he came upon the two young girls that were already bringing their horses around, not only rested, but also well groomed. Rakas stepped past him and thanked the young girls as he took the offered reins. Dephithus, too confused by his fast swinging emotions to say anything and spurred on by the fading light of dusk, took his reins and mounted up in silence. Rakas mounted up as well and they turned westward toward the cave.

Since the creation of the web, only two dragons had ever broken from it. It was ironic that both were of the original sixteen. The first web breaking had occurred over a century ago.

Theruses, the Death Dragon, had used the power of the web and the daenox to break loose and, in using powers that were more or less permitted to him, he guaranteed himself the independence to roam free of the oversight of the council of dragons, at least until he was imprisoned with the daenox years later. Much more recently Vanuthan, the Mother Dragon and a dear companion of his, had committed a dreadful offense by using the natural powers to break free of the web. In using that power, she cursed herself to live out her life in whatever prison she had chosen.

Siniva, the Fire Dragon, was not one of the original sixteen—currently fourteen—dragons, and the web vexed him in many ways. Being born into the web, he had not been given the choice that the original sixteen dragons had been given, though none of those had turned down the opportunity to be a part of it. He did not have the knowledge or the daring to use the daenox in conjunction with the power of the dragons to free himself, and he was not willing to accept the imprisonment Vanuthan now suffered. Even if he could be free, Siniva was not certain that he would give up the combined power and security of the dragon web. Such were the things he pondered while mourning the loss of Vanuthan and waiting to see if the second dragon-child would escape from the cave and free them.

The web was meant to be a source of sanctuary and assistance so that no dragon would ever be left needing. It gave them the ability to give power to one another and to call upon each other for assistance regardless of distance. It also allowed the original council of dragons to keep watch over the others.

For more than a century, the web's power had been limited by their imprisonment, but they needed little protection as long as they were trapped in stone. The most overpowering complaint he had with the web was the extra privilege its creators allowed themselves. The original sixteen were the only ones allowed to completely block out their connection with the other dragons in order to hold private council and other such nonsense. Any dragons could hold private conversations over the web, but their emotions were always common knowledge for whoever might be paying attention. The original dragons were also permitted to make crucial decisions without first consulting the rest of the web. The decision to place the power of the dragons within the child Dephithus and his eventual offspring had been one of these decisions, but Siniva had known about it before hand because Vanuthan kept very few secrets from him.

Nearly two days ago, the remaining original fourteen dragons had closed themselves off from the rest of the web. Siniva worried over what absurd ideas they were considering this time. They had only recently given up trying to connect the web to Vanuthan and use that connection to pull in more power through her. The idea was sound enough if one ignored the fact that she had used a forbidden power to escape the web. Campaigns such as that were what had convinced Siniva that intelligence was passed on to each new generation, leaving the original ones with something of a dearth in that area. If the web-builders would come out of their council he could tell them that the first dragon-child, Dephithus, had only just passed through Kithin.

The constant presence of the web faded away and the fourteen remaining web-builders became the only dragons he could sense.

Dread folded Siniva in an unwelcome embrace.

Whatever scheme they were hatching, he was being drawn involuntarily into it.

"Siniva, Fire Dragon of the web."

Despite the careful guard the elder dragons kept on their emotions, Siniva could sense the tension in the fourteen like a faint hum. He could also feel that familiar and less concealed sensation of being looked down upon.

If only once he could get away with snubbing them and not suffer for it.

"R'Gos, River Dragon of the web-builders," he greeted in turn. "I sense some dire purpose to this meeting that you have drawn me into."

Dire purpose indeed. Undoubtedly, they had another fool idea and he was unfortunate enough to be part of it this time.

"Have you no respect for the elders?" Colvan, the Storm Dragon, hissed in his mind. "R'Gos, I think we err in using him."

*Using?*

That word brought Siniva no comfort. Still, he waited with forced patience to hear the web-builders out, reminding himself that they could sense his emotions all too easily.

"We have no other options," R'Gos stated. "Siniva, you must break from the web and go after the dragon-child. We can wait no longer, and Theruses is too dangerous with her in his clutches."

The words were spoken as if R'Gos truly expected him to jump up and go to it right now. Siniva was appalled, and he knew they could feel it. "Dephithus has only just passed through Kithin on his way to the cave. He will save his child."

This statement was met with surprise, but it won Siniva no escape. "You know we cannot trust him. The daemon-seed is still in him. It must be you."

Frustration swelled in Siniva. Did he really have to explain to them why this was not possible? Were they not supposed to be the wise elders? "There is no way for me to break the web. I haven't the knowledge and you know I can't access the kind of power needed to do so."

The brief, emotionless silence that followed filled Siniva with a surge of misgiving that would have made his physical body shiver if he were not stone.

"As soon as the people of Kithin go to sleep you will use the power of the web to set the village on fire. Fire is your skill, so you should not need to use much. Then you can use the natural powers of their fear and death to break from the web. You must do this and go free the dragon-child."

A hollow began growing in his mental awareness of himself, as though just the knowledge of what they wanted him to do was changing him. "The people of Kithin deserve better."

"They serve the daenox."

"Because of proximity." He could feel their patience wearing thin, so he changed tactics, appealing to their compassion as fellow dragons yearning to go free. "If I do this, then I will be made a prisoner while the rest of you go free."

"No. If you turn yourself mostly human as we did

often before we were imprisoned you will still be free to roam the land."

Siniva directed a mental scowl at Rythis, the Song Dragon, for her words. "Yes, I will be free, trapped forever in a human form." His growl was meant for all of them.

"We will focus on trying to restore you once we are free," R'Gos assured him. "For now, there is no other way. You must do this for the good of all the dragons."

He did not need to ask why they chose him. Like the people of Kithin, he was doomed by his proximity to the caves. "I feel you give me no choice. I will go."

"Good. The power of the web is open to you. Use it wisely."

The web-builders dropped the block that had kept the rest of the web out of their conversation and their overpowering presence receded along with a fading sense of satisfaction. It was a satisfaction that Siniva did not share. Concern washed towards him from several areas of the web where other dragons could undoubtedly sense the mixture of anger, fear, and resignation that filled him. He turned back their inquiries with an aggressive mental growl.

The power of the web was open to him, R'Gos had said. Siniva could feel it. The unrestricted power that he now had the ability to take from all the dragons. It might have been a heady sensation under different circumstances. But the knowledge of what he was meant to do with it made it an unwelcome privilege.

Did the web-builders always have this ability? If so, it explained their superior manner.

Fire was his proficiency. With this much dragon power at his disposal, limited though it still was by their imprisonment, the village of Kithin was close enough that he could incinerate the buildings there in only a few moments. So many innocents would die. People that he had no desire to kill. Even though they served Theruses, they were a good people, making a best of the life they were born to.

Siniva started to draw upon the power of the web, then he hesitated, his conscience getting in the way. The distracting emotions of the other dragons faded away again, and he could only sense Rythis, the Song Dragon. In his mind he could see the beautiful silvery-white dragon as she was in the flesh. Her presence was reluctant this time, rather than confident and overbearing as it had been only moments ago. It captured his attention.

"I cannot do this to these people or to myself, Rythis." The words came with no conviction. He knew the decision had already been made for him.

"You must go. Thousands have suffered and died because of the daenox and its followers. That number will continue to rise if we cannot intervene. It is for the greater good that these people must die, and you, my son, will suffer more than they."

It crossed his mind to mention Dephithus again, but he had sensed the daemon-seed in the boy as well as the daenox in his companion. They could not trust Dephithus, and he was no match for Theruses. Still, Siniva did not see how the web-builders could expect him to face down Theruses either. The Death Dragon was several hundred years his elder.

Rythis bathed him in comforting warmth, sympathy and compassion that had been missing when she faced him as one of the council. Siniva took what she gave and drew upon the power of the web again. This time he did not falter. Focusing on the nearby village whose graveyard he overlooked, he began to spread that power under the buildings.

With the elements of fire clear in his mind, he forced that power up into the buildings and ignited it, leaving himself no time to think it over. The bitter shrieking of the natural power of life being forced out of the people in mass was excruciating in his mind. Already awash with a deep loathing for himself and the web-builders, Siniva took hold of that power and manipulated it to the results he desired.

He did not realize he had been closing his eyes until the warm night air brushed against his eyelids. Opening them Siniva, scanned his surroundings with catlike eyes that would be the same fire-bronze color as his scales were in dragon form. Red hair, intermixed with high-lights of bronze, was blown into his face by a strong smoky wind full of the smell of burning flesh and wood. Tempering the sudden wave of nausea by focusing on his rage, Siniva began to walk down the hill on human feet. He touched his fingertips to the scales reaching out along his cheekbones and his jaw line, wishing they covered all of him as he scowled at the world around him.

Even before he got to where he could see the village, he could see tendrils of flame leaping up against the tinted sky. With the light of the fire reflecting off the rising smoke, the sky took on a blood red cast. He could not bear to think of what he had done, but when he rounded the bend he could no longer hold back the torment of it. The village of Kithin was a massive ball of fire. With heat from the towering flames making his human skin tighten, Siniva walked down the hill into the village.

To drive home that he had done this and there was no turning back, he forced himself to walk down the main street rather than skirting around the village. Almost instantly his nude, muscular body was covered in a sheen of sweat from the scalding heat of the fire. The buildings were becoming skeletons as the fire ate away at everything it touched. Most of the rooftops had already caved in, vanishing into the intense raging flames below. Here and there, toward the outer reaches of the village, the consumption of the homes had been a little less than the instant incineration towards the center of the power focus. A burning body hung partway out one window and another failed escape attempt lay burning in a doorway.

Siniva had seen these people many times. Against the traditions of their land and heritage, these people did not ignore their dead once they were buried. Like most, they did hold a death celebration, but they held it in the graveyard. They came often and read stories and sung ballads over the graves because they believed it would help the dead resist the daenox powers that resided so near. Siniva had enjoyed those stories and ballads from his stone prison. This was a vile way to repay them for the only reprieve he had from the dragon web for so many years.

Before he was fully out of the village, he stopped and turned back, tears running down his cheeks and sweat itching as it ran over the mixture of scales and skin that made him not quite human and not quite dragon. Finding it hard to simply turn away, he stood there, not really caring that he had a purpose. Then the sound of bitter weeping tugged at his awareness. Peering into the shadows cast by towering flames he noticed a burly shepherd kneeling on the ground hunched over with misery. The shepherd, obviously a night watchman that Siniva had forgotten to consider in his decimation of the village, noticed him at the same time. Looking up with eyes that were beyond surprise and beyond accusation he reached one large hand out to the Fire Dragon.

"You did this," he stated in a voice torn by his sorrow.

Siniva only stared back at him, unable to deny the words.

"Please. Take me too. I don't want to go on without them."

Siniva still held his silence and turned to gaze back down the main street as the tears continued to run down his face unchecked. A few moments later, the man walked past him, heading down the street completely naked. Siniva was weary from all the power he had drawn upon, but he was not about to deny this man his request. Pulling on all the remaining power he could, his chest twisting with a fresh swell of hatred for himself and his elders, the Fire Dragon focused his skill upon the departing figure. Flames pulled in from both sides of the street and engulfed the man.

He made no sound that could be heard over the roar of the fire.

Glancing down, Siniva regarded the shepherd's clothes, a sort of morbid offering in exchange for the favor he had asked. He put on the pants, which were several inches too short, and the boots, which were a touch tight. The shirt did not fit at all, so he fed it to the flames. As he turned away from the fire, Siniva began to sing one of the ballads he remembered a young village girl singing in the graveyard. It spoke of a love that lasted beyond life and he hoped it brought as much peace to the dead as it once had to him. His voice, deep as the wind and elegant as a well-played harp, rose up strong over the sounds of the fire.

**E**ven seated upon his proud stallion in the surprising brightness of a new morning, Dephithus could feel his confidence drifting away like dead leaves in the wind. Before him the gaping maw of darkness beckoned, daring him, almost mocking him with its ominous blackness. He had been in caves before. Mostly lava tubes around Dalynay as a young boy. Many times, he and Myara had gotten in considerable trouble for wandering into such places alone. Once a rescue party had even hauled them out after spending most of the night in one such lava cave, though they had never once admitted to being lost.

This time, his beloved Myara and their child had been taken in and he meant to go bring them out, but his nerves were failing him. It was unlikely that death would let him cheat it twice and he was certain that death hid somewhere within that darkness. If only he could avoid it. Vanuthan would not be flying in to revive him this time. She was trapped in her new prison and it was his child the dragons wanted now. Not him. There was no more reason to keep him around once his child was free.

As his feet touched the ground next to Hydra, Dephithus was struck with a sense of panic. Taking hold of the saddle with both hands he steadied himself. All he really wanted at that moment was for this nightmare to be over. The life he had once known was destroyed, thanks in large part to the man who travelled with him, and he had missed out on nearly five years already. Now it seemed he was riding a fast course toward missing out on the rest. How had all of this happened?

The answer was simple. The daenox and the dragons had caused all this suffering in their careless efforts to be free. Of course, it went back even farther than that. Humankind had imprisoned them. Could they really be blamed for trying to be free again? What would happen if the dragons went free now? Would they help counter the chaos the daenox was creating? Or would they add to it?

Dephithus could feel the daemon-seed pulsing bitterness through him. He would not consider leaving his child in captivity, even if the dragons did make things worse. Indeed, he could think of no more pleasing thing than to defy the daemon-seed and smother his child in all the love and kindness he possessed. Yet, that chance might never come to him even if he did manage to free them. He had to survive, and he had to convince Myara that he had a right to be a part of the child's life, which he was not sure he did.

Dephithus grimaced his distress at no one and leaned his cheek against Hydra's neck in search of comfort. The stallion made a soft nickering sound and lowered his head to lip gently at his rider's pants.

"We should go in before I lose my nerve," Rakas suggested, raw fear plain in his voice.

Glancing at his undesirable companion, Dephithus saw that the man looked at least as nervous and out of sorts as he felt. "I haven't found mine yet, and your being afraid of a place you used to live is certainly not helping."

Rakas managed a shaky grin, though his blackened

eyes were locked upon the cave mouth. The welcoming mat of moss along the inner and outer edges of the opening created quite a contrast to the foreboding black of the unknown regions beyond. The entrance was perhaps two horses high and twice as long, which seemed a little backwards to Dephithus, but he was thinking in terms of a manmade doorway. The powers of nature that made this doorway were not concerned with catering to anyone.

"I hope to see you soon," he said to Hydra as he rubbed the stallion's nose before joining Rakas at the edge of the darkness. "What about light?"

Before Dephithus could hope that they might have to go back to the village to acquire some appropriate lighting, a sphere of pale light appeared in the air before them. The light brightened and dimmed and changed in size until it settled at a tolerable output level and a size just larger than a man's fist.

Dephithus gaped at the creation in surprise, but he noticed a problem with it as soon as Rakas began to walk in and the light accompanied him. "Wait."

Rakas stopped and glanced askance back at him.

"What if something happens to you? I have no light."

Rakas sighed, his fear plain in his features even with the blackness of his strange eyes. Another sphere of light appeared next to Dephithus, and he felt as though someone were probing inside of his gut. The sensation passed quickly, but Dephithus snarled at Rakas and dropped his hand to the sword hilt.

Rakas raised up his hands to ward him off. "I did not touch you. I simply linked the sphere to the daemon-seed so that it will not leave you even if I die."

Dephithus took a step toward him and there was subtle tugging in his gut as if there were a leash connecting him to the glowing ball. It was not unpleasant so much as it was simply a peculiar sensation. "How do I get rid of it if you die?"

"Well, you can either die in the cave or it will fade away when you leave the cave again. Come on."

As Rakas turned away, Dephithus caught a glimpse of that old desire in his expression as well as the frustration it caused him. With a huff of pent up irritation, he followed the other man toward the darkness.

They had barely gotten into the cool entrance, not yet beyond the reach of the light, when Rakas held a hand back toward him, motioning him to stop. Dephithus stopped and watched the other man who now had his head cocked slightly to one side as if listening for something.

"What is it?"

"It feels like—"

Rakas was thrown aside like a ragdoll seconds before pain burst through Dephithus, seeming to come from somewhere inside him. He fell to his knees, the pain so excruciating he could not even voice a scream. It had taken his breath away.

Amahna stepped out from the shadows.

Not Amahna as he had last seen her.

A long gash opened one cheek. The edges were blackened as though someone had burned it to stop the bleeding. One sleeve of her dress was torn and bloodied, revealing another series of deep, burned wounds, and there was blood around some holes in the torso of the dress. Her hair was a mess with a few twigs and leaves tangled in it and her eyes shone with a glee that bordered on madness.

She walked over to him, one hand held in a fist in front of her, her teeth showing in a wild snarl. With her other hand, she grabbed Myara's sword and yanked it from the sheath.

"The great thing about the daemon-seed in you is

how vulnerable it is to manipulation with the daenox."
She lowered her face closer to his. "So close only to die
again and I will see to it that you don't come back this
time."

She backed up, raising the sword. From the angle of
her position, she meant to behead him this time. That
would make it harder to come back, even if Vanuthan
were able to help him.

This would be the perfect time for Rakas to redeem
himself. He could see the man in his periphery, however, and he was getting up slowly, shaking his head as
if dazed. No help would come from that quarter. Not in
time, at least. He was on his own, though not without
options.

Pain still wracked him, but he focused on the things
that might save him. He looked at Amahna, at her hands
on Myara's blade, and rage swelled in him, reddening
the edges of his vision. He embraced that rage. That
unparalleled hatred for this woman who had brought
about so much of his suffering. Of Myara's suffering. Of
his child's suffering. A child he had never even laid eyes
on and would not if he did not do something now. He
let the anger sweep through him, feeding the daemon-
seed. Giving it all the power it could want.

Myara's sword started to fall. Then, suddenly, the
pain was gone. The daemon-seed was his power now.
Dephithus grabbed the dagger at his belt and surged up
under the path of the sword, slamming into Amahna
and driving the dagger blade deep into her side. She
cried out, her scream of pain bringing a pulse of pleasure deep within him. That was the daemon-seed, he
knew, but right now he was willing to go along with it.

The sword fell from her hands and he spun, catching the hilt before it hit the ground. He spun back as
Amahna fell to her knees on the rough rock and raised
the blade. Her hands were wrapped around the hilt of

the dagger protruding from her side. Her eyes were wide with surprise.

"You thought it was over, didn't you?" he growled.

Her eyes rose, not making it past his hands on the hilt of Myara's sword. Her gaze then shifted toward Rakas who was walking over to them.

"Help me."

Rakas placed a hand over the ring-shaped scar on his chest and backed away. Dephithus swung. The blade bit deep into the side of her neck, not quite cutting through. He pulled it back and she toppled over, her life bleeding away in the entrance of the cave.

Dephithus turned to Rakas. The other man glanced down at Amahna with a pained expression and closed his eyes. Rage flowed, powerful and invigorating, through Dephithus, feeding the daemon-seed. He stared at Rakas, his hands tightening on the hilt.

Dephithus closed his own eyes and took a deep, trembling breath. He turned from Rakas and cleaned the blade on Amahna's tattered clothes. Then he made himself sheath it.

"Let's go."

## CHAPTER FORTY TWO

The cave was relatively plain for some distance. They traversed around several treacherous hidden pits that Rakas made visible for him. Dephithus could see no bottom to them.

As they roamed deeper, he noticed the increasing strangeness of the surroundings. Peculiar formations of rock grew upon the walls, ceilings, and floors. Tooth-like formations grew up from the floors and down from the ceilings in varying lengths and thickness. Some even met in the middle, creating pillars that the light turned into serpent shadows on the uneven floor. Magnificent formations spilled off the walls, glossy with dampness, giving the illusion of living masses. In some areas the floor was of the same nature as those wall formations, and in others it was white and powdery. In the white areas there were numerous bush formations that seemed to be formed of a white crystal. And these were only a few of the wonders within the chambers and passages they traversed. In different circumstances, he would have liked to study these things more.

In its strange way, the cave was beautiful. Unlike the lava caves he had been in, this vast cave was a haven of new colors and shapes. It was also distinctly more open than some of the lava caves. Though he did see many smaller passages that would require crawling or even squirming on one's belly to get through, the direction they took never met such discomfort. As he gawked in wonder at a group of white crystal formations that dropped down from the ceiling Rakas hissed back at him.

"Watch your step," he snapped in a low voice.

Glancing down in front of him Dephithus discovered he was about to walk heedlessly over the edge of a drop. It was only perhaps twenty or so feet to the next floor, but the possibility of such an unpleasant landing sent a small wash of energy through him, leaving him feeling even more on edge. He continued after Rakas, this time a bit more attentively.

When they had been walking for what seemed an extraordinarily long time the spheres of light suddenly dimmed and Rakas turned back to him. With his finger on his lips, he expressed the need to be quiet.

Dephithus nodded, seeing the pale light that came out of an opening just ahead of them. Peeking into the chamber, Rakas crept past the doorway and motioned Dephithus to follow. Dephithus began to comply, but he stopped a few inches past the edge of the doorway. Within the oddly illuminated chamber was a large pool surrounded by a stone shelf. Numerous people, most scarcely dressed, lounged around the pool gazing into the crystalline waters or engaged in intimate delights with one or more of their companions. With the sparkle of the water glinting off his silver-green eyes he was captured by the beauty of the room and understood instantly the desire to know pleasures on the shelves around that pool.

"We do not help anyone by standing here trying to get caught," Rakas hissed as quietly as possible.

Dephithus nodded and lingered for a moment longer, then tore himself away from the utopian scene. Moving deeper into the cave, they entered a long, broken down group of passages. This section was no less amazing than the rest, for the cave had included the breakdown in its decorating. Younger formations hung down from the sides of large boulders already promising of future magnificence.

As he was admiring this creation process an icy heat moved through Dephithus, bringing with it an unpleasant ache of sorrow. A voice that seemed to come from all around as well as within him spoke.

"Go, see your daughter. Then I will kill you, dragon-child. She will see you fail and despair."

Dephithus stopped, frozen to the spot by the chill of the voice. Rakas, realizing he was continuing alone, stopped and glanced back at him. Dephithus could not hide the fear from his face and Rakas looked concerned, though he had obviously not heard the same thing.

He moved close and whispered, "What's wrong?"

"I heard a voice." Dephithus replied, not concerned about how crazy that might sound.

Rakas shrank before him. His whole carriage and demeanor deflated. "Theruses knows we are here."

Shaking off the chill, Dephithus forced himself to begin walking. "He will let me see her. If we can get that far, there is still a chance."

Rakas nodded, looking resigned, but his steps when he continued were strong and determined.

*What of Myara?*

Why had the voice had only mentioned his child, his daughter? A girl was good. Myara would like having a girl child to teach and to corrupt with her mischievous ways. He smiled inwardly, though there was also a sinking feeling in his chest as he did so.

Realizing Rakas had gone on without him again, Dephithus began to follow the way the other man had headed. He took two steps and stopped again. Odd as it seemed, he was compelled to try a different direction.

The feeling grew fast until it was overwhelming and Dephithus forgot his companion. Walking in the direction of the pull he came upon what appeared to be a dead end. Confused, he studied the area and discovered an opening at the bottom of the wall. As he dropped down to his hands and knees the scabbard hit the floor with a dull clank.

Scowling, he glanced around the chamber uneasily then dropped more carefully on to his stomach and pulled himself through the opening. The sphere of light accompanied Dephithus, lighting the passage which rose up immediately to a crawling height. After several feet of crawling on the reasonably smooth stone, the small passage curved to the right and opened into a slightly larger room. It was about the size of a private bathing room, though the ceiling was low enough to keep him slightly bent over.

Alongside of where he entered the chamber was a deep, clear pool. Dephithus took a moment to gaze down at the formations under the water before he looked around for where he was to go next. Across the pool from him was a passage as tall as the room itself, though this was discouragingly not the way he was being drawn. Directly across from the passage he had come out of was another crawling passage. This was the one he needed to continue down. As he deliberated there, he wondered how long Hydra would wait for him. Hours? Days? He hoped that the stallion would not stay too long if he did not return within the day. Making sure the scabbard touched down gently this time, he returned to his hands and knees and moved on.

For at least twenty feet Dephithus continued on his hands and knees, then the passage closed down more and he was forced to squirm along on his stomach. It did not take long for him to start feeling the effort of this awkward movement in his muscles. It occurred to him that this might just seal off and he would have to back out on elbows and knees that were already feeling tender. It seemed like this dreadful passage might go on forever when he finally saw a larger area ahead at the edge of the light's reach. Dephithus focused his full attention on moving as fast as he could toward this new opening. The reckless effort won him several lumps on his unprotected head and he was developing a headache by the time he poked out of the hole.

The headache was suddenly the least of his worries.

In his careless rush to get out of the confining belly crawl, Dephithus had failed to consider that this new area might be occupied. He emerged lying vulnerable in the face of a twisted daemon-beast with his head and arms sticking out and the rest of his body, including his weapons, still in the crawlway. The beast, which was vaguely dog-like in form, looked as if its skin were slowly melting away. The fleshy lips around its mouth appeared to have already sloughed off, leaving its teeth bared in a permanent snarl. The creature put its nose in front of his and emitted a gurgling growl.

As Dephithus tried to search his panicked mind for some way out, the compulsion that had drawn him here vanished. At the same moment, the daemon-beast raised its head and peered down one of the passages leaving this chamber. Seeming to have forgotten him, it turned and loped away in that direction. Dephithus pulled himself quickly from the hole and stood up. The overhang he had failed to notice put an abrupt stop to his standing and the force of the impact dropped him back down on his knees. He knelt there with his hand to his head and struggled to fight off the pain.

There was a small gash on top of his head and his fingers came away bloody, but it was no reason to dally.

Fighting the pain, Dephithus wiped the blood on his pants, which were already dirty enough from crawling that it would make little difference. Remembering that he still had to face Theruses, he took a quick moment to stretch a few knotted muscles before trotting in the direction the beast had gone. Rounding into the passage the creature had taken he caught a glimpse of its hind legs vanishing down yet another passage on the right. Without a thought to how little he knew of what was ahead of him, Dephithus broke into a run. He could not let this animal get away from him.

They darted down assorted passages, all thankfully tall enough for Dephithus to stay upright. Keeping a sharp eye on the swift daemon-beast he leapt over rough spots and dodged around obstacles. The beauty of the cave was no longer important, for he was close to what he was searching for. He could feel it. Dephithus darted around another corner and barely had time to stop before running into an oddly out of place barrier of bars. The daemon-beast was somehow able to pass through the bars, and it disappeared into the dark beyond the reach of the sphere of light. Startled and confused, Dephithus peered into the darkness.

A figure stepped into the light.

Dephithus stared, awestruck by the delicate, lovely young girl who stood on the other side of the bars, barely within the reach of the sphere of light. The daemon-beast stood beside her now like a twisted guardian. Her long, brassy black hair framed an elegant face with brass tinted black scaling peeking out from under the locks. The clothes she wore were drab brown things and no shoes protected her dainty feet. Tilting her head a fraction to one side, a motion the daemon-dog eerily mirrored, she regarded him with striking black eyes that were also intermixed with burnished highlights.

"Father."

## CHAPTER FORTY THREE

Dephithus continued to stare in awe-struck silence at the creature before him.

This girl was far too old to be his child, but he had distinctly heard the word she spoke. She had called him Father. Perhaps this was some deception of the daenox. While his mind told him it was impossible, something deep inside disagreed with logic. As he fumbled to make some sense of what he was seeing, the young girl stepped closer to the bars. Like a wild animal, he hovered between bolting from this strangeness and moving closer to feed his soul on the beautiful enigma.

The young girl stopped only a few inches from the bars and gazed at him.

"Father," she stated again, though her voice trembled close to uncertainty as her strange eyes searched his face for some response.

Dephithus finally defeated his fear of the mystery before him and stepped in next to the bars. Reaching his fingers up he paused inches shy of touching her cheek. "How can this be?"

"I am very young as a dragon lives," she replied, as if this should be answer enough for anyone.

Both her voice and her manner where more those of a young woman than a child, though there was also a distinct innocence in the way she did not seem to know what it was to be so young. He understood that the power of the dragons was much greater in her, giving her more of their traits, but it was still hard to accept this.

Dephithus touched her cheek then, very gently because he almost expected her to shatter under the soft weight of his fingers. There was very little of Myara in her appearance, which was almost disappointing. Still, her beauty was all her own and that could only be a good thing.

"What is your..." he hesitated, feeling awkward at having to ask his own child her name.

"They call me Raine."

"They? Don't you mean Myara, your mother?"

Raine shook her head and met his gaze steadily. "Mother left us. She could not handle the pain of her life."

Dephithus felt as though his chest were being crushed. Sinking to his knees he leaned his head against the cold bars.

*Myara.*

All this way he had come for her only to find that he had already lost her. Now she would never understand why he had wronged her and he might never have the freedom of her forgiveness. Raine sank to her knees with him and he looked up at her, thinking that she shared his suffering, but it was only curiosity he saw in her eyes. Reaching through the bars, she caught a tear off his cheek and rubbed it between her thumb and forefinger. For a moment she gazed at the damp spot and then turned to regard him again.

"You are mourning her? She chose to leave, so it seems logical to assume she would be happier this way."

Rage surged up with her words. The idea of Myara so alone and miserable that she chose to take her own life was more than he could bear. It took a great deal of restraint for him to check his temper before speaking. "When death is your only freedom, where is there happiness in that?"

Raine shrugged and waited patiently for something more. Dephithus had to remind himself that she had been raised in this place, isolated and surely not loved. Despite her apparent maturity, there was much she simply was not going to understand. As he bowed his head and fought to control his anguish he remembered the sword he was supposed to give to Myara. Glancing down, he laid a hand on the hilt of the grand weapon. "This was your mother's. I suppose it is yours now."

Raine scowled. "What use have I for a weapon such as that? I know nothing of such things." Surprisingly, she seemed to recognize the hurt as it appeared in his eyes at her words. Her voice and expression softened as she reached through the bars, touching the hand that still rested on the hilt. Her fingers were cold. "This sword is best served in your hands, I think."

Dephithus collected himself, realizing there was still part of his quest he could complete. If he succeeded in this, there would be time later to teach her the things she did not know and perhaps find redemption in so doing. "How do I get you out of here? Is there a door?"

"There is no door, but you and I have the same blood and the same powers within us. We can use these things to breach these bars."

Dephithus shook his head, trying to hold down his impatient temper. No door? What kind of enclosure was this? "I don't know how to use these powers."

"I have had much time to think on this. Give me your hands."

Raine's expression was full of determination, if not quite confidence, as she took hold of his offered hands. Her slender hands were so cold, but her grip was steady as she wrapped her fingers into his palms. With an eternally patient gaze she waited for him to close his fingers over hers. As he did so, a flood of irritation swept through Dephithus. Did she not understand the danger they were in? Her calmness was maddening.

Raine gazed intently at the space between their clasped hands.

She was so strange, and yet, how could she not be? Her years were much less than the age she appeared to be. Not to mention, those few years she had lived were spent here, isolated from the world with no one to love and teach her.

Her eyes unfocused and he felt distinctly alone in the moments that followed.

Where was Theruses and why was he waiting so long? Perhaps Rakas had proven to be a useful distraction after all.

Just then, little tendrils of light, like brightly colored worms, appeared in the space between their hands and began to wind up their arms without ever touching their skin. Dephithus did not realize he was trying to pull away from the strange spectacle until Raine's grip tightened. Her focus had not changed and he forced himself to relax as more and more of the sinuous lights wound ever faster up their arms and over their bodies to vanish back into the space between them where the bars still separated them.

He had to trust her.

A wave of nausea passed through him and Dephithus had to close his eyes as the chamber seemed to waver around them. The nausea was gone as fast as it came and he opened his eyes to find Raine looking at him with no bars between them. Dephithus was too stunned to say anything. Raine smiled in response to his silence, though there seemed to be little in the way of real feeling behind the expression.

"Enough!"

The booming voice that raged around and within them caused them both to jump and Dephithus could feel his pulse pounding through him, thumping like a hundred drums in his ears. Before the word had finished echoing, he caught a glimpse of movement out of the corner of his eye. Positioned as he was, he had to move very little to grab his belt dagger. Taking hold of the hilt, he flung the weapon toward the movement and leapt to his feet, pulling Raine with him by the hand he still held. The roar that followed could have been anger or pain, but Dephithus was not going to wait around and find out which.

It seemed that Raine knew as much about the cave as he did for she followed along without a word. The pace she kept, staying close enough that he could almost feel her breathing, encouraged Dephithus onward. Perhaps she did have some idea of the danger they faced, for her breath came in short uneven gasps. With no idea of how to get out, Dephithus picked their way by turning down passages they could move through quickly and hoped for the best.

A young woman stood in one of the side passages as they ran past and Raine stopped, pulling her hand away and turning back to her. Dephithus stopped with her, his nerves screaming at him to run. The woman had black hair and eyes like Rakas, but she reached for Raine's hands, taking them in her own. She stared into Raine's eyes. Her hands shook visibly, and a tear ran down her cheek.

"I'll delay him." The woman's voice shook when she spoke.

"You'll die."

The woman nodded. She leaned in and placed a light kiss on his daughter's lips, then she released her hands. "Run."

Whatever their relationship, Raine didn't hesitate.

She turned, grabbing his hand, and they ran again. As they darted into a large chamber and headed for the next promising opening across the room, another figure stepped into their path, this one blocking the passage.

A woman's scream echoed through the passages behind them. Raine flinched.

Dephithus stopped to face the stranger, keeping hold of Raine as she halted beside him. Though the individual before them had dragon traits, it was immediately obvious that this man was not Theruses. He had cat-like eyes that blazed with the fiery heat of their strange bronze coloring and the pants he wore were plainly borrowed for the hem ended above the boot tops, revealing more of the scaling that showed on his bare chest and arms. He was no bigger than Dephithis and he had no tail or clawed feet. If the physical traits were not enough, his expression of concern and relief marked him as a possible ally.

"They should have trusted in you," he snarled under his breath. "Dephithus. I am Siniva, the Fire Dragon. I came to lead your child out of here."

The dragons had not trusted him to succeed. As much as he wanted to be offended, he could not blame them. Still, he hesitated at trusting this stranger with the child he had only just found, but they had few options. Someone had to slow Theruses and Siniva had gotten in. He would know how to get out. As he opened his mouth to accept the offer a growl filled the chamber.

"Siniva," the voice growled from somewhere further behind, speaking the stranger's name in octaves almost too deep to register.

Siniva looked past them, his eyes narrowing a fraction.

Icy terror filled Dephithus at the prospect of facing what came behind them, but he knew that his journey would fail if he did not.

"You know how to get out?"

Siniva nodded.

"Get her out of here then," Dephithus hissed, nudging Raine forward.

Raine turned to him and touched his hand, a hint of awkward in the contact. She met his eyes. "She still loved you. Despite…"

His chest tightened. "I didn't deserve her love."

"No."

He swallowed hard. "Thank you. Now go."

For a second, she leaned closer as if to hug him or kiss his cheek, then she drew away and turned, giving Siniva a nod. She glanced back at Dephithus once more with reluctance in her eyes though she was already breaking into a run and Siniva turned, bolting down the passage with her.

Drawing his sword, Dephithus turned to face Theruses. The imposing figure entered the passage a few heartbeats after Raine left.

Unlike Siniva, Theruses, with his pale gold scaling and black hair and eyes, was inhumanly large. He bore almost more resemblance to the dragons than to a man. A long barbed tailed snapped back and forth behind him and his feet were large clawed things that forced him to stand with his knees slightly bent. When he grinned, Dephithus could see the vaguely pointed teeth that lined his jaws. Theruses bore no weapons and there was some small satisfaction in the blood that ran down his leg from a wound below his ribcage. Dephithus had thrown the dagger to penetrate the chest of the average man. Obviously, this had been an underestimate, but at least the beast was wounded.

"Raine is much stronger than you, boy, but she will fall just as you are going to now."

Dephithus did not disagree with that last part, so he held his silence. There was little doubt that Theruses had an advantage over him. Several advantages. All he could hope for was to delay him long enough. If they were swift, Raine and Siniva would be free of the cave before he fell.

Standing his ground between Theruses and the passage they had gone down he waited with Myara's sword ready.

Theruses growled his impatience and advanced suddenly. Dephithus dodged to the right, swinging his sword low to try to catch a leg and cripple the beast. The blade made contact, but it slid across without breaking the skin. Remembering what had occurred when he attacked Rakas at the inn, Dephithus knew his only chance was to surprise Theruses. He dodged the beast twice more without striking back. The third time he feinted to the side then lunged into Theruses. The sword made contact this time, cutting a deep gash along the monster's ribs.

Spinning back toward his opponent, Dephithus realized he had overestimated the effect the wound would have on him. Theruses had already recovered and was coming at him again. As Dephithus struggled to salvage his misjudgment, Theruses caught hold of the sword blade and growled, the sound vibrating through the weapon. He did not take the time to protect himself, ignoring as the weapon cut into his hand, sending rivulets of blood streaming down the blade.

"Enough playing," Theruses snarled.

"She's probably already free," Dephithus shouted at him.

Theruses smirked. "Not yet."

Before Dephithus could do more, he was thrown back with tremendous force, though he was sure Theruses had not touched him. The force that threw him also caused him to let go of the sword hilt as he was slammed into the rough rock wall several feet above the floor. As he hit the floor his legs gave out and he slumped over, trying desperately to recapture the air that had been knocked from him with the impact.

There was so much pain. Broken ribs at the very least.

He sat gasping, not aware of Theruses approaching until the large hand closed on his throat and lifted him from the floor.

Already short of air, Dephithus could feel his life ebbing away and he thrashed against the strangling hold, but Theruses was too strong and he was weakening fast. Blood trapped in his skull pounded ferociously as he stared into the face of his enemy with rapidly diminishing coherence. Theruses moved his face in close enough that Dephithus longed for at least enough strength to bite him, but he could only dangle helplessly in the grip that was probably going to be his death.

"You have failed, Dragon-child."

There was a lack of conviction in the words that brought Dephithus a strange blissful pleasure despite his predicament and his lips found the strength to smile. Theruses threw him even harder this time and he flew across the room like a rag doll with no control of his abused body. Theruses was already turning to leave when Dephithus hit one of the chamber walls headfirst. The impact brought a flash of blinding light and pain. He landed on his side and was able to roll onto his back, but it was hard to draw in a breath. Strange shadows moved across his vision in the light that Rakas had left him with. An overwhelming need to close his eyes and rest clouded his thoughts.

Just when he thought he might go ahead and close them, Rakas leaned over him with Myara's sword in hand. The man knelt beside him, his face twisted with remorse and his lips forming words Dephithus could not focus enough to understand. This was not the image he wanted to hold as he lay here. Raine was on her own now, and he had to believe that she would escape. Maybe the dragons would continue to help her. Whether she escaped because he had delayed Theruses, or simply because she was determined and strong he did not care. His daughter would be free.

Pulling up a picture of Myara in his mind he closed his eyes to rest. Her image was perfect, sitting in the Mother Tree with her golden beauty and laughing. He could hear her laugh as though he sat there with her. Indeed, it seemed as if he was sitting in the Mother Tree with her, a warm summer sun folding them in warmth. The bark rough under his hands. Reaching out he took hold of her hand and smiled.

## CHAPTER FORTY FOUR

Siniva and Raine rounded another bend and entered the twilight zone of the cave, the area where the light from the entrance permeated the darkness. Raine stopped so fast that she almost fell over her own feet. Throwing her hands up in front of her face she began to back away from the invasive sunlight. Siniva turned and caught hold of her arm before she could vanish back down the way they had come. Pulling her arms down he saw sheer terror in her wide eyes as she stared past him toward the entrance. She had looked no more than a hint uneasy while they were running from Theruses, now she looked near tears with terror.

"Theruses is coming," he hissed.

"I can't go out there. It hurts."

"Out there is your freedom," he replied, pointing roughly toward the entrance. His nerves burned with the certainty that Theruses would be upon them any minute. "You'll die in here."

Raine brushed a tear from her cheek brusquely, perhaps hoping he would not notice it, and shook her head.

Siniva snarled. This child's fear was nothing to the people he had killed, and he would not let their deaths be in vain. Grabbing her arm with bruising force, he hauled her after him. Small stings of pain assailed his hand and arm as she tried to fend him off with daenox, but she either was not willing to really hurt him or simply did not know enough to cause him significant pain. He rather hoped it was a little of both.

At the entrance he shoved her ahead of him and she staggered falling to her knees in the brilliant afternoon sunshine that was so much harsher than the lights she had known in the cave. Siniva watched her struggling to open her eyes in the bright sun. Pity was all he could feel. Pity and anger. Unlike the dragons, she was afraid to be free, something he did not think even she knew until now. He would give anything to be free. Free of the body that would remain his prison even now with the dragon-child free.

The stallion Dephithus had left and another horse were both standing to the side of the entrance. Hydra, the stolen king's horse, stepped up to Raine and looked down on her with his neck arched up in an almost regal posture, intrigued by this new creature. Siniva sank down on the rocks, fighting against the misery of the freedom he could not have and realized he had no plan from here. Getting the child out had been the extent of his goals. What would he do now?

Theruses burst from the cave entrance and lunged into the air on blinding gold wings. Circling above them, the Death Dragon focused in on Raine with eyes that were still as black as pitch, marking him for life as a creature of the daenox. Siniva could see blood on his ribs and abdomen. Dephithus had gotten in a few good strikes before he fell. Neither he nor Raine had any weapons to fight a dragon and Siniva was too drained to pull upon what powers might still be available to him now that he was split from the dragon web.

Raine crouched closer to the ground when the Death Dragon dove at her.

When he rose up again, she got back up onto her knees, seeming unaware of the hard, rocky ground beneath them. Her focus turned inward and daenox began to stream from the cave in visible dark violet tendrils, gathering around her. Behind her, Rakas sprinted from the cave entrance, glancing once at the girl and the power gathering around her before he leapt up on the other horse waiting there and kicked the animal hard down the hillside. He would go free as well, but Siniva was too enthralled by Raine to care. She had the power to hurt him earlier, that much was becoming obvious fast.

Theruses dove down at Raine, his claws bared before him to grab or tear at her. When he was within inches of her the daenox gathering around her swept up into a violet barrier.

The dragon's outstretched claws struck, and he reeled back with a scream of pain and frustration. Theruses touched down with his hind legs to redirect himself away from this barrier. In the few moments that he was on the ground, Hydra reared up next to Raine striking out with his hooves. The first two hits tore into the Death Dragon's wing as he lunged skyward. The damaged wing slowed his ascent, but he was still clear of the stallion's reach before the animal could attack again. Raine looked up, her eyes starting to adjust to the light, and watched as Theruses circled again. This time the circles were rough and graceless because of the injured wing. Finally, with a growl so deep it vibrated through the air between them, Theruses left, his vast gold form disappearing over the ridge.

Raine glanced at Siniva, her expression unreadable and the brassy highlights of her hair and eyes shimmering like moonlight on a dark pool as she stood.

"He will go to heal," Siniva said, feeling like he should put something out into the stretching silence.

"Yes. Then he will hunt for me."

Siniva nodded, still troubled by his own uncertainties.

What now? They were both outcasts among human and dragon kind, but Raine had a link to the powers of the daenox, and the dragons would have linked her to the dragon web to facilitate their freedom. She was a creature of many worlds, made unique by the powers that had fostered her. Finding acceptance for her might be even harder than it would be for him.

"Eventually," he agreed. "Though he will have many other things to occupy his time outside of finding you."

"Yes." Raine's gazed down at her hands as though expecting to find something there.

He saw the same realization in her that he experienced. They were alone. They did not belong here. They were lost in this world.

The magnificent stallion stepped closer to her, his head dropping in a peculiar mimic of her own bowed posture.

"Shall we go back for Dephithus? He's likely to need help."

Raine shook her head. "He is gone."

Siniva was startled by the silent tears that slid down her cheeks. "And you would mourn this man you never knew?"

"No," she shook her head and wiped at tears with the sleeve of her rough made shirt. "I mourn the loss of what he might have been to me. A mentor. A companion. A father. I mourn because I am alone."

Hydra nudged her hand with his soft nose and Raine glanced up at him, her face twisting in a curious expression that made her look almost as young as she really was. She tentatively touched his soft nose. Hydra pushed his head into her hand. Encouraged, Raine got to her feet and stepped closer to stroke a hand down his stark white neck under the beautiful black of his mane.

Siniva smiled sadly at the two. "Not completely alone."

She smiled wistfully in return. "It seems that my silver dragon left me his wings."

*

Vanuthan was woken from her hibernation sleep by a surge of power that coursed through her like fire in her veins. Startled, her head snapped up, her burnished red cat's eyes unfocused as she tried to turn her gaze inward on this surge of power. Despite her efforts, the Mother Dragon could not control it. Before she could understand what was happening she was assailed with a barrage of images. She saw each of the dragons as they went free. Though there were hundreds of them all leaving their stone prisons in the same moment, each individual image was perfect in her mind.

R'Gos, the River Dragon, with his gleaming violet-blue scaling, massive horns that curled uselessly down and a long, beak-like snout, rose to the sky in a flash of brilliance. He was the one who had originally designed and presented the idea of the dragon web. Undoubtedly, the freed dragons would converge around him. Arrogant and temperamental though he was, R'Gos was a strong leader and had long been the one the web-builders turned to. Where he was heading, Vanuthan could not tell from the short vision, but he departed his prison in Corbent Calid with a challenging roar that probably terrified the residents of the city.

Colvan, the Storm Dragon, leapt into the air, head down so that his horns curved up and back before him. Vanuthan had seen him kill with those horns, proving they were for more than just show. Colvan was a massive creature and he looked very much like a storm with his burnished charcoal coloring as he flew up against the backdrop of a pale blue sky.

Not far from him, Tikat, the Hope Dragon, rose up

on gently curved pale bronze wings. Ever sensitive to the suffering of others, the Hope Dragon looked almost sad as she rose up over the troubled land.

The long, snakelike, green and gold form of Cyrsyth, the Sea Dragon, did not rise to the sky on his wings, but rather he dove from his seaside cemetery into the raging waters of the Illtide coast. That Cyrsyth had ever conceded to the building of the web had always surprised Vanuthan. The magnificent Sea Dragon, who could navigate the sky and the water with equal skill, though he seemed to favor the latter, had never been much for unity. Yet, his solitude was something he preferred for himself and did not encourage in the other dragons. Vanuthan could see him so perfectly that she even noticed the gills on his neck flaring open as his webbed front claws touched the surface of the rough sea.

Rythis, the silvery-white Song Dragon, was blinding to see in the bright afternoon sunshine. Her crystal eyes and elegant form had always won admiration and Vanuthan envied her now more than ever. Then the beautiful Song Dragon screeched in pain and the Mother Dragon could see blood welling around an arrow in her foreleg. A woman stood at the edge of the graveyard, apparently thinking she was safely out of harm's way, but Rythis, indignant at her injury, was quick to prove her wrong. With amazing speed, the Song Dragon launched herself into the air over the woman's head and whipped her tail out underneath her. The muscular tail struck the woman and sent her flying. Blood sprayed from her mouth with the impact and she landed limp like a child's doll, all in the few seconds the vision lasted.

Cylan, the War Dragon, Simpar, the Moon Dragon, and hundreds more went free within the same instant. Vanuthan witnessed all of them, and Rythis was not the only one to encounter problems. Ovith, the Fear Dragon, was attacked by a pack of daemon-dogs who had been digging in the graves and were enticed by the opportunity for fresh meat, despite the daunting size of their quarry. Ovith escaped the attack with only minor flesh wounds and considerably healthier than his defeated assailants.

Fyth, the Dream Dragon, was freed amidst a band of well-armed Silent Watch who were preparing for that evening's burial. Unpleasantly surprised by her sudden movement, they hid their fear behind a vicious attack. Fyth was struck from several sides at once with the long-handled halberds the Silent Watch expertly wielded. Gashes opened in several places unleashing streams of dark blood over her blue and gold scaling. Disadvantaged by her confusion, Fyth lunged desperately skyward, suffering several more brutal wounds before she was clear of their reach. Vanuthan wondered if she would survive the injuries as the blue and gold dragon struggled skyward. The world they had left was not the one they were returning too. People did not know the dragons like they once had and were not likely to be very accepting in this dark time.

The only one dragon Vanuthan did not see was her favored companion, Siniva, the Fire Dragon. Before she could question this omission, the power left her suddenly empty and alone. Recognizing the power as it departed, Vanuthan laid her head on the cold floor and faced her misery. It was the power of her son's death that had visited her, and she could do nothing for him this time. At least she knew he had kept his promise. His child was free, so the dragons were now free, those who had not trapped themselves in another way as she had. The child was free now. No longer needed by the dragons. Set loose in a world that would never accept her.

Vanuthan mourned for them all.

**THE END**

# ACKNOWLEDGEMENTS

As always, there are many people in my life I'm leaving out here for brevity sake. All of you are still very important to me and I am always thankful for you.

To my mom Linda for your loving support and for helping me work out and refine my ideas.

To Kai for your support and for being the most amazing creative and life partner.

To Rick and Ann for being two of the best of friends anyone could ask for and for being willing give honest feedback on my books.

To Aradia for knowing I would succeed from the first time we met and being an inspiration in your dedication to your own art.

To my cover artist, Rob, my editor, M Evan, and my interior designer, Brian, thank you for your fantastic work and for being such wonderful people to work with.

To my fans for being awesome people and continuing to follow my work. You inspire me to write even when my muse goes on hiatus.

To my sixth-grade teacher, Mr. Johnson, for being so pleased and excited when I told you I was going to be an author and to my eighth-grade algebra teacher, Mr. Siebenlist, for almost letting me flunk because you were so delighted that I was writing books in class rather than notes.

# AUTHOR BIO

Nikki started writing her first novel at the age of 12, which she still has tucked in a briefcase in her home office. She now lives in the magnificent Pacific Northwest tending to her sweet old horse and a wondrous cat-god. She feeds her imagination by sitting on the ocean in her kayak gazing out across the never-ending water or hanging from a rope in a cave, embraced by darkness and the sound of dripping water. She finds peace through practicing iaido or shooting her longbow.

•

Thank you for taking time to read this novel. Please leave a review if you enjoyed it.

•

For more about me and my work visit me at http://elysiumpalace.com.

# OTHER NOVELS by NIKKI McCORMACK

CLOCKWORK ENTERPRISES
The Girl and the Clockwork Cat
The Girl and the Clockwork Conspiracy
The Girl and the Clockwork Crossfire

FORBIDDEN THINGS
Dissident
Exile
Apostate

THE ENDLESS CHRONICLES
The Keeper

STANDALONE WORK
Golden Eyes

Made in the
USA
Columbia, SC

80634889R00239